All Aboard

Neive Denis

Book 4 of the Merivale Retirement Village series.

Copyright

Cataloguing-in-publication data
Creator: Denis, Neive, author
Cataloguing-in-Publication details are available from the National Library of Australia www.trove.nla.gov.au

ISBN: 978-1-7635109-6-8 (paperback)
ISBN: 978-1-7635109-7-5 (eBook)

Cover: T A Marshall, Mackay Australia

Contents

Chapter 1

"Does anyone know who that toffee-nosed, would-be-God creature I just passed on my way here might be?" Cilla Longhurst asked as she entered the Recreation Room for the morning's mahjong session.

"Is he a new resident?" Marjorie Bosworth asked.

"Well, that was going to be my next question, but nobody appears to know who I'm talking about," Cilla replied, looking back over her shoulder to see if the bloke in question was visible outside.

"Tell us about him. If there is a new good-looking resident on the loose, we should know all about him," Alice Logan remarked.

"Why?" Frank Risdale demanded.

After giving Frank a withering look, Alice continued, "What does he look like?"

"I'm not sure about 'good-looking'. Arrogant might be a more apt description. He was getting around as though he had a bad smell under his nose," Cilla replied before trying for a more helpful description. "Let's see... Over six feet, maybe somewhere between six feet two inches and six feet four inches... whatever that equates to in the new measurements."

"They are hardly 'new', Cilla. They've been in use for several decades now," Ted Furlong reminded her. "Almost six decades."

"Whatever... Anyway, the bloke is a bit overweight – fairly round-looking – and well-dressed. Wearing a jacket and tie just to stroll around the Village, if you don't mind."

"But it is a bit cool today," Janet Furlong suggested.

"He sounds more like a prospective resident scoping the place before buying," Ted suggested.

"No, I think he already is a resident," Janet murmured. "I've seen him around before this, and he is always well-dressed."

"His name would be useful so I can contact him," Marjorie stated. "As the Village's librarian, I need to ensure he is aware of our library and the services we provide for residents."

"Give me a minute to think about it," Luigi Giordano said. "I'm sure I've heard his name mentioned. Yes... Yes, that's it. If we are talking about the bloke that I think we are, his name is Baxter McCormac, or something like that."

"Baxter McCormac...! What sort of name is that? Who would burden their child with such a label?" Bernard Stuart-Parnell scoffed.

"That's rich coming from someone with a double-barrelled surname," Luigi responded.

Rod Maguire, standing beside the urn stirring his coffee, chuckled but refrained from entering the conversation. I had elected to follow his example until I heard my name called.

"Marion, have you seen the man we all appear to want to know more about?" Cilla asked.

"Me?. No, I can't say I have. At least, if I have, he didn't register with me."

Having spent little time out in the Village over the last few days, it was unlikely I had encountered the man in question. Still, all this talk now had me intrigued. I wouldn't mind getting a look at him. I thought I felt Rod's eyes boring into me, but didn't look around to check. Then, Rod chose to enter the conversation.

"You are right, Luigi. His name is Baxter McCormac. He is a new resident who has moved into the house on the corner of the street where Zorka Weinhardt used to live," Rod announced.

"Zorka's house...!" Janet exclaimed in horror. "Does he know the history of that house and the people who lived there?"

"If he does, why would it worry him?" I asked. "I doubt ghosts or any other malevolent remainders from the previous tenants inhabit the house."

"God, there will be patrols through the Village now as everyone tries to get a look at the bloke, " Cilla exclaimed.

"I almost feel sorry for him. Never before has a new resident caused such a flurry of excitement. I think you will find he is nothing more than an ordinary mortal who happens to prefer to be well-dressed."

"Not so ordinary, perhaps," Janet said quietly.

"Oh, no...? What have you heard about him then?" Bernard demanded, sarcasm dripping off every word.

"Important in some way, I believe, or he has been," Janet replied. "Ex-military or something along those lines, I should think. He was walking along the street the other day at the same time as I was. A car pulled up and the driver called out to him. I heard the visitor address the resident as 'Major'. The 'Major' got into the car, and they drove out of the Village."

"Major, eh? That is interesting," Cilla mused. "Worth looking into, perhaps?" she asked, shooting her partner, Joe, an enquiring look as she did so.

"Cilla, you didn't finish telling us what the bloke looks like. Please don't keep us in suspense any longer. Come on, what's he look like?" Alice demanded.

"Hmm... Well, tall, overweight, with a thick, snowy white, slightly wavy thatch on the roof and a luxurious, Stalin-type, 'cookie-duster' moustache to match. Can't tell you much else. If you are so keen to know what he looks like, you will just have to keep your eyes peeled. Now, are we going to play mahjong this morning, or should we all go home again?"

"For goodness sake, we're here to play mahjong. Let's get on with it. Ladies and gents, to the tables, please," I commanded.

The sound of chairs being dragged out from tables filled the room, and was soon replaced by the click of tiles as the morning's games got underway. Today, everyone appeared focused on hurrying home for lunch. No stragglers lingered after the games, leaving just the usual trio – now plus one extra – to clean and tidy before locking up.

"Anyone want another coffee before I turn off the urn?" Rod called out, causing something of a stampede as the other three of us rushed for our mugs.

"While I admit to being a newcomer to mahjong mornings," Joe began, "even I noticed today was a wee bit different. Is the group always so interested in the arrival of new residents? Do they expect a newcomer to be introduced to everyone when they move in?"

"Of course not," I replied, "but I do agree. Today's performance was a bit exceptional... And it is all down to you, Cilla. If you hadn't mentioned a good-looking new resident, it would have been a normal mahjong morning."

"That's right, blame me. But I must say, some of the ladies showed an exceptional interest in the new bloke," Cilla chuckled.

"I can't help but wonder what sort of stir my arrival in the Village must have created," Joe mused.

"None at all, my dear," Cilla replied tartly. "You were just an addition to an existing household, not someone new and possibly available."

Joe nodded his acceptance of Cilla's comments while Rod and I tried not to giggle too much. Then, the conversation adopted a more serious tone when Cilla continued. Although it was obvious she was mainly addressing Joe, Rod and I became involved.

"So, what about this 'Major' title that Janet believes she overheard? Should we take a closer look, Joe? What do you think?"

"Yeah, probably worth a bit of digging. I can't say I'm familiar with the name. It is unusual, though, for an Australian bloke to continue to use his rank after retirement. It sort of waves a bit of a flag for me. Janet's comment sparked my interest. I might have a bit of a poke about the next time I am away."

"When are you off again?" Cilla asked. "The last time we talked about it, you didn't know."

"Still not sure, but depending on what happens by the end of this week, I could be off again next week for a few days."

Despite itching to know more about Joe's frequent absences from the Village, I knew it would be pointless to ask about them. Having been put in my place by Cilla on more than one occasion, I had no desire to experience it again. Anyway, I didn't need to be too bright to work out that Joe's frequent disappearances continued to be something to do with his previous work (that we can't talk about) in far-off places (that we mustn't know about). I had long ago decided he was a spy of some sort working for ASIO or some such Australian security organisation. Neither Rod nor I believed his real name was Joe... but that's okay. He is a decent sort of a bloke who has fitted in well with the rest of our crew.

Lost in my own thoughts, I had almost decided to try arranging a 'chance encounter' with the new resident when Rod's voice cut across my thinking.

"Now, what about those bus trips? It was a week ago now that we agreed we needed to look at the bus trips schedule and rejig it a bit. Does anyone have any thoughts on when we might do that? I feel it has become a wee bit critical and needs to be soon."

"We have nothing on this afternoon," Cilla volunteered. "How about you come to my place for coffee, and we spend some time on it then?"

I surreptitiously tested the weight of the container I was carrying. Damn! Judging by its weight, there weren't many scones left from morning tea. Coffee at Cilla's house this afternoon meant I would have to produce something else for afternoon tea or at least make another batch of scones to augment the ones left from this morning.

Chapter 2

"Right... Coffee and then down to work," Rod announced as we were ushered into Cilla's dining room.

While Rod and Joe made themselves comfortable at the table, I followed Cilla through to the kitchen to help with the coffee.

"Oh, good... My favourites, blueberry muffins," Cilla cooed as she surveyed the contents of the container I placed on the bench.

"With one solitary scone left after this morning's efforts, I decided on muffins for this afternoon: quick, easy, and no fussing about with jam and cream."

As Cilla and I set out the afternoon tea, Joe cleared his throat. "Ahem, Rod, I'm not sure what I can contribute to this meeting. Apart from the fact that I am still fairly new to all things Merivale Retirement Village, I thought everything was going well with the new bus."

"It is. At least, what is being offered is going well, but the bus was intended for more than shopping trips. So far, other trips are not happening. The bus is sitting around doing nothing for much of the time. As the board of directors has charged our group with the responsibility of ensuring the bus justifies its purchase, it's time we devoted some thought to the matter."

"I see," Joe replied in a way that indicated he didn't.

"Just bear with it, Joe," Cilla suggested. "You will soon get the hang of how things happen around here, including how bus usage is scheduled."

While I still had a mouthful of muffin, Rod decided it was time to start work.

"Okay... I think it's fair to say we all agree the scheduled shopping trips are working well. According to reports, the bus has been full for every trip. But, apart from that, there has been only one other social event involving the bus." We all nodded and murmured our agreement.

"If the one social event you're referring to was the trip to the opening of that new gallery up the valley, as I recall, it wasn't without its moments," Cilla said.

"True... but it ended well. It would have been naïve of us not to expect some glitches with the first such event, and it went pretty well, really," Rod conceded.

Finally, having swallowed the last of my muffin, I joined the conversation. "Have the residents complained about the lack of social events being offered?"

"No, not as far as I'm aware," Rod replied.

"So there is no urgency in scheduling any trips?" I didn't quite understand the need for the meeting.

"There has been no comment from the residents, but I doubt it will be much longer before the board of directors starts asking questions. After all, they have appointed a bus driver and employed another staff member on the strength of it. Soon, they are going to ask why they are spending money on a driver when the bus does so little."

"Good point...," Cilla conceded. "As they are the people who make all the arrangements with intended venues, shouldn't Maria and Alice be at this meeting as well?"

"Look, as I see it, there are two aspects to this bus usage thing we need to think about: those social outings we've been alluding to, and those extra trips on the side we had envisaged for limited numbers."

"What exactly are those 'trips on the side'?" Joe asked.

"Well, you might find it difficult to understand, but here goes." Rod took a moment to marshal his thoughts before continuing. "Management has supplied a dedicated bus driver for shopping trips and other social outings that are open to all residents but restricted by the capacity of the bus. We also envisaged various occasions restricted to specific groups of people. On such occasions, the bus would be driven by one of our group who holds the appropriate licence, rather than by the management-appointed driver."

"In case that added to your confusion, Joe, here's an example," Cilla suggested. "Suppose one of our group has a birthday, or there is some other event special to just our group happening somewhere in the area. Then our group would take over the bus for the day or evening, and one of our members would drive it."

"How come such events haven't happened in the past – before the arrival of the bus?"

"They did occur, but we used private vehicles and loaded as many as possible into each vehicle." Cilla looked pleased with her explanation.

"I see," Joe said again, without any indication he had experienced a lightbulb moment.

"Think of this as a look-and-learn session, Joe," Rod suggested. "It won't take you long to get the hang of what we are trying to do here."

"Okay, Rod. What are we looking at in particular today?" I asked. "Are we going to try scheduling social trips for the residents?"

"That's our priority. I brought copies of the list of possible outings we compiled earlier, so let's start by looking at those."

About half an hour later, four possible trips had been scheduled for the coming month, and I think we were all feeling a bit pleased with ourselves and much relieved that Rod seemed happy with our efforts.

"Now that's done, what happens next?" Joe asked.

"Rod will post the proposed schedule on the Village's Facebook page and alert the office staff that residents will start trying to book seats on the bus for the various trips," Cilla explained.

"It appears the bus driver will be a bit busier after this. Do we have to be on all these trips as well?" Joe asked.

"No, not all of them, and not necessarily all of us, for that matter," Rod assured him. "For those trips to specific venues that involve the provision of morning tea or lunch, Alice and Maria will need to be on the bus. As they make all the arrangements with the venues involved, they need to oversee things. The first couple of scheduled trips aren't to specific venues and residents will be expected to make their own arrangements for coffee and lunch. I think at least a couple of us should be on those first trips to help ensure they go well."

"If they are just going up the coast to spend a few hours wandering around in that little beachside village, what can possibly go wrong?" Joe asked. "They board the bus, get off at the village and wander around at their leisure, buy a coffee or lunch, get back on the bus and come home. It all seems fairly straightforward to me."

"Your 'newness' is showing, Joe. Some residents are a bit prone to expecting everything to be done and laid on for them. They might be horrified by having to fend for themselves. The fact that we are there won't change anything. They will still have to fend for themselves – but with plenty of advice and encouragement from us."

"When is the first trip scheduled?" I asked

"Two weeks from today," Rod reminded me. "The short timeframe should generate some urgency about booking a seat. I'll post it on the Facebook page tonight."

"We have a full bus for our trip up the coast," I told Rod as I climbed aboard the bus before it set off to collect the rest of the passengers. "Our new resident, Baxter McCormac, also booked himself a seat."

"Good to see him becoming involved in Village life."

"I wouldn't have thought this trip was something that would appeal to him. He looks as though he would be interested in things of a more highbrow nature, a bit like Bernard, if you know what I mean."

"Ah, yes, but even Bernard is booked on this trip... And here he comes now. I'm a bit surprised that he didn't wait to be collected from in front of his unit."

The bus set off and collected the first half a dozen passengers without incident. At the next pick-up point, everything went to hell in a handbasket. Bernard followed Rod's example and alighted from the bus to assist the women onboard. While Rod stowed their walkers in the luggage compartment, Bernard helped them safely negotiate their way onto the bus. Then the problem arrived.

"You cannot bring that onboard," Bernard bellowed at the two approaching women. Scrambling out of my seat, I peered out the window to investigate the cause of the fuss.

An indignant Mrs Carr had drawn herself up to her full height. The other woman who accompanied her looked about to burst into tears. Taken aback by what was happening, I hesitated for a few moments while I tried to work out what to do to help remedy the situation. There was only one thing for it. To help sort it out, I need to get off the bus again.

Bernard standing defiantly on the ground with his arms folded across his chest and a fierce look on his face, blocked the entrance – and prevented my exit.

"Excuse me, Bernard. Please let me off so I can help sort out whatever is the problem."

"There is nothing to sort out. The woman cannot bring that thing on this bus. That's all there is to it," Bernard snarled in response, but didn't move out of my way.

Rod, finally having dealt with a particularly cumbersome walker, marched up to investigate the apparent problem.

"What the hell is going on here? If we don't get a move on, it will be too late to bother going. Bernard, what are you carrying on about? Step aside and let these two women board the bus."

"The women may board the bus any time they like... but that thing cannot." Bernard pointed an accusing finger at a small, hairy dog that one of the women had on a bright blue lead.

"To the best of my knowledge," Rod began, his voice a low rumble, "there is no rule in place that prohibits dogs on this bus. So, please, Bernard, be so kind as to step aside so I can help these ladies onboard."

"I will not travel on this bus with that dog onboard."

"Fine, I see you are quite adamant about this. So, step aside and move away from the bus, please, Bernard. You are free to do whatever you wish, but the dog *will* board the bus with its owner. It's your choice. Do what you please."

After a few spluttered attempts at a response, an offended Bernard stalked off towards his unit.

"Ladies, if you would board quickly, we will be on our way... at last," Rod said as he ushered the women and the dog onto the bus.

"That went well...," I quipped as I went past Rod to follow the women onto the bus. He did not find the comment amusing.

Once we arrived at our destination, everyone was left to their own devices to fill the time until we were to gather at the bus again at two o'clock. Rod and I walked the length of the esplanade to a quiet little hole-in-the-wall type coffee shop at the far end of the village.

"My preference is for something a good deal stronger than coffee, but decorum suggests that, at this hour of the morning, I should stick with coffee," Rod moaned as we drew out chairs and parked ourselves.

"Are you expecting fallout from this morning's encounter with Bernard?" I asked quietly. "You know how he is. I have no doubt he would have been straight over to the admin building to lay a complaint."

"Yeah, that's probably a fair assumption. What are your thoughts on the dog being on the bus?"

"If I'm honest, I would have to admit to being a bit undecided. A well-behaved little pooch is unlikely to be a problem, while a bigger dog wouldn't be acceptable. However, I understand how some people might not see why a dog should accompany its owner on a social outing involving the bus. I suppose it's another instance where a Board's ruling on the matter might be necessary."

"On our way here, I sent the chairman of the board a text requesting an urgent meeting. Let's wait to see what they think about the matter."

"If the chairman discusses it with the board and our director before arriving at a position on the subject, we could be waiting a while. Will you continue with the social outings in the meantime, even though the matter of the dog might persist until you receive a ruling on it?"

"Having set something of a precedent this morning, I don't see what else I can do except to allow the dog to come with us."

The coffee was excellent, and the cheesecake was deliciously calorific. Still, there is only so long that good manners allow you to occupy a table without buying something more, especially in such a small establishment. We stood for a few seconds on the pavement out front, blinking in the bright sunlight as our eyes adjusted from the low lighting in the coffee shop. A scan of the esplanade revealed some of our passengers wandering around the shops and along the foreshore. I was surprised by what I saw in a more secluded spot beyond the esplanade and the immediate foreshore.

"Well, look at that. I was surprised when he came, but it appears he had no intention of mingling with the residents."

"What are you on about, and where is this surprise you found?" Rod demanded a bit testily.

"Look... way along there. See... That's Baxter McCormac sitting on a bench all alone and away from everyone else."

"He might have viewed this trip as a way of escaping the confines of the Village for a few hours while not having any real interest in this place or what it has to offer."

"Isn't that true of all the residents who came on the bus today? Hmm... but it is a long way to come to just sit by yourself and stare out to sea. Do you suppose he is all right? Should we check on him or something?"

"God, no. That would be an intrusion on his privacy. He might be a loner by nature, or he might be dealing with some personal situation we know nothing about. In any case, he doesn't need us annoying him. Anyway, the fact that there is a bench there suggests it might be a favoured spot by those who just want to sit in solitude to watch the ocean."

"For me, his behaviour today just adds to the mystery of the man. Is there anyone in the Village he has become friendly with since moving in?"

"I wouldn't know, but it certainly isn't me. Keep an eye on him if you must, but just leave him be to establish his life as a Merivale Retirement Village resident."

Now feeling in a bit of a huff after having been put in my place by Rod, I announced, "I am going to look in some of the shops.".

As I walked away, it occurred to me Rod had appeared a bit tense, a little offside somehow today. Had I done something to cause it, or was it the incident involving Bernard and the dog?

My wander through the shops produced no surprises. There was just the usual cheap, commercially produced tat that I suppose was meant to appeal to tourists. After a quick tour of two such shops, I paused outside a third shop that seemed to have more going for it. This one looked as though it was dedicated to selling the wares of local artisans. The shop's windows' artful display of high-quality pottery, jewellery, and leatherwork beckoned me inside. By almost planting my nose up against the window, I could see some of the shop's interior, where framed artworks adorned the walls.

"This is more like it," I thought aloud and headed for the entrance.

The sound of voices made me pause before entering. I looked around and saw a gaggle of Merivale bus passengers making their way towards their rendezvous with the bus waiting in the parking area. I was surprised to see it was fast approaching time for us to leave. Remembering Rod was not in the best of humour, I did not want to be last to return to the bus. Besides, I was expected to be there to help some of the less agile to board. "You seem to have managed about as much shopping as I did," I commented as I caught up with Cilla and Joe also heading for the bus.

The usual chaos of loading passengers and stowing walking frames in the luggage compartment prevailed briefly. Not everyone had returned yet, but stragglers were on their way.

A headcount a few minutes later revealed we were all present and accounted for – except for one. Baxter McCormac had not returned and was nowhere in sight.

"There's just that McCormac bloke missing," Cilla told Rod after taking another headcount of those already occupying their seats.

"Didn't we see him somewhere this morning?" Joe asked

"Yeah, but that wasn't long after we arrived," Cilla replied. "He didn't look too interested in anything, but I think he went to buy a takeaway coffee."

"I think he did have a coffee when I saw him a bit later. He was wandering off in that direction," Joe said, gesturing towards the south.

"Isn't there a lookout a bit further around the point over in that direction?" Cilla asked. "If I remember correctly, there used to be a bench seat there. He might've gone to sit and admire the view and lost track of time."

"Right, come on, old girl, let's go and look for him," Joe said, taking Cilla by the arm and dragging her off towards the southern end of the village.

After watching the couple head off, I glanced at Rod. Something about his demeanour suggested he didn't agree with Cilla's suggestion about the missing passenger's whereabouts.

"Rod, you don't appear convinced that pair will find Baxter along there somewhere. Is there anywhere else he might be? I remember we saw him as we were leaving the coffee shop, but that was some time ago."

"No, I have no ideas regarding his current whereabouts, but I do remember seeing him sitting by himself over there just before you went off to explore the shops. He appeared to be okay and happy to be on his own," Rod said as he turned to look towards the northern end of the village. I followed Rod's example and turned to look towards where we had seen the missing passenger sitting by himself.

"Well, he appears to have moved from there, but might we follow Cilla and Joe's example and check out that lookout area where we last saw him?"

"Yeah, I don't know what's further around the coast from that lookout area, but I suppose he could have decided to explore further along from here."

As if by some mysterious command, an apparent sense of urgency seemed to invade both of us. We strode off rapidly in the direction of the lookout. It wasn't until we were about thirty metres away from the area that a truer picture of the situation at the lookout became obvious.

"Something has happened to him, Rod," I gasped as I focused on the bench seat in the lookout area. "Looks like he might have taken a turn of some sort."

Baxter McCormac was slumped over face down and sprawled along the length of the bench seat, but with his legs still hanging over the edge of the seat.

"Oh, God, Rod, what do we do? Can you manage to turn him over so we can check if he is still alive?"

My question was unnecessary. Rod was already checking for a pulse. He looked up at me and gave a slight shake of his head. I caught my breath. My pulse stepped up a few notches. What the hell were we supposed to do now?

Rod took out his phone and moved a few paces away. He made a brief call before returning to stand with me beside the body.

"Luigi is going to drive the bus back to the Village," he said quietly.

"Didn't he want to know what was going on? I would have thought Luigi would have a mountain of questions, but your call was brief."

"Yeah, he had a truckload of questions, but I shut them down – a bit roughly, perhaps. Of course, he was confused and concerned when I asked him to take the bus back to the Village. I told him we would make our own way back when we were done here."

"And how long is it likely to take before we are done here?" I demanded. Rod shrugged and turned his attention to the body.

"Marion, give me a hand to roll him over, please. He is a big man and rolling him over on this narrow bench, without dropping him on the concrete, won't be easy."

He was right. Even with the two of us struggling with the uncooperative and pudgy mass, Baxter McCormac remained sprawled along the bench... But we saw all we needed to see.

I gasped and jumped with fright when a voice behind me said, "Interesting. Very interesting, eh, Joe?" Cilla and Joe had joined us.

Then, I was being shoved out of the way and Rod also was elbowed further along the bench as Cilla and Joe commandeered the scene.

"Better give Richard Wilson a call, Rod," Cilla suggested. "I think this needs to be dealt with at his level and not by the officers on duty."

"Why would you call our district's top cop about someone who has had a heart attack or something similar?" I demanded. "Surely the officers on duty aren't called to deal with a death by natural causes? I doubt Richard will appreciate being annoyed about something as routine as this."

"If it were a routine 'natural causes' type of event, he wouldn't be interested – and we wouldn't be calling him." Cilla's response still oozed condescension when she continued. "The claret all over the front of his otherwise pristine shirt clearly suggests this is neither a routine nor a natural causes event."

"What?... He's been stabbed. Christ, he's been murdered," was all I could manage at first as Joe stepped back, allowing me to see the blood on the front of Baxter's shirt.

"She's finally worked it out," Cilla murmured.

"Fair go, Cilla," Rod said sharply. "Marion hadn't seen the body since you helped me roll it over properly."

"Who would do this? Why would anyone want to murder an ancient retirement village resident?" I mumbled as I tried to deal with the shock of the scene before me. "Still, even if it is murder, wouldn't the officers on duty be expected to deal with it – at least in the first instance, anyway?" I asked as I tried to grasp the full extent of the situation in front of me.

"That would be true, Marion," Joe began quietly, "if the man was nothing more than an elderly retirement village resident." I swung around to face Joe as I tried to formulate a suitable response, but Joe motioned for me to settle down before continuing. "There were things about the man that suggested he was more than that... perhaps much more than that."

Chapter 3

Nothing was making any sense. I glanced at Rod in the hope that he might provide some explanation. He appeared deep in thought as he stood with head bowed and studying the toes of his sneakers. Sneakers...! Why hadn't I noticed them earlier today? I didn't know Rod owned anything other than the sandals he always wore. I was brought back to the here-and-now when he suddenly looked up and glared at Cilla.

"So, what do you know about Baxter McCormac?" he demanded. "If I call Richard Wilson about a murdered retirement village resident, he will demand to know why I thought it necessary to worry him about it. If McCormac was not just a fellow resident, what was he? Come on, what do you know about him?"

"We don't *know* anything, Rod," Joe said quietly, "but we suspect there was more to his story than that."

"A Spook? A spook of some sort? Is that what you're suggesting?"

"Rod, please settle down," Joe said, shaking his head. "As I said, Rod, we don't know anything – yet. We had initiated some careful enquiries based on suspicions we both held, but nothing has come to light so far."

While continuing to glare at Cilla and Joe, Rod took out his phone and flicked through his contacts list. Again, he wandered away a short distance to speak to the person he called... presumably Richard Wilson. As Rod walked back to where we stood next to the body, I noticed Cilla appeared to be conducting a visual scan of the area.

"What are you looking for, Cilla?" I demanded. "Might we be told so we can help you look for whatever it is?"

"If you must know, I was checking if there was a possible murder weapon somewhere in this area. No, don't go tramping around looking for it. We've already stuffed up the crime scene enough to render it virtually useless to the investigators. Rod, what were Richard's instructions?"

"Argh... He said not to touch anything more and, Cilla, you are to take charge of the crime scene."

"Right, that's as I expected. Now, who is he sending to deal with this?"

"I don't know who is coming other than Richard himself. He expects to be here in about ten minutes. We are to wait here with the body. That is all he said." Rod concluded his report with an emphatic nod at Cilla.

Cilla wasted no time in taking charge, immediately ordering us all to stand still and not touch anything else. Again, she moaned about how badly we had corrupted the crime scene and how it would reflect on her professionalism. Rod went to say something but seemed to think better of it and stopped. I had no doubt it would have been an angry response to Cilla's high-handed approach but, after all, she was only complying with Richard Wilson's instructions.

It was more than fifteen minutes later before Richard arrived at the small seaside village and promptly rang Rod to find out where we were. As Rod gave him directions, a second vehicle pulled in beside Richard's car.

"Looks like the cavalry has arrived," Joe indicated with a jerk of his head towards the car park.

"I hope we all have our stories straight about what we saw and what we know about what happened here today," Rod said with an edge to his voice. "And, while I think of it, Cilla and Joe, did you find anything relevant when you went to explore that lookout site at the other end of the village?"

Joe shook his head and muttered, "No sign of the bloke ever having been there, although I suppose it's possible. Unless he left a wrapper or something lying around, you'd be unlikely to find any evidence anyone had been there."

Any further discussion was curtailed when Richard Wilson strode up onto the lookout area. He was followed by two men in suits who I assumed were detectives. Immediately taking charge of the scene, Richard said a few words before handing the three of us over to the two detectives, who promptly shepherded us down to the esplanade in front of the shops. Cilla remained at the lookout with Richard.

Conveniently for the detectives, four picnic tables with attached benches were evenly spaced along the esplanade. We were singled out, and each of us was sent to sit at a separate table. Feeling more than a little bit offended by this turn of events, I stormed off to the table I'd been allocated and threw my bag down on it in disgust. Then, I sat drumming my fingers on the table and glaring at everything and nothing in particular as I waited for my 'interview' to take place. It was while I was thus venting my displeasure that Cilla marched to the spare table on the esplanade. It was obvious she was not happy about being relegated to the ranks of those to be interviewed by the detectives. Whatever had been said at the lookout after we left appeared to have trampled on Cilla's ego in no small way. I had little time to ponder Cilla's situation. A large, gruff detective demanded my attention as he plonked himself opposite me at my table.

"Right, let's have your particulars first before we get down to the important stuff," he said as he flipped open his notebook. "I will be making notes as we go along, but I need to inform you that this interview will be recorded on body cam."

Charming, I thought... but said nothing, choosing instead to just level my gaze at him across the metre of greyed timber between us.

Finally having settled himself and apparently having found a blank page in his notebook, he looked up and barked, "Now, let's have the basics: name, address, age... you know, all the usual personal particulars."

Not feeling in the least bit accommodating, and with ice dripping off every word, I stated my name and gave my address as the Merivale Retirement Village.

"Age...?" he barked.

"Over 65," I snapped, "and before you say another word, be aware it would be politically incorrect for you to pursue that question further... and complaints might follow." He glared at me – but heeded my advice.

"Okay, now, in your words, tell me what you know of the deceased." And so the interview proper began...

Applying judicious brevity, I told the detective of seeing the victim sitting alone at the lookout and then later, going with Rod to remind the victim it was time to leave. The detective confined his interview to querying a couple of points of what I had told him before snapping his notebook close and telling me, "That will do for now". Interview complete, he told me 'stay put', before hauling himself up off the bench seat and leaving me to my chaotic thoughts once more.

What did Joe and Cilla tell the detectives during their interviews? I doubted they could have told them much. That pair wasn't aware of anything until they arrived and helped Rod turn over the body. Why would thoughts of what Joe and Cilla told the detectives gnaw at me as savagely as they did? Activity at one of the other tables brought such pointless thoughts to an end.

The detective who had been interviewing Rod stood up and started to move away from Rod's table. Rod followed his example and began to scramble to his feet, only to be told to stay where he was until he was told he could leave. The second detective promptly moved along the line of tables, ensuring we all received that same message. I was over this particular detective's rude, officious manner.

"How long are we likely to be held here? And, more to the point, why are we being held here?"

"Eh? Oh, didn't I say...?"

Apparently, we were to remain at our tables until Richard came down from the lookout area to talk to us.

Richard, striding with his phone to his ear towards the esplanade, came to a sudden halt for a few moments. Then, the call apparently ended, he strode briskly to join us on the esplanade.

"Why are you still sitting at separate tables? Did a row about something erupt between you? Anyway, please, everyone, come up to this table so I can talk to you all together."

About to give Richard an angry response, as I drew myself up to my full height, I glanced at Rod. He shook his head and motioned for me to 'leave it'. 'Leaving it' would not help cool my anger one bit, but I took Rod's advice and bit my tongue.

"Right... your pleasant day at the seaside appears to have gone a bit awry. The detectives who conducted your interviews will now begin searching the area around the lookout and further along the coast for any evidence. They will be joined in a few minutes by several uniformed officers to help cover the area as quickly as possible. Now, how were you four planning to return to the Village?" Rod explained about sending the bus back and how we planned to make our way back – somehow.

"Well, I can give you all a lift back if you don't mind being a bit friendly in the back seat... And perhaps there might be a coffee when I drop you off," Richard said with a grin.

Yes, there was coffee and muffins at Rod's place when Richard dropped us off. I found it strange that during the half hour or so that we sat around drinking coffee and munching muffins, not once was Baxter McCormac or his demise mentioned by anyone of us. I had expected at least some discussion, if not a post-mortem, of what had happened to our recently deceased resident, but not even a hint or veiled reference occurred.

After Richard left, no one appeared inclined to linger and chat. Cilla and Joe left Rod's house a couple of minutes after Richard. I stayed behind to help Rod clean up after our afternoon tea. After that exercise was carried out in almost complete silence, I also went home.

Tonight would involve several hours of solitude. On the premise that everyone would be too tired after their day out, our usual evening happy hour at Rod's had been cancelled at the time the bus trip was scheduled. It meant I would be at home on my own for dinner and the rest of the night. There was always a chance Rod might invite himself to dinner with me but, somehow, I didn't think it likely. And that's when the rot set in.

Images and questions from today churned through my mind at breakneck speed, tumbling one after another through my mind as I prepared dinner and later as I sat in my dimly lit lounge room. Why is there nothing worth watching on TV when you desperately need a distraction? In the end, I gave up the fight and tried to work my way logically through everything. One by one, the questions paraded through my mind.

What did Cilla and Joe really know about the late Baxter McCormac? Did they know anything, or were they assuming the overheard title of 'Major' meant more than it did? Of course, it was possible, even probable, that the man had been military at some time. That's true of a lot of people. So what? No, that's not it. It was as though they were suggesting something else. After all, they didn't argue or even raise an eyebrow when Rod asked if they believed McCormac had been some sort of spook.

Would Richard know? If he didn't know, would Richard be able to find out easily the truth about McCormac's true identity and possible background? Did Cilla share with Richard her and Joe's suspicions about the victim? I doubted either of them would have said anything to the detectives about their suspicions. Cilla probably would have thought the information too hush-hush to discuss with the rank and file. But would she have mentioned it to Richard during that first (private) discussion she had with Richard before she was sent to be interviewed by the detectives? The little voice in my head told me she wouldn't have said anything.

Apart from all the others, the BIG question underlying all of this was the suggestion that Baxter McCormac was more than just an elderly retiree. And, if he was, so what? He wasn't the only one on the bus today who could be described as being more than just a retiree. Cilla continued to be actively involved with the police services both here and in New South Wales. And then there's Joe. While what his occupation was before he settled here is a closely guarded secret, I think it is a fair assumption that he probably was a spook working for some Australian agency and appears still to have some connection to it. Rod, who continues to work as a journalist, might also be considered more than just a retiree. Hmm... when I think of it that way, I am the only one of our quartet that the label of 'elderly retiree' does fit. Is that significant in any way? Probably not, but it does set me aside as different.

The tsunami of questions searching for answers churning around in my mind accompanied me for a shower and came to bed with me... and that gave rise to another couple of questions. How difficult was it going to be for me to find sleep tonight, and how much sleep would I manage before the sun came up again?

After a very late start to my day, and in something akin to a zombie-like trance, I managed to make and drink a mug of coffee before feeling sufficiently together to make breakfast – and another mug of coffee.

As I sat in a semi-stupor, hunched over my empty plate and half empty coffee mug, the shrill call of my doorbell snapped me back to reality. It was 9.00AM. I wasn't expecting visitors today. After opening the door, I stood for a moment, blinking in surprise at Rod's presence on my doorstep.

"Was I supposed to be somewhere this morning?" I blurted out as I searched my memory banks for some forgotten appointment.

"Not that I am aware of," he chuckled. "I was on my way home from my morning run and stopped to invite you to morning tea. Are you able to join me at about ten o'clock?"

"Sounds lovely. Yes, I'll be there. I'll bring something to have with our coffee – seeing as how we probably ate all your muffins yesterday afternoon when we had coffee at your place." I hoped I had now recovered sufficient intelligence to remember the recipe for whatever I was going to make.

Rod jogged the rest of his way home along the footpath. As I stood watching him, I couldn't help wondering who else might be joining us this morning. While I held a slim hope it might be just the two of us, the little voice in my head told me I knew better than to believe that. By the time I was ready to leave for Rod's, I had accepted the probability that Cilla and Joe also had been invited for coffee.

For more than a week now, Rod had appeared tense and on edge about something. While I know we all have things going on in our private lives that we don't share with others, Rod's current state of mind – his demeanour – was impacting our relationship. Relationship...! What relationship? Do we really have one, or is such a situation no more than a figment of my imagination? I genuinely thought for some time now that we had been in a close personal relationship. Whenever I start to believe that, Rod's behaviour manages to shatter my rose-tinted glasses. Some significant private matter always comes along to impact Rod's life. It eventually intrudes and creates havoc with whatever exists between us. Then, it is not until the matter troubling him is dealt with that 'former relations resume'.

My spirits soared when it appeared there would be just the two of us for morning tea. I was only halfway through my first cupcake when they were dashed again by the sound of the doorbell.

"Apologies for the late arrival," Cilla chirped as she drew out a chair and collapsed onto it. "On top of everything else this morning, an unscheduled early meeting ran on longer than expected."

I struggled to keep the disappointment out of my voice when I asked, "Will Joe be joining us? If he is, I'll fetch an extra plate and mug ready for him."

"No, he won't be. That's the other thing I've had to deal with. I had to take Joe to the airport to catch the early flight south. He likely will be away for the best part of next week unless they manage an early breakthrough."

"Aren't you concerned about his being out in the field again?" I asked – before I had thought it through and received the response I should have expected.

"Sorry, Marion, I haven't a clue what you meant by that comment about 'being out in the field'. But, regardless, no, I am not concerned by his absence."

Rod launched a discretionary move to manoeuvre the conversation in a different direction and diffuse the building tension.

"So, in between everything else you've had happening, have you heard from Richard Wilson since you left yesterday afternoon?"

"Not a murmur. Our top cop either hasn't uncovered anything yet or hasn't seen fit to share his findings with me."

Still stinging from my earlier skirmish with Cilla, I defiantly aimed my next questions at Rod. "Were you expecting to hear something so soon? I would have thought Richard and his team have barely had time to open a file on the case, let alone discover anything of interest. Was there anything in particular you thought he might have discovered?"

"Yeah, I agree it's a bit soon, but I thought he might have uncovered some background on the victim. Even confirmation that the bloke's name was Baxter McCormac would be a start."

"Well, if that was the first step in the investigation that they took, it's not surprising we haven't heard anything. Confirming someone is who they say they are is a complicated process, usually requiring other supporting information to guide it in the right direction. Confirmation of the bloke's identity is the last thing I would have expected at this early stage." Almost from the moment Cilla started speaking, I saw Rod stiffen in response to her condescending tone.

By the time Cilla finished speaking, Rod's jaw was firmly set. Silence reigned for the next few moments, during which I studied the cupcake crumbs on my plate, and Rod stared fixedly at some indeterminate point in the distance. I was devoid of ideas of how to remedy the situation – short of announcing I was going home. The only one of us who appeared not to notice the prevailing hostile atmosphere was Cilla. As she completed freeing the last of her cupcake from its paper case, she sat back and glanced around the table.

"I don't suppose either of you has heard or remembered anything more about yesterday's victim?" We both shook our heads, and Cilla continued. "Hmm... it's unlike the inmates of this Village not to have winkled out every last detail of his life by now. That must tell us something about Mr Baxter McCormac."

"Major Baxter McCormac," I corrected her. "At least, there is some evidence to suggest that might be the case."

"Unlike in some other countries, it is unusual for Australian ex-armed services personnel to continue to use their former rank in their retirement," Rod mused.

"Perhaps McCormac didn't continue using his rank. Perhaps the bloke who used it when he picked him up was someone from McCormac's earlier life, and the bloke simply used the rank as a mark of respect for his former officer," I suggested.

"Anything is possible, I suppose," Cilla began, "but there is a major flaw in any such thinking. If the victim was a former member of the armed services, he didn't enlist as Baxter McCormac."

Her comment suggested she knew more than she was saying. It tended to indicate that the victim's identity had been researched. It also made me pause to rethink the suggestion I was about to make. Nevertheless, I went ahead and launched it anyway.

"We are assuming the victim previously had been a member of one of the Australian armed forces. Might the victim have previously been a member of some other country's armed services, for example, one of the British services? Has anyone commented on his having an accent of any sort?"

"Hmm... That's something worth thinking about. The British do like to hang onto their rank after they retire. I haven't heard any comments about an accent," Rod admitted, "and I don't know that I even heard him utter a word when he boarded the bus yesterday."

"Ah, might he be keen to keep a telltale accent a secret?" I murmured.

"Oh, for goodness sake, stop with the speculation," Cilla exclaimed. "At the rate you're going, before we've finished our coffee, you will have the man heading up some international spy ring or worse."

"Cilla is right," Rod conceded. "We don't know anything about the man. We could be doing him a major disservice by speculating about his past in this way. We should just wait for Richard to come back to us with accurate information."

"That seems like wasting time to me," Cilla announced. "We could do a bit of digging of our own. Rod, you must have a discussion as soon as possible with our village director, Tanya Jellicoe. She needs to be officially informed of yesterday's events and that one of her residents is now deceased... And while you are about that, Rod, you might think to ask a few pertinent questions about McCormac."

"You're right, but Tanya won't be back in the village till first thing Monday morning. That's when I intend to go across to her office to enlighten her about yesterday's events. I can think of a couple of judiciously worded questions I might put to her regarding the deceased. If she passes on any information, how useful it might be will depend on how honest Baxter McCormac was with all the paperwork he submitted when he applied to become a resident here."

"True... But whatever she tells you will amount to more than we know now. Do you need a hand to formulate some appropriate questions?" Cilla asked.

"Thanks, but no. After all, I am a journalist and well-practised at asking appropriate questions to obtain the information I need."

Morning tea did not drag on today. As soon as she had drained her mug, Cilla left, and after helping Rod clean up and stack the dishwasher, I also went home. Had we achieved anything this morning, I wondered as I strolled home along the footpath. I don't know that morning tea this morning was designed to be a revelation or an enlightening experience of any kind, so perhaps none of us should be disappointed with the outcome. But, as I unlocked my front door, I knew that wasn't the case. I was feeling disappointed. I just didn't know what I was disappointed about.

Chapter 4

I hadn't seen or heard anything of Rod or Cilla since morning tea. As I prepared nibbles to take to happy hour at Rod's place this evening, I realised I had no enthusiasm for an hour or so spent with our usual happy hour attendees. Many of them had been on yesterday's bus trip to that seaside village and, no doubt, our absence from the bus on the trip home will not go unexplored tonight.

Damn! I should have thought this morning and established what line we would take when the questions start flowing this evening. As I picked up the container of nibbles and headed for the door, I had no doubt I would manage to say the wrong thing at some point tonight, while both Rod and Cilla would reel off glib stories that everyone believed. "Too bad," I hissed as I locked my front door. "They should have schooled me up properly this morning if they didn't want me to say the wrong thing."

Soon after arriving at Rod's place, I realised Rod and Cilla seemed almost as subdued as I felt. More than that, the whole gathering felt a bit flat tonight. Of course, there were questions about our absence from the bus on its return trip to the Village, but no one pressed me for more details. On the odd occasion when I was asked, I brushed aside the questions with the lame explanation 'that something requiring immediate attention came up unexpectedly'. I would have given anything to know what replies the other two were dishing out. No doubt, they would have been infinitely more believable than mine.

The prevailing subdued atmosphere saw everyone leave Rod's place much earlier than usual after happy hour. Cilla followed the first of them out the door and seemed in a hurry to be home. For a moment, I wondered if she might be expecting

29

a call from Joe. Then I remembered that Joe was familiar with happy hour arrangements and wouldn't bother calling Cilla until later in the evening when she was likely to be home. That left just me again to help Rod clean up after everyone left. The atmosphere did not improve and resulted in only the odd word exchanged during the twenty minutes involved, but no conversation as such. Accepting the situation for what it was, I gave up and went home in a sour mood.

Monday morning found me in no better humour than I had been for the previous couple of days. After an extended period of reluctance, I finally hauled myself out of bed and set about my normal morning routine as though I had weights strapped to my ankles. A coffee before I set off didn't help but did result in a later start to my morning walk than usual. For something a bit different, and in the hope it might help brighten my day, today, I headed off in the opposite direction to the way I usually go. Once I closed my gate behind me and was out on the footpath, I turned left instead of right as I usually do.

My late start meant the street was starting to come to life as I strode past Rod's and Cilla's houses. Before crossing the street at the corner, I paused on the footpath in front of the house formerly occupied by Zorka Weinhardt and, recently, by Baxter McCormac. It looked like every other house on the street, except for its front yard now in urgent need of attention. Zorka and her partner had not been gardeners and it appeared neither was McCormac. I chuckled to myself as I thought about the reputation now attached to the house. Many of the residents who had lived in the Village for longer than the last twelve months would now view anyone moving into that house as placing their life in jeopardy.

As I strode through the small park separating the Village from the adjacent residential area, I became aware of a heavy silence surrounding me. Most days, I have the company of birdsong, the sound of the breeze rustling through the trees, and the conversations and laughter of other walkers in twos and threes also traversing the park. Today, there was nothing other than the sound of leaves being crunched under my feet. The walkers I usually encounter were absent.

Going in the opposite direction meant that, at the end of my walk, I re-entered our street almost opposite my house. Most mornings, when I'm on my way home along our street, I encounter Rod on his way back from his run, and it often results in our having morning tea together. I was too late this morning. He would have returned home soon after I set off for my walk. With my hand on the latch of my gate, I paused to ponder the last couple of days. More precisely, to ponder when and what had gone awry between Rod and me. While I stood there, Rod strode out of his yard and strode off away from me in the direction of the Admin Building... And, no doubt, to meet with our Director, Tanya Jellicoe.

By the time I pushed open my gate and marched up my path, I had resolved that if Rod's attitude towards me hadn't changed by this evening, I would be demanding an explanation, regardless of what the cost might be. Far from being improved by my walk, my mood now had acquired a belligerent undertone. Then, as it was too early for morning tea and too late for breakfast, a decision was required. I chose breakfast and vented my feelings on everything I touched in the process.

With nothing demanding urgent attention scheduled for the rest of the day, the outlook for improvement as the day wore on was dismal. So, with my empty plate and mug still in front of me on the breakfast bar, I took a few moments to ponder exactly what was wrong with my outlook on life at the moment. No enlightenment was forthcoming. Then, on an impulse, after checking the time, I reached over and grabbed my phone.

"Rod's meeting with Tanya should be finished by now," I murmured aloud as I keyed his number. He answered on the second ring. "I wondered whether you might be interested in lunch today," I asked and hoped my voice sounded more relaxed than I felt.

He sounded a bit brusque, but he accepted my invitation. As I had made a move to call him, I intended to invite him for coffee, but I realised he probably had coffee with Tanya before he left her office. So, now he was coming for lunch, I had to work out what to feed him. After a brief deliberation, I settled on an omelette with a side salad. I promptly set about preparing the mushroom filling for the omelettes and the salad. When Rod arrived at noon, all that remained to do was to cook the omelettes using two small frying pans. I held my breath as I folded them over their mushroom fillings and breathed a sigh of relief when both were perfect. Rod turned down my offer of white wine, settling instead for soda water with a dash of lime juice.

It was predictable that my self-restraint wouldn't last long. By about the second mouthful of lunch, I launched into the inevitable questions.

"Have you briefed Tanya on Saturday's events yet?"

"Yeah, I saw her first thing this morning. She was shocked, of course. But she was concerned about how the Board would react to the news and how it might impact the future of similar bus trips."

"They can hardly blame McCormac's death on the bus trip. Surely, he just happened to be in the wrong place at the wrong time... unless you know something different."

"No, I don't know anything different."

"What about the information in his file? Did Tanya share any of that with you?" That would be my last question, I told myself, unless Rod became a little more communicative.

"The information in his file was quite basic and suggested he was 'ordinary'. There was nothing of interest in it. What's with all the questions? Why are you so interested in the man's background?"

What a silly question – given recent events. Still, in the hope of better things to come, I tried to diffuse the tension I sensed building on the other side of the table.

"There was nothing unusual about the questions, Rod. I simply wondered whether you learned anything that might shed some light on the man and maybe provide a clue as to the reason for his death. It seems I was wrong ... or maybe it's just that you are not prepared to divulge what you learnt."

"That's not the case, Marion. Why would I withhold anything I learned from you? If anything, his file painted him as a bit too 'ordinary'. It felt like a story down pat to suit the particular situation."

"I suppose it's too much to hope that you've heard anything more on the matter from our top cop... or Cilla?"

"Not a word yesterday or so far today. Perhaps Richard and his officers are finding the 'real' Baxter McCormac just as elusive as we are."

"Rod, do you think Cilla might be withholding information from us? I don't know why I say this, but Cilla's behaviour in regard to this event is not quite right, not quite as I would expect Cilla to behave."

"If I have to be honest, I'm inclined to agree that she might be holding something back, but I have no idea what or why."

"Might it be that she considers whatever she has discovered is too sensitive to share with the likes of us?"

"Anything is possible, I suppose, but I do agree. Her behaviour since the incident is a bit out of the ordinary for Cilla."

As there wasn't anything more to say on the matter, I let the topic die... but I did feel a twinge of pride in myself. I had managed to carefully avoid suggesting that, if Cilla did know something, withholding the information might be nothing more than 'grandstanding' on her part. Was she simply fuelling her need to be important by knowing more than everyone else?

"It's probably no more than one-upmanship... if she does know anything, that is," Rod suggested, breaking the brief silence between us.

"What about Joe, Rod? Do you believe his absence results from his employers requiring his services, or do you think he has gone south on a private mission to do some digging for anything in McCormac's background?"

"The latter, I am inclined to think. Maybe he and Cilla have sniffed out a whiff of something about McCormac, and Joe has gone to poke around for more information."

"Or to confirm what they already have discovered?"

"Quite possibly, I suppose. As there was no happy hour on Saturday evening after the bus trip, I went for an extra run at dusk and changed my route to run through that small park next door. I encountered Joe strolling through the park and we stopped for a chat. Joe confided that a call from his 'employers' would have him heading to Canberra in the next day or two. He was waiting for confirmation of his travel arrangements. He admitted he still does the odd bit of work for 'The Agency', as he calls it, but was careful not to divulge any details of what exactly that work was."

"I don't suppose we can expect him to share too much of his life with us. Still, I find it strange there's been nothing from Richard yet."

"To my way of thinking, it's too early to really expect anything from Richard. I suspect it won't be easy to dig up anything on McCormac. What I find strange is the absence of contact from our chairman or any members of our board of directors regarding the McCormac incident. I expected to be bombarded with questions and please-explains."

"As you say, it all seems a bit strange at the moment. But, there must be something we can do instead of just sitting around wondering."

Rod left no doubt he was sceptical about our being able to do anything to progress the investigation into McCormac's death or to establish anything about the man himself. After a few moments of thought, he did come up with the suggestion.

"If you're up for it, we could take a trip back to Jackson Cove where it all happened."

"What is that likely to achieve? It's been so long since the incident occurred, I hardly think we'll find anything now that we didn't find on the day."

"That's true. There's a fair chance it will prove nothing, but maybe talking to the locals might turn up something. Someone might have seen something, even if they don't think they did."

After a brief discussion of how such a visit might occur, it was agreed we'd go first thing the next morning. Although having agreed to revisit the site of McCormac's demise, I couldn't muster any enthusiasm for the idea, and the whole thing left me feeling flat all day. Another subdued happy hour tonight did nothing to improve my outlook on the whole idea. At first, I found it strange that nobody at the happy hour even mentioned McCormac, but I suspected his death was occupying everyone's thoughts. Maybe it's their particular way of dealing with the shock of the situation.

Probably for the first time ever, I was the first to leave Rod's place and long before happy hour had concluded. I wasn't feeling particularly sociable. I suspected nobody else was either, as the evening's atmosphere seemed quite flat. Although a particularly early departure wasn't scheduled for the next morning, I told myself an early night might go some way to boosting my enthusiasm for tomorrow's trip.

Our arrival at Jackson Cove, the seaside village where McCormac went to meet his maker, didn't appear to spark any interest amongst the locals. When we arrived in the village, Rod drove straight to the far end of the street and parked in front of the coffee shop.

The early morning rush was over, and the owner was busy wiping down and preparing tables for mid-morning arrivals. She recognised us from our previous visit and stopped to chat with us. Her topic for the conversation she initiated was predictable.

"Good to see the events of your last visit haven't put you off this place altogether. Have you found out what actually happened?"

I expected Rod to answer, but he just shook his head before asking his own question. "Has there been any talk around here about what happened or why?"

"No, nothing. The whole village is still in shock. Things like that don't happen often here, so it has rocked the whole community."

"That's only to be expected, I suppose. Has there been much talk about it – or much speculation, should I say?"

The woman considered Rod's question for a moment before offering an opinion.

"Although nobody really knows what happened, there has been plenty being said about it ... in hushed tones and quiet corners, if you know what I mean."

"So, I take that to mean the rumour mill is alive and working overtime at Jackson Cove...?" I suggested. "What's the favoured version of the event?"

She laughed. "Take your pick. It ranges from 'the Chinese did it' to its having been part of a gangland war. You don't have anything more exciting – or plausible – to offer, do you?"

We both shook our heads. I thought it might bring the subject to an end, but I was wrong. Rod had entered journalist mode.

"As you say, it is only to be expected that the incident would shock the village. I imagine such events don't happen around here too often. Would it be too much to expect that someone saw or heard something of any use regarding the incident? There appeared to be a few locals around on the day. People who might notice anything out of the ordinary that happened so close to the main street."

"It's fair to say everyone is curious about it, but no one is talking about it. I don't think they are game to talk about it too much. Still, there is one woman you might find it worth talking to. She owns the local art shop and runs what amounts to the local art hub. You might have picked the right day to pay her a visit. The local art group are having their monthly meeting in the art shop at eleven o'clock. You never know what might come out of a chat with them."

While I expected Rod to leap up and dash along to the art shop, I was mistaken. He was sceptical.

"Well, I will try for a chat with them, but there might not have been artists around that Saturday morning when the incident happened. They were probably all at home working in their studios."

"No, I think you will find that's not the case. Just about everyone belongs to that art group – even those who only crochet fridge towels or make fluffy coat hangers. Even a jam and pickle maker is a member."

"How does a jam and pickle maker qualify as an artist?" I demanded. "I would have thought that to belong to an art group, you would have to be involved in producing art of some sort."

Rod was not happy about my interrupting proceedings and gave me a filthy look. I ignored him and focused on the coffee shop owner, who launched into an explanation.

"You need to understand that the art group is more of a social club than a group of people dedicated to the production of fine art. It's a reason to meet with fellow residents and chat about everything and anything. Even the jam and pickle maker is genuinely involved with art. All her products have fancy artwork on their labels, and even those fiddley bits of fabric she attaches over the lids feature hand-drawn images of what's in the bottles."

I was intrigued. "So, a bottle of strawberry jam would have drawings of strawberries on a scrap of fabric covering its lid?"
"That's correct...."

Another filthy look from Rod warned me not to pursue this discussion further. There followed a few moments of silence before Rod took charge again.

"What about you... Cheryl?" he asked as he peered at her name badge. "Did you notice or hear anything out of the ordinary that Saturday morning?"

"Apart from murder having been committed along there at the lookout...? No. All I noticed was a herd of police and paramedics swarming over the place... and presumably that all happened after the event."

Her tone suggested Rod's question had stretched the friendship a touch too far for the coffee shop's owner, and her comment being delivered over her shoulder as she returned to her position behind the counter confirmed it.

"As I said, maybe your best bet would be to take your questions along to the art shop and put them to the art group meeting."

As their arrival at the art shop would have been too early to meet any of the art group, Rod suggested we revisit the crime scene. I trailed along behind as he marched off in the direction of the lookout.

"Rod, what do you hope to achieve by coming up here again? The police combed the site on the day and it's not likely they missed anything. There won't be anything new that's appeared here since then."

"I don't expect to find anything, certainly nothing new. I just want to copy McCormac; to re-enact what he was doing and maybe get some feel for why he was here and what he might have seen or heard. Besides, it's a pleasant way to fill in time until the art group meeting. How about we agree to return to the art group about fifteen minutes before their meeting is scheduled to begin? Maybe we'll be able to speak to some of the early arrivals before the meeting gets underway."

With no other prospects of anything to entertain me until then, I agreed and plonked down on the seat where the dastardly deed was believed to have occurred. That soon lost its appeal. After about a minute of sitting staring out across the bay, I was bored.

"There's nothing to see up here, Rod, except for a few white caps on the breakers way out there beyond the bay. What would McCormac possibly have found here to hold his interest for anything longer than about a minute?"

"Perhaps there was more activity on the bay that morning. Maybe surfers or sailboats, or some other such activity happening out on the water."

He had a point, I suppose, so I thought about it for a few moments before my memories came back into focus.

"No, that wasn't the case... not while we were here that morning, anyway. I remember sitting at one of those picnic tables along the Esplanade waiting to be interviewed by the coppers. To fill in time and bring the morning's activities back into perspective, I sat there studying the bay. Nothing was happening out there. I have clear recollection of thinking how boring it all was."

"Okay... Maybe McCormac just wanted to sit in peace and quiet and enjoy the solitude."

"Why would he take a bus trip all the way to Jackson Cove with a group of people he didn't seem to have much time for? He could have stayed at home and pondered the world from his back deck in complete peace and quiet. And, if he'd stayed in the Village, he wouldn't have had to suffer the sing-along that seemed to last the entire bus trip."

"Yeah, perhaps that's true, but maybe there's another reason. Maybe he expected to see something specific here, like sailboat races, or fisherman bringing back their catches. Yes, maybe he was hoping to buy some fresh fish or other seafood."

"That's unlikely," I said after a moment's thought. "No, if that were the case, he would have brought something with him to keep it cold until we returned to the Village. The fish or whatever he might have bought would have gone off by the time he was home again unless he had an esky or something to keep it cold."

We lapsed into silence for a brief period before a new line of thinking occurred to me and I shattered the silence between us.

"Maybe he was waiting to meet someone. This lookout is an ideal place to meet if you don't want others to know about the meeting."

After a moment's consideration, Rod conceded my suggestion was a possibility, but quickly shot it down again.

"If we stick with that idea, who would he need to meet covertly and why? McCormac appeared to be a newcomer to our area with no previous connections to the district at all. How would he even know this was a good place to meet someone covertly?"

Right, I had to admit Rod had a point, but I still liked my idea of the meeting and put forward further supporting arguments.

"What about that bloke who Janet heard call McCormac 'Major'? What was the connection there between those two? We must quiz Janet about that when we're back at the Village. She might remember something about the car – maybe even its registration number."

"This is Janet Furlong you're talking about," Rod reminded me. "How much do you really think she will be able to tell you?"

"Still, it is something worth thinking about. And, maybe Richard can find some CCTV footage of the car coming or going from the Village. There must be cameras somewhere reasonably close by that would have recorded it."

That generated some positive discussion. After agreeing we should talk to Janet about the car, Rod supported my suggestion that CCTV footage might be a possibility. That generated speculation about where CCTV cameras in the vicinity of the Village might be positioned along the main road that runs past the Village. Encouraged by Rod's positive response to my suggestion, I aired the rest of my thoughts on the matter.

"If Richard can locate some footage of the car, it could indicate which way it went after leaving the Village and from which direction it returned."

"Now, that is interesting," Rod began. "We don't know when McCormac was dropped back at the Village. Was it a short or long absence?"

While Rod was speaking, I checked the time.

"Rod, it's now about half an hour before the art group meeting is scheduled to begin. I know it's a bit early, but might it be worth going down to the art shop now? We could talk to the shop owner until the art group members start arriving."

Chapter 5

The art shop owner, Hazel, who had issued such a warm welcome when we first entered, soon dropped her enthusiasm for our presence once she discovered we weren't there to buy anything. Although reticent to talk to us initially, Rod soon sweet-talked her around. Not surprisingly, perhaps, Hazel didn't have any information to offer.

"A few people were coming and going from the shop that morning, so I was a bit busy. And, anyway, I can't actually see that lookout area from here in the shop. So, I don't have any useful information to give you. There has been plenty of discussion and speculation around town, but I haven't heard anything of any substance. I doubt the art group members will have anything useful to offer either, but I'll take you in and introduce you once the meeting comes to order. You'll be able to ask your questions, but I doubt you'll get anything useful."

When some early art group members arrived, we were still talking to Hazel, and it resulted in our missing the opportunity to talk to them before the meeting. Then, a group of members, laughing and chatting amongst themselves, came in together and again, the opportunity to question them was lost. The last few members rushed in right on the dot of eleven o'clock, just as the meeting was being called to order.

Then, it was 'showtime' for us as Hazel led us through to the meeting in a back room. After introducing us and explaining our connection to and interest in the events of last Saturday morning, Hazel handed over to Rod to begin asking questions. His opening gambit was designed to put the members at ease and, hopefully, avoid the likely negative responses to our presence.

"I know the police were fairly thorough on the day and interviewed most of the people who were in town at the time. It's more than likely that if any of you were in town that morning, you would have been interviewed as well. Our hope in talking to people today is that someone, thanks to the passage of time, might now recall something they weren't aware of at the time. While that 'something' they now recall might seem trivial to them, it might prove vital to the investigation."

It was hard to judge the group's reaction to Rod's statement. At first, the only reaction I detected was blank looks all around that lasted a few moments ... Before the questions began.

Who was he?... Was he someone important?... Was there a gangland connection?... Was he the local drug dealers' supplier?... Was it simply a random attack by someone suffering mental illness?... Were the townspeople safe?... Was the culprit likely to strike again?

Overwhelmed by it all, I felt tempted to bolt out of the store. I looked to Rod for salvation and noted he was looking a bit frayed around the edges. It was a relief when Rod called a halt to it all.

"Ladies, please... Let's take a moment to draw breath. While we share your questions and concerns, we don't have any answers. That's why we've returned today in the hope that somebody might've recalled something that they hadn't been aware of at the time. We've taken up enough of your meeting time already and apologise for our intrusion this morning. Thank you for your time. If anyone should happen to think of something, regardless of how irrelevant they might think it to be, for the next hour or so before we leave Jackson Cove, we will be at the coffee shop. So, if anyone thinks of something they want to pass on, that's where we will be."

Once we were out on the street again, I was itching to put to Rod something that occurred to me while we had been at the art group meeting, but I was of two minds about sharing it with him.

"Right... What now, Rod? I know you told them we would be at the coffee shop for the next hour, but I wonder about the wisdom of that. I think we came close to outliving our welcome in the coffee shop this morning."

"Nah, I don't think so. Besides, I don't think she's so busy she can pick and choose who to serve. It's a bit early for the lunchtime rush – if such a thing happens here – so the coffee shop should be quiet while we have an early lunch before heading back to the Village."

"Do you really expect anyone to come to talk to us over lunch? It seems like wishful thinking to me."

"You might be right, but there's always hope. Anyway, we need to have lunch. We will be starving by the time we return to the Village if we don't have something to eat before we leave here."

Our reception when we entered the coffee shop was decidedly frostier than when we arrived this morning. Nevertheless, as the only customers in the shop, she probably felt obliged to serve us. We sat in silence for a few moments after we ordered and I felt myself starting to relax. I hadn't realised how tense I had become and couldn't quite work out why. Yes, the art group members mounted a fairly solid 'inquisition', but none of it was confrontational. As I searched for the cause, I found myself slowly accepting my tension was self-inflicted. It stemmed from the thoughts I'd had while we were at the art group meeting. Although I knew it wasn't going to go well, I decided to share those thoughts with Rod.

"Rod, I've been thinking. What is there past that lookout?"

"Eh...? What do you mean by that?"

"A bit of the track carries on away from that lookout point. Doesn't look like it's had a lot of use, but I wondered where it went."

"I've no idea, but I suppose it leads further around the coastline until whatever comes next. If, as you say, it doesn't look as though it gets much use, it probably doesn't lead to anywhere exciting. Why are you interested in where it goes? Come on, spit it out. What's niggling at you?"

"Argh, all right... I know what you're going to say, but here goes, anyway... What if the crime didn't happen at the lookout?"

"What? What are you suggesting? I'm afraid you're going to have to explain further if you want me to answer that question.

Why do you think it didn't happen there? And where else do you think it might have happened?"

"Yep, that's about what I expected. Well, there was nothing at the lookout, no evidence of any sort. We didn't find anything, and nor did the police. That seems just a bit off to me."

"Ye-es, I admit the lack of evidence is a bit odd."

"A bit odd? It's bloody odd that a bloke can be stabbed to death without even a speck of blood lying around apart from what was on his shirt. I know that's where the body was found, and I also know that some wounds such as his can bleed internally, rather than leaving great pools of blood lying around at the crime scene."

"Hmm... I hear what you're saying and I think I understand your reasoning, but..."

"No, Rod, there is no BUT involved. As a crime scene, the lookout doesn't fit with the body that we found. There wasn't a drop of blood anywhere around at the scene. We didn't even see any until we rolled him over and saw the front of his shirt."

"We don't know what the autopsy had to say about his wound, but I am inclined to agree that there probably should have been more blood around. His wound looked serious enough to suggest death would have followed within moments. So, if the crime actually occurred somewhere else, would he have been capable of returning to the lookout where we found him?"

"You haven't mentioned anything I haven't thought about but, no, I don't have any answers.

Oh, maybe we'll have to shelve this conversation for the moment. Rod, I think that's one of the ladies from the art group meeting that's just entered the shop. Is it possible she is coming to talk to us?"

She was coming to talk to us, and it was obvious she was very tentative about it. After hesitating for a moment, she slowly made her way to our table. Rod sprang up and pulled a chair out for her before asking if she'd like something to drink or eat. She shook her head, then changed to mind.

"A mineral water would be nice, thanks. Look, I don't know that I've got anything useful to tell you but I thought maybe I should come and speak to you. By the way, I'm Jolene. I'm fairly new to Jackson Cove, and an even newer member of the art group. That's why I didn't want to say anything at the meeting. The art group is a bit of a clique, you see, and I don't think I've been fully accepted yet."

Once her mineral water had been delivered and she had a few sips, Rod felt it safe to press her for whatever information she thought she had to offer.

"It goes without saying that I didn't know the man who was murdered or anything about him, but I had seen him around. As I said, I'm only new to the area and I'm still trying to set up my home. I've had all sorts of minor repairs that needed doing and a little bit of painting and... well, you know how it is, you're in and out of the shops every other five minutes to get something you need for whatever you're doing at home."

"So, you think you saw the victim around here at Jackson Cove prior to last Saturday morning?" I asked quietly to encourage her to go on with whatever she came to tell us.

"How sure are you that it was the same bloke as the victim?" Rod asked.

"Well, he kind of stood out, didn't he? I mean, the way he dressed and looked – and maybe the way he moved about the place as well. It sort of set him apart as different from the locals and, somehow, he didn't look like just another tourist."

"That's interesting... And, yes, you're right about him. He did tend to stand out a bit. How often did you see him?" Rod asked. "Was it just the once, or was he something of a regular visitor?"

"I don't know that I would call him a regular visitor. Now that I think about it, I probably saw him in town about three or four times. I don't know whether that makes him a 'regular visitor' or not. But, I suppose he could have been staying somewhere in the area because those occasions when I saw him occurred over the week or ten days before he ended up dead at the lookout."

Jolene might not have thought she had anything important to tell us when she came in, but she now had me sitting on the front edge of my chair. There were so many questions I wanted to ask. Respecting Rod's superior journalist's ability to question people, I sat quietly while he asked the questions. But, the time came when intrigue got the better of me.

"What great information... Thank you, Jolene, for passing it on. Although, there is one detail I am keen to know more about. On those occasions when you saw the victim around town, where did you see him? Was he going in and out of shops or just ambling about? Did you see him in much the same place every time?"

"He probably came in here once or twice, I think. She might remember him," Jolene flicked her head at the woman behind the counter. "Apart from that, whenever I saw him, he appeared to be coming from the lookout or heading for it. I'm sorry, but that's about all I can tell you. I apologise for interrupting your lunch, but I didn't feel comfortable mentioning this at the meeting. Oh, and I wasn't interviewed by the police. I was on my way home from town last Saturday morning just as the police and ambulance were arriving."

"You didn't think to contact the police later?" Rod asked a little too sharply.

I saw Jolene flinch at what amounted to a rebuke, and I felt compelled to ease the situation. I noticed she appeared to have become fidgety. If I didn't know better, I'd say she was keen to leave.

"It's not surprising. I probably wouldn't have thought to contact the police either. Jolene, while we've been talking, I haven't noticed the art group members leaving the art shop. Had the meeting ended when you left?"

"Oh, yes. The meeting doesn't take long at all, usually less than half an hour. Then, those who aren't in a hurry to do something else stay on to socialise for a while. After that, a few either come in here for lunch or go to the pub for a meal."

"So you gave up socialising with the group to come and talk to us. That was kind of you. Are you sure you wouldn't care to have lunch with us?"

"Thank you, Marion, but I really would like to go now... if there's no more you need to ask me, of course. I don't usually stay to socialise as I'm not really accepted yet. And, if it's okay with you, I would like to leave now as I don't particularly want the other members to know I've been chatting to you."

By the time she finished speaking, Jolene was on her feet and had her bag over her shoulder. Rod added his thanks to mine before we watched her walk briskly out of the shop.

"Should we go, too?" I asked as I watched Jolene scramble into her car and drive off.

"No. Let's just wait a few minutes until everyone leaves the art group meeting, so we can watch where they go for lunch. I have a feeling we have managed to kill today's lunchtime crowd for this coffee shop. Something tells me all the members will elect to lunch at the pub today. I suspect we might be considered best to be avoided."

"What do you hope to achieve by hanging around here?"

"Probably nothing... but I don't think it would be a good look for us to bolt out of town before the meeting ends or the moment after it ends."

A couple of minutes later, people spilled out of the art shop. While a small group headed to the pub, the remainder of the meeting attendees climbed into their cars and drove off. We followed their example soon after. As we started back along the street, I spoke softly to Rod.

"No doubt you were aware the coffee shop proprietor kept a watchful eye – and probably an ear – on proceedings at our table. I hope Jolene doesn't think her chat with us will remain a secret for long, not in a small place like this."

"If any of that art group has lunch in the coffee shop, that's about as long as her chat with us will remain confidential. Anyway, Marion, now that we are out and about again, I suspect you'll want to explore that track leading further along the coast from the lookout area. Shall we do that before we head home again?" Sometimes, he does ask the silliest questions!

Mother Nature had smiled on us while we were in the coffee shop. A light sea breeze had sprung up and a thick covering of heavy, grey clouds had rolled in, making the trek to the lookout a reasonably pleasant stroll.

As if in response to some subliminal command, we both simultaneously dropped down onto the long wooden bench seat that occupied the majority of the lookout area. I immediately sprang up again.

Startled, Rod looked up at me and demanded, "What...?"

"Sitting where we had so recently found a body doesn't appeal to me."

"What are you doing now?"

"I came up here to explore that track leading off to the east from here. So, that's what I'm going to do." I started towards the track in question.

"Hang about. I'll come with you. I don't know what you think you're going to find or achieve by trudging off along that track."

He was right. There was nothing obviously appealing about it, and it didn't become any better once I started along it. Nothing more than a rough dirt track dotted with small rocks and pebbles and bordered on both sides by spiky, spinifex-like grass and small shrubs. The first fifty metres followed closely along the cliff line. Then, it took a somewhat significant detour inland to skirt around a jumble of large rocks and boulders perched for quite some distance along the edge of the cliff. After about another eighty metres or so, the track again veered over to follow closely along the cliff line. To avoid damaging a toe or tripping over on the rough track, I trudged along with my eyes focused on the ground beneath my feet and risking only occasional glances up ahead to survey my surroundings.

On one such occasion, a short distance up ahead, I noticed the cliff line curved outwards a little way, creating a brief interruption to the continuous curve of the cliff line around the bay. Already regretting my decision to explore the track and questioning my thinking that now had me where I was, I strode up and stood close to the edge of that piece of the cliff jutting out over the bay. I hoped it would allow me to see some distance further ahead and hopefully prove there was nothing more to be achieved by continuing along the track. That wasn't quite how it happened.

"Look at that! Rod, look what's up ahead... Rod, where are you?"

I spun around to search for him and found him sitting on a rock along the side of the track some distance further back. He was fully absorbed in digging a small pebble out of the tread of his shoe. Once the excavation was completed, he eased himself onto his feet and started towards me.

"What are you on about now? I don't see anything out here to get excited about."

"If you don't want to be here, Rod, go back to the lookout and wait for me there. You didn't have to come with me."

"Of course, I had to come with you. God only knows what sort of mess you might have gotten yourself into if I hadn't come with you. This track you were so keen to explore hasn't seen much traffic in a long while, if ever. Now, what is it you think you've found?"

"From here on this bit of the cliff that pokes out, you can see further along the coastline. There is a little bay up ahead. I can see a number of houses there. I didn't know there was another village along here. It only looks quite small... And I can't see any road leading down into it. In fact, the only thing that seems to link it to anywhere else is this dirt track."

While I had been speaking, Rod had come up beside me and had focused his attention on the buildings I had indicated.

"Hmm... Shacks... Not houses as such. They are just shacks, probably weekenders or maybe fishermen's shacks. You're right about there being no village along here, and there are no roads leading off the main highway to anywhere along this stretch of the coast except the one to Jackson Cove."

"Okay... But if there is no road in, how do the owners of those buildings get into that bay?"

"By the look of it, I imagine it's boat access only. That certainly fits with them being fishermen's shacks. Although, they could be getaway places for people who own small boats and like to escape to solitude for the weekend."

"Is it likely McCormac visited that enclave of shacks before he was killed? Maybe something happened there that resulted in his death. Somehow, he didn't seem dressed or prepared for a hike in the countryside. His leather-soled brogues tend to be a bit of a giveaway.

Do you think that might be the actual crime scene? That's where he might've been stabbed?"

"Marion, how far do you think those shacks are from the lookout? We walked about three or four hundred metres just to be here, and those shacks are at least that much further again ahead of us. If McCormac were stabbed in the vicinity of those shacks, he would never have made it back to the lookout. His body, when and if it was found, would have been discovered somewhere along this track – and probably quite close to the scene of the crime."

"Yeah, I suppose you're right. His wound looks serious enough to have prevented him from going too far from the crime scene before he died. So, I suppose it means that, if the crime scene isn't the lookout, it has to be somewhere quite close to where we found him. And, yes, I still think this track was somehow involved. What's your take on all of this? Come on, Rod. Share your thoughts."

"The one thing I will agree is that the crime scene either had to be at the lookout or somewhere quite close. Perhaps we should return to the lookout and devote a bit more thought to the situation."

It's hard to argue with common sense when it slaps you in the face. I took one last look at the shacks in the distance before preparing to head back along the track, but a stray thought that slammed in from left field delayed matters for a few moments.

"Rod, what surprises me a bit is how peaceful he looked when we found him. Yeah, sure… He was dead, but he looked as though he was just sleeping. There were no signs of a struggle or that he'd been thrashing about in his dying moments. Maybe the experts wouldn't find that a bit strange, but I do. Anyway, on our way back to the lookout, there is something I want to explore before we abandon this track."

"I'm almost not game to ask what that might be."

"Soon after we started along this track, I noticed a disturbed area of grass leading off from one side towards a clump of scrubby-looking trees and shrubs. It wasn't a track as such, but it looked as though someone had gone that way in recent times and trampled the grass and a few other plants along the way. It might be nothing. I know that. But, now that we're here, it won't take me long to put my mind at rest about whether it's relevant or not."

No time was wasted as we hurried back along the track as quickly as possible without incurring injury.

"Look… See, over there… See how the grass has been trampled as though somebody· ran through it on their way over to that clump of scrub. Come on. I want to follow it to see where it goes and if it leads to anything interesting."

"No… Stop! Marion, don't go charging along there. What if it's important? What if it leads to the crime scene? We don't want to go charging over to that patch of scrub and destroying whatever evidence might still exist. Best we continue back to the lookout and I give Richard a call about our suspicions."

Of course Rod was right, no matter how much I wanted that not to be the case. It was all I could do not to charge off towards the scrub. But, if it was connected to the crime scene in some way, I did not want to be responsible for messing it up. Rod whipped out his phone as soon as I agreed not to go charging off through the grass. By the time we were back at the lookout, Rod had shared our suspicions with our top cop, Richard Wilson, and was in the process of sending him an image he had taken with his phone of the area of interest. Job done, he slid his phone back into his pocket. It was a signal to me that it was now safe to talk to him.

"What do we do now, Rod? Do we go back to the Village, or do we wait here for Richard and his merry men to turn up?"

"We wait here as Richard instructed us to do."

"And how long might that be? Maybe we should go back and sit in some degree of comfort at one of those tables along the Esplanade. I definitely don't feel inclined to sit on that seat where we found McCormac – and I don't feel like standing around up here for however long it takes for the others to arrive."

"If you can stop moaning and are happy to stand around here at the lookout for about ten minutes or so, the others will have joined us by then. We can show them what we need to show them and then go home. Richard and a team of his officers have been working out in this area and were just about to head back to the city. They will now detour in here to have a look at what we want to show them, and hence, it will only take them about ten minutes to arrive."

Suitably chastised and feeling decidedly grumpy, I turned my back on Rod, leant on the railing around the lookout area, and spent the time studying the complete nothingness happening out on the bay.

Chapter 6

True to prediction, Richard and his officers arrived about ten minutes after Rod called him. From the outset, it was obvious Richard was sceptical about our suspicions regarding possible evidence of the crime scene of McCormac's murder. Richard bowled up to Rod and started asking questions before asking to be shown the area we thought might be of interest to McCormac's case. It was as though I wasn't there. As I watched Rod lead the cavalcade of Richard and his officers along the dirt track, and despite having first drawn attention to the area in question, I realised I wasn't being included in any of what was happening – and probably wasn't going to be. It darkened my already filthy mood.

I heard Richard instruct his officers to follow the line of trampled grass to the patch of scrub but to leave a clear area along both sides of the trampled area in order to preserve any possible evidence. Then, they were to search the patch of scrub for any relevant evidence.

It seemed like only moments later when Rod and Richard, returned to the lookout. Richard was voicing his opinions about the exercise as they stepped up onto the lookout.

"...Doubtful they will find anything there, especially all this time after the event. There probably was nothing of interest for us there to begin with. We might be inspecting the equivalent of the local 'lovers lane'. You know the sort of place I mean. Somewhere the local youth come to sow their wild oats."

Richard marched over and plonked down on the bench seat without a moment's hesitation. More cautious, Rod gently lowered himself onto the end of the bench further from where the body had been. It would have been awkward for all three of us to perch on the bench. We would have looked like pigeons on a fence, but that wasn't going to happen. There was no way I was going to sit on that bench, even if it wasn't already occupied by the other two. With Richard now apparently comfortable and relaxed, it was question time.

"Why did you choose to visit Jackson Cove today? I mean, what prompted you to come back here today? Did something happen to suggest you should come back and explore that track?"

"No-o, nothing happened," Rod replied. "After we returned to the Village, Marion and I were discussing the day's events, and I suppose we developed a couple of hypotheses about the crime. Anyway, that was enough to bring us back here today. Our intention, if you could call it an intention, was to talk to any of the locals who might have been in town the morning of the murder. Yes, we knew the police had interviewed those who were around, but we had the notion that, after some time to think about things, maybe someone had remembered something they didn't report at the time."

"And was your fact-finding mission successful?" There was no mistaking the sarcasm in Richard's question.

As I went to answer, I caught Rod's stern look, and I thought I detected the slightest shake of his head. Although I had no idea what Rod's message was all about, I thought it prudent not to deliver the response I had intended. Instead, we both simply shook our heads at Richard, who replied with a condescending nod and smile before continuing questioning.

"So, obviously you chose to come back up here to the lookout. What did you hope to find?"

"We-ell...," Rod began tentatively as he seemed to choose his words carefully. "Well, Marion was curious about where that dirt track might lead to, and after we had a bit of a look around up here, we decided it might be worth exploring it just to see where it went."

"And did it go anywhere nice?"

"It might, but we only went part way along it before we returned to the lookout."

Richard's attitude seemed to undergo a rapid change. He had been officious to the point of being obnoxious, but in a sudden about-face, he became Richard again – the Richard I was familiar with. He was interested in the track, where it led, what we saw and what our thoughts were on why it existed. Although I threw in the odd comment, Rod took charge of answering the questions. To be honest, there wasn't much to tell. When Rod mentioned the ancient shacks nestled in the small alcove, Richard's eyes lit up.

There was little we could tell him about the shacks. After all, we had only seen them in the distance. We hadn't visited them and really didn't know anything about them other than they were there and we assumed their only means of access was by boat. Richard tried a couple more times to elicit more information from us about the shacks but eventually accepted that we really didn't know anything about them other than they were there.

At that point, his interrogation seemed to come to an end and no further questions were forthcoming. I waited a few moments to confirm that Richard was done with questioning us before I felt it was safe for me to drive the conversation.

"While we've nothing more to tell you about today, I am curious about what you might have found out about McCormac's real identity and background. Have you uncovered anything at all about the man?"

My question caused Richard to shake his head and heave a sigh.

"If only.... The man's a ghost. No, that's not right. If he were a ghost, there would be information about him to be found without too much trouble. That's not the case. So, in answer to your question, other than he doesn't appear to exist in any records, I haven't been able to establish anything about the man."

"What about a driver's licence and bank accounts? Surely he had those sorts of things and, in order to have those sorts of things, he would have had to prove who he was."

"Oh, those things do exist, but there is no information behind them. How they came into being is a mystery. The search for information is ongoing, but I hold little hope of finding anything anytime soon."

Rod shot me a strange look. I didn't understand it and just shrugged in response. I expected Rod would explain, but he didn't. Instead, he decided to throw in a question of his own.

"Richard, I was wondering about CCTV cameras in the vicinity of Merivale Retirement Village. Are there any cameras located along that main road that are close to the turnoff into the Village?"

"Are they important in terms of the McCormac investigation?"

"Don't know yet, but they could be."

"Let me think... Yeah, there are two cameras along that road running past the Village. They are both located just a short distance on either side of the Village entrance. So, are they likely to be important?"

"Nah, I don't think so. I was just curious in case something should emerge later regarding our murdered fellow resident."

Rod shot me another hard look as he replied. I understood this one of Rod's repertoire of looks and, just in time, did my best to look as though I had no idea what Rod was on about as Richard shot an inquiring look in my direction.

Then, the third degree appeared to be over for the time being and the lookout lapsed into silence for a couple of minutes until Richard became impatient. He stood and looked around before announcing, "I might go and check on my officers to see if exploring that track and its surrounds has been a waste of time."

He stretched and was about to set off when his phone came to life. While Rod and I tried not to look interested, we both listened to Richard's one-sided phone conversation. We gained little information, but it was obvious the officers had found something. Whatever it was, appeared to generate a degree of excitement in their boss. It was only a short call. After telling us to stay and wait at the lookout, Richard rushed off to join his officers.

We did exactly as we were told to do – for a few moments. But, that's about as long as I could stand it before curiosity got the better of me.

"You can continue to wait here at the lookout if you like, but I am going for a stroll along that dirt track."

"Marion, be sensible. We were told to wait here. The police have now taken over that area. You can't just go marching in there."

"I'm not going to go anywhere we – and the police – haven't already been, so there is no chance I'll be messing up evidence. Anyway, I intend only to venture along the track as far as where the trampled grass leads off it.

The argument raged for some moments. In the end, Rod lost the argument but still refused to go with me. That was not how I envisaged it would end but, fair enough. It was his decision and it wasn't going to stop me. I flounced off to the start of the track and then paused to check out what was happening further along. From what I could see, no officers were visible and everything looked quiet. I guessed Richard and his officers must be hidden as they searched the patch of scrub. As I took the first couple of steps along the track, I heard Rod's phone play its tune.

"It's Richard...," he yelled at me before answering the call.

I rushed back and stood beside Rod, hoping to learn something from Rod's end of the call. I was disappointed. I didn't learn much at all and sought to remedy that situation as soon as the call ended.

"Well, what's happening? What have they found?"

"Don't know...Richard didn't say."

"So, why did he call you? What was the call about?"

"Okay, I know this won't suit you, but here goes.... He told us to go home. He was quite emphatic there was nothing more for us to do here, and he would contact me later if he had anything interesting to report."

"You are right... that doesn't suit me at all. I'll bet he is already on the phone to Cilla giving her all the details of what's going on and what they have found."

"That could well be. As Cilla works with the local cops in some mysterious capacity – in some sort of advisory role – Richard probably would contact her. The way this case is shaping up, it probably is strange enough to warrant her involvement."

His comments did nothing to improve my mood, and I sulked all the way back to the Village. I was not at all happy about the way the day had turned out. The drive home provided time to devote to the question of what to do next – and reach a decision. While I won't be telling Rod about it in advance, I will be visiting Janet Furlong as soon as we return to the Village, and I will be quizzing her about that car that collected McCormac, and about the car's driver who called McCormac 'Major'.

My plan unravelled about five minutes after I arrived home. I called Janet intending to invite her for coffee but, as the phone started dialling, I realised it was too late in the afternoon for coffee. I quickly changed my strategy to ask instead if I might drop by for a chat. In the end, it didn't matter what I planned to say. My call went through to voicemail and I ended the call without leaving a message.

With nothing much of the afternoon remaining, it left me with only two things to think about: a shower to freshen up, and what nibbles to prepare to take to happy hour this evening.

My outlook on life hadn't improved by the time happy hour rolled around. I decided to be there a little early in the faint hope Richard might have called Rod to share with him the outcome of this morning's search. Arriving at Rod's a little early would allow a few minutes for Rod to share it with me before the others arrived.

The result of that manoeuvre was much in keeping with the rest of my day: a total disappointment. The moment I arrived, Rod let me know he had anticipated the motive behind my early arrival.

"Before you ask, no, I haven't heard anything from Richard and, if I'm honest, I didn't expect to. We both know sending them to look at that location was a long shot that could produce nothing of interest."

"Still, it would have been courteous to at least tell us they hadn't found anything. After all, we were only trying to help with their investigation. I don't suppose you have heard from Cilla either?"

"No, I haven't heard from her. Why would I? Were you expecting her to call me about anything in particular?"

"Argh... No, I suppose not. I just wondered if she might have called to say she wouldn't make it to happy hour this evening."

"And you would take such a phone call to mean she wouldn't be coming tonight because she had suddenly become too busy helping Richard with the McCormac case?"

"Yes. Well, it wouldn't have come as a surprise, would it?"

The arrival of Maria, Alice and Luigi brought our discussion to an end, not that it was a problem. Our conversation wasn't going anywhere anyway. Within the next few minutes, the rest of the happy hour gang arrived while I was still setting out bowls of nibbles on the table on Rod's back deck. The rest of the evening, at least as I recall it, was subdued and nothing of any import occurred. Happy hour that night also was notable for its brevity. The last of the gang departed for home barely an hour after they arrived.

It was a fitting end to the kind of day I had endured. Cilla bolted along with the first of the guests to depart, leaving just me to help Rod clear away and tidy up afterwards. And, despite my best efforts to lure Janet away from the mob to ask her about the car that collected McCormac the other day, it seems she and Alice and Maria had found an enthralling subject that kept them in animated conversation for the entire hour.

Nevertheless, I did manage a quiet, surreptitious word to Janet as she was leaving.

"Will you be around tomorrow?" She nodded and looked bemused. "Good, how about joining me for coffee at ten o'clock tomorrow morning?" She still looked bemused but readily accepted my invitation.

What is wrong with me this morning? I feel about as nervous as I used to before an important job interview. It's just Janet coming for coffee, I told myself. What can be so scary about that?

Ten o'clock seemed to arrive much quicker than normal this morning and, about five minutes before it did, I realised I hadn't prepared for it. The coffee and cake were organised and ready, but I hadn't planned how to elicit the information I wanted from Janet. Then, Janet was ringing the doorbell, and I still hadn't thought out a few well-worded questions to put to her. With the usual welcoming faffing about out of the way, we were seated in my lounge room. Our coffee and cake were accompanied initially by light conversation of no consequence while I tried to work out how to initiate conversation in the direction I wanted.

"Out of the blue, sometime yesterday, it occurred to me that it was ages since we had been able to sit down and just have a chat. I suppose that's just an indication of how busy life's been around here. So, come on tell me what you've been up to these days. You've always been so busy with other things besides what's happening here in the Village. Are you still involved in all of those things? I must admit, I don't know how you found time to fit it all in."

"Yes, I'm still involved in much the same things. I don't know what I do all day if I didn't have all those things going on in my life. I'd probably end up sending Ted up the wall by annoying him all the time."

"So, you're still helping with the remedial reading at the school?"

"Oh, yes, there is an ongoing need for that."

"What about the school plays competition? Is that likely to happen again this year?"

"Yep, that's on again, and I think there's even greater interest in the competition this year."

"That's good news, but it looks like we're all going to be busy again towards the end of the year when all those plays are being staged here in our theatre. The Village always seems to have so much happening all the time. So much for retirement being a time to sit around and worry about becoming bored. I suppose, now that we're running bus trips, there's even more for residents to do to fill in their time."

"Marion, speaking of bus trips... Do you know when the next bus trip is scheduled and where we are likely to be going?

"If I'm honest, I'd have to say I'm not sure after what happened with the last bus trip. I know Rod is still expecting some problems to come from the board of directors as a result of incidents regarding that trip, especially what happened to McCormac. But there is also Bernard's fuss about the dog being allowed on the bus."

"Bernard is not likely to do anything about that, is he?"

"Argh, I suspect he would have gone straight over to the director to complain, or maybe directly to the Board chairman."

Anyway, given all that happened last Saturday, I imagine the organisers will probably let things die down for a bit while they wait to see what fallout there is from the Board before scheduling another bus trip."

"Surely the Board can't blame the bus trip for what happened, or think any of the residents were involved."

"We-ell, the way the Board thinks sometimes is a mystery to we mere mortals on the outside. I suppose the Board – like the rest of us – will be struggling to come to terms with what actually happened and why. There's so much mystery surrounding Baxter McCormac's death. Perhaps if we knew more about the circumstances that led to his death, it would help sort things out a bit. What's compounded the situation, I think, is the fact that nobody seems to know much about McCormac. I can't say I recall ever seeing him before that bus trip. Oh, that's right... You said something once about having seen him being collected and driven off in a car."

"I've thought about that a bit after what happened on the bus trip. I don't know what the director is going to do now. Tanya is going to have a hard job finding anyone who wants to live in that house now that it's jinxed the way it is. Even if she puts a newcomer in it, it wouldn't take them long to learn about the history of the place and demand to be shifted."

"I don't really believe the house is jinxed, Janet. I think it's as safe to live in that house as it is in any of the other houses in the Village. Perhaps, it all comes down to knowing more about the background of the people involved in those two incidents. In Zorka's case, her background suggested what happened to her and her partner always was a strong possibility. But, as we don't know anything of McCormac's background, what happened to him just remains a mystery."

Janet remained silent for a few moments when I finished speaking. She sat there just nodding and staring at some indistinct spot on the floor. Then, she looked up at me and agreed with everything I'd said. I decided to jump in and ask the questions I'd been itching to ask since she arrived.

"If you think back to that day the car came to collect McCormac, what do you remember about it? Do you remember anything about the car? What sort of car was it?... What colour...? Anything at all? I don't doubt you wouldn't remember much. It was such a 'nothing' sort of event."

"Oh, that's not true. I've thought about that day a lot since last Saturday. I don't know why, when it didn't seem particularly important at the time, but seeing McCormac picked up by that car seems to have stuck in my mind fairly clearly. The car was a sedan, not a little one. It was a big silver-coloured one. Well, I suppose it was really grey, but it had that metallic look about it. And, the thing I noticed most was its bright yellow number plate. It was one of those fancy ones. You know, not the run-of-the-mill sort issued by the transport department."

"Good heavens, you have got a good memory. What about the driver? Was there anything about him that sticks in your mind?"

"Hah hah... I was going to say he was young, but anyone aged less than sixty looks young to me these days. No, I think it's more like he was in his late forties... or probably early fifties. He was smartly dressed. Wasn't wearing a suit, though. I think he had on a sports jacket, but no tie. What else can I tell you about him?... Oh, that's right. I remember thinking at the time that he looked fit. You know, like people who work out a lot or play sport and have that hard, fit look about them. A bit like Rod does, I suppose."

"Wow, it has stuck in your memory very well. I think I remember you saying that the driver called McCormac 'Sir', or something."

"No, it wasn't 'Sir'. He called him 'Major'... And he dropped McCormac a sort of salute as he did so. Not a proper salute, though. No, it was more like a mock salute. Maybe it was meant as a joke of some sort. I hope it wasn't meant as an insult. That would be terrible – especially now poor man is dead."

There was nothing more to mine from Janet's memory banks about the incident. I changed the subject by asking what Ted was doing today and, after her brief response, moved to bring our get-together to an end. I glanced at my watch.

"Goodness, look at the time. Ted will be getting anxious about whether he is going to get any lunch today. I shouldn't keep you any longer or he will be phoning me to ask where you are and if you are coming home to feed him. It's been lovely to just sit and chat with you, and how good your memory is amazes me. If I learn anything more about the McCormac mystery, I'll share it with you either at happy hour or our next mahjong morning."

Then, this morning's interlude with Janet was over. I stood at my open door watching her rush along the footpath towards home and wondered what sort of stories Ted would be told about this morning.

Chapter 7

What had I learned from Janet this morning? Had I learnt anything? Lunchtime provided an ideal opportunity to review any possible outcome from it. While it might not be much, I decided I had learned some things that could be useful.

When it came to describing the vehicle that collected McCormac from the Village that morning, Janet proved not as vague as I thought she would be. Yes, it was only a vague description of the car, but it might be enough to help identify the correct vehicle on any CCTV footage Richard can locate. I realised that wouldn't tell us much. While I didn't know what the others might be interested in, I wanted to know where that vehicle went. If we knew where it went after it left the Village, we might be able to determine what McCormac was involved in and how it might have led to his death.

Indications were that the vehicle had come into the Village, left again soon after and then returned again at some unknown time later to return McCormac, before departing once more. Perhaps, if they can identify the car leaving or entering the Village, maybe they might be able to track it through the city or to wherever it went. After giving that idea some thought, I realised I didn't know the first thing about what might be involved in doing so, or even if it were at all possible, not to mention how much time and cost might be involved in such an exercise.

Now, what about the driver of the vehicle? Based on what Janet said previously, I had been inclined to think he was, or had been, military of some sort. Now, his reported actions tend to confirm that. So, does it then follow that McCormac was from a similar background?

My initial disappointment at the outcome of coffee with Janet had disappeared. I sensed a tingle of excitement running up and down my spine. Maybe this was the breakthrough we needed to progress this case. The problem now was whether to share with Rod tonight what I had learnt this morning or to keep it to myself until I see what else might emerge from other sources. I held no doubts that both Joe and Cilla were working flat out behind the scenes to uncover at least some details of Baxter McCormac's life prior to moving into Merivale Retirement Village.

The problem remained unresolved in my mind as I left early for happy hour at Rod's place. By the time I reached his gate, I had more or less decided to say nothing for the moment. Of course, there was always the possibility that Janet might tell Rod about our conversation this morning, but somehow, I was inclined to think Janet would see our conversation as nothing more than an amiable chat over coffee. At least, I was hoping that was the case, and I wouldn't be forced to admit to Rod what I had been up to.

In the end, I needn't have worried. Almost from the moment they arrived, Janet, Maria and Alice began another enthralling conversation that continued throughout happy hour and stayed with them on their walk home. Cilla was late arriving, seemed not in the mood for socialising, and left early, precipitating something of a mass exodus soon after. That left just Rod and me to tidy up after the others had gone.

Cilla's behaviour tonight had me curious. I decided to ask Rod about her mysterious behaviour.

"Have you spoken to Cilla at all today?" He shook his head. "She didn't seem her usual self tonight and I thought she might have said something to you."

"How do you mean? Why do you think she wasn't her usual self? I didn't notice anything."

"Well, she arrived late and left early for a start and, yes, I know she could have had something else happening. She didn't socialise tonight. She did wander around for a bit and dropped the odd word here and there as she went. Most of the time she was here, she spent standing off to one side on her own. I don't think her behaviour was because she was missing Joe. Something is going on with her and I thought she might have mentioned it to you."

"Now you mention it... No, she wasn't her usual self. I haven't had any contact with her at all and, I suppose, if I thought about it at all, I would have assumed she was busy with the work she does for the Police Services, either here or in New South Wales."

"Maybe she has been brought in to help with the McCormac case, and she is not coping well with the fact no progress has been made so far. I am assuming Richard hasn't contacted you either?"

"No, there has been nothing from Richard since this morning. I think that simply means he doesn't have anything of any substance to share with us."

"You're probably right, but I thought he might at least have let you know whether they found anything useful or not. If we don't hear anything in the next couple of days, are we supposed to assume he has nothing to tell us because they found nothing?"

This conversation was not going well. My voice was becoming more shrill by the minute. I knew it wasn't Rod's fault he couldn't tell me anything new about the McCormac case, but my frustration was getting the better of me. It was at that point, I realised I should go home before I said something I might regret.

My slow stroll home in the cool night air did little to clear my head or help improve my mood. With nothing worth watching found on TV, it resulted in an early night. At least, I went to bed a lot earlier than usual, but sleep took forever to arrive. My mind was just a thick soup of 'suppose-if' facts about McCormac and his demise. Somewhere in amongst it all, it did dawn on me that I knew nothing about Baxter McCormac. I also knew nothing about what happened to him other than he was found murdered at the lookout at Jackson Cove.

Tuesday morning found me searching for even the slightest hint of some vague illness I might have contracted overnight. The last thing I felt inclined to do this morning was to join the others at the Recreation Room for a morning of mahjong. And, after a night of little and disturbed sleep, I felt less inclined to bake something to take for morning tea. It took a second mug of coffee with breakfast before I accepted what lay ahead this morning. Nevertheless, a quick batch of brownies was the best I could persuade myself to make... And the fact that they were not part of our usual morning tea fare attracted plenty of comment.

Cilla was again late arriving, but Cilla arriving late for mahjong wasn't unusual. What was unusual this morning was how late she was. The click of the tiles had already filled the room by the time Cilla strode into the Rec Room. She downed a brownie while she surveyed the tables.

"I see you have enough this morning for all the teams and don't need an extra player. That's good. There are other things I could be doing." With that, Cilla turned on her heels and strode out again.

Stunned by her performance, I spun around to face Rod and raised my eyebrows at him. He shrugged and turned his hands, palms up, towards me. No one in the room made any comment, but I noticed an almost deafening silence lasted a couple of minutes after Cilla's departure. It replaced the previous click-clack of the tiles.

Whether due to Cilla's performance or what seemed to be a pervading feeling of unease, the morning ended a little earlier than usual. No one hung around for an extra cup of coffee or to finish off the few remaining brownies.

"Not one of my better ideas," I murmured as I returned the brownies to the container they arrived in. "Reminder to self: don't deviate from the normal in future."

Rod chuckled. "I thought you would know by now that this group is allergic to change. I hope you realise you've probably upset their whole day by introducing something different this morning. So, come on. Tell me what prompted this drastic break with tradition this morning. What prompted the brownies?"

"A general state of mind and a massive dose of frustration... That's about the best explanation I can give you. Truth be told, I'm not really sure why I decided to make brownies. But, if I'm honest, I gained a certain degree of satisfaction from upsetting them all."

"You haven't seemed yourself the last couple of days. I'm sure the brownies are a result of whatever the underlying problem is. So, come on, Marion. What is bothering you at the moment? I'm not suggesting I can fix it for you, but talking about it might help."

"Oh, it's just the Baxter McCormac stuff. Nothing is happening. I know it's still early days and the police are probably doing all they can, but it's difficult to believe no one has been able to discover anything yet, either about the man or why he would be murdered in the way he was. It's almost impossible to accept that, in this day and age, the powers that be aren't able to at least discover something about a member of the community – or of the wider population of this country."

"Give it time, Marion. All sorts of people are probably working flat out on trying to solve this case. Given all of today's technology and what have you, it's almost impossible for anyone to remain hidden and completely anonymous, and I'm sure that includes Baxter McCormac."

Of course, Rod was right. I knew everything he said was true, but it didn't help the way I felt, and I wasn't sure what I could do about that. Yesterday's chat with Janet flashed through my mind. Was this the right time to tell Rod about what I'd discovered? What had I discovered...? The bit I'd managed to glean from Janet was little enough.

Unable to decide whether to tell Rod or not, I reverted to repeating local idle gossip. While I knew it was a stalling tactic, in the back of my mind, I think there was a faint hope that, if Rod knew anything more, discussing McCormac in an oblique way might shake it loose and he might, inadvertently or otherwise, share it with me.

"The notion that Zorka's house where McCormac was living is cursed seems to be gaining support amongst the residents. It's amazing how quickly such nonsense can spread and infect so many people who are otherwise intelligent, clear thinkers. The next thing we know, they will be taking up a petition to hand to the board about having the building pulled down as now unsafe to be inhabited."

"Perhaps it hasn't reached that level just yet, but I know there appears to be considerable support for the idea that the house is cursed."

"Rod, why are you carrying your phone around like that today? Normally, it's in your pocket and we never see it. But, all morning, it's been either in your hand or on the table while you were playing mahjong. Are you anxious about something or someone and waiting for a call about it?"

"I tried calling Richard this morning. He was tied up with something else at the time and couldn't talk. He said he'd call me back as soon as he was free. I'm sure we are both keen for me not to miss Richard's call when it comes."

"Are you and I the only ones concerned about what happened to McCormac and why? It seems to mean none of the rest of the group is interested. Even the board members don't appear too concerned about it unless you've heard something from the chairman or Tanya that I don't know about." Rod shook his head, so I continued, "What about the fuss Bernard made about the dog being allowed on the bus? Has there been any blowback from that? I don't doubt that Bernard complained to all and sundry about not only the dog but also about the fact that he didn't get things his way."

"No, there has been nothing from anyone, and I agree it seems a little odd. I was thinking about calling the chairman this evening, but now I think about it, I might try to talk to Tanya after lunch instead."

Guilt or whatever was getting the better of me. Might it be time to share with Rod what I had learned from Janet? If I do, it has to be handled delicately and not just blurted out. After giving it some thought for about two seconds, I decided it was the right thing to do, but I needed to do it in the right atmosphere. I invited Rod to lunch... And immediately wondered what on earth I was going to feed him. Then I remembered I had a couple of nice fish fillets in the fridge. Grilled fish and salad would go well for lunch. Rod accepted my invitation but wanted to go home and freshen up before coming for lunch.

I don't know whether to blame it on the weather, the McCormac incident, or Cilla's recent strange behaviour, but since Saturday, everyone seemed to be uptight somehow – and that includes Rod. I began to doubt that the lunch invitation was the cleverest thing I'd ever done, and sharing with him what I'd learned from Janet might not be in my best interest. Still, the invitation had been issued and accepted. The best thing I can do is play it by ear when the time comes.

The table had been set and the salad half made by the time Rod arrived. He still appeared uptight or preoccupied and it didn't bode well for an enjoyable lunch. After a glass of wine with him before I started cooking the fish, I noticed he seemed to relax a little. He was still sitting at the kitchen bench as I dished fish and salad onto our plates. It seemed like a good time to test the water, so to speak, so I dived in.

"Rod, tell me to mind my own business if you think it's necessary, but I noticed you appear to bit uptight today. Has something happened that I might be able to help you with?"

"Eh...? No, I'm not uptight. Oh, all right, I suppose I have been a bit. There's nothing to be done about it though. It's just that the continuing complete silence surrounding McCormac's death is getting to me. Maybe it's frustrating the journo in me. It wants to investigate and find answers... And I can't because I don't know anything that I can use as a launchpad for an investigation."

"Hmm... I may not be a journo, but I can relate to what you're saying. Maybe that's what's wrong with our whole group at the moment. Maybe that sense of not knowing is getting to them all.

No one appears to be behaving normally since the weekend."

As we settled ourselves at the table, I poured us both another glass of wine. Then, lunch was delayed when Rod's phone played its tune. He took it out onto the back deck to deal with it and was back at the table in a matter of moments.

On his return, he announced, "That was Tanya. I have an appointment with her at 1.30PM. Apologies, but it looks like I'm going to have to eat and run. Wish me luck."

"Well, it is something. How do you plan to handle it? Are you going to talk about the McCormac incident, or will you endeavour to establish if Bernard has been in her ear about his tantrum over the dog?"

"Now I have an appointment with her, I'm probably going to try to discuss both of those matters. I'll need to go cautiously, though, until I have a feel for what Tanya is thinking and what her mood is. I don't expect to learn much, but I aim to find out if the chairman has had any discussions with her."

"Bernard must have told at least someone of his unhappy incident regarding the dog last Saturday. It seems a bit strange to me that nothing about it has filtered down from on high. Come to think of it, Rod, Bernard has been conspicuous by his absence from happy hours since then. And, of course, it follows that Marjorie also is boycotting happy hours in solidarity with Bernard."

"Yeah, I noticed his absence. I must admit I don't find that a real problem. Whether he turns up or not is up to him. As he is not exactly great company when he does attend, I don't think anyone is too concerned about the current situation. Nevertheless, I have been wondering if I should cancel happy hours for a while – say, until the end of the week, perhaps. I get the distinct impression everyone is turning up out of habit as opposed to any other motivation. And now, with Cilla also acting weird... Yeah, maybe I will cancel them for the rest of this week."

"Okay, that's not a bad idea. Cancel them for this week and then see what the response is like after that before you decide whether to continue with them or scrap them altogether. At first, I thought that being a bit flat was only a natural reaction to Saturday's incident, but I had expected things to have picked up again by now.

Is it possible there is something we are not aware of behind it? Something going on, I mean? And, what about Cilla? She seems to be treating us as though we are lepers to be avoided at all costs. Putting the rest of them aside for the moment, do you have any ideas on how we might go about finding out what is wrong with Cilla? Might Richard know if something has gone haywire in her life?"

"There's no denying Cilla is definitely offside with us at the moment. If something has gone amiss with her life, she is not coping well with it."

"Might something have soured between Cilla and Joe? After all, Joe's current sudden trip away is a little unusual. Maybe there is more to it than work or looking into McCormac's background. Whatever it is, her behaviour at mahjong this morning suggests it's something major."

"Er... I think I might invite her for coffee this afternoon. I know there's always a chance she will say no, but I think it's worth a try. Whether she accepts the invitation or not, Marion, please come at three o'clock and we'll have coffee together regardless."

"That sounds like a good idea. I agree there is a fair chance she will turn down the invitation, but I'll bring something to have with coffee anyway."

About half an hour later, Rod reported back on his invitation to Cilla. "Cilla was a bit offhand at first. I didn't push her, but she eventually came round and accepted the invitation. I thought I should let you know in advance, because I'm not sure what her manner is going to be like – or if she will actually come, for that matter."

I already had most of a leftover cheesecake in the fridge, so no baking for afternoon tea was required. By a few minutes before three o'clock, I felt my stomach tightening as I strode along the footpath to Rod's house. There was every chance this afternoon would not be one of our better occasions together – if Cilla even turned up.

Three o'clock came and went without Cilla having made an appearance. Rod and I sat at his kitchen bench and waited. There was no conversation. Just a heavy silence filled the room. At about five minutes after the appointed hour, it appears we both felt it was time to address the situation.

"Rod, it seems we've been stood up. Cilla is usually quite punctual."

"It would appear so. I'm not quite sure how to proceed. Should I call her to see if everything is okay with her, or should we just ignore her absence and have a coffee without her? Or, if you prefer, you could go home again and not worry about coffee."

"Don't be ridiculous. I came to have coffee and that's what we're going to do. Whether there will be three of us is another matter, but I don't think I would recommend calling Cilla. The fact that she hasn't turned up tends to suggest she never intended to."

"Right... Well, time is away. Let's have coffee. What treat have you brought us for afternoon tea?"

Rod made our coffees as I sliced up the cheesecake and took it, side plates and forks, through to the dining room table. We had just sat down with our coffee when Cilla arrived. It was 3.16PM – and not at all like Cilla to be so late.

For a moment or two, I wondered whether her tardiness was due to indecision – indecision about whether to honour her acceptance of Rod's invitation or not. But then, Rod was busy in the kitchen making Cilla's coffee, and it fell to me to try to put her at ease and make her feel welcome. It felt like mission-im-possible from the outset.

Cilla seemed hostile, and it was obvious to me that she didn't want to come. She continued to be abrupt and rude after Rod brought her coffee and joined us at the table. In his usual fashion, Rod tried to be the diplomat. Throughout this whole performance, I had sat biting my tongue in the hope Rod would do some good. He didn't and I decided enough was enough.

"Why did you bother to come, Cilla, when it is so obvious you don't want to be here? If you don't want to spend time with us, why did you accept Rod's invitation in the first place?"

Not surprisingly, I suppose, all I managed to do was make her angry. Then, after a couple of vitriolic outbursts, she calmed down. An apology of sorts followed. Afterwards, she remained withdrawn and not talkative. Then, it was Rod's turn to lose patience with his guest.

"Despite your apology, it's obvious you are still not happy about being here, and we aren't particularly enjoying your presence. Maybe you should drink your coffee and then leave."

More apologies from Cilla followed, but she decided to do as Rod suggested. She stood up to leave, but Rod had a final suggestion to make.

"If your mood hasn't improved, it might be best if you don't attend happy hour until it does."

I watched as Cilla flounced out. I waited until we were alone before saying anything to Rod.

"Your comments hit home, I noticed. Maybe they might be what Cilla needed to hear to help her get over whatever is gnawing at her."

Chapter 8

A few minutes after Cilla left and while I was helping Rod clear away the afternoon tea stuff, Rod's phone demanded attention. He answered it out on the back deck, so I remained unaware of who the caller was until after Rod returned.

"That call was from Richard Wilson. He wants to meet with us as soon as possible. Later today would be good for him."

"At last...! Well, I would suggest we meet either at the police station or at my house." I saw Rod's eyebrows crawl towards his hairline in surprise. "I don't think it would be wise for Richard to come to your place given Cilla's current mood ... unless, of course, she is to be involved in the meeting as well."

"No, I sounded him out about Cilla and, no, she is not invited. I had much the same thought as you had about a location, so I suggested the Rec Room as a good place to meet. Richard will meet us there at four o'clock."

"It's as well Cilla went home when she did. The meeting would have been difficult to arrange if she hadn't. As it is, we don't have much time to waste if we are to meet Richard at four o'clock."

"You're right. We need to head to the Rec Room now. Just so you're clued up before Richard arrives, I told him I'd suggested the Rec Room because we were already going to be there doing some tidying up. So, we need to go now so we can look as though we're in the middle of doing something when Richard finally arrives."

"Clever thinking. When you first mentioned the Rec Room, I had thought I would drop the rest of that cheesecake off at home on my way past, but now I think about it, I might take it with us. Who knows? Perhaps we might be able to interest Richard in coffee and cake while we are there."

Having tidily put all the tables and chairs back against the wall after this morning's mahjong session, we hastily pulled a few out and scattered them around at one end of the room. The scene looked fairly authentic when Richard arrived about five minutes earlier than expected. When Richard knocked on the door, Rod was pushing a stack of chairs over towards the wall and I was carrying another chair across to add to another stack. A stray thought flashed across the front of my mind as Richard came in.

"Perhaps I should leave these chairs and the last table until I determine whether Richard might like a coffee and a slice of cheesecake," I shouted to Rod over the noise he was making.

"Oh, yes, Richard would love a coffee and a slice of cheesecake," Richard said with a wry grin. "It's been a helluva day with no time for coffee or lunch."

We finally settled with our coffee and cake at the one table still out in the middle of the room – and with me almost bursting with curiosity. I wasn't about to stand on ceremony and got straight down to business.

"Richard, was your search of that patch of scrub near the Jackson Cove lookout worthwhile? Did you find anything useful?"

"Well, that's what I wanted to talk to you about. What prompted you to explore that track leading further along the coastline from the lookout?"

Rod jumped in to answer while I was still trying to put together a suitable reply. "Exploring the track wasn't part of our original intention when we revisited the lookout, but, once we were there, the track seemed worth a look."

I was not happy with Rod's version of events and felt obliged to deliver a more comprehensive explanation.

"It wasn't that we thought evidence might have been overlooked at the time of the incident. It was more a case of the fact that nothing was found there that kept niggling me. By the look of McCormac's wound, there should have been more evidence of a struggle – more blood around at the scene, and there wasn't. There wasn't anything to suggest a murder had been committed except for McCormac's body laid out on the lookout's bench seat. I knew that nothing that wasn't there on Saturday would suddenly have appeared during the intervening couple of days, but I wanted to look at the site again."

"So, what did you hope to achieve by revisiting the site?"

"Argh, it's not that I had anything particular in mind. The thing that stuck in my mind was that the lookout was where the body was found, but there was no evidence there to suggest it was the crime scene... And that came through strongly to me again when we were once more standing at the lookout. So, if that wasn't the crime scene, where else might it have been? I decided to see where the track that appeared to lead further along the coastline led."

Richard regurgitated what appeared to be his standard repertoire of questions – and then, threw in a few extra ones for good measure.

"Okay, so you decided to explore that track leading off from the lookout. Where did it lead? What did you see? Did you find anything?"

My answers were brief and to the point, but I wanted to know about those shacks we saw in the alcove further along from that little promontory that was as far as we went along the track.

"We didn't follow the track all the way to those shacks, and I don't think it went the whole way. I don't know why I say that but I think the track we were on stopped some way short of the alcove where those shacks were located. And, I don't think there was any road access to them either. At least, I couldn't see any road access."

That's interesting, I thought, as Richard tried to fob off my question about the shacks. It only offered an invitation to press him further about them. Eventually, he admitted he didn't know who owned them, why they were there, or anything else about them, but he was quite interested in them. By then, I had run out of patience. We had answered Richard's questions and received nothing in return so far. It was time for another direct approach.

"You and your officers went to investigate the flattened grass leading to that patch of scrub while we waited at the lookout. Then, you called Rod and told us to go home. I assume by then you were searching the patch of scrub. What did you find? Did that sidetrack through the grass reveal anything? And, what about the scrub? Did you find anything interesting in there?"

"Er, yes... There was a bit of evidence. Well, we found enough to suggest it was the crime scene. Don't get too excited. I don't have any more to add to that. We're still waiting for the forensic info to confirm that it was the crime scene."

A wave of disappointment flooded through me. I had hoped for something a bit more positive, but the fact that it might be the crime scene gave me some scope for hope. I didn't have time to dwell on it anyway before Richard was in interview mode again.

"Right, what do you two know about that bloke McCormac? I want to know about his hobbies, his past life, where he might've lived before moving to Merivale Retirement Village, and anything else about him that might be helpful to our investigation."

"Huh... There's nothing we can tell you." After a moment's pause, Rod continued, "I don't think Marion or I had even laid eyes on him until he joined us on the bus on Saturday. Before you ask, there is nothing on his Village file that provides any clues either."

"How can that be? That's not normal, is it?" Richard demanded. "Surely an applicant has to provide all sorts of information to allow them to be assessed as suitable potential residents."

After taking a moment to consider Richard's question, Rod replied. "No, it's not normal. Now that I think about it, I'm not sure how McCormac ever came to be a resident. He seems, somehow, to have circumvented all the usual application requirements."

In response to Rod's reply, I felt a thought slam in from left field. "What about the chairman, Rod? Would he know something about McCormac? Maybe he does know something about the man and arranged for all the usual application process to be waived."

"Hmm... You're right. That would be the only way he could have been accepted without providing all the usual information. And that's especially so after the Zorka Weinstein fiasco that made the place tighten up on rules and regulations. I suppose I could question the chairman about what he knows about McCormac," Rod offered.

"No, don't do that," Richard said without looking up from the notes he was making. "I'll follow up with the chairman. As part of an official investigation, your chairman will have to think twice about withholding information."

Neither Rod nor I appeared to have any further questions for Richard, and he appeared to have run out of questions to ask us, but my conscience bothered me. I decided to come clean about my morning coffee with Janet Furlong.

"Whether you will be able to do anything with any of this or not, I don't know, but I thought it might be useful."

"Anything and everything is useful at the moment," Richard said as he dragged his notebook out of his pocket again. "You have the floor. Please share what you know."

"The word 'know' might be a bit of an overstatement, but here goes. On her way to mahjong one morning, another of the residents saw the vehicle collect McCormac and drive out of the Village. The driver of the vehicle, who was in civilian clothes, dropped McCormac a mock salute and called him 'Major'."

Rod's demeanour left no doubt he was not impressed at having been left out of the loop, but I was grateful he didn't make a scene about it. Richard, however, seemed excited and keen to explore the matter further.

"Is she sure it was McCormac she saw? Earlier, you suggested that few of the other residents claimed to have seen McCormac before the bus trip."

"She is quite sure that's who it was, and he was collected from out front of what we now refer to as Zorka's house and where we now know McCormac was living."

"Okay, what about the vehicle? What did she say about the vehicle?"

Richard was still scribbling in his notebook as he asked the question, so I paused for a moment to allow him to catch up before I replied.

"The details of the car are a bit sketchy but they are better than I expected to get from her." I relayed the scant details Janet had provided and Richard again was scribbling frantically.

"Did she have anything else to tell you? I mean, anything that might be useful in terms of our investigation."

"No-o, that was about all she had to offer. I wondered whether it might be possible to identify the vehicle on the CCTV footage from the traffic cameras close to the Village. I don't doubt it would be difficult to do, but, if we could track where that car took McCormac before it brought him back to the village, maybe it would provide some clue about the man."

"You're right. If we can identify the vehicle. Tracking it will be time-consuming but, as you say, it might provide the only breakthrough we have so far."

With his head cocked to one side, Rod studied Richard for a moment. I held my breath as I waited for Rod to share whatever he was thinking.

"I'm a bit amazed by your comment that there has been no breakthrough in the case so far. It is difficult to believe you haven't been able to establish anything about the man or his past life from the resources available to you. What about inter-state resources, haven't they provided anything either?"

"Not a thing."

Shaking his head as he replied, Richard looked uncomfortable. My heart went out to him. Rod had sounded very much like he was in investigative journalist mode. The one in which he barks questions and hounds his 'victim' until he is given what he believes is the truth and the whole story. I risked incurring the wrath of both men when I threw in my next question.

"What about Cilla and her Special Operations team across the border? Haven't they been able to find anything? I assume you have involved Cilla in this case."

"Uhm... Ye-es, Cilla was brought in to assist, but there has been nothing forthcoming from her end of things either. The problem is... McCormac doesn't exist, not under that name or any other that we have been able to find. His prints have not turned up anywhere and there is no record of matching DNA anywhere in this country. The search for any such evidence has been extended to overseas agencies as well. If, as your fellow resident suggests, McCormac might have some military connection in his background, his prints and DNA would be on file somewhere.

By the way, since she has been mentioned, is there something going on with Cilla at the moment?"

Both Rod and I shrugged and invited Richard to explain his question.

"Dunno what it is. She seems a bit uncommunicative – a bit frosty – somehow. I wondered if the cause was something that was amiss in her life, or whether it was something I had done to upset her. If it were down to me, whatever I did was unintentional."

"Does that mean she isn't helping you with your investigation?" I asked.

"Oh, she has accepted the case and supposedly is working on it, but it feels as though she had a quick look and then said, 'no, sorry, nothing to be found'. It is not like her. Normally, you have to hold her back with a tight rein or she takes over the whole show. This time, she doesn't seem even the least bit interested. Argh, look, I'm just whinging. I know all avenues have been explored and there just isn't anything to be found anywhere. We even explored whether he might have been a member of one of the overseas armed forces... but, no."

"Those in the Village, who had seen McCormac around before last Saturday, have said that the way he dressed and behaved suggested McCormac was from overseas, probably England," Rod told us. "I don't usually give such gossip any credence, but as we still seem to have nothing else...."

"If only that were the case," Richard sighed. "Then, we would have found his real identity from his prints and possibly DNA."

"Unless he was a Spook...." I murmured.

Where did that come from? I couldn't recall having any such thought, but the words had come out of my mouth, so I must have thought it. My words made an impact. I had been studying the toes of my sneakers as I made the statement. When silence descended like a lead balloon over us, I looked up to find both Rod and Richard regarding me with shocked looks. Richard recovered first.

"Anything further to add to that, or any other bright ideas to offer?"

Feeling suitably chastised, I shook my head. While Richard appeared to consider my response, I glanced at Rod. He was gazing off into the distance and appeared to be wrestling with troubling thoughts. Then, Richard again questioned the thinking behind my comment.

"When you suggest he was a spook, were you thinking here or overseas?"

"I've no idea. I don't even know where the thought came from."

"It doesn't matter whether it was here or overseas, his prints and DNA would have been recorded by the agency he worked for," Rod said.

"Yes, I accept all that," Richard began. "But, perhaps there is an agency somewhere whose files we haven't explored yet. Don't ask me which agency or where, because I haven't a clue. But, as I don't have anything else, it's worth thinking about.

Anyway, you haven't responded to my questions about Cilla. Have you noticed anything strange about her in the last few days, or is it just me that she is offside with at the moment?"

"No, you are not being singled out for any special treatment. We are all shut out at the present time. Our efforts to explore the matter earlier this afternoon did not do well. We don't know what the problem is," Rod assured Richard.

With nothing more to be added or revisited, our meeting went into 'wrap-up mode'. Richard just finished telling us a couple of officers would be assigned to identify and track on CCTV footage that grey vehicle with the yellow number plates that Janet had described, when Rod's phone played its tune. He glanced at the caller's ID on the screen before almost knocking over his chair in his hurry to dash outside to answer it.

Richard raised his eyebrows in question at me and asked, "Any ideas...?"

"Not a clue, but it might be worthwhile hanging around to check out his facial expression when he returns."

From past experience, I know some of Rod's calls can be quite lengthy affairs. I had no idea how long this one might take, but there seemed little else to do but wait. So, wait, we did – in almost complete silence. After the silence stretched on for a few moments and neither of us had found anything to talk about, although I expected Richard to decline, I suggested another coffee.

"Yes, please, and another slice of that cheesecake if there is any left."

Coffee and cheesecake were on the table in record-breaking time, and I had just sat down again when Rod returned. I know Rod well enough now to be able to tell when he is deliberately blanking his face. I think the giveaway is a kind of glint he can't keep out of his eyes. It proved a relatively short call by Rod's standards.

In well under five minutes after he left, I watched Rod enter the Rec Room again. He was texting on his phone as he made his way to our table. At one point he glanced up in our direction. I saw that glint in his eyes. Was it too much to hope that he had learnt something regarding our case? Intuition suggested that the moment Rod sat down again, Richard would ask if the call had anything to do with Richard's investigation. That was not how I wanted the next few minutes to go down, so I jumped in before Rod actually reached the table.

"We decided to have another coffee while we waited. Shall I make you one?" I asked as I stood up.

"Good thinking. You dish up the cheesecake while I make my coffee."

As we stood side-by-side with our backs to Richard, I hissed a warning to Rod, "Don't you dare say anything until we are both sitting down again. I don't want to miss a word of it."

At that point, my phone pinged to announce an incoming message. "Damn..." I muttered.

"That will be the message I just sent out," Rod told me. "I cancelled happy hour for tonight and until further notice. I hope the message went out in plenty of time so nobody is too inconvenienced by it."

"I doubt anyone will be inconvenienced. The way things have been the last few nights, they will probably find it a relief having no happy hours."

"Is that anything I should know about?" Richard asked as Rod and I took our places at the table.

"Nothing for you to worry about, Richard," I assured him. "It's just a Village matter."

"Oh, good, I don't need another problem to deal with," Richard said with a wry grin. "I suppose it's too much to hope the call you just took might have been about our current case?"

Rod grinned and his eyes sparkled. "Funny you should ask that. The call was from a... er, from a colleague. Yeah, just a former colleague of mine."

It was obvious Rod was being obtuse. The call might have been from a *colleague*, but I suspected *connection of some sort* might be a more accurate description of the caller. The finer points of such a differentiation appear to have passed over Richard's head without being noted, and he continued to press Rod regarding any possible information he might've received.

"Well, I didn't gain anything of substance. In a phone call with that colleague earlier this morning, I mentioned our 'mystery man' and asked if he had heard any scuttlebutt about what had happened here. He hadn't, but afterwards, he spoke to a number of his contacts in various circles. That mostly drew a blank everywhere... until the last one he spoke to on his list. The others hadn't even heard of the incident that happened here and asked questions about it before admitting they knew nothing. The last bloke he spoke to never even blinked when McCormac's name was mentioned, and asked no questions about the incident. It was almost as though he already was familiar with the incident that happened here."

"Don't stop there," Richard demanded. "What did he find out?"

"Nothing... That final contact he spoke to said he had never heard of McCormac and claimed to have no knowledge of whatever might have happened up here. But, my colleague had detected a slight – maybe involuntary – reaction to McCormac's name,"

"So, your friend thinks he might've hit a nerve?" Richard suggested.

"Yeah, apparently so and, based on that, my colleague is now digging around in the area it might have suggested."

I was feeling exasperated at being shortchanged on detail and felt the red mist starting to descend. The last thing I wanted was to give Rod a hard time in front of Richard, so I controlled my venom.

"If every avenue has already been explored, Rod, where else is there to look? I hope your colleague is aware of all the work already done and won't waste his time going over the same ground again."

We received solemn assurances from Rod that it would be his friend's time. What he did with it was up to him. However, Rod believed his friend was astute enough not to waste time unnecessarily.

"True enough," Ricard agreed. "But what avenue is your friend exploring now?"

Rod claimed he didn't know... And our brief period of excitement was lost.

Not too surreptitious glances at watches by those at the table quickly brought the meeting to an end. Then, after farewelling Richard and locking up, Rod and I made our way home. I had an ulterior motive when I suggested Rod might like to go home to freshen up before returning to my place for dinner.

Chapter 9

It was a balmy late afternoon stroll across the grassy area to the street where we lived. It seemed to provide the ideal environment in which to begin my campaign to discover exactly how much Rod had learned from his 'colleague' earlier this afternoon. It did require a bit of prodding but, eventually, he opened up.

"I'm not just being difficult, Marion. I don't really know any more than I've already told you."

"Okay... You might not *know* anymore, but you do have some assumptions. It's those assumptions I want to hear about. I understand you might not want to share them with Richard, but I want to know why you are being so coy about sharing them with me."

By then we had crossed the street and were standing at my gate. We couldn't continue this conversation where we were so I clarified what would happen next.

"Tell me, Rod, are you still coming for dinner?"

"Yes, I said I was, didn't I? I'll slip home for a shower and then be back in time for a drink before dinner... if that suits you."

Of course, it suited me and it's as well he confirmed his acceptance of my invitation. There is more I want to know – need to know – about that phone call. If he had tried to renege on his earlier acceptance of my invitation, I would have dragged him inside, then there and held him captive until he did tell me.

Once I was inside, the problem of what to have for dinner hit me. A check on the contents of my fridge confirmed a pack of two nice-looking steaks continued to languish there, and I had a good variety of vegetables to choose from. I decided the steaks would be accompanied by jacket-baked potatoes and a garden salad. Main meal sorted, now, what to have for dessert? After pigging out on cheesecake this afternoon, neither of us needed more sweet stuff tonight. A platter of fruit and nuts and another of cheese and crackers would suffice instead, and we could take them out onto my back deck to have with coffee and port later in the evening.

The salad was made and I threw the potatoes in the oven as Rod rang the doorbell. We left the steak on the bench to come to room temperature and took glasses of wine out onto the deck. A starry night and the smell of newly mown grass drifting in on the light breeze made for a pleasant interlude as we sipped our wine. Somehow, I managed enough self-restraint not to ruin the night so early by asking the questions I was dying to ask. That self-restraint managed to last until we were out on the deck again with coffee and port and platters of nibbles to keep us company. It was a lovely evening, and I knew it was risky, but the time had come.

"Rod, what did you make of the information your colleague gave you this afternoon? I accept that the conversation might have been light-on for information, but what did you make of what he did tell you? What assumptions have you come up with?"

"All right, all right... I know you are dying of curiosity. But, you need to understand that any assumptions I've made are not based on any real facts or hard evidence. It would be more appropriate to describe them as feelings I developed during our brief conversation."

"Okay, I understand that, but what are those feelings? And, where next might your friend search for information?"

"This is pure guesswork on my part – gut feeling if you like – but I suspect the place my friend will concentrate on might have something to do with the mob Joe works for. I don't know what pointed him in that direction and, of course, I could be completely on the wrong track."

"Joe's behaviour has been strange. Yes, I know that he supposedly has retired, but he still disappears occasionally to visit his old 'Firm'. This time his disappearance feels a little more odd than usual. It was so sudden. I feel it can only have been triggered by what happened to McCormac. He's only been gone a couple of days, but I feel confident that, if he has discovered anything, he hasn't shared it with Cilla."

"We don't know that."

"No, we don't ... But, if he had discovered something, I feel sure Cilla would have been crowing about it, at least to Richard, if not to us. And, Richard as much as said Cilla was acting strangely and that he hadn't heard anything from her about the case."

"Maybe her investigation has met with the same level of success as ours has – nothing found so far. What are you thinking? You look as though you've just had an awful thought."

"It was. Rod, here's something to ponder. What if Joe did go back to his former 'employers' to search for information for our case? And what if something happened there? Something bad, I mean. What if we haven't heard anything from Joe because he has gone missing – or worse? It might help explain Cilla's current behaviour."

"Yeah, I guess it's a possibility, as much as anything else is, I mean. Speaking of a certain strangely-behaving resident... I noticed Cilla's car garage was closed when I returned home after our meeting with Richard, and it was still closed when I left to come here for dinner. She only closes the garage when she is away."

A brief discussion followed during which we both agreed she could have gone out for dinner or simply gone to visit a friend. Somehow, it didn't ring true for me, so I devoted a few moments of silent thought to the matter before offering further comment.

"What friend? Cilla doesn't seem to know anyone outside the Village. She wasn't a local, so doesn't have any family connection around here."

"Good point. Maybe Joe is returning on a late flight tonight and she went to collect him. Although, she wouldn't have closed the garage if she was only going to be away for an hour or so to collect Joe"

"The late flight would have landed a while ago. If Joe was on it, they would have returned by now, but I haven't heard any vehicles on our street tonight."

As I finished speaking, I noticed Rod nodding in silent agreement. So, it was no surprise that, as soon as we went back inside, we both rushed to the kitchen windows. There was still no sign of life at Cilla's house. No lights on and the garage remained closed. The mystery of Cilla's absence continued to occupy both of us as we sat in the lounge room sipping another glass of port in relative silence. Although it wasn't said, I knew we both thought the port was a nightcap before we called it a night. Perhaps it was the alcohol consumed over the course of the evening, but I felt bold enough to ask the question rattling around in the back of my mind all evening.

"Rod, it is late. There is a heavy dew tonight. You might find it a bit cold and wet if you plan to walk home... Or you could stay."

"As I wasn't planning to walk home, the heavy dew is not likely to bother me tonight."

I awoke to the sound of Rod bustling about in the kitchen and set about hauling myself out of bed. Cereal and juice already were laid out on the kitchen bench for me. Rod wanted to have breakfast ready for me before he headed home to change and go for his morning run.

"What about you? Aren't you having breakfast this morning?" I asked as I glanced in the sink. No evidence there of breakfast already having been eaten.

"No, I'll have breakfast at home after I've been for my run."

"Okay, but would you at least consider having a coffee with me before you go?"

He allowed himself to be persuaded to stay for coffee and seemed suitably guilty as we sat together sipping our brews. It was then I remembered how he hates to have anything to eat or drink before he goes for a run. Then, with coffee dispatched, as he walked to the door to leave, his phone played its tune. I saw him check the caller ID and watched concern spread across his face. He flicked me a farewell wave before rushing outside.

My pulse rate stepped up a notch. It was obvious the call was important, and I know Rod's mysterious friends and former journo mates always seem to call at strange hours – like so early in the morning. Might the caller be the same one who was going to dig into the mob Joe works for to see if he could find out anything about McCormac? It was obvious Rod wasn't returning to share whatever he learned from the call, so I turned my attention to my untouched breakfast.

"Maybe Rod had the right idea," I told my empty kitchen. "Perhaps it does make more sense to go for my walk before I have breakfast. And, who knows? I might even encounter Rod again on his way home from his run. There's always a chance he'll mention his early morning call." Decision made, breakfast would wait.

By the time I had dressed and laced on my shoes, it was still earlier than usual when I closed the gate behind me and paused for a moment on the footpath. Although a creature of habit by nature, I decided to try something different today. This morning's walk would be in the reverse direction. I normally cross the street and walk directly over to the small park running along the side of the Village. Then, my walk takes me through the park, back into the Village and, finally, back onto my street. That allows me to go past Rod's and Cilla's houses before arriving at my own gate. This morning, my 'reverse direction' walk would start out along my street. It would allow me to check out Cilla's place as I went by.

It was a beautiful morning. Nobody else was out and about yet, so instead of power walking this morning, I strolled along the footpath and had a good look at Cilla's place as I went by. Still no sign of life inside and the garage remained closed. Cilla is usually an early riser. I had no doubt that, if she were at home, she would be up and about by now.

Primary mission achieved –Cilla's place checked out. I stepped up my pace and continued around to the park. There were so many things churning around in my mind. I didn't even chat to the birds on my way through the park like I usually do. I wasn't enjoying this morning's walk, but with so many things occupying my thinking, I didn't notice anything around me. That included the dark clouds gathering overhead. I remained unaware of them until the first drops of rain caught my attention.

Not wanting to get soaked, I stepped up my pace after having dawdled through the park. As I was about to cross the street to my house, Rod ran round the corner on his way home. It was at that point that the heavens opened properly.

"Come inside, Rod, so you don't get drenched. We can have breakfast together."

Yes, there was an ulterior motive for inviting him in. I wanted to know about that call he received as he was leaving this morning. But, how do I ease into that conversation without being too obvious? Luck was on my side, and it didn't take long for an opportunity to occur to bring up Cilla in the course of our conversation.

"I noticed Cilla's garage was still closed as I went past this morning. It does tend to suggest she might be away. I wondered if something had happened to Joe. Have you heard anything?"

"Nah, I don't know anything and nor does my contact. I had a call from my contact earlier this morning. He didn't know much but said *his* contact had suggested some internal ruckus was happening. It was all being kept hush-hush, with only senior staff at the agency appearing to be involved or in the know. He said his contact didn't think it involved anything out in the field, either here or overseas."

"Some sort of fifth column activity detected perhaps...? Or some other form of security leak?"

"Perhaps you're 'fifth column' description might not be quite fitting in this instance. A 'fox in the henhouse' might be more accurate."

After considering Rod's comment for a moment, I sought clarification. "Does that mean there might be only one bad apple – a lone miscreant – in the barrel? If that is the case, was McCormac the 'bad apple'? And, was he eliminated by The Firm? Or, was McCormac one of the good guys who was tracking down the rogue and ended up being neutralised by that rogue? "

"While I don't have any hard evidence to go on, I admit my gut feeling is that, somehow, McCormac was involved in some way in The Agency's current problem."

"Here is something else to think about. How might Joe be involved in any of this? Has he been sent into the field to weed out bad apples? What about Cilla? Apart from worrying about Joe perhaps, what else might have sent her rushing off to places unknown?"

Rod looked up from running his spoon around in his empty cereal bowl and shrugged and shook his head in response to my string of questions. His response took long enough for me to think of something else.

"I remember you had a friend who had a friend who found passenger flight information for us in the past. I was wondering if...."

"A message has already been left for him to call me, but there's been no contact so far. What do you expect we will achieve by talking to him?"

"That's a good question. I suppose your friend might be able to find out if Joe and Cilla flew somewhere, but that won't provide us with any clues about why they did. I guess our best bet is Richard, and I can't help wondering how long it might be before he has anything to tell us. I'm dying to know how things went with tracking the vehicle Janet told us about."

"In Richard's world, I'm sure the last thing on his mind is reporting back to us. I might be wrong, but I think the first thing we'll hear about that car is after his men found out where it went and why."

"You're probably right about the car. But, what about Zorka's house? Did Richard's officers go through the house and McCormac's possessions? I can't say I've seen anyone there or noticed any activity around the house. I would have thought the house would be the first place they would search for information on McCormac's identity. The man must've left something behind that provides a clue about him, even if it's only a hint that can put Richard and his men on the right track."

"Interesting... Now that you mention it, I'm fairly sure no police have searched that house yet. During my meeting with Tanya, she asked me what I thought she should do about the house. The list of applicants to move into the Village is growing and she doesn't have an empty house to allocate. I told her the house had to remain locked until the police completed their investigation or said it was okay to clean it out."

"As it is pretty obvious McCormac will not be back, once the police release the house, what will Tanya do with McCormac's possessions? If she doesn't know anything about the man, she can hardly contact his next of kin or other relatives to sort out what happens to his belongings."

"I suppose the answer to that might depend, at least in part, on what the police investigation manages to unearth on McCormac's identity and his past life."

"And if they don't discover anything?"

"Yeah, that's looking increasingly possible. Then, Tanya will have a problem. I admit I don't know what the practice is in such cases, and I'm not sure Tanya knows either, but I'm sure there must be one."

"It must be difficult to know what the best thing to do is when the resident hasn't provided any indication of what is to happen. Still, I don't imagine McCormac is the only resident who has died without leaving details of next of kin."

Such talk made me think about my own situation. With no close family, there is no one for Tanya to contact should I drop dead tomorrow. Of course, my will makes provision for what happens to anything of any value I still own at the time of my death, but other stuff, like clothes and household bits and pieces, probably are destined for the tip. They were sobering thoughts. To take my mind off them and onto something less depressing, I tried returning my attention to the matter of Richard's investigation.

"Would it be inappropriate to ask Richard whether his men have had any success in tracking down that car Janet told us about? I know he is busy with other things, but I thought that, if we knew a little more about the car in question, we might be able to do something more to help with the investigation."

"No, I don't think it would be a good idea, and I certainly won't be annoying him for updates on the case."

Rod's reply left me little room to manoeuvre and I was forced to drop any ideas I had about maybe helping the police with their enquiries. No further discussion of the matter followed, and I felt more than a little unhappy about what I perceived as a lack of progress so far on everyone's part.

Later, when sitting alone on my back deck, a thought slammed in from left field. It wasn't a new or unique thought. It was the same thought that had occurred to me the last time there was an incident involving the resident of that house on the corner of our street: if you want to know something about someone, ask their neighbour about them.

Mavis Grimshaw... Yes, ask Mavis what she knows about her recent neighbour, Baxter McCormac. So, when might be the best time of the day to happen to be 'just passing' Mavis's house? I knew she spent a lot of time out in her front garden attending to her roses. That suggested late this afternoon might be a good time to catch her in her front garden. With no happy hour to worry about this evening, I wouldn't have to worry about keeping an eye on the time.

For whatever reason, it was a little before four o'clock when I decided the time was right to go for a walk along our street. Mavis, dragging a hose behind her, walked out into her front garden just as I reached her front fence.

"Your roses are looking as beautiful as ever," I called out to her as I continued along to stand at her gate. "It must take up a lot of your time to keep them looking that way. Still, it's a lovely time of the day to be outside."

"If I didn't spend time with my garden, what else would I be doing? I'm not one for craftwork and all that other stuff."

"That's one of the benefits of being retired. You have the time to do the things you really want to do, as opposed to the things you have to do. And, this is a lovely quiet place to indulge in the things you love to do. I suppose that's something of a relief after the ruckus that went on with the last residents of that house next door."

As I added my last comment, I jerked my head in the direction of the house on the corner, the one most recently occupied by McCormac.

"I'm not sure that is the case anymore. Maybe they should pull that place down and build a new one there. At any rate, anyone who knows anything about this place would not live there, not after all that's happened to the last couple of residents."

"Oh, of course, that bloke... What was his name? ... The one who died while on that bus trip?"

"McCormac... That was his name. Baxter McCormac. I suppose he was all right. Yeah, a bit strange perhaps, but nowhere near as strange as that last lot. This bloke did get out and about a bit. Dressed a bit too fancy for the Village, if you ask me, but each to their own I say."

"Well, I have to admit, I don't think I ever laid eyes on him until that bus trip. Had he been a resident for any length of time before he died?"

"No, not long... maybe only about three weeks. I don't think any of the other residents got to know him while he was here. He didn't leave the house much either, but he did get out and about more than the last pair of residents did. He was nice enough to speak to. A bit toffee-nosed, perhaps, but pleasant enough."

"The poor bloke barely had time to settle in before he was no longer with us. Do you know if he was a local before he moved here? I only ask because nobody seems to know anything about him."

"Not a local, I don't think. I only say that because of comments he made about this being 'a lovely part of the world'.

I don't think he meant the Village specifically, but the area in general. He tended to keep himself to himself. Didn't leave the Village much and didn't have more than a couple of visits from friends. I was a bit surprised when he went on that bus trip. I was too late putting my name down and the bus was booked out by the time I did."

"It seems he must have known some people in the area if visitors came to see him."

"Yes, I suppose that's true. He only had two that I am aware of, both men and both a bit younger looking than him. One of them came to visit twice. The second time, he took McCormac somewhere in his car. They didn't return until late that evening, and I was beginning to develop an uneasy feeling about it. Well, you know, after what happened to Zorka and all that. I was beginning to think Baxter might have been abducted, too... And then, look what went and happened to him anyway. I know some of the residents are saying the house is cursed. While I don't believe in that stuff, I'm starting to think that, in this case, there might be something in what they are saying."

"Argh, I don't think you can blame whatever happened to him on that house. Maybe something from his previous life caught up with him. It's hard to tell what that might have been without knowing anything about the man or his background. When you think about it, we didn't know anything about Zorka either, but she had quite a background that finally caught up with her and her partner here in Merivale Village."

"While I don't know anything about the man, I suspect he might have had something to do with one of the armed services – Army, maybe. I don't exactly know why I say that other than it was sort of the way he was. And that younger bloke who took him for a drive saluted him... well, sort of saluted Baxter when he picked him up."

"Sounds intriguing, doesn't it? You must have been dying of curiosity to know more about your neighbour. It's only natural to want to know about who is living next to you."

"Oh, I was curious. So curious, in fact, that I took a sneak peek at his mail one day. When the mail was being delivered, I met Charlie as he started down our street. He handed me my mail and I offered to put any for Mr McCormac in his letterbox as I went past on my way to the hairdresser's. Charlie handed me a couple of things. One was a letter of some sort and the other was a magazine. Both things had an emblem – a badge – of some sort stamped on them. There was no return address on either one, but they were both postmarked New South Wales."

"You've done well to discover that much about the man. Who knows what you might have discovered if he had hung around a bit longer?

Well, if I'm going to go for my afternoon walk through the park, I had better be off. Nice talking to you again, Mavis... Catch up again, soon."

Chapter 10

Oblivious of the birds keeping me company and the murmur of the trees swaying in the breeze, I strode resolutely through the park adjacent to the Village. What had I learned from Mavis? Did anything useful come out of our chat? I slowed my pace to amble along as I replayed in my head our conversation.

No return addresses on McCormac's mail was interesting but probably insignificant. On the other hand, the New South Wales postmarks could be quite interesting... Canberra, perhaps? Mail from Canberra would tend to back up the suggestion of some sort of military connection. The whole matter of mail begged other questions. Presumably, if McCormac received those two items of mail, there might have been other mail received as well since his arrival... And any mail received was likely to remain in the house. Surely it would provide some clues.

So, why hadn't the police searched the house yet? Did the police know something about McCormac that somehow prevented them from going through the place? Oh hell, I don't know whether the police searched the place or not. I assume they haven't because I haven't noticed anyone there, but that doesn't mean it hasn't been done. Should have asked Mavis about it. Could I be so lucky that she might still be out in the garden? It's worth a try.

I spun around on my heel and stepped up my pace as I headed back the way I had come. As I turned the corner onto my street, I caught a glimpse of Mavis still out in her front yard. She was just finishing gardening for the day as I approached her fence. A couple of dead flowers remained on the end bush of the garden bed running along the inside of the fence.

"You've missed a couple of dead ones here on this corner bush," I called to her as she picked up the last of the dead-headed flowers lying on the ground. "You probably can't see them from inside, and you'll need to come out onto the footpath to reach them."

Heeding my advice, she rushed onto the footpath, reached over the fence, and nipped off the offending dead flowers. While she was so occupied, I stood surveying McCormac's house and, as I had hoped, Mavis noticed my apparent interest in her neighbour's house. I had to think of something to initiate another conversation.

"Looks like this one was no more of a gardener than the previous resident," I said, nodding at the house's front yard.

"No, but he did mow the grass and that's more than Zorka or her partner ever did."

"It must've been upsetting to you to have the police tramping around everywhere and going through that house again. All those memories from the last time must've come rushing back."

"Well, no. It probably would be upsetting, but the police haven't been through the place, no one has. I assumed they must know all they need to know about the man without having to turn his house inside out."

"If they had wanted to go through the house, I suppose they would have to talk to Tanya first and get a key from her to access the place. Although... Maybe they wouldn't need to get a key. McCormac probably had his house key in his pocket and that would now be part of the evidence the police had collected. So, if the police wanted to go through the house, they could just let themselves in."

"Maybe McCormac didn't have his key on him at the time. It's possible the police wouldn't have needed a key to get in anyway. On one occasion, he commented that this place was so safe, you didn't need to lock your doors. I thought he was joking until I was walking over to the gym one morning a few days later. I knew Baxter had gone out for a walk, but his front door was wide open. It was still like that when I came home later. He didn't come back until at least another hour after I arrived home. So, it's possible he left the place unlocked when he went on the bus trip."

Mission accomplished, I walked the rest of the way home at a sedate pace that was at odds with the turmoil in my head. My mind was now working in overdrive. It definitely was worth going back to talk to Mavis, but the BIG question remained. What to do with what I had learned? How to capitalise on it?

Any likelihood of arousing Richard's interest in a few words of say-so from a neighbour was pretty remote. If Richard was out of the question, that left Rod to consider. For the moment, I parked to one side the thought of the conversation I would need to have with Rod. Instead, I turned to thinking about how we might gain access to the house without raising too much attention.

Harebrained thoughts of scaling the back fence and breaking into the back door galloped through my mind before being dismissed. If the house wasn't locked, there would be no need to break in. We could simply let ourselves in through the back door. And, yes, entry would need to be via the back door. In this place, too many eyes would note anything happening at the front door. Did we need a plausible excuse for what might amount to illegal entry? Something left turned on, or food left out on the bench to rot? Shouldn't someone at least check if everything was all right inside?

I could spend the rest of the night asking myself questions and coming up with equally silly answers. There was nothing for it. I need to have another carefully managed conversation with Rod. The problem is how to initiate it now that there is no happy hour to use as an excuse for us to get together. Well, there might be no happy hour this evening, but there is nothing stopping me from dropping in on Rod on my way home to suggest a drink between friends this evening.

By the time I rang his doorbell, I had more or less worked out the conversation I would have. Without too much fancy footwork required, it should easily segue into how we might explore the contents of McCormac's house. Rod looked a little surprised when he opened the door and found me standing there still in my walking gear.

"Yes, I do know there is no happy hour this evening," I rushed to explain, "but I wondered if you might be interested in a drink anyway. Apologies for arriving looking like this. I had intended to ask you earlier but I was held up chatting to Mavis on my way past."

"A drink sounds like a great idea and, as it is almost happy hour time anyway, come on in and let's have a drink to put the day to bed."

"Oh, but I haven't had a shower after my walk, and I had intended we would have a drink at my place."

"You don't look as though you've just completed running a marathon, so don't worry too much about not having a shower, and we'll have a drink here. Come on in. We'll go through to the back deck and relax into the evening."

For the first few moments, we sat in companionable silence just drinking in the ambience of our surroundings as the sun went down, until Rod unwittingly began the conversation I wanted to have.

"You said you'd been chatting to Mavis... How is she holding up after McCormac's death? She must be feeling a bit twitchy after having her last two neighbours meet with tragic ends."

"It has unnerved her a bit, I think, but she seems to be trying to maintain as much normality as possible. She was out in the front yard deadheading her roses when I came along the footpath and I drew her attention to a couple she had missed. I felt sorry for her anyway, and thought she might need a conversation to help keep her on an even keel after what's happened."

"Well, I have no doubts the conversation quickly focused on Baxter McCormac. Did she have anything enlightening to say?"

"Actually, Mavis confirmed a couple of things for us. She recounted the story of a man, a bit younger than McCormac, who dropped McCormac a salute when he came to pick him up and take him somewhere. This has given Mavis the belief that her neighbour had at some time in the past been a member of one of the armed services."

"Okay. Well, that backs up Janet's story about the bloke in the car that came to collect him. Did she say if McCormac had any other visitors since he'd been here, or had she picked up any interesting gossip about her new neighbour?"

"Huh, you know how Mavis is. Once Mavis started on the topic of McCormac, she had quite a bit to say. Apparently, her neighbour had two visitors since his arrival. The one in the car who took McCormac off somewhere was the second visitor. The first visitor had come a few days earlier. That first man also looked a bit younger than McCormac. He was taken inside but didn't stay long; maybe just long enough for a quick cup of coffee. There had been no other visitors, but she didn't see anything strange about that as he had been there for such a short time."

"Interesting... No, I don't mean that he had two visitors was interesting. I meant it was interesting that Mavis didn't know a whole lot more about him. It's not like her not to have squirrelled out everything there is to know about the man."

"O-oh, that wasn't all she had to tell me. She had only spoken to him a couple of times, but was curious about him as he didn't seem to be making much effort to fit in with the Village. Then, she had a bit of good luck one morning, on her way back from the hairdresser's. She met Charlie as he delivered residents' mail and was just about to start down our street. She asked if there was any mail for her as she would take it now and save him having to deliver it. After scratching around in his bag, Charlie said there were only a couple of things for McCormac to deliver along our street but nothing for Mavis. Mavis volunteered to put McCormac's mail in his letterbox as she walked past."

"Now, that's sounding more like the Mavis I expected to hear about... And what did she learn from McCormac's mail?"

"As I said, there were two pieces of mail – a letter and a magazine. There was no return address on either of them, but both had the image of a badge of some sort on their envelope and both had New South Wales postmarks. She didn't recognise the badge but, in her mind, it tended to confirm McCormac had some past connection with one of the armed services."

"Interesting they were both sent from New South Wales..." Rod murmured, "Canberra perhaps...?"

"Perhaps some flight information from your friend's friend might be useful after all. Maybe we do need to check to see what he's managed to find."

"Don't get your hopes up. My contact called to say his friend had found nothing useful so far, and asked what other information I might be out to give him to work with."

"Rod, I've just had a terrible thought. What if both Joe and Cilla did take flights somewhere? The fact that they haven't been able to be located on any passenger lists might be because we don't know what names they were booked under. When you think about it, we don't know what Joe's real name is, and he probably has more than one that he uses in his line of work. And, if you think back, some time ago we learnt that Cilla's real name was Gina something or other. But, is that really her name or, in her case, is Gina just another name she uses from time to time?"

"Well done... Thanks for shooting that down so quickly. Yeah, you're right. We don't know under what names their flights might have been booked. Regardless, I still think Canberra might figure in the mystery. Hmmm, it might be a big job, but it might be the only way to find out. It might mean checking the flight lists of who flew from here on the right days for the same names on passenger lists of those who flew into Canberra soon after. I don't know what our chances are, but, if it can be done, we might also find out about the names they were using."

"Yeah, I don't like our chances, but it's worth a try. The other thing I was thinking about was Cilla's car. Might your friend in airport security be able to check whether Cilla's car is in the long-term car park?"

"I suppose that would be one way of confirming that she had flown somewhere, but I've got a better idea. Instead of bothering my friend at the airport, we are going for a drive in the morning. Be ready to go at 8.30 tomorrow morning and wear sensible walking shoes."

Things seem to be progressing satisfactorily along my desired path. I wondered whether this might be the right time to tell Rod about that other information Mavis passed on to me – and to suggest what we might do with it.

"Uhmm... That mail Mavis told me about has sprouted a germ of an idea. At least those two pieces of mail are probably lying around in that house somewhere, and who knows what else might be there. Mavis confirmed that the police had not searched the house, and nor had anyone else been through the place to look for anything."

"We suspected the police hadn't searched the house, and I still find that odd. I'm finding Richard's silence also a little odd. Perhaps Richard knows something more than we do and that's why he's not interested in the house. Still, I agree with you. There's a real chance the house contains at least something useful to the investigation. Well, we're just going to have to wonder about it, because there is nothing we can do to find out what might be in that house."

Time to reel him in, I thought and jumped in to share the rest of the information Mavis had given me.

"Perhaps... But something else Mavis told me might indicate something different." I saw Rod sit forward on his chair.

"Do tell...."

"There were two bits of information that, at the time, I dismissed as being insignificant. Mavis was recounting bits of information from a conversation she'd had with McCormac. At some point, McCormac had commented that this was a wonderful part of the world. He wasn't talking about just the Village. He was talking about the whole of this area. To Mavis, and to me when I heard it, it tended to confirm he had not been a local before coming to reside in the Village. But, he also gave the Village a good wrap as well. He commented on how everyone seems happy to just mind their own business while also keeping an eye on what's going on around the place. He claimed it was so safe here in the Village that you never needed to lock your door. Mavis confirmed that the man often went out, leaving his front door wide open when he was gone."

"Now, that is interesting. I had assumed McCormac would have locked up before he joined the bus trip and probably had his house keys in his pocket when his body was found. In that case, his keys would now be securely in Richard's evidence locker. But, if the man was inclined to leave his doors unlocked, might he have been so generous on this occasion?"

"Only one way to find out how accommodating he might've been, I suppose."

"Marion, do you know of any particular time when Mavis leaves her house?"

"Yeah, first thing every morning. She goes to the gym every day, except in summer, when, on two or three mornings a week, she goes to the pool instead. But, every morning, she leaves home around eight o'clock."

"Perfect... Well, maybe perfect but tricky. I need to give it a bit more thought. Leave it with me."

With that, the discussion of McCormac and his house was left in abeyance. Rod went to the kitchen to refill our glasses and came back with extra crackers to go with the remaining lump of cheese, looking a little forlorn on an otherwise empty platter. Our conversation didn't return to anything to do with McCormac, instead degenerated into various brief discussions about inconsequential matters.

A glance at my watch told me more time had elapsed than I had thought and I was feeling in desperate need of a shower. I moved the conversation towards ending the evening and heading home for dinner. Rod had been quiet for a few moments and I took it as a sign that it was time to go home. Then, as I went to stand to leave, he came to life again.

"Right... Yes, we do need to take a look inside McCormac's house, but we would need to be careful not to be seen entering or leaving the place, and it's paramount we leave no evidence of our 'visit' behind. I've decided that tomorrow morning, as soon as Mavis leaves home, will be a good time to implement our investigation. If Mavis normally leaves home around eight o'clock, you will need to be here by about 7.30. We'll keep an eye out until we see her leave, and then go straight into action."

"Uhmm... Yes, okay... But, Rod, what are we going to do if we find anything? And, exactly what will we be looking for? I think I might find it helpful if I knew beforehand how this might play out."

"I haven't worked that bit out yet, but what we do will depend on what we find – if anything. Here's how it will go.

As soon as we see Mavis leave home to go to the gym or the pool, we'll implement our plan. We'll go in over his back fence, and hopefully, he has left his backdoor unlocked. Be here by 7.30, dressed and ready for action, and you will need gloves."

"Rod, haven't you forgotten something? Tomorrow morning, we were supposed to be going to the airport's long-term car park to look for Cilla's car. What's going to happen now? Are we still going to go to the airport after we've done McCormac's house?"

"Argh, shit, I had forgotten about that arrangement. Looks like McCormac's house will have to wait until the following day, but the same arrangement will be in place when it finally happens."

"Well, I think I would prefer to give McCormac's house priority. Finding Cilla's car in the long-term car park won't really tell us anything. All it will do is confirm what we think has happened. McCormac's house holds the promise of finding some real evidence. If you're so keen to know if Cilla's car is in that long-term car park, perhaps you could contact your mate in airport security and ask him to look for the car."

I thought I'd lost the argument. Rod seemed reluctant to change tomorrow as planned but, after thinking on it for a few moments, he eventually agreed that McCormac's house was more likely to produce the most useful information and should probably be given priority. "After we've had a look in McCormac's house, if Cilla is still not home and there has been no word from Richard, we'll decide whether to go to the airport and check out the car park or contact my friend and ask him to look for the car."

My departure was further delayed as we finalised arrangements for our early morning mission. Rod saw me sneak another glance at my watch and suggested I stay for dinner. I declined his offer. I wanted a shower and an early night. I needed time alone to prepare and get my head around everything about tomorrow morning's operation. So, at seven o'clock I was eating eggs on toast in front of the TV news at home. After the news, I showered and then ransacked my wardrobe to put together an appropriate outfit for tomorrow's 'housebreaking' expedition. Just to be on the safe side, I laid it all out ready for the morning.

If my alarm didn't work or I slept in and wasn't at Rod's place on time, I knew he would have no hesitation in investigating that house alone. I had done too much work to make this happen. I was not going to miss out on being there for the 'main game'.

Chapter 11

Just as well I had laid out my outfit last night. Although I was awake before my alarm went off, I didn't seem able to think straight and was all thumbs as I tried to do up buttons and tie shoelaces. I gave breakfast a miss. Although I had plenty of time for cereal and maybe even a coffee, I didn't think I would be able to keep it down. My stomach was a roiling mass of trepidation.

The time I had to spare before heading to Rod's place, I put to good use making sure I had all the necessary equipment I might need for the exercise. Then, at last, it was time to go. For a few moments, I considered leaving my house via my back fence. That way, no one would see me going into Rod's house at such an early hour. But, as we would be climbing over other back fences in the course of our operation, I didn't need to add to the list. So, a couple of minutes prior to the appointed hour, I sauntered along the footpath and rang Rod's doorbell.

Rod's offer of coffee was refused. I just wanted to get the show on the road. This morning, time seemed to be chugging along in slow motion. I noticed Rod eye me up and down yet again.

"What are you doing, Rod? Why are you looking at me like that?" My sharp tone indicated the tension I felt.

"No reason... I was just checking out your choice of outfit this morning. I'm sure it was put together with a particular purpose in mind, but I can't quite work out what that was."

"Whatever I wore today had to be fit for purpose. My outfit had to be bland so I wouldn't be noticed; no bright colours, but with plenty of pockets for all my equipment."

"Equipment...? What equipment?"

"All the stuff I might need when we are searching the house."

"Like what?"

"Well, for a start, I have two pairs of gloves – in case one pair is torn or damaged somehow – and a notebook and pencil. Then, there is my phone...."

"Who do you intend to call while we are illegally on a crime scene? Richard, perhaps?"

"Of course not, but I might want to photograph things we find."

"Anything else in those pockets you haven't told me about?"

"Only my cap."

"The only time we will be in the sun is for the few seconds it takes along the track from here to McCormac's place. The rest of the time, we will be indoors."

"Oh, I wasn't worried about being out in the sun. The cap is to make it harder for anyone who happens to see us to recognise me."

"All I can say is, I hope you have a strong belt holding up your pants if you're carrying around so much stuff."

That brought the discussion to an end. For me, the tension was mounting. I figured my blood pressure must be approaching a critical level. I needed to keep busy to help take my mind off what we were about to do.

While Rod kept watch from his kitchen window for a glimpse of Mavis leaving home. I wandered out onto his back deck and began pacing about. One of the chairs from the deck had been positioned against the back fence, no doubt in deference to my lack of physical fitness. Rod might simply vault up and over the fence, but, without the aid of the chair, I would struggle to haul myself over it. That then brought another unpleasant realisation to the forefront.

I was facing two more occasions on which I had to climb over a back fence. On neither of those occasions, would I have the benefit of a chair to assist me. Oh, hell, how am I going to manage this, I asked myself as I stood eyeing off the chair against Rod's fence. Still, manage it I must. The alternative was not to take part in searching McCormac's house – and, for me, that wasn't an option.

Having paced around on the back deck for what seemed like an eternity, I was about to go back inside when Rod rushed out onto the back deck.

"Mavis just left home. Come on, it's time to go," he said as he locked his back door behind him.

"What's the plan? I need to know how we are going to do this before we start."

"You wait until now to ask that? It's simple. We go over my back fence and then along the track on the other side of the Village's perimeter fence until we reach McCormac's back fence. Then, it's over the fence, across his backyard and deck to his back door. We don't run or rush unduly while we are about any of that, but we don't dawdle either. The longer we are wandering around out there, the more chance there is of being seen. Now, for God's sake, please stop yapping and let's get moving."

No further encouragement needed, I hurried after him to his back fence. As I went to climb onto the strategically placed chair, I saw Rod place his hands on top of the fence and, in one smooth move, vault over it. I was endeavouring to follow him over the top with as much dignity as I could manage when I heard him hiss at me from down on the dirt track outside the perimeter fence.

"Come on... If you hang about up there, you'll only draw attention to yourself."

Needless to say, by the time I was safely down on the dirt track, the red mist had started to descend and my mood was becoming darker by the minute. Regardless, I didn't have time to stew over it. As soon as my feet were back on terra firma, Rod strode off along the track. Ignoring his instruction about not hurrying, I almost had to jog to catch up and follow along close behind him.

In a matter of seconds, we were standing at McCormac's back fence. Rod looked perfectly calm and collected as he casually looked around, while my head was bobbing about as though I was watching a football match.

"Right, over you go," Rod whispered.

I eyed the fence up and down. I wasn't being defeatist, but there was no way I could haul myself up over that. But, Rod was insistent. He gave me a hoist up and I found myself clutching the top of the fence. I'd heard him grunt as he boosted me up. How embarrassing! Mental note to self: must lose the excess weight. Almost at the same time as I landed in McCormac's backyard, Rod vaulted over the fence and landed beside me.

"Right... Gloves on now and don't take them off again until we are back at my place," Rod hissed.

Gloved up and, after a quick look around for anyone who might be interested in what we were up to, we were striding across the back lawn and up onto McCormac's back deck.

"Let's see if our luck holds and the back door is unlocked as we expected," Rod said as he marched across the deck to the back door.

"Please let it be unlocked," I whispered to no one in particular, and not game to even ask what we might do if the door was locked.

If there was a Plan B, I'm not sure I wanted to know what it was. Even the prospect of having to go over that fence again so soon did not appeal. If the door was unlocked and we could get inside, going over the fence again after having spent some time searching the house would be soon enough for me.

While I held my breath, Rod, looking completely unfussed by what he was about to do, tried the door knob. The door eased open three or four centimetres and then stopped abruptly.

"What's happening? Why did it stop?"

This was not what I expected and it alarmed me. When he didn't respond to my questions, I studied Rod's face. He remained quite still and obviously focused on what he was doing. It only took me a moment to realise he was listening... And probably didn't appreciate my questions. Then, the reality of the situation occurred to me.

Of course, the next stage of our operation required caution. In recent times, some of the residents had installed various security systems in their houses. Had McCormac done the same? Would we set off alarms the moment we went through the open door? Rod continued to stand stock still and listen, while I pondered the possibility of encountering security alarms if we entered. After a moment's thought, I decided it was a possibility but unlikely. If McCormac had been so concerned about security as to have a system installed, he would hardly be so cavalier about leaving his doors unlocked.

In the few moments it took me to reach that conclusion, Rod, having heard nothing to concern him, decided to proceed. He pushed the door about half open and stepped inside. Still unsure, I continued to hesitate outside until he impatiently beckoned me in.

"You're not going to find anything of consequence hanging about out there. Let's get on with it, or if you've changed your mind about the whole exercise, feel free to go home."

No further encouragement needed, I stepped over the threshold and took a few bold steps inside.

"Does anyone actually live here?" I asked as I cast my eyes around the open-plan living area.

"Yeah, it's a bit stark, isn't it?"

"Might be a good thing, though," I murmured. "By the look of it, it won't take us long to go through this place. Although, I don't know that we will find anything. There doesn't seem to be much of anything to find."

Rod shrugged. "Maybe not... Doesn't look as though he was planning on staying long. Either that or he's not into creature comforts. Don't let's get ahead of ourselves. Where do you want to start?"

Good question, but I didn't have a clue how to answer it, so I applied a well-tested approach: when in doubt, let someone else make the decision.

"I'm easy, Rod. Where do you want me to search first?"

"Well, we are standing outside the kitchen. How about you start searching the kitchen while I tackle the lounge room?"

Nothing to argue about with that allocation, so I took a couple of sideway steps into the kitchen as Rod continued further along into the lounge room. I stood just inside the kitchen and ran my eyes over everything. Nothing excited me. I know we shouldn't get ahead of ourselves and jump to conclusions, but the kitchen looked more like one that might exist in a display home. It certainly didn't look like one where someone prepared meals on a regular basis. I gave myself a mental talking-to. Stop whining and get on with the job. Who knows what might be lurking in those cupboards, or in the fridge? I made a beeline for the fridge and yanked open the door.

"Okay, that's interesting," I told the universe – just in case it hadn't been looking over my shoulder and hadn't seen the contents of the fridge for itself.

Now what am I supposed to do? Although I don't know what exactly, the state of the fridge means something. So, how do I record it? After all, I'm the only one doing the kitchen at the moment. Ah, yeah, that's why I brought my phone. I clicked off a couple of shots of the interior of the fridge before checking the freezer compartment. The contents of that part of the fridge would not stave off starvation either. More photos for later.

Feeling a little more inspired about the task I'd been allocated, I moved along from the fridge to the first of the cupboards and threw open the two full-length doors. This was serious storage space. It also was seriously empty. I took a few moments to stand in front of the cupboard and ponder its emptiness. No enlightenment – or bright ideas of any description – came to me, so I closed the doors and moved on to check out the rest of the cupboards.

As I reached for the handles on the doors of the last of the cupboards, I almost felt afraid to open them. So far, all my search of the kitchen had netted me were several photos of mainly empty cupboards. How can a man live in a house and not eat? O-oh, what about the bin? Maybe McCormac was one of those neat freaks who thrived on clean and tidy. The kitchen bin proved just as disappointing as the rest of the room. A small torn scrap of paper lay in the bottom of the liner bag – a new, clean liner bag.

When was the last garbage collection day prior to McCormac's death? I stood in the middle of the kitchen and thought about it. There was something about the garbage collection last week. What was it? Ah, yes. The garbage truck broke down or something. So, instead of our regular garbage collection on Wednesday, the truck came on Thursday. Logically, McCormac would have emptied his kitchen bin in accordance with the Wednesday rubbish collection. Might he have emptied it again when the truck didn't come until Thursday?

Did it really matter whether he emptied it on Wednesday or Thursday? Either way, it meant his kitchen bin should have contained at least two days' rubbish before McCormac joined everybody else on the bus trip on Saturday morning. I was still pondering that question when Rod's appearance in the kitchen startled me.

"Have you finished in here?" I nodded. "Good... Find anything interesting?" I shook my head. "Ri-ight, then... Are you okay to continue?" More nodding on my part.

At last, I found my voice. "Yep, I'm finished in here. I think you'll find I have nothing to report from the kitchen. Where do you want me to go next?"

"Well, I'm going to have a go at the main bedroom. I don't know if the spare bedroom was being used or not, but it still needs to be searched. You never know, it might have been used as a storeroom to hold all sorts of treasures."

"Yeah, yeah, I can hardly wait to get stuck in." My less-than-enthusiastic response earned me a dark look from Rod, but I ignored it and bustled about to return my notebook and phone to my pockets from the bench where I had them during my inspection. Anyway, I shouldn't feel too bad about having found nothing. I hadn't heard any whoops of joy from Rod in the course of his search of the lounge room, so it was a fairly safe bet he hadn't found anything either.

By the time everything was back in my pockets, Rod was already on his way to the master bedroom. I was about to follow his example and set off for the spare bedroom when a sudden thought stopped me. I hadn't photographed the kitchen bin.

While it might not seem like a monumental oversight, everything else I looked at had been photographed, so the bin should be, too. Anyway, the state of that bin bothered me. I dragged my phone out of my pocket again and opened the kitchen bin. A quick shot of its all-but-empty interior, and I was about to put my phone away again. Another thought slamming in from nowhere stopped me. Was there anything on that torn scrap of paper?

After carefully retrieving the paper from the bottom of the bin, I flattened it out on the kitchen bench and photographed it. Why did I bother photographing a blank bit of paper, I thought as I picked up the paper to return it to the bin.

"Whoa...," I squeaked. "Hang about. There's something on the other side."

A quick check over my shoulder to see if Rod had heard me and rushed back to check what the fuss was about revealed I was still alone in the kitchen. I flattened the paper out on the bench again and took a close look at the faint words written in pencil.

"Oh, now, that is interesting," I murmured as I moved in as close as possible with my phone to photograph the words. Not confident my shot would have picked up the words clearly enough, I wrestled my notebook and pencil out of my pockets again ready to make a note of the words before I even checked my shot. I need not have bothered with the notebook and pencil. My phone's camera had brought the words up even more clearly than they were to the naked eye. But, just for good measure, I made a note of them anyway.

Then, with the paper returned to the bin and all my bits and pieces back in my pockets, I took one final look around the kitchen before heading for the spare bedroom. As I walked the short distance down the hallway, I could hear Rod opening and closing doors and drawers in the main bedroom but, again, I heard no howls of delight emanate from that room. I took a deep breath, partially opened the door, reached in and switched on the light. A room as stark as the rest of the house greeted me.

The room's furniture included only a single unmade bed and a small chest of drawers, apart from built-in cupboards occupying the length of one wall. It was obvious no guests had come to stay with McCormac since his arrival in the Village. In fact, what I've seen of the house so far tended to suggest that no one had stayed in this house since McCormac supposedly arrived. After a couple of shots of this stark room, I began my search with the built-in cupboards. A quick look and more photos soon had the built-in cupboards dealt with.

No, this room was not an Aladdin's cave. There was no horde of exciting treasures to be found. I giggled. Exactly what am I supposed to consider constitutes 'treasure' in this 'treasure hunt' we were undertaking? No, of course, we were not looking for a stash of gold and jewels or even a swag of money. I suppose I had hoped we might find mail or photographs that would provide clues as to the resident's background. So far, I had found nothing, nothing at all, never mind anything that might indicate something about McCormac or his life.

Feeling more than a little deflated by my morning's effort so far, I flopped down and sat on the bed's bare mattress. Reaching out, I ran my hand over the mattress. Its lumpiness surprised me. Could this be where McCormac hid stuff he didn't want people to find? Get a grip, I told myself. Still, a look under the mattress might prove worthwhile. After all, the only other thing I had to search was that small chest of drawers and I had no doubt it would produce nothing either.

Several moments later, all that remained for me to check was the pine chest of drawers. Larger than a normal bedside cupboard, it was about 400mm wide and contained three drawers, each about 120mm deep. After a shot of the chest of drawers in situ, I opened the top drawer. No surprises there, and another shot of an empty space to add to my collection.

The second drawer proved no more rewarding than the top one. The temptation was not to bother with the third drawer. After all, why would it be any different from the other two? In the interests of thoroughness, I chided myself, you must check the third drawer as well. So I did – and was surprised.

No, it wasn't empty like its counterparts. Okay, no, it wasn't loaded with treasure but it did contain one object. An old, dog-eared book was the lone occupant of the bottom drawer. It was lying face down in the drawer, so I took a shot of it as it was, before flipping it over to reveal its cover. After another shot, I took a moment to study the cover. This was not a book I had read or was familiar with in any way. Temptation won out. I picked it up. It was an ancient hardback with its cover bound in a greenish-coloured canvas of some sort and sporting gold lettering. A look inside the cover revealed the canvas originally was a deep forest green, but it had faded and become grubby through age and use.

Its title page offered some enlightenment. The book purported to be a collection of 'stories and poems' written by a name I did not recognise. What really caught my attention was the tiny print at the foot of the title page. It told me the book was first published in 1899 by a publishing house in the UK. While all that was interesting, it told me nothing to suggest it might be of any use to our investigation.

Nevertheless, a few more shots of various parts of the book before I returned it to the drawer as I had found it. Closing the drawer, I stood for a moment pondering my find. Why would an elderly man keep what was obviously a children's book of stories and poems? Had it been a childhood treasure McCormac couldn't bear to part with? Perhaps it had been left behind by a previous occupant and missed when the place was cleaned out before its new resident moved in. None of that rang true for me. If it was such a treasured keepsake, why was it lying abandoned in here?

With no answers or any other form of enlightenment forthcoming from any source, I shoved thoughts about the book to the back of my mind, stuffed my camera back in my pocket, and went in search of Rod.

Rod was sitting on the edge of the bed in a room only a little less stark than its counterpart. Apart from a double bed (not a queen or king sized one, I noted), there were a pair of bedside cabinets and a chest of drawers similar to that in the spare bedroom. A cheap student desk with a beige melamine finish resided in one corner of the room and was accompanied by a standard-looking kitchen chair. A row of built-in cupboards also occupied the length of one wall.

All of this I registered in one swift glance around the room before my focus returned to Rod... and the collection of material strewn around him on the bed.

Chapter 12

"Ooh, what have you found?" I cooed as I came into the room. "It looks as though you've struck the mother lode. Can I help with anything?"

While I don't know about wanting to help, I sure wanted to get my hands on some of the stuff that Rod had found. It looked like it was all paper and that some of it was magazines. It struck me as odd – and unfortunate – that there didn't appear to be any envelopes amongst it. As I walked towards Rod, he reached into a drawer of the bedside cabinet nearest to him and drew out a notebook. Later, I realised it wasn't a notebook so much as a scribble pad.

My immediate thought was that it could be useful. If McCormac had used it to make notes, during telephone calls, for instance, we might have been able to retrieve some valuable information. I thought of scenes from television shows where a detective scribbles all over the impressions left on a page to bring out the last message written on the pad. No such thoughts seem to occur to Rod, and he casually threw the scribble pad onto the other stuff already spread out on the bed. But he wasn't finished with the contents of that drawer.

Reaching in and scrabbling around a bit, he brought out a plastic bottle consistent with those that hold prescription medication. I strained my neck for a better look at the bottle as Rod rolled it around in his hands. I didn't notice a label, but there would have to be one.

"Rod, is there a label on that bottle?" He shook his head.

"No, if it was prescription medication, the pharmacist's label has been removed."

"What about a proprietary label that identifies the contents of the bottle? Even if we don't know who it was prescribed for, the nature of its contents could be useful."

"Yep, it would have been, if a label of any sort was present. The residue from where the labels were removed suggests it might have been prescribed medication. I suppose a pharmacist might be able to identify the contents." He shook the bottle and then unscrewed the cap. "If he took whatever these are on a regular basis, he would have needed to visit his pharmacist very soon for a replacement. There are only three or four tablets left in this bottle."

I sat down on the end of the bed, reached across, and dragged the nearest magazine over to me. I could say I don't know what I expected to see, but that wouldn't be the truth. I thought I knew what McCormac's taste in reading matter would encompass and, in my mind, I had imagined the magazines spread out on the bed probably had something to do with weapons or other material relating in some way to war or the military. I was wrong.

The magazine I had snagged was about restoring old cars. It must've been a subject McCormac was interested in because the magazine looked well thumbed through, and the corner of one page was roughly turned over. Whether that was accidental or intentional, it was impossible to tell. Still, I thought the page merited a photo, so I wrestled my phone out of my pocket and took a quick shot of the page in question.

"What's so special about that particular page that it's worth photographing?" Rod demanded with a distinct edge to his voice.

"I'm not sure it's important at all, but I thought I'd photograph it anyway. You know, just in case...."

Rod's tone of voice had told me his morning hadn't gone any better than mine in terms of what he had found. I half expected him to announce that the whole project was a waste of time and we should get to hell out of the house and go home before someone discovered we were there. Even if he did, I wouldn't be leaving until I'd looked at all that mail and other stuff that was spread around on the bed. It's not that I don't think Rod is astute enough to recognise something is important. It's more a case of worrying that his darkening mood might lead him to overlook some significant piece of evidence.

As I dragged over another couple of magazines, I asked, "Are all the magazines about old cars?"

"Some are, but the others are about restoring old machinery."

"There are only five magazines. Who are the letters from?"

"They're not letters as such. They are circulars advertising various events and auctions. And, surprise, surprise, there is nothing of any use in any of this."

"All it seems to tell us is that McCormac appeared preoccupied with old things. Right, what do we do now?"

"We still have the bathroom and the laundry to search. I don't expect to find anything useful there either, but you do the bathroom. I'll check the laundry after I put this lot back as I found them."

Apart from what brand of toothpaste he used, what else are we going to find out about the man from his bathroom, I grumbled under my breath as I marched along the hall to the bathroom. It was as stark and pristine as the rest of the house. White tiles everywhere, with the only splash of colour the black towel, hand towel, face cloth and bath mat. A new cake of soap lay in the soap holder in the shower recess.

"This does not look promising," I murmured as I turned my attention to the vanity unit and the mirrored cabinet affixed to the wall above it. I elected to start with the vanity unit.

The cupboard space contained four rolls of toilet paper, an unopened box of toothpaste and an unopened cake of soap, but that was it. The space was devoid of the cleaning materials I expected to find there. Next, it was time for the unit's two small drawers. The first drawer I opened was completely empty. Its mate contained one solitary item, a zippered wet pack – also empty.

I'm on a hiding to nothing from this lark, but at least I'm maintaining my average. I don't know what I would do – probably collapse from shock – if I actually found anything useful, I told myself as I gingerly opened the cabinet on the wall. No need for caution… There was nothing shocking about its interior. All that resided there was an ordinary-looking razor, a can of shaving foam, a can of some exotic-sounding deodorant, and a comb. Yep, maintaining my average well.

After one last look around the bathroom, I was out in the hallway again. That was when I noticed what I presumed was a built-in linen cupboard in the wall adjacent to the bathroom door. Of course, it needed to be searched, and in the absence of Rod, I guessed it was up to me to do it. I marched over and stood in front of it for a moment before flinging open the two cupboard doors. I expected to find spare sets of bed linen and bath towels neatly stacked on the shelves. Wrong again. This pristine cupboard remained unsullied by people shoving stuff in it. A shot of the interior of the cupboard, and I was off in search of Rod.

He stepped out of the laundry and into the hallway as I approached. The disgusted look on his face told me he had found nothing either.

"Well, that's that then," he said, sweeping his arm in an arc around him. "There are no more rooms; nowhere else to search. It's time we were gone." He peeled his glove back a little and checked his watch. "Jesus, has it taken us that long to find nothing? Perhaps Richard knew something after all in not rushing to search this place."

Yep, that was one disgruntled Rod Maguire. Since that was exactly how I felt as well, all I wanted to do was go home. Without further discussion, we headed along the hall towards the backdoor. As Rod was about to open the door, I voiced a thought that had just arrived.

"What about the garage? This house has a garage, the same as all the others. We should have a look in there before we leave."

Without a word, Rod turned on his heel and led me back down to the dining room and the door in the far wall that opened into the garage. He flung open the door and then stopped abruptly. I slammed into his back.

"Sorry, but you shouldn't stop abruptly like that. What's up? What have you found?"

"Not a bloody thing… At least, not at first glance anyway. Let's see what's in those cupboards, but I'll bet my socks they are empty."

Two sturdy cupboards of the sort handymen might purchase from hardware stores to store their tools were against the garage's rear wall. Rod's prediction was right on the money. They were empty. A couple more photographs and then Rod was holding the door open for me to go back into the dining room. I stepped through the open door and came to a sudden halt before turning around to stand in the open doorway.

"Where's his car? For someone who was so interested in old cars, he seems to be without wheels of any kind, not even a mobility scooter. Look at the floor tiles. No tyres have been over those tiles in the last three weeks or so."

"Hmm… Something to ponder over a coffee, I think. Let's get out of here."

Rod was already halfway to the backdoor by the time he finished speaking. I didn't argue. I was more than ready for a coffee. When he reached the door, he opened it cautiously and peered out.

"Wait here while I check our surroundings," he told me over his shoulder as he eased out of the door and onto the back deck.

He stood just outside the door and casually looked around before moving to stand at the edge of the deck to have another look around. Without a word, he motioned me to join him. As I stepped outside, he pointed to the door. Really? How insulting can he be? Did he really think I'd leave the door open? I made a show of closing the door before striding across to join him at the edge of the deck.

"I can't see anyone about. I suspect Mavis came home while we were busy inside. I think I can hear her TV over there," he said with a nod in the direction of Mavis's house.

"She's never usually gone for more than an hour, so she's probably been home for a while. I think when she comes home, she has a shower and then sits down with a cup of coffee in front of TV. Anyway, she is not usually out in the yard at this hour of the day."

"Right then… Come on, quickly across the grass and over the back fence."

I groaned internally at the prospect of needing him to hoist me up again. Nevertheless, the next stage of the operation seemed to happen in a blur. We strode across to the fence. Rod boosted me up. I climbed over the top and landed on all fours on the dirt track outside. Rod landed lightly on his feet beside me.

"Let's not hang about out here for too long," he said as he turned to walk back towards his house.

"You can go that way if you wish, but there is a different route I'm going to take."

He stopped and spun around to face me, his face a mask of confusion.

"A bit further along this fence, there is a gate that opens onto that dead-end street in the Village. I intend to avail myself of that gate and walk home along the footpath in comfort. Are you coming with me, or are you going home over your back fence?"

"At least put your cap in your pocket. I wouldn't want the neighbours thinking I was taking a strange woman home."

Probably no more than a couple of minutes later, Rod was unlocking his front door and I felt my pulse rate and blood pressure beginning to return to normal.

We were soon sitting on his back deck with our mugs of coffee and slices of toasted fruit loaf. The silence that prevailed between us allowed my mind to create its own turmoil as it sifted through every aspect of this morning's exercise. I don't know how long that situation lasted, but, eventually, I heaved myself upright on my chair and took another bite of my now barely lukewarm toast before asking my first question.

"Should we have a debrief?" Rod gave a half-hearted nod. "Okay, what is your assessment of this morning's outcome?"

"An utter and complete failure, not to mention a waste of the morning. So, what are your thoughts?"

"Ah, yes… Well, I have only one real observation to contribute. For me, this morning was more about what *wasn't* there, than what *was* there. How long had McCormac been living there? Three weeks…?"

"Yeah, about that – or maybe a bit more. From what I understand, he moved in around the middle of the week, so he would have been here for three weeks and two days before he died on that Saturday. Is that important?"

"Dunno exactly. To me, the place looked like it should belong to a recent graduate who had just moved out of home and was setting up his own pad. He had a few bits of furniture from his parents but nothing much else. And, in the case of a recent graduate, probably not much cash to rapidly improve his situation."

"Okay, would you like to explain that a little more?" Rod suggested.

"Was McCormac really living there? I can't be sure after going through that house. There was no food in the fridge, no groceries in any of the cupboards, no pots and pans, and nothing but empty cupboards and an empty bin – and that's just in the kitchen. But, the rest of the house seemed to follow suit. Think about the main bedroom that you searched. There was nothing personal. While you were dealing with the magazines and whatever, I searched the wardrobes as you asked. Again, there was nothing. Well, there was one pair of well-polished shoes and a folded jumper on a shelf. That was it.

People talked about McCormac being a walking picture of sartorial elegance, and his standard of dress being well above what was considered standard in the Village. Any description of him mentioned his tie and jacket. He wasn't wearing his jacket when he was killed at Jackson Cove. So, where is the jacket he reputedly wore around the Village on a regular basis? And where is the tie he used to wear? He wasn't wearing one of those either when he was killed."

"Anything else? Don't hold back. Let's hear about everything you considered abnormal or worthy of note."

"Let's stay with the main bedroom for the moment. That chair parked where it was suggested that student's desk was going to be used as a desk by McCormac. As we didn't find another desk or an office of any description anywhere in the house, I feel that's a reasonable assumption. But, there was nothing on it; no paper, no writing equipment, nothing. Apart from the scribble pad you found in the bedside cabinet, there was no writing material anywhere. And, what about a laptop? I didn't see one of those anywhere. I find it hard to believe he wouldn't have had one, and that desk appears strategically placed at the power outlets just above the skirting board in that corner.

Come to think on it, we didn't find a phone either, but he probably had that on him when he was killed. Still, I didn't see a charging cable for a phone anywhere. Did you find one?"

I found it a bit unsettling that Rod was saying so little while I rattled on at great length about what I considered to be anomalies in that house. He didn't do anything to stop me, so I dragged my notebook out of my pocket and continued.

"Moving on to the bathroom, there was a little personal stuff there inasmuch as I found a comb, razor, and a couple of cans of product he would have used. But where are his toothbrush and opened tube of toothpaste? Those weren't anywhere in the bathroom or anywhere else I searched. And, the linen cupboard in the hallway was full of the same emptiness as so many other cupboards I checked.

It's not worth mentioning the garage. We both saw what wasn't there. I can accept that he might not have had a vehicle. But, when combined with everything else that appears to be missing, it makes me wonder. What about you, Rod, what are your thoughts?"

"Good question. I suppose the key thing is that, from the moment we walked in, I was struck by how stark the place was. I'm inclined to agree that the place didn't look lived in, but we know he was living there. Apart from the fact that he was seen around the Village, Tanya has him registered as the current resident. I must admit, I hadn't particularly noted all the facts you mentioned, but I'm not about to argue about any of them. I think I'll take some time to sit quietly and think about this morning."

"Rod, here is something else to think about. Was McCormac really living there? I know a couple of people said they had seen him around the Village, and that includes Mavis, his next door neighbour. But that doesn't give him a high profile in the Village. I know it's not going to make any sense when I say this, but to me, it looks as though a few bits and pieces were thrown into that house to create the impression someone was living there. So many of the basic necessities were missing, it would have been impossible for anyone actually to be living in that house at the time McCormac was supposedly the resident."

No argument from Rod was forthcoming. Basically, he agreed with my assessment of the situation and, while that might have been reassuring, it was not in the least bit helpful. I was hoping for some creative thinking on his part. We lapsed into silence again. This time, it dragged on for about a minute before I brought it to an end.

"Thanks for the coffee, Rod – and for an interesting, if frustrating, morning – but I think it's time I went home and tried to make some sense of what we discovered. One thing that has come out of it though, is that my curiosity about what Richard is up to has just about gone through the roof. Do you think it's because he's got nothing to tell us, or is he just playing us…? Pretending to keep us in the loop while deliberately excluding us from everything?"

Of course, Rod had no answer to my questions. I didn't expect he would but, regardless, they were my current thoughts about Richard and his investigation. The ongoing silence from Cilla doesn't help matters either. I knew I would spend the afternoon churning through all my thoughts, notes and photos from this morning. With little prospect of having developed any clear line of thinking by bedtime tonight, there was every chance I'd be in for a long, restless night of staring at the ceiling.

This morning found me feeling decidedly below par. My prediction about last night was spot on. Sleep was elusive, and when it did come, it lasted only briefly and was dogged by disturbed dreams. I slept in and didn't hear the alarm. I now sat at the breakfast bench with a strong cup of coffee, trying to decide whether to go for my usual morning walk or to stay home and prepare myself for the miserable day that lay ahead. The option to stay home eventually won out. So, straight after breakfast, I armed myself with another coffee and went to sit at my desk.

"Now that I'm here, what do I do first?" I asked my empty room. "Do I start with my photos or my notes?"

Somehow, dealing with the photos seemed the easier option. But why did I think that? What was there to do with them? I opened the camera roll on my phone and looked at the first couple of shots I took in the kitchen of McCormac's house. I had taken a lot of photos and it was going to take me a while to go through them all. Looking at them on my phone wasn't an efficient approach. Decision made, I created a separate file and dumped all of the photos of McCormac's house into it. Then, it was a simple matter to upload that file to my computer so I could look at the photos on the big screen.

After looking at the first couple on the big screen and feeling a bit smug about my efforts, it occurred to me there was a better way of doing it. Moments later, my colour laser printer was spitting out page after page of prints of my photos.

"That's more like it," I told the universe as I gathered up the pile of printouts… But now, what to do with them?

I decided to spread them out on the dining room table. Of course, there was only room on the table for a limited number at any one time, so I decided to examine the prints room by room, and in the order in which they were taken. It meant that, within moments, I was revisiting McCormac's kitchen. After bending over the table for a few minutes to examine the printouts, I was slowly easing my stiff back into an upright position when my doorbell rang.

Rod stood on my doorstep. "I didn't see you out walking this morning and was concerned you might not be all right. As soon as I had a shower after my run, I came along to check."

"Oh, thanks for your concern, but as you can see, I'm fine. Well, maybe a bit the worse for wear from lack of sleep, but apart from that, I'm fine… And I could do with another coffee. Can I interest you in one, too?"

While I fussed about in the kitchen making coffee, Rod, having spied my prints spread out on the table, detoured to the dining room to examine the photos.

"Is this all of them? I mean, are these all the photos you took?"

"No, they're just the ones from the kitchen. I decided to look at them room by room. Now you're here, we can do that together. Who knows what we might uncover?"

"Yeah, who knows? Probably nothing. But, let's deal with our coffees first and then get down to the serious business of examining your prints."

Chapter 13

We were soon heads down and poring over the prints spread out on the table. At the rate we were progressing, we would still be examining the prints at Christmas. I couldn't work out what Rod found so absorbing. We were still dealing with the shots of the kitchen and I failed to find any new or exciting detail in any of them. Then Rod asked if I had a magnifying glass. Good God, what has he found to make him think he needs a magnifying glass? I couldn't help myself. That question was out before I could bite my tongue.

"Eh?... No, I haven't found anything of interest. I just thought that a quick scan with a magnifying glass might pick up some little thing we hadn't noticed, or at least confirm there was nothing to find."

As I was already on my way to find the requisite piece of equipment from amongst my craft gear, I continued and returned a few moments later brandishing it.

"Rod, if we carry on like this for each of the rooms, we will be bent over this table until next week. Can we speed things up a bit? Did you take any shots of the living area as you searched?"

"No. I didn't find anything to photograph. Why do you ask about that area?"

"Because I didn't search it and I don't know what it was like."

"Oh, I see. Well, could we look at the shots you took in the bathroom first? Then we can sit down while I tell you about the living area."

It seemed a reasonable request, so I agreed – and the bathroom was a small area. It shouldn't take too long to look at all the shots taken in there. How wrong could I be? Granted, we did get through the shots from the bathroom more quickly than those taken in the kitchen, but it still seemed to take inordinately longer than I imagined. But, even all good things must come to an end.

Despite good intentions, it was almost five o'clock by the time Rod gathered up all the bathroom shots and stacked them in a pile next to the pile from the kitchen.

"Is it too early to take a drink with us out onto the back deck?" I asked as I did a few weird bends and stretches to loosen my now stiff and aching back.

"Soda water or an iced tea perhaps, but I would prefer to hold off on alcohol until a bit later."

While Rod settled himself on the deck, I loaded a tray with our drinks… and had a quick scan of the contents of my fridge. It was likely that, within the next hour, it would be polite to ask Rod to stay for dinner, and I could hardly serve the man baked beans on toast. I found a pack of two steaks and a pack of two chops that weren't frozen. Either would provide a quick and easy dinner.

After the usual brief period of faffing about settling down and pouring drinks, it was time for Rod to report on his search of McCormac's lounge and dining rooms. He stretched back in his chair and clasped his hands behind his head. Then, staring off across the neighbouring paddock, he began a running commentary of his findings.

"There really isn't much to tell. All I can offer is a similar report to those discussed so far, but without images to support it. I started in the dining room. Nothing in that area other than a basic, fairly dated dining suite. One chair appeared to be missing but was later found in the main bedroom. There were no cupboards or any other storage devices in the dining room.

Then, I moved across to the lounge room. The centrepiece was an ancient, over-stuffed three-piece lounge suite. There were no coffee tables, side tables, or footrests of any description. There was no TV set and no unit that might hold one. One basic set of shelves, presumably intended as bookshelves, sat against one wall. It was about 1800mm high, by 900mm wide, and the shelves were probably not quite 300mm deep. Whatever its intended purpose, there was nothing on any of the shelves, on top of it, or behind it. There were no cupboards, lamps, or any other adornments in the lounge area."

"That house really paints a bleak picture. Given its appearance, I struggled to believe someone actually lived there or even wanted to live there. From what I saw and what you've just described, I find the furniture interesting. It all appears to be old – not that there's anything wrong with old furniture. But, McCormac's furniture appears as though it was acquired from a charity shop. For me, that doesn't fit with the image I have of a toffee-nosed bloke who wandered the Village on a regular basis in a jacket and tie. Am I missing something in that assessment?"

"No, I think that's fairly accurate. But, we do have to remember that McCormac was not a young man. I don't know how old he was, but it was obvious he had lived a fair slice of his life before he came to the Village. It's possible that, while his furniture is dated, they may be treasured pieces that he has held onto over the years and been reluctant to part with for whatever reason."

"Okay, I can buy that, but there are too many other anomalies… No food in the fridge or anywhere else in the kitchen… No clothes in the wardrobe… No toothbrush in the bathroom… And everything too pristine and unlived-in looking. Did Richard know what that house was like? Does that explain why he hasn't bothered to search it? And, why haven't we heard even a murmur from Richard for so long? He hasn't called you, has he? And, Cilla has been strangely quiet for too long. It's unlike Cilla to go so long without a call given the circumstances that probably lured her away from the Village."

"While I was out running this morning, I received a call from my colleague who was in contact with his friend about who was on which flights recently. He didn't have anything definite to tell me but said he would be out of contact for a couple of days and thought it best to update me before that happened. It seems his friend who is doing the searching for us thinks he might have found something interesting, but he couldn't confirm it yet. What the call actually amounted to was that my colleague's friend might be onto something interesting but we wouldn't hear any more about it for at least the next couple of days."

"It's as though the whole world is working against us. If only we could think of an excuse for a phone call to Richard… You don't happen to have any bright ideas, do you?"

Rod shook his head and went to say something in response, but his phone played its tune at that precise moment. "Pour me another one," he said, pointing to his empty glass as he went inside to take the call.

My mind kept me entertained while Rod was busy with his call. Thank goodness it wasn't a long call or I might've died of mental exhaustion while waiting for him to return. I glanced up at him as he came back onto the deck, and caught my breath. The look on his face told me the call had unsettled him in some way. He hesitated before pulling out his chair and sitting down again. I waited patiently, the whole while silently willing him to share details of his call. After studying his glass for a few moments, he took a deep breath and looked up at me.

"That call was from Richard. No, he didn't tell me anything, but perhaps you might like to fetch another glass. Richard was on his way here when he called. He'll probably arrive in the next five minutes or so."

"I know you said he didn't tell you anything, but how did he sound?"

"Like Richard… How else would he sound?"

While that was not the answer I was hoping for, I know Rod well enough to know that was the only answer I was going to receive. I took his advice and took the tray inside. After putting another long glass for iced tea on the tray, I had another thought. Three wine glasses, an ice bucket and a cold bottle of Chardonnay went on the tray as well. After all, it was late enough to indulge in alcohol, and who knows, we might need it after Richard tells us why he needed to come here.

As I plonked the tray down on the table, it occurred to me that some cheese and crackers would probably go well with it too. I was on my way to the kitchen again when I heard a car pull up out front.

"Richard has arrived, I think," I called over my shoulder to Rod as I disappeared inside.

He followed me in and answered the door when the doorbell rang. After the usual pleasantries, Rod led Richard out onto the back deck and I followed along behind with a platter of cheese and crackers. We then went through the usual time-wasting of settling at the table and asking polite questions about how everyone's day had been. I waved my hand questioningly at the pitcher of iced tea and the bottle of wine.

"Yes, please. Get the top off that, if you don't mind," he said, indicating the wine. "It's been one of those days – correction, another one of those days."

At last, everyone was sipping wine and munching crackers. I noted a certain tension surrounding the table. Then, just before I thought I was about to burst, we finally got down to business. Richard cleared his throat a couple of times and seemed a little uncomfortable as he pushed his glass of wine around on the table.

"Have you heard anything from Cilla?" he asked. Both Rod and I shook our heads before Rod answered.

"No, not a word."

I thought the question a bit odd considering the fact that Cilla works as a consultant to Richard's mob.

"Should we be concerned?" I asked as innocently as I could muster.

"No idea… I haven't heard anything either."

"Uhmm, Richard, isn't Cilla working with you on the McCormac case?" I asked.

It earned me a hard look from Rod, but I had no idea why. It seemed like a perfectly logical question to me.

"Well. No, that didn't end up being the case. We did discuss the case, of course, but that was soon after the crime scene was established. The consensus at the time was that I would contact her if I needed to bring her in on the case."

"And...? What happened?" Another dark look from Rod shot my way.

"At the time, I didn't know it was going to be such an impossible case. There was no indication the bloke would turn out not to exist. Then, by the time we had established that fact, Cilla had disappeared and had turned off her phone."

Rod's phone played its tune, halting proceedings briefly while he checked the caller ID.

"Sorry, but I do need to take this. It shouldn't take more than a moment," he said as he strode back inside.

Richard raised his eyebrows in question at me. I shrugged and continued to cast my mind about for something 'safe' to talk about while we waited for Rod's return. In the end, I decided to hell with safe and just waffled on aimlessly about the case.

"I must admit I find it hard to comprehend that, in this day and age, someone can become completely non-existent, not just anonymous, but non-existent. If you think about it, these days, everyone has email accounts, bank accounts, receives mail, has a driver's licence, and so many other things that indicate who you are. It almost seems impossible for someone to completely hide their identity."

"You would think so, wouldn't you? I certainly thought so until I started trying to find something – anything – relating to Baxter McCormac. However he went about it, he is proof that it is possible to completely disappear."

"Perhaps not 'disappear' exactly. He was still here, so he hadn't disappeared. It was more like anything and everything relating to him and his life had disappeared."

"Yeah, I hadn't thought about it that way, but you are right. I suppose that means the question is, how can a person exist here in the flesh while existing nowhere else in any form."

It was a relief when Rod reappeared. As he pulled his chair out from the table, he gave me a look I couldn't interpret. I had no idea what he was trying to tell me or what I should make of that look. So, I did my best to look blank. If Richard noticed, he didn't comment. I thought it might be wise to let Rod know what had been said during his absence, and gave him an executive summary.

"We were just marvelling at how someone can manage to lose their identity and everything else about themselves these days."

My reward was something I interpreted as a relieved nod from Rod. Then he attempted to resume the conversation from where it left off when he went to deal with his phone.

"Is it possible Cilla's services were urgently required by your southern counterparts? Although, if that were the case, surely you had first dibs on her time, Richard."

"If only that were the case. Because I didn't know how complicated the case would be, I hadn't actually signed her up to assist with the investigation. By the time I did realise what I was up against, she had disappeared and had gone incommunicado. It would be handy at least to know what she was up to, and whether she is able to be involved in my case. Even just knowing where she is and how long she might be gone would be helpful."

"While I don't know much about what she might be up to, I can tell you there is strong suggestion Cilla flew out of here soon after McCormac's death. Her partner appears to have left here either on Sunday or early Monday after McCormac's demise, and Cilla and her car disappeared from the Village late on Monday. Cilla's car has been in the long-term car park at the airport since Monday evening, according to the ticket on the dashboard. It remains there this evening."

Richard took a moment to respond to Rod's information, but, when he did, his tone made it clear he was not impressed.

"I could have done with this information a lot sooner. Is there some reason you chose to withhold it until now?"

"A fairly reasonable one, actually. I didn't know about her car being at the airport until I took that call a few minutes ago. I suspected she might have flown somewhere, probably south of the border, but I couldn't substantiate it."

Rod's reply was delivered in a completely neutral tone. I saw Richard appear to visibly 'deflate' as he sat back on his chair.

"So, Sydney, you think?" Richard asked after a moment to consider Rod's information.

"Dunno, but I assume that's where she went."

"What about Joe's absence? Did he fly to Sydney, too, or what's his story, do you suppose?"

"No idea about Joe, I'm afraid. I'm guessing he probably went in the same direction, but I have nothing to base that on, other than a gut feeling."

Conversation lapsed for a while. The two men appeared to be considering recent comments. Although I sat quietly while they got on with their pondering, internally, I was bouncing up and down. I had questions for Richard and I was determined to ask them. But I didn't know how to ask them without incurring the wrath of one or both of my companions. Eventually, it got the better of me.

"Richard, I can't understand how someone can leave absolutely no trace of themselves. Surely, McCormac had a bank account somewhere and credit cards linked to that account. He must've had a phone and an internet connection and, therefore, there must've been contracts and regular bills associated with those services. Is there nothing you can glean from the evidence in his house?"

I carefully avoided looking at Rod, but out of the corner of my eye, I saw the scowl he directed at me. Too bad… We've been dancing around the situation for too long. It's time we found out why Richard hasn't searched that house.

"All of that is true. I'm sure he had a phone and, in this day and age, it would be unlikely for him not to have some sort of internet connection. But, all our efforts so far to locate his providers have hit dead ends. None of the banks or other financial institutions know anything about a Baxter McCormac."

"What about his phone, Richard?" Rod asked. "Isn't it possible to extract something from his call history or the phone's details?"

"Do you know where his phone is? We don't have it… And that means it wasn't on his body when we found him."

My mind was racing at breakneck speed. What else wasn't on the body when he was found? One way to find out, I suppose, is to ask the question. So, I did.

"While that sounds a little odd to me, I suppose there are people who don't carry their phones with them at all times. I suppose, some people value their privacy and don't want to be bothered by calls. What about his wallet? Did that contain anything that might help with your investigation?"

"No wallet… Yes, I did find it strange that he wasn't carrying a wallet on a day's outing to the seaside. Didn't he plan to buy himself a coffee or lunch? When we went back to check that patch of scrub and the track leading off to it, we paid particular attention to looking for a wallet and a phone that might've been lost in those areas.

This was becoming more intriguing with every question I asked and I had at least one more to throw into the mix.

"What about his house keys? I have trouble accepting that he might not have carried his phone or a wallet, but I expected he would have slipped his house keys into his pocket when he left home to board the bus for Jackson Cove."

"The answer is the same: no keys. No keys of any sort in any of his pockets."

That question earned me another threatening look from Rod. I chose to ignore that one too, and carried on to expand the discussion of McCormac's house keys.

"So, you would have needed to obtain a master key from Tanya, our director, in order to search McCormac's house. Didn't you find any clues in the house?"

"We haven't searched the house yet. Before you ask, there are a number of reasons why we haven't. The primary one being our need to establish beyond any doubt the identity of the body found at Jackson Cove. In the absence of that clear identification, a mountain of paperwork needs to be completed and approved before we can go rummaging through someone's possessions. Having said that, the way this case has progressed so far, it almost has me believing a search of that house will produce exactly the same results as we've encountered everywhere else.

Anyway, I have a meeting with your chairman of the board and the Village's director in a few minutes' time. As they want to talk about the situation with the house, it will be the time to discuss searching the premises."

Rod, finally, elected to join the conversation. He sat forward on his chair and leaned on the table. I detected a hint of excitement in him. I tried to remain focused on Richard and ignore Rod's renewed interest in proceedings. Although I didn't really know what I expected him to say or ask, his question surprised me.

"Whose idea was the meeting, yours or theirs?"

"Theirs… Does it make any difference who requested the meeting?"

"Perhaps not to you, but I find it *v-e-r-y* interesting. There has been no word from the chairman since the day the incident occurred. I did have a meeting with the director, for what it was worth. She didn't seem to know much at all and McCormac's file, which she allowed me to flick through, told me nothing. So, as I said, it's interesting that they suddenly decided they needed to speak to you. No doubt, it's because they've got a long list of applicants waiting for a house to become available – and the Village now has one that no longer has a resident."

As Rod finished speaking, Richard's phone demanded his attention.

"Speak of the devil… I'll take this and probably be back in a minute."

Richard wandered inside to take the call, and I took the opportunity to ask a question that had been gnawing at me since Richard arrived.

"Do you happen to have any steaks in your fridge, Rod? I only have two steaks. If you have one I could 'borrow' for the evening, I could ask Richard to return here for dinner with us after his meeting with the chairman and Tanya."

"It just so happens I do have a couple of steaks in my fridge. If he accepts your dinner invitation, I'll dash home to fetch the steaks when he goes to the meeting."

His brief phone call over, Richard returned and sat down on the chair he so recently vacated. As he shoved his phone back in his pocket he gave us a wry smile.

"Looks like you're stuck with my company for a bit longer. That was your venerable chairman calling to tell me he'd be about ten minutes late after being held up at a previous meeting. I had better stick with iced tea after this, seeing as how I have to drive home this evening," he said as he picked up his half-empty glass of wine.

Seize the opportunity, I told myself, and rushed to fill the void in conversation.

"Unless you need to be elsewhere tonight, why not come back and have dinner with us after your meeting with the chairman? It won't be anything too fancy, but it will be edible, and you will have our sparkling company to help you recover from your meeting."

"I don't know that any recovery process will be necessary, but if it's not an imposition, thanks for the invitation. I'll return as soon as I've discovered why I've been summoned this evening."

"Prepare to be questioned," Rod said. "We also would like to know why you were summoned – and what was said."

Nothing of any consequence was discussed during the next fifteen minutes or so until Richard deemed it was time to leave for his meeting. About two minutes after Richard's taillights disappeared in the direction of the admin building, Rod jogged along the footpath to his house and returned soon after with the promised steaks.

As soon as Richard departed, I threw three potatoes in the oven and began preparing a salad. Well, I had warned him it would be nothing fancy, and there was no way jacket potatoes and salad could be considered fancy. Nevertheless, I was concerned about the jacket baked potatoes. They do take an hour or so to cook, and I doubted Richard's meeting would last that long.

In the end, I needn't have worried. Richard's meeting ran on much longer than any of us had anticipated. By the time the steaks were ready, the potatoes were done and my stomach was rumbling.

Chapter 14

Richard's meeting with the chairman and director stretched on longer than any of us expected, including Richard. He returned looking a bit shellshocked. He and Rod perched at the kitchen bench as I cooked the steaks and dished up dinner. While Richard looked as though he was happy to settle in at the table for as long as possible, as soon as I dished up desserts, Rod suggested – fairly strenuously – that we take them out onto the back deck.

In the interim period, the sultry early evening had been replaced by the darkness of night. A breeze had sprung up and was a pleasant relief from what had been a steamy afternoon and early evening. I could see stars everywhere against the dark backdrop of the night sky and the evening breeze had a crispness to it.

"You looked a little battle weary earlier when you returned from your meeting. Did you achieve what you wanted, or was it just an exercise in frustration?" I asked as soon as we were settled.

"As you would be aware, I'm not exactly a rookie at interviewing people, but I had never encountered anything like it before," Richard said, shaking his head in disbelief. "I wouldn't have believed it possible to discuss an important matter for so long and actually say nothing. So, did my meeting achieve anything? I will think about it overnight, but my immediate answer is, no, not a thing."

Rod's interest appeared well and truly fired up by Richard's comments. He pushed his empty desert bowl out of the way, shuffled forward on his chair and clasped his hands on the table.

"Well, Richard, if it's not too top-secret to discuss with us, perhaps there might be a chance we could throw a little light on some of the things you asked them about."

"Nothing top-secret about it. I was simply chasing information on Baxter McCormac, and I had this outlandish idea that his file and his application for residency documentation might contain at least a few grains of what I wanted to know. The meeting concluded with me still none the wiser about our mystery man. I don't know if they were just being obtuse, or if they just didn't have the information I required. I find it hard to believe the latter might be the case. Surely, they require prospective residents to provide considerable information for the organisation to consider before they accept them as residents."

"Perhaps not in this case," Rod murmured. "I went to see Tanya on the Monday after the incident to give her details of what had gone down over the weekend while she wasn't around, and I also asked about McCormac's background. I probably asked much the same questions as you did tonight, but my objective was to have his family or next of kin advised of what had happened. Tanya produced his file and gave it to me to read. I asked where the rest of it was and she just looked stunned.

There was nothing in the file. Well, nothing of any consequence and certainly nothing like what must exist in any of the other residents' files. How that bloke was accepted without having provided a skerrick of information about himself or his background remains a mystery for me."

"So, they weren't just being difficult or trying to fob me off. That's not what I wanted to hear, but it certainly confirms what came out of the meeting."

"What about McCormac's house? Did they give you a key so you can search that place?" Another black look from Rod winged its way in my direction after I asked the question.

I knew Rod probably was concerned I was going to let slip about our 'treasure hunt' earlier today. I wanted to shout at him, give me credit for some intelligence, but settled for ignoring his looks. Some later time, when we are alone together, I probably will deliver that message, but, for the moment, I'm concentrating on maintaining my dignity.

"Yeah, I did mention that, in the absence of any personal information on McCormac, accessing the house to go through his personal possessions might be the only way we will find out anything about the man – and who to notify about his death. That really did earn me a fob-off by the chairman. As I half expected by then, he quoted all sorts of possible legal ramifications associated with allowing access to a resident's personal property."

"What was the final outcome?" Rod asked.

"Well, I did try to acquaint him with the legal issues surrounding the current situation. I thought I was being patient and persuasive, but nothing changed. Rather than create a confrontation, I decided to leave it without further argument. I ensured the meeting ended soon after that. My patience only stretches so far. Anyway, by the time I was on my way back here, I had decided I would seek a warrant to search the premises first thing in the morning. There won't be any problem obtaining one, but the difficulty will be extracting a key from Tanya – or, more likely, the chairman. Miss Jellicoe looked most uncomfortable while the debate about a key raged. Something is not right about the whole matter of McCormac's presence in this village."

"Right, not a particularly productive meeting for you," Rod began. "I didn't think you would need to obtain a warrant to search that house. The resident was murdered, doesn't that open the door for you?"

"Normally, yes… But, because we can't prove the man's identity beyond any doubt, it becomes a bit more complicated."

"That sounds like some form of Catch 22 scenario. You can't prove who McCorman was, because you can't get entry to the house… And you can't gain entry to the house because you can't prove who McCormac was. Does that about sum up your situation?" I asked.

"Exactly…."

"We-ell…," I began tentatively, while resolutely not looking at Rod. "Well, I don't know if it will be any use to you, but

McCormac was not in the habit of locking his doors – told his neighbour he didn't think there was any need to in this Village."

"Now, that is interesting … and possibly useful to know. But I'm surprised he was so blasé about the security of his property." Richard appeared deep in thought as he studied his empty dessert dish.

He appeared so intensely focused on his own thoughts, I thought I could almost hear the cogs of his mind turning.

"Probably because there is no property there to be concerned about," Rod said quietly.

Without looking up, I saw Richard's eyebrows come together across the bridge of his nose in confusion at Rod's comment. Then, he looked up at Rod. He did not look pleased.

"What exactly is that comment supposed to mean? Am I to take it you know something of the state of the interior of that house? And how might you have gained such knowledge?"

Although a seething mass of trepidation, I couldn't let Rod be the only one to suffer what might follow. So, I cleared my throat and jumped in while Rod and Richard were engaged in something of a hostile gaze exchange.

"By the most obvious means, of course. We had a look, and Rod is right. There is no evidence anyone was actually living there. Before you argue about that, yes, we know McCormac was seen around the Village, and he supposedly was one of the Village residents on the bus to Jackson Cove that fateful day. His neighbour speaks of having seen him around his house."

"As you say, he supposedly was living in that house on the corner. How is that possible if there is nothing in the house? And, when you say there is nothing in the house, what exactly do you mean? I'm afraid I'm not understanding any of this."

"Perhaps, if you have a look at some photos, you might better understand the situation," Rod suggested. "Marion, could you dig out those photos from this morning, please? We might have to go inside so we can spread them out on the dining room table."

Richard's face had lost its scowl. He now looked… stunned. Best to have him looking at those photos before he finds his scowl again, I told myself as I sprang up and rushed inside. A few moments later, while Rod rinsed the dessert bowls and added them to the dishwasher, I spread out on the dining table all the photos from McCormac's kitchen. When Richard and Rod joined me at the table, I gave Rod a look that I hoped he understood was an invitation to deliver the commentary on the display before them.

Silence reigned for a few moments as Richard slid his eyes slowly over all of the photographs. He then straightened up and took a more long-range view of the panorama laid out before him before giving Rod a questioning look. A look that Rod interpreted as an invitation to go ahead with his spiel. After a few moments of Rod's commentary, I quietly returned to the kitchen and set about making coffee. This could develop into a *long* night and, while I didn't know about the other two, I would definitely need caffeine support long before it ended.

My assumption was correct. It was almost midnight by the time the session with the photographs crawled to an end and the three of us stood around the dining room table stretching our backs after being bent over for so long.

"Marion, if I could impose on you for another coffee, perhaps we could return to your back deck to talk about a few things?" Richard asked.

I quickly threw crackers, cheese, a few dried apricots, and a handful of roasted almonds onto a platter and handed it to Rod to take with him as he led Richard out to my back deck. A few minutes later I loaded a tray with fresh mugs, coffee, glasses, and a bottle of port.

While I was over everything to do with Richard, McCormac and his house, I was interested in how soon I might be able to go to bed. The other two did not appear to share my inclination. It was a couple of minutes after one o'clock when Richard climbed into his car and drove out of the Village. It was too late to even think about Rod going home for what remained of the night. So, while the loaded dishwasher was set about its business, there were a couple of quick showers and then lights-out.

Rod was long gone when I finally crawled out of bed this morning. No doubt, he had gone home to change and then went for his usual morning run. I admired his stamina but my thinking was that I might give going for a walk a miss this morning. Then, by the time I had finished my first coffee for the day, I had built up sufficient guilt to have me lacing on my sneakers.

Although it was still early, more people were moving about in the Village. I gave Zorka's/McCormac's house a long look as I strolled past on my way to the end of my street. I had turned the corner and taken a couple of steps along the street leading to the small park adjacent to the Village when the little voice in my head brought me to a standstill. It reminded me that, although it hadn't really registered with me, I had seen something at that house as I went past. I turned around and moved back to the end of my street.

"O-oh, that is interesting," I whispered to the universe.

From behind the house, I saw Richard wave to three men coming in through the gate in the perimeter fence. The three officers, all wearing navy blue boiler suits and carrying bundles that looked like rolled-up white scene of crime suits. In response to Richard's signal, they strode across to the house. I stood anchored in the middle of the intersection for about a minute – and probably with my mouth hanging open.

So, Richard had decided to take matters into his own hands and circumvent Merivale Village's powers-that-be. No doubt, our discussions last night were the motivation behind this morning's move. Although Richard was adamant he had every right to search the house as part of a crime investigation, I couldn't help wondering about the ramifications of his show of authority. It was likely his officers' search constituted nothing more than an exercise in ticking every box. His examination of our photos last night told Richard exactly what they were likely to find in that house this morning. Perhaps, once he officially knows about the unusual situation regarding that house, it might create other avenues for him to explore with his investigation. I realised that by standing where I was in the middle of the intersection, before too long, I was bound to attract attention – not only to myself but also the operation currently happening at McCormac's house.

I spun around to head off in the direction of the park again and barrelled into Mavis Grimshaw on her way home from the gym. My watch told me her workout had finished early this morning.

"What do you make of that?" she asked as soon as I'd finished apologising for almost knocking her over.

"Do you reckon they might be the police? Or are we about to experience a repeat of the Zorka episode? If it's the latter, they've left their run a bit late."

Mavis hadn't waited for a reply and barely drew breath before continuing. I had managed to slip in a shrug in response to her question. That was as much as I was going to give Mavis this morning, but it didn't matter. She obviously hadn't expected a response and simply drew a long breath before posing the next question.

"Should we let Tanya know what's going on? I mean, we don't really know what's going on anyway, but the way they slipped in through the backdoor like that tends to suggest they might be up to no good. If Tanya called the police to report something funny happening here, they would either confirm or otherwise that it was their officers in the house. In any case, then we would know whether to prepare for another showdown like the last one or to just go home and have a coffee."

"Yes, I can understand your concern when you live next door as you do. I don't think we are in for a repeat of the Zorka episode. Somehow, that type of event doesn't happen in broad daylight and, as you say, they've left it a bit late if they were planning to abduct McCormac. Anyway, on a different note, isn't this a bit early for you to be on your way home from the gym? Isn't your workout usually longer than this?"

"Uhmm… Yes, it is, but I happened to glance out of the window and saw people making their way to my neighbour's house. Oh, I wasn't worried about Zorka's house – or McCormac's house if you prefer. I was worried about my place. They could be a mob of looters about to ransack places along the street. I thought it best to hurry home, just in case. What are you going to do? Are you going to go home again and keep watch over your place?"

"No. My routine already was shot this morning thanks to a late start, so I'm just going to continue with my walk – and hopefully, my house will be intact when I return. I'm sure you'll be all right, Mavis, but if you have reason to be concerned, call Tanya, or maybe the police."

That's when I looked up the street and saw Rod on his way home from his run. He waved and beckoned me to join him. It required a quick 'two-step' for me to disengage from Mavis.

"On second thoughts, Mavis, I think I'll give going for a walk a miss today. Come on, I'll walk with you to your gate."

She didn't argue. There was little conversation until we reached her gate.

"Are you sure you feel okay about being on your own now?" After she assured me she would be and I had watched her disappear inside her front door, I strode off along the footpath to Rod's place.

"That was poor management on your part, allowing yourself to be cornered in the middle of the intersection like that. Were you heading out for or returning from your walk when you encountered Mavis?"

"Neither… By the time Mavis came along, I already was stalled at the intersection, as I watched Richard and three of his officers hurry around to the rear of McCormac's house. I suspect he dispensed with the need for a warrant to enter the premises and went ahead as you might expect the senior investigating officer to do in such a situation."

"And Mavis caught them in the act? Is that likely to cause problems of any sort?"

"Not sure, but I don't think so. She was all for calling various people about the matter, but I think I convinced her whatever was going on was part of the investigation into McCormac's demise – and, perhaps, it's best not to become involved."

"Good work. Now, have you had breakfast?" I shook my head. "Nor have I. So, come in and let's get that out of the way while we discuss what to do about Richard."

What to do about Richard...? What is Rod on about? Richard is finally doing what we have wanted him to do since last Saturday...although a fat lot of good, it will do his investigation. It is likely to be as useful to him as our 'treasure hunt' was for us. This is so frustrating. I have absolutely no ideas about what we might try next, and Rod doesn't seem able to come up with any bright ideas either. For my money, our only hope was for one of Rod's contacts to come up with something for us to work with.

As I picked up our coffees to take them out onto Rod's back deck, I saw him grab something off his desk before following me outside. As we settled at the table, he slapped a pad and pencil on the table in front of each of us.

"...To note anything that emerges as we brainstorm this McCormac thing," he said, indicating my pad and pencil with a jerk of his head. "Now, where to start? The usual practice is to start from what you know."

"Well, that won't be difficult. There is only one thing we do know: McCormac is dead, murdered. Ah, no, wait a minute. We don't know that at all."

"What do you mean by that? Of course, we do. McCormac *is* dead. We found his body."

"No... we found a body. The body of a person who purported to be Baxter McCormac. But, we don't know who that body really was and, so far, nobody else has been able to find out either."

"Christ, you are right. The only solid *fact* we have is that there was a body. The body of a man who had been murdered. Right, so where do we go from here? Do you have any suggestions, Marion?"

"None whatsoever. Unless one of your contacts comes up with even the tiniest clue, all we are doing is thrashing about in quicksand – and probably about to go under for the third time."

As I finished speaking, Rod's phone played its tune. It sounded deafening in the stillness of the morning. Rod checked the caller ID, immediately shoved his chair back from the table, and stood up.

"Speak of the devil…," was his intriguing comment as he rushed inside to take the call.

It probably wasn't a long call, but it felt like it went on for ages. After fidgeting on my chair for a while as I waited for his return, the tension and excitement were at dangerous levels. I bounced up off my chair and began pacing about on the deck. I had no doubt that his comment regarding the caller indicated it was one of his contacts. Please, God, let it be good news that will allow us to make some progress, I thought as I stepped down off the deck and onto Rod's back lawn. I had completed a couple of circuits of the backyard before I heard Rod sit down on the deck again.

"Find anything you liked?" he quipped by way of letting me know he had returned.

"What? I just thought I wouldn't feel so guilty about missing my morning walk if I wandered around out here while I was waiting for you to come back. Did the 'devil' who called you have anything useful to share?"

"Possibly… At least, it might be if we are able to confirm it. All right, all right. Come and sit down and I'll tell you about it."

What is wrong with the man? Couldn't he see I was sitting opposite him and almost salivating for details of the call? I gave him a steely look. He read it correctly and promptly launched into his report on the call.

"My caller was my colleague who has a friend who can check flight passenger lists. If Cilla and Joe were on flights recently as we assumed, they didn't fly under the names we know them by. By a process of elimination, he seems fairly certain Cilla flew to Sydney under her 'Gina' name. He hasn't found her – under any name we know her by – flying on from Sydney to anywhere else, so it appears she is still in Sydney."

"Okay, so she went to Sydney. That doesn't mean her trip had anything to do with our investigation. It might have been something to do with her consultancy contract with the Special Operations team there. We can't dismiss the fact that it might all be coincidental. Something has just occurred to me. Cilla might not still be in Sydney. There is nothing to say she didn't hire or borrow a vehicle and drive to somewhere else. She could be anywhere in that New South Wales by now … Or anywhere else for that matter. Anyway, what about Joe? Did we learn anything about him?"

"Maybe… It appears that a male who flew from here on about the right flight for him to be Joe also flew to Sydney. The same man, a day later, boarded a flight to Canberra. He doesn't seem to have flown anywhere else since then."

"Sounds promising, but it could all be circumstantial. We don't know about any other names Joe might use, so we have no way of knowing whether that man was Joe or not. But, I must admit that man's travel arrangements are tantalising. We don't know who Joe works for, but there is a fair chance that whatever the agency is, it's likely based in Canberra. So, come on, what name did this intriguing man use?"

"Theo Rothwell… And, no, my colleague has been unable to find anything on anyone with that name, but he hasn't had much time to do any research since his friend gave him the name.

Chapter 15

"Theo Rothwell..?" I repeated. "Is that likely to be Joe's real name, do you think? Or is it just another one he uses to suit the occasion?"

"I have no idea. I have to admit I admire Cilla and Joe for the way they never did slip up when using the only names we know them by. They undoubtedly know each other's real names, but they've never slipped up by using them – not in front of us, anyway."

"You are right, Rod, it's an assumption on our part that Theo Rothwell is Joe. It could be anybody and, yes, I know it would be a huge coincidence if it were someone else behaving exactly as we would expect Joe to do. I suppose, the big question now is, do we pass on the Rothwell name to Richard, or do we try to establish a reasonable connection to Joe before we pass on the information?"

"We probably should, but, first, let's see how he wants to play the game. Let's see if he is kind enough to tell us what his search of McCormac's house produced."

"How can it produce anything other than what we found? Nobody else has been in there?"

"Maybe... But let's wait and see. By the way, I've been meaning to ask you about Mavis. Is she likely to have called Tanya about strange people sneaking into her neighbouring house?"

"It's hard to be sure, but I don't think so. I tried hard to convince Mavis that, if she were concerned about anything happening next door, she should call the police rather than bothering Tanya about it. She would save a lot of time by cutting out the 'middle man', Tanya, and going straight to the police.

Would you mind fetching your copies of the images we took of McCormac's house?"

"Why? There will be nothing in them that has changed overnight." I gave him a withering look.

"There's something about the photos that niggled me last night. I can't pin down what it is that's annoying me. Maybe another look at them might help. Of course, if it is too much trouble to fetch them, I could go home and look at my own copies."

"All right, all right. Don't be like that. I'll fetch them."

After studying the images for a while, Rod became fed up with it and declared it a waste of time. I wasn't so sure.

"No, Rod. I don't think it is. This photo is trying to tell me something. I don't know what it is, but there is something about it that keeps drawing me back to it. Either go and find something else to do, or shut up and let whatever it is come through to me."

A few seconds later, I let out a yelp that startled Rod who was on his way to the kitchen for something. He rushed back.

"At last…! Yes, I knew there was something I hadn't thought about. Don't look at me like that. I haven't lost the plot. It's an important point that we haven't considered.

Look at this image... The magazines… We dismissed them without giving them enough thought."

"Well, we commented on them at the time, but what more was there to say about them?"

"Think about how they got here. They would have been mailed in plastic sleeves and would have had an address sticker of some sort on the front, and there probably was some information about the sender. We found no plastic sleeves anywhere, even for the latest edition. But, for them to arrive in the post, McCormac must've had a subscription."

"Not necessarily. He could have bought them at the local newsagents and they wouldn't have been in plastic sleeves with the name and address on them."

Rod was right, of course, McCormac could have bought them at the newsagents. There was something about that notion that didn't sit comfortably with me. I knew there was something wrong with it, but exactly what it was took a while to come through to me.

"All those flyers we found are related in some way to the magazines. The only way McCormac would have received those flyers was if he had a subscription to the magazines."

"Hmm… Yes, you could have a point there, but I need to think on it a bit longer."

"Ah hah, now I remember. I remember Mavis telling me that McCormac had received a magazine in the mail. I didn't ask if she checked the name and address on it. I don't know why, but it didn't occur to me at the time."

"I'm surprised Mavis didn't tell you anything about the name and address. To me, that suggests it's exactly what she expected to find on it."

"Yeah, that's probably true, but I still think that an enquiry to the publisher might be interesting. The name and address might be exactly as it should be for now, but, maybe, there might be at least a previous address to be gained by such an enquiry."

"Good thinking… While there's nothing we can do, it might be something we could suggest to Richard. Before that, though, we might have to go back into that house to retrieve the publisher's details from those magazines before we try igniting Richard's interest in talking to the publishers."

He made sense and I left it up to him to decide what our next step might be and when it would happen. Then, I remembered that he was on his way to the kitchen when I realised what it was about the photo that was bothering me.

"You were on your way to do something before I interrupted you by talking about magazines and publishers. What were you going to do, and do you need help with it?"

"It was nothing urgent or important. I thought I might wander out into my front yard to see if anything was happening at the end of the street."

"Anything like what? Are you expecting trouble?"

"No. I just thought I would check for any sign of activity – or if Tanya's car might be parked in front of Mavis's house. I will just have a quick look while you organise another drink. I'll have an iced tea this time, thanks."

It didn't take long to open the fridge and pour two long glasses of iced tea, but I had finished before Rod came back inside. We returned to his back deck and took a couple of swigs of our drinks before conversation resumed.

"Nothing at all happening at the end of the street. Well, nothing obvious, that is. If Richard and his officers came in through that gate in the perimeter fence, their vehicle probably is parked somewhere along that dirt track out the back. I might wander out to the fence to see if there are any strange vehicles out there." Rod pushed his chair back from the table as he finished speaking, and stood up.

"Before you go rushing off, do you think Richard and his men are likely still to be at McCormac's house? It's been a while since they arrived, and we know how little there is to find in there."

"Richard will ensure the place is searched thoroughly and that there can be no question about his men having missed anything. If you think back to how long it took us to go through that house, it's likely the police are still there. I'll just go and check the track for stray vehicles. It won't take long."

Rod had taken only a couple of steps across the back deck when his front doorbell interrupted. We exchanged surprised looks as he rushed past me on his way to the front door. Moments later, I heard voices, and they were becoming louder as they came towards me. Then, Rod was giving somebody instructions.

"Take a seat. I'll bring your iced tea out in a moment."

Not sure what to expect or whether I should sit or stand, I eventually decided perhaps I should be on my feet when the visitor arrived. I sprang up and faced the backdoor just as our top cop, Richard, stepped out onto the deck.

"I was hoping you might both be here," he said as he collapsed onto a chair. "It's surprising how finding nothing can be so absolutely exhausting. I noticed you out there at the intersection so, no doubt, you are well aware of the search we carried out this morning. Before you ask, no, unless somebody has let her know, your director is unaware of our presence in the Village today."

By then, Rod had joined us at the table and we allowed Richard a few sips of his tea before Rod fired his first question at him.

"Did you find anything we overlooked?" Richard shook his head.

"There were no surprises this morning. I didn't expect to find anything new or that you hadn't already discovered, and that was the result of our morning's efforts… Zero… Nothing useful at all. I don't suppose you pair had any bright ideas of where we might go from here? I have no clue about where else we might go to progress this investigation and, so far, I have nothing to show for our efforts since finding the body."

His demeanour spoke volumes about his level of frustration. I assessed it as being about the same level as mine. I waited to see if Rod would mention magazine subscriptions, but when no mention was made for a few moments after Richard had basically asked for help, I decided to speak up – while carefully avoiding eye contact with Rod.

"At the risk of wasting your time, I do have a couple of things I wanted to bring up. One is a particularly weak suggestion, while the other is a question that's been bothering me for a couple of days."

Richard indicated I should go ahead, so I did. After recounting my lightbulb moment about the magazines, I floated the idea of how a possible subscription might provide at least a glimpse into McCormac's past. Richard managed to only look mildly interested but hastily scribbled himself a note. Then, I moved on to a more important matter I had been itching to ask him about: the CCTV footage of that car that collected McCormac and took him out of the Village for most of a day. My enquiry appeared to hit a nerve and seemed to cause Richard a good deal of embarrassment.

"Argh, you've caught me out, I'm afraid. I have to admit I've spent little time in my office since I set those couple of officers to search CCTV footage for the car you mentioned. I've spent most of my time with the major task force down south that is searching for McCormac's identity. There probably is a report regarding that vehicle hiding under a pile of paper that's built up on my desk in my absence. I'll have a look for it as soon as I return to my office. I promise I'll let Rod know if I have anything to report."

It seems Richard's promise caused Rod a change of heart and he decided that one good turn probably deserves another. After a moment or two of deep thought, Rod gave Richard the recently discovered name, Theo Rothwell.

"Never heard of him. I can't say I've come across the name in my searches so far. What do we know about him, and how might he be important in terms of their investigation?" Richard asked as he made himself another note.

After Rod explained the name's possible connection to Joe, and admitted that assumption could be based on nothing more than a major coincidence, Richard scribbled a few more words in his notebook before shoving it back in his pocket.

"All this sounds like I have a bit of work to do and that I had better get back to my office and make a start on it."

"Did you walk here from McCormac's house?" I asked. "I don't remember hearing a vehicle pull up out front."

"No, it's parked back along that dirt track, probably about behind your house. And, if I'm going to make a start on that work I've got to do, I had better start hoofing it back to my car."

"How fit do you think you are?" Rod asked, and Richard nodded confidently in response. "Well, if you think you're up to it, you could scramble over my back fence. It would save you having to trek all the way around again, and I could position a chair against the fence to help facilitate the undertaking."

"Uhm, I'm not sure it's fitting for the district's top cop to engage in such an endeavour." With that, Richard grabbed a chair and said, "Come and hold the chair for me. It's bad enough being seen scrambling over a fence, I don't want the world to see me fall flat on my face while I'm about it."

We both walked Richard to the fence to see him off. As Rod and I stood at the fence watching Richard make his way back to his vehicle, another thought occurred to me.

"Rod, about the other officers… Are they still at McCormac's house and, if they are, where is their vehicle?"

"When I looked along the track earlier, there were two vehicles parked out there. Obviously, the second one was the officers' vehicle and that's now gone. So, I think it's safe to assume there is no continued police presence in McCormac's house."

"Well, now that we've suggested to Richard that he look into those possible magazine subscriptions, do we still need to revisit McCormac's house?"

"No-o… I think we should wait to see what Richard's enquiries manage to produce and then reassess what we need to do."

It was time for me to go home. Rod walked with me as far as his gate and opened it for me. I stepped through and then stopped and looked across the road at Cilla's house. I heaved a sigh and shook my head.

"I wish I knew where Cilla was and what she was up to. I know it's ridiculous, but I feel concerned about her and even more so about Joe."

"Yeah, I know what you mean. I've thought about calling her but I need to think of a good excuse for the call before I bother her. Of course, there is every chance she won't tell me anything anyway, but it's worth a try."

As I walked home, I was accompanied by the realisation that the rest of my day held little promise of anything exciting or even interesting… And that's about how it panned out.

By the time I was home again, it was almost lunchtime. I told myself there was no point in trying to start anything. I should just settle for an early lunch instead. Following what seems to have become my usual practice, I took my lunch through to the loungeroom and settled into my favourite chair to watch TV as I ate – and immediately regretted it.

Apart from various elections, there appeared to be nothing else happening in the world at the moment. The news broadcasts on all channels consisted of a procession of talking heads espousing their opinions on the outcomes of the various forthcoming elections in various parts of the world. Lacking interest in any of it and not inclined to suffer it for long, after a couple of minutes of surfing channels, I muted the sound and settled back to think.

One solitary thought kept running through my mind. There must be something we've overlooked in the McCormac investigation. How can there be no clues about the man, no hint even of his existence? I was no more enlightened when I opened my eyes about an hour later. My 'thinking' had lasted a matter of seconds before I dozed off in my chair. It was well over an hour later before, stiff and dopey, I opened my eyes again. After a couple of tries, I managed to turn off the TV. My limbs seemed unable to coordinate with my thoughts. It finally resulted in my dropping the remote on the floor. I eyed it as it lay there on the floor and knew it would remain there for a while … at least until I was sufficiently in sync to be able to pick it up without ending up headfirst beside it.

A strong coffee achieved little, but a second one managed to have me functioning relatively normally. Now, what am I to do with the remaining hours of the afternoon and this evening that stretch out before me? Of course, there is always housework… Nah, I'd sooner sit around being bored. And that is pretty much what I did until about five o'clock when my phone demanded attention. It was Rod calling with an invitation to come for drinks followed by dinner. I had an hour in which to become human again and do whatever was necessary before arriving at Rod's at six o'clock.

The wonderful aroma of the roast in his oven wafted around me, enticing me along the footpath to his front door. When he opened the door and ushered me in, Rod was on his phone. He pointed to the wine and glasses waiting on the kitchen bench before gesturing towards the back deck. His message was clear enough. I gathered up the wine and glasses on my way past and relocated them to the table on the deck. I had just opened the bottle and poured myself a drink when Rod joined me.

"I'll have one of those, too, thanks. Apologies for the poor welcome earlier. That was Richard on the phone. He's on his way to join us."

"Has there been a development?"

"No idea why he wants to talk to us. He didn't say what it's about, but I thought I might have detected a hint of excitement in his voice."

"In that case, I hope it won't be too much longer before he arrives, and he has something positive to share. If he is excited, it might mean he has had his first breakthrough in the McCormac case. We need something to start going our way. Now, if only we knew what Cilla was up to. There certainly has been nothing of note happening in my life all afternoon. What was the rest of your day like?"

"Well, let's see… I tried calling Cilla several times during the afternoon, but she did not answer. So, still nothing to report on that front, but I will try her again tonight."

"What about Joe? Do you have his number?"

"Joe's number…? You must be joking if you think anyone was going to give me Joe's number, especially as we have never even been told his surname."

"If Richard arrives shortly, will he be staying for dinner with us?"

"That might depend on what he has to tell us. If we are a bit excited by the news he has come to share, I'm almost sure he will be invited to stay for dinner."

"Good thinking… Well, it seems your afternoon wasn't any more exciting than mine. Have you had any bright ideas about what we might try next to gain some traction with our investigation of the now deceased Baxter McCormac – or whoever he was?"

"Fresh out of ideas about what to do next, but inspiration might dawn after we hear Richard's news. Oh, there was one other thing of note that happened this afternoon. The chairman of our board of directors called me. He wanted a chat and scheduled it for tomorrow morning."

"Uh oh… How did he sound when you spoke to him? It's taken him long enough to contact you. Did he say what he wanted to talk about?"

"He didn't sound excited, if that is what you are asking me. And, no, he didn't say what the meeting was about, but he did ask how the residents had responded to the new bus."

"Hmm, is that a clue about what he wants to discuss with you? I mean, I find it amazing that neither he nor Tanya seems perturbed by McCormac's death. I half expected the incident might curtail further bus trips for a while."

"Well, in reality, it has had that effect. We have no bus trips planned for the remainder of this month, and as our group aren't spending time together at the moment, we don't know if anyone is interested in further trips."

"Do you think there might be any chance of asking the chairman and Tanya about the lack of information in McCormac's file and how he managed to become a resident without supplying the mandatory personal information?"

"I doubt it, not unless they bring it up or they mention being questioned by Richard."

Richard's arrival curtailed further discussion of Cilla, Joe or bus trips. Our top cop was unceremoniously bustled through to the back deck and promptly supplied with a glass of wine as Rod and I took our positions on the front edge of our chairs in readiness for the exciting news we hoped Richard was about to share with us.

Chapter 16

"Apologies for interrupting your evening, but I have a couple of pieces of information I thought you would be keen to hear."

Both Rod and I rushed to assure Richard he hadn't interrupted anything special and that we were more than eager to hear whatever he had to pass on.

"Okay, in that case, the first piece of news I have for you relates to McCormac's magazine subscription. We managed to contact the supplier McCormac had used and the supplier has agreed to follow up on details of the subscription and get back to me as soon as possible. He said he had no immediate recall of McCormac's subscription being a renewal but can't be certain until they carry out a search of their records. He did tell me he doesn't supply more than a handful of subscribers in this area."

"Hmm… Interesting but not particularly helpful so far," Rod suggested.

"No, maybe not, but it is a step in the right direction. Anyway, after that, I contacted the magazine's publisher. They told me a few copies were sold through one of our local newsagents, but they had only three direct subscribers in the area. Apparently, most people prefer a subscription with a supplier rather than directly with the publisher."

"Despite the publisher's comments, I'm a bit surprised more locals don't have subscriptions with the publisher."

I wondered if we might be lucky enough for McCormac to be one of the three who obtained their copies directly from the publisher. Somehow, what little I knew of McCormac suggested that would be the way he operated.

"Well, the publisher did say that originally and for many years, they did not offer direct subscription to individuals, preferring instead to deal directly with suppliers who purchased bulk copies. But, eventually, a growing tide of enquiries combined with problems with a dodgy supplier convinced them to trial individual subscriptions. They also opened up the magazine to subscribers who wanted to send in stories for inclusion in the magazine. Now, with about 200 such subscriptions across the country, the move is proving worthwhile. They, too, are checking the subscriber records for anything relating to McCormac."

While the information about the magazine subscriptions was interesting, and might even prove useful somewhere along the line, I was impatient for news about whether CCTV footage shed any light on that car Janet saw collecting McCormac.

"Richard, did you find a report from your team who were checking CCTV footage of that car we told you about? Were they able to find anything useful?"

"Ah, yes, I did find their report buried under a pile of other paperwork that had come in. The report indicates they believe they identified the correct car on footage from cameras in the area, both when it arrived at and left the Village."

"Wow…! That's something positive to chalk up. Were they able to track it?" Although I didn't expect a positive response and I tried to remain calm, I could feel excitement pulsing through my veins.

"Not without some difficulty. It appeared that those involved were determined not to be followed – or tracked. My men tracked the vehicle as it travelled a convoluted, roundabout route through obscure and often unmarked backstreets and roads. At one point, the officers lost the car for a part of its journey. They were about to call an end to tracking it when, by accident, while looking for something else for another investigation, they discovered the car on totally different footage. It was while they were examining a truck's dash cam footage in relation to a vehicle accident it might have captured, they got lucky. Only the relevant car's rear number plate was evident for a few moments at the distant edge of the dash cam footage."

"Damn… For a moment there, I thought we were about to hear some good news." I felt my earlier excitement now replaced by disappointment.

"Yeah, but it was something, I suppose," Rod added. "How did they manage to lose it? And is it too much to hope that your officers somehow managed to locate that car again on footage from cameras elsewhere?"

"Well, as the car was travelling much faster than the heavily loaded truck that was towing a loaded dog, it soon disappeared out of the range of the truck's dash cam. The officers had noted the direction in which the car was travelling and took a punt on its continuing in that direction. They trawled the car's anticipated route in the hope of finding CCTV cameras somewhere in the vicinity. They found one at a major intersection not far from where the vehicle left the truck in its wake. After that, they were able to track it through to where it turned into a light industrial area."

"Light industrial…?" I echoed. "What would McCormac want with a light industrial area? Was there anything interesting about the businesses operating in that area?"

"We are still working on that one. Nothing else is known about what went on at that location until about seven o'clock that evening when the same car was picked up by cameras elsewhere as it took a different route – a more direct route this time – back to here."

"Anything else turned up since then?" Rod asked, and Richard shook his head.

"What's the next move?" I asked, with frustration clearly evident in my voice. "Is there anything we can do to assist?"

"No, nothing you can do at the moment. As for our next move… My officers noticed the light industrial area was equipped with its own security lights and cameras. They didn't want to chase up footage from the cameras until they knew about the place and had my approval. We don't want to rush in heavy-handed and risk stuffing up the investigation."

"So, what happens now, then?" While I understood the possible need to proceed with caution, I felt as though the whole investigation was going nowhere and was unlikely to produce results any time soon.

"I met with my team last thing this afternoon and suggested a low-key approach was necessary, starting with where to go and who to ask about security CCTV footage from that industrial site. It won't be possible to implement anything until tomorrow. So, until then, we won't know anything more about McCormac's visit to that area. And, before you ask, I have absolutely no ideas about why or for what reason he might have gone there. All we know so far is that, whatever it was, it took all day to do it."

Frustrating though it was, I was happy enough that, at last, something was happening. I knew Richard was doing his best, and everything 'by the book' in case things went pear-shaped locally, but the investigation seemed to be moving at a snail's pace. Then, it was Rod's turn to air his frustration.

"That's great news, Richard, and I don't suppose I need to tell you how anxious we will be to hear how things pan out. But, while your team follows up on that lead, what's next? What else can we look into while we wait for your team to unearth camera footage or anything else useful regarding that industrial site?"

"Look, I understand your frustration… but that's not all of today's news. I tried following up on that Theo Rothwell name you gave me. For a while, it looked as though I had struck out. Then, almost as a desperate last resort, and after several calls had gone unanswered, I finally managed to make contact with an old friend who, in another life, used to work for Interpol. My friend thought he might have had a vague recollection of a similar name but couldn't remember why. Anyway, we left it that my friend would call me back if he manages to dredge anything useful out of his memory banks."

"Is that likely? I mean, how confident are you that your friend might remember something? How long ago are we talking about here, and what chance is there that it's the right bloke he is thinking about?" Rod quickly apologised for being so negative and Richard laughed.

"There are no guarantees in this game, of course. But, off the top of his head, my friend thought he recalled the name from a joint operation some time ago. No, I don't know what sort of timeframe we are talking about here, but he seemed pretty sure Theo Rothwell was a spook of some sort. This bloke's memory borders on encyclopaedic, so I don't think we will have to wait too long to know one way or the other."

Rod appeared satisfied and silence hung over us for a few moments as we sipped our drinks, but not for more than a few moments before Rod asked his next question.

"Richard, come on. Off the record, forget about the official position, what are your thoughts about what McCormac was doing at that industrial site? You have to admit, it seems an unlikely place for the bloke to spend so many hours."

"No idea, I'm afraid, Rod. I genuinely don't have a clue. I checked the businesses registered at that address but none of them rang any bells for me. The bottom line is, I didn't find anything likely to keep someone like McCormac entertained for such a long stint."

It appears Rod considered there was little else to be said on the McCormac matter and opted to change the subject.

"Do you have somewhere else to be this evening, Richard, or would you care to stay and have dinner with us?"

"Nowhere else to be and thank you. I'd love to stay for dinner, if I'm not intruding, of course."

We both rushed to assure him he would not be intruding, but I did wonder what we might have to talk about over dinner. In the end, it wasn't a problem. As Richard and Rod were acquainted long before I knew Rod, they had plenty to reminisce about that kept the conversation flowing all through dinner. Then, with dinner over, we were about to make our way back out onto the deck when Richard's phone brought a halt to proceedings.

"Sorry… I know it's rude to eat and run, but I do have to go. Thanks again for dinner. It was way better than the baked beans I probably would have had at home – and the company was an added bonus, too."

As we walked Richard out to his car, Rod took the opportunity to ask for advice.

"Before you go, Richard… The chairman of the board has requested the pleasure of my company in the morning at a meeting with him and Tanya, our Village director. I don't know what it is about but, as there was a bit of an incident here at the Village before we left for Jackson Cove the other day, I've been waiting to hear about it from the powers-that-be. I've no doubt the McCormac thing will feature in our discussions. I know Tanya is keen to clear out the house and move a new resident in now that McCormac will no longer be requiring that house. And, of course, there is the problem of what to do with his belongings. She has already asked me what she should do with them. I don't know any more than she does, or than I did then for that matter, but I'm sure I will be asked the same question again tomorrow. Do you have any suggestions regarding what I should say – or shouldn't say – about anything to do with the McCormac case?"

"I don't have any suggestions about what to tell them other than to claim ignorance of all matters relating to McCormac. What I might suggest, though, is trying to find out – carefully – why there is such a lack of information on McCormac's file. Lay it on a bit heavy if you like that, if all the usual information had been provided by the resident, they wouldn't have a problem dealing with the situation now. But, whatever else you say, stress the fact that they must not enter or remove anything from the house without first obtaining my permission."

"What to do with his belongings seemed to be the main item of contention when Tanya asked me about it previously and, no doubt, that will still be her main concern."

"Well, as we all know, clearing McCormac's belongings out of that house is likely to take all of five minutes – once they are given the go-ahead to do it. With so few things in the house, it's hard to believe the man actually lived there. Anyway, until a next of kin is identified and contacted, they have no authority to touch anything or even to enter that house."

By the time Richard had delivered the last of his advice to Rod, he had his car door open and quickly slid in behind the wheel. After dropping us a mock salute, he drove off and we watched his taillights all the way out of the Village before we went back inside.

We elected to postpone cleaning up the kitchen, opting instead to take coffee and glasses of port out onto the back deck where, for a few moments, we sat sipping in silence. But, that was as long as I could restrain myself. Something had been bothering me since we spoke to Richard earlier and I wanted – no, needed – to know the thinking behind what had happened. Although it might ruin the evening, I decided to ask the question.

"Rod, although I was a party to it, something we did has me confused. Why did we give Richard Theo Rothwell's name? I know how we came by the name and all that, but that's not what bothers me."

"Well, I would have thought it only natural for us to pass on to Richard anything of relevance to a case. I'm surprised you have concerns about it."

"No, it's not giving the Rothwell name to Richard that bothers me. It's the inference we attached to the name. We kind of led Richard to believe Theo Rothwell might be a name sometimes used by McCormac. That's not what I understood about that name."

"Of course not… I can't imagine what led you to think we suggested Rothwell and McCormac were one and the same."

"You know that's exactly what we did, Rod. Oh, we didn't say it in so many words, but we definitely led Richard to believe the Rothwell name could be significant in the McCormac case. Why? What did you hope to achieve?"

"If you think that is what we did, then you are as guilty as I am of any deception that occurred."

"Yeah… I supported you in this. Now, please tell me what I was supporting and why we allowed that situation to develop."

"All right, all right… I still don't know anything more about McCormac than I did before, but I figured creating some interest for Richard in the Rothwell name might turn up something worthwhile – like whether it is possible Rothwell is Joe. Don't ask me why I think having that confirmed, or otherwise, is important. I don't know what's prompting it, but my journo's nose is telling me it is."

His comments gave me pause for thought, and I took a couple of moments to consider Rod's explanation before I commented.

"That might prove not to be such a bad move. Both Cilla and Joe's reaction to McCormac's death appeared a bit odd to me. At the time, I felt – and I still do – that his death triggered some form of emergency response from both of them. But it was particularly noticeable in Joe. I can't help feeling they knew or thought they knew, more than they claimed about possible circumstances surrounding the McCormac incident. And, not a word from Cilla since she disappeared from the Village is odd."

"She doesn't exactly need to report back to us, you know. She could be working on some case in Sydney with her special investigations team. It could be that the investigation needs to be kept hush-hush. But, you are right. Her behaviour this time is odd and doesn't fit with the way she usually operates. At the very least, she usually tells us when she is going to be away from the Village for even just a few days."

"You are right, but everything about her absence this time doesn't feel right. Still, I suppose, if she doesn't want to take your calls, there's not much point worrying about it when there is nothing we can do about it … Unless, of course, she *can't* take your calls."

"Don't go there, Marion. You will just give yourself more to worry about, and it will be stuff we can't do anything about."

At that point, Rod's phone brought our discussion of Cilla's behaviour to an end. Rod checked the caller ID and quickly raised his eyebrows in surprise at me.

"What?" I demanded before thinking and amending my tone. "One of your contacts…?" I whispered.

Rod shook his head as he answered the call. Now it was Rod's behaviour that was odd. I had expected him to take the call inside, but instead, he continued to sit facing me at the table on the back deck. My curiosity was piqued by his first words, and the one-sided conversation coming from the other side of the table only heightened the intrigue.

Cilla, good to hear from you. How are things? ... Good, good. Look, first things first, I must apologise for bothering you when you are working, but I wondered whether you had picked up anything about McCormac while you have been away ... Yes, I appreciate it's not your highest priority at the moment ... Oh, no, I didn't expect you would have heard anything but I thought it worth asking. It's just that I've been summoned to a meeting with our chairman of the board and our director tomorrow morning. I have no doubt the main item on the agenda will be McCormac ... Nah, I don't think they will want a report on the investigation into his death. If they wanted that, they would talk to Richard. ... Yeah, it's likely to be about his house. Tanya has already been in my ear about the long list of applicants waiting for a vacancy to occur in the Village and how she really needs to be able to reallocate McCormac's house ... Here? No, nothing new to report from here. Richard still seems as much in the dark as he was when it happened ... No, I don't think it's an act. I feel sure there genuinely hasn't been any progress made so far ... Well, you could be right. His superiors down south appear to have taken over the investigation, so I don't know whether Richard is being kept in the loop or not ... Oh, I see. Well, that is disappointing, but not surprising ... Have you heard from Joe? How is he? ... Ah, right, of course ... Okay, talk to you again when you return.

After the call ended, Rod appeared lost in his own thoughts. I allowed the situation to drag on for at least a minute before I could restrain myself no longer. I cleared my throat a couple of times in an attempt at a subtle intrusion into his thoughts. It didn't work. So, I adopted the more 'sledgehammer' approach of a direct question.

"I deduced from what I heard that your caller was Cilla. Is there anything from her call you might care to share with me?" He chuckled for a second or two before answering.

"Yes, it was Cilla and, safe to say, she was not best pleased with my attempts to call her, but I think things became a little more civilised as our conversation progressed – until right at the end when I almost blew it again."

"Well, don't stop there. I would like to hear the gist of Cilla's side of the call as well as your contributions to the conversation."

"My mentioning tomorrow's meeting seemed to ease the initial tension a bit. But, according to Cilla, she doesn't know anything new about McCormac and hasn't heard anything useful. She claims to be too busy to become involved in what is basically another State's investigation. Mentioning Joe seemed to rekindle the earlier hostile vibe, but she assumes Joe is okay, and hasn't heard anything to suggest he isn't. Her side of the conversation ended by making it clear that what was happening in the Village was not her concern right now. It was made clear to me that I should not contact her again, except in the case of an emergency."

"What constitutes an emergency?"

"Nothing short of her house burning down, perhaps. It wasn't defined for me."

"Right… Well, you didn't gain anything to help you with tomorrow's meeting, so what's your approach going to be?"

"That's easy. I will be in a state of complete bewilderment as to why the meeting has been called."

What had shown all the promise of being a romantic evening for the two of us had effectively been derailed by Richard's arrival and finally scuttled by Cilla's phone call. It was fairly obvious it felt the same way for both of us. There was no question of staying over until after breakfast tomorrow. As soon as the dishwasher was doing its thing and order had been restored to the various areas of Rod's place, I made moves to be on my way home.

"You need time to prepare for tomorrow's meeting. I know there isn't much you'll be able to tell them regarding McCormac but, as Richard suggested, it would be good to know why there is so little detail on McCormac's file. And, you must remember that the meeting might not be just about McCormac. It also could be about your run-in with Bernard about that dog being allowed on the bus. You do need to have your head on straight before you go into that meeting tomorrow. So you have time to consider it all, I will head off home for an early night."

There was a token protest, but we were soon on our way to my house. Of course, Rod insisted on walking me home. We set out from his place in a companionable silence that lasted only until I asked the question that had rattled around in the back of my mind for the latter part of the evening.

"How long do you think it will take before Richard discovers that Theo Rothwell is not a name associated with McCormac?"

"Possibly a day or two – hopefully."

"Then, what will happen? Will we need to apologise for leading up the wrong track? And, how will discovering the truth likely impact Joe?"

"Not at all. All we did was give him a name that cropped up at about the same time as everything else was happening. I doubt he will discover Rothwell is connected to Joe, but what he does find out about Rothwell could be useful to us. Don't ask me how, because I don't know yet. It is just a hunch at this point in time."

By then, we were at my front door and saying our goodnights. I knew it would be much later tonight before I fell asleep. There was far too much to think about before that happened.

Chapter 17

Sleep was a long time coming last night, failing to arrive until sometime early this morning. Confident my routine was now well established, I did not set my alarm last night. Then just to prove me wrong, I slept way past my usual time. When I finally did wake up, it was so late, I decided not to go for a walk. That resulted in my spending an extra hour in bed dozing on and off.

Although I didn't know what time Rod's meeting was this morning, I knew it was early. As Tanya doesn't start work until eight o'clock, I guessed the meeting was scheduled for soon after she arrived at her office. While waiting for my morning coffee to be ready, I checked the time. It was eight o'clock. My mind flew to Rod. I felt my stomach start to tighten.

I knew discussing the McCormac matter would not be an issue. After all, as we knew nothing of any substance, the chairman was in for a disappointment if obtaining information about McCormac was his motivation for the meeting. It was the possibility of that *other* matter that bothered me… the matter involving Bernard and his objecting to the little dog travelling on the bus with its owner.

There was no doubt in my mind that Bernard had made the board of directors, probably directly via the chairman, aware of his objection to the little dog being allowed on the bus. Ever since the incident occurred, I was concerned there could be serious repercussions after Rod overruled Bernard's objection on the day. I feared Rod could be in for a rough time over it at this morning's meeting. While thinking about it as I finished my coffee, my doorbell rang.

Rod enquired about the availability of coffee as I opened the door and ushered him in.

"Coffee will take only a couple of minutes. Rod, aren't you supposed to be at a meeting this morning? Surely, it can't be over already."

"Yep, been there and done that already, and now I'm more than ready for a coffee. I'll save the details until we can wash them down with our coffee."

We filled in time with small talk about nothing in particular while we waited for the coffee. Then, armed with coffee and raisin toast, we settled in the lounge. My curiosity was approaching danger level by then, so we had barely sat down before I demanded a full and detailed report of the meeting.

"Well, I have to admit to being a bit bewildered about what the chairman hoped to achieve from the meeting. Yes, I had expected McCormac would be discussed at some point, but I was surprised to discover McCormac ended up being the only item on the agenda. As we had discussed previously, I maintained my 'no knowledge' position on why or who in relation to the man's death. I assured them several times that Richard had not given me any information or even clues regarding the matter.

"I told them I was surprised they thought Richard might have passed on anything about his case to me. Why would he when it was none of my business?"

"That is the truth. Richard hasn't passed on anything to us. So far, the information flow has all been in the opposite direction. So, having disappointed the chairman on that score, where did the discussion go after that?"

"While you might expect that was the end of the McCormac discussion, it wasn't. Talk then turned to the matter of McCormac's house still sitting there empty when there is a long list of applicants awaiting a vacant house. Again, I assured them I couldn't tell them anything useful, and explained that the house was likely to be a part of Richard's investigation into the murder. As such, only Richard could tell them anything regarding the house, including when they might be granted access to the place."

"Not quite an accurate statement, perhaps, Rod? Does Richard consider the house relevant to his investigation?"

"Yeah, perhaps not, but, while the man's belongings remain in the house, Richard must consider it to be hands-off for now. Anyway, I reminded them that the place, more than likely, wasn't empty unless someone already had removed McCormac's belongings from it. It gave me a certain degree of delight to suggest that a lack of information on the deceased next-of-kin could result in that house remaining off-limits for some time."

"Good points-scoring move there, Rod. What sort of reaction did your suggestion trigger?"

"Ha, ha… It worked like a charm at shifting the focus to why there was so little information on the man's file. I have to thank Tanya for grabbing the opportunity after I opened the door for her. She confirmed that they would not be able to help Richard with next-of-kin information as they had nothing on file."

"Of course, you would have been forced to state your surprise that such a state of affairs might exist in the Retirement Village's records."

"That's exactly what I did. I questioned why it wasn't on file when such information is part of the details every applicant has to provide as part of an application to reside here. The chairman looked uncomfortable and tried his best to move the conversation in a different direction. Tanya ambushed his efforts by demanding to know how it was that the requisite information wasn't on file."

"Goodness, I didn't think Tanya had it in her. She always seems so subservient to the chairman and other board members."

"Her job demands that I suppose. Anyway, on this occasion, her questioning of the chairman hit a nerve. He became stirred and told us in no uncertain terms that it was none of our business, and that McCormac had been appropriately vetted and approved. Tanya snapped back, 'by whom' and looked shocked by her own impertinence. I was compelled to jump in to deflate the chairman who had puffed up enough to look as though he might explode."

"Did you manage to defuse the situation?"

"Yep... I told him he was right. It did have nothing to do with me, but it was a concern for Tanya who was in danger of being seen not to be running the place properly if residents' records were not in order. I then went on to play my ace. I told him that, while it might be none of my business, it would be of interest to the police. Because of their interest, he should expect a visit from the police... And they will be most interested to know the reason for the lack of information on McCormac's file."

"Oh, dear… You weren't out to win friends, were you? How did the chairman take your comments?"

"He laughed – or gave a forced attempt at a laugh – before demanding to know why I thought the police would be interested in Merivale Retirement Village's files."

"Did he not realise it's a murder investigation and the police will expect information important to their case to be in those files?" I couldn't believe the chairman of our board of directors was so naïve.

"I explained that the police would expect to find certain important information in McCormac's file and, when they didn't, they would demand to know why. As Tanya's question indicated, she doesn't know why it's not there. When she tells the police that, they will turn their attention to you, the chairman of the board. Under those circumstances, you will stand a fair chance of being seen as complicit in McCormac's murder."

"How I wish I had been a fly on the wall… Of course, given everything you told him probably is correct, how did he react to it?"

"You would have enjoyed witnessing it. The chairman turned white and spluttered for a moment or two before admitting he really doesn't know anything about McCormac's background. He went on to claim he had been pressured into taking McCormac as a resident, *even if it meant tipping an existing resident out of their house to make way for him.* But they appeared to already know that Zorka's house was still vacant after the incident that happened there.

It goes without saying that I quizzed the chairman about who the 'they' were, but he claimed he doesn't really know."

"What do you think? Is any of that rubbish likely to be true, or is it all fiction?" I never had the chairman pegged as creative, quite the opposite. It all sounded a bit far-fetched to me.

"Well, his being pressured into this unlikely situation sounded like fiction, so I asked how it was possible for such pressure to be applied. It took him a while, but he did eventually admit there was something in his past that might be enough to render him ineligible to hold the various positions in the community that he does."

"Ah ha, the plot thickens. How did this juicy bit of conversation end? Did he explain this mysterious past of his?"

"Don't get your hopes up. There was no great revelation. When it was obvious he wasn't going to share further details, I told him that when the police came asking questions, I hoped he had something to prove his story about being pressured.

At that point, I decided it was time to either end the meeting or to return it to its original intent. So, I asked why this morning's meeting had been called, especially as I didn't know anything more about McCormac than the rest of the residents. Tanya confessed the meeting was her fault. She said the board didn't want that house sitting empty for too long. She didn't know what to do and asked the chairman for direction. He told her just to empty everything out and store it in one of the sheds in the Village until someone claimed it. Tanya doubted the legality of such a move and wanted confirmation from elsewhere that it was okay to do that."

"And they thought you would tell them it was okay to do that?"

"Apparently so… I told them they thought wrong, and I strongly counselled against even entering that house without prior police approval. That concluded discussion of McCormac and his house. So, before the meeting ended, I brought the chairman's attention back to his earlier comment by reminding him that he previously had mentioned the bus. So I asked the question: What about the bus?"

"Are you mad, Rod? That was just inviting trouble for yourself... All right, tell me about the chairman's concern regarding the bus."

"Relax... All that happened was the chairman said he had noticed the bus hadn't been used for a few days and asked if there was a problem with the bus. I told him it was fine as far as I knew, but the residents were still in shock and not keen to go on another bus trip yet after the horror of the last one. After commenting that 'surely they don't expect that to happen every time the bus goes out', he seemed to accept my explanation and the meeting ended."

After taking a moment to process the last of Rod's report, I had two major questions to ask but, as I was about to ask them, Rod suggested another coffee. A search of my fridge while I waited for the coffee pot to do its thing, I produced more raisin toast. We took our coffees and toast out onto my back deck and once we were settled, I was again ready to fire off my questions.

"So, what happens now, Rod? And, how do we go about finding out what's hiding in the chairman's past?"

"Two good questions, Marion, but here is another one to add to your list. Should we concern ourselves with either of them?"

"Well, I thought it might be worth our while to know what secret the chairman has."

"Why do we need to know? If you're thinking of holding it over him in some way or using it to have him chucked off the board, forget it. Better the devil you know than one you don't, and this one is just about trained to perfection. As to what next as far as the investigation is concerned, there isn't anything more we can do until we receive more information from somewhere. Oh, and that reminds me. I have a couple of things I need to do and I had thought to go into the city today."

"Stay for lunch. We can have an early one."

"Thanks, Marion, but I really should go."

Having declined lunch, Rod was soon out on the footpath and heading for home. I heard his phone play its tune as he strode along.

I figured having lunch alone provided an ideal time to ponder Rod's report of his meeting with the chairman and promptly got on with the job as soon as I sat down with my lunch in front of TV. I don't believe I'd achieved anything before I fell asleep in the chair with the afternoon's programs happily continuing to roll across the TV screen. It was just after three o'clock when I awoke groggy and disoriented. Somehow I managed to struggle into the kitchen and made a coffee to get me going again. Then, for want of something better to do, I decided to tackle the pile of ironing that mysteriously had developed and was begging for attention.

While waiting for the iron to heat up, my mind drifted to mahjong. I should talk to Rod about it. Reinstating our mahjong mornings might provide the first small step towards getting things back to normal for at least some of us in the Village. Thinking about mahjong seemed to help both time and the ironing slipped by faster than normal. Soon, the pile of ironing had disappeared and I was rummaging in the fridge and the freezer while trying to decide what to have for dinner. My foraging was interrupted by the sound of my doorbell.

Rod was on his way home from the city and called in. Whatever brought him to my door remained a mystery but I thought it might have something to do with Richard. As I poured us both long iced teas, on the spur of the moment, I asked Rod to dinner – and immediately panicked. I hadn't even found anything for myself to have for dinner, let alone what to have when there would be a guest as well.

"Ah, dinner… Uhmm …Well, that would be lovely if you could handle two extras for dinner."

"Two extras? I don't imagine that would be impossible, but who else did you have in mind?"

"Richard… He called me as I was on my way home from the city. No, don't get excited. I don't know anything more yet, but I might find out something later this evening. He said he'd come and see me at about six o'clock, so we could meet here and then stay for dinner – if you can manage the extra person."

Of course, I could handle two extra for dinner! But God knows what I'm going to feed them. Rod sent Richard a text of the new meeting arrangements. Thankfully, Rod said he had to take care of a couple of things before returning for our meeting and dinner and rushed off. I immediately raced to the kitchen on an urgent foraging trip. The only thing I found that I could remotely turn into a reasonable meal by six o'clock was the leftover roast leg of lamb in the fridge.

"Not the most glamorous meal, but shepherd's pie is what will be on the menu this evening," I told the universe as I surveyed the amount of meat recoverable from the leg of lamb.

By the time Rod returned, the pie was ready to go in the oven and I was preparing the vegetables to go with it. As he came in, he announced he had an interesting phone call while he was at home. I felt my pulse step up a notch, but, at that point, Richard pulled up out front and Rod hurriedly told me he would tell me about his phone call later tonight – after Richard had left. My mind immediately applied itself to ways and means of ensuring Richard didn't hang around too long after dinner. I wasn't sure I would get through dinner before I burst from the buildup of curiosity and intrigue Rod's comment had created. As it turned out, Richard also had news to share and it helped, at least for a moment or two, to take my mind off whatever Rod might have to share with me later.

Richard didn't waste time getting down to business. As soon as we were comfortably settled on my back deck with glasses of wine and a platter of crackers and cheese, Richard shared the news he had promised us.

"You remember that former Interpol friend of mine I told you about? He got back to me about Theo Rothwell. It seems Rothwell was a spook for MI5 or MI6 for a few years before transferring to ASIO and working undercover in various countries. Other details my friend had to share suggested Rothwell was a younger man than McCormac, and he believed it was possible Rothwell might still be working for that Australian agency.

My friend also thinks that Theo Rothwell, or whatever identity he currently is using, might have encountered a spot of bother recently. Some of my friend's contacts who are still in Interpol think there could be a hit out on Rothwell but they don't know why or anything else about it."

"Wow, that all sounds a bit cloak and dagger – but I suppose that's what the world they inhabit is all about," I blurted out and received a filthy look from Rod. "I'm sorry, Richard. I didn't mean to interrupt. Did your friend have anything else to offer?"

"No, that was the extent of it, but he has asked his contacts to keep him informed of anything new that comes to light.

Anyway, regardless of the information I received, I'm almost convinced Rothwell must have been McCormac and the hit that was out on him was successful."

"Hmm, I'm not sure, but you could be right," Rod murmured. "Do you have anything else that points to that being the case?"

I sat forward on my chair. Rod might be happy to accept Richard's position on Rothwell, but it didn't fit with what we thought we knew and I wanted to challenge his conclusions. Another seriously threatening warning look from Rod made me change my mind. Rather than settle back on my chair without saying a word, I flounced off in a huff to check on dinner. My return to the back deck was midway through a lull in conversation between Rod and Richard, so I immediately jumped in to take advantage of the situation.

"Have you had any success at tracking down the CCTV footage from those cameras your men identified at that industrial site McCormac visited?" Richard nodded enthusiastically.

"Yes, my officers were successful and collected some recordings just before lunch. I have officers working on the recordings now but there is no information available yet."

"That site has me a bit intrigued, I must admit. I can't for the life of me think what interest McCormac would have in such a place. What businesses are located there and do any of them look interesting in terms of this investigation?"

Richard rattled off a short list of the names of the businesses located on the industrial site. None seemed exciting or even interesting until he remembered one last name he forgot to mention. I glanced at Rod as mentioning that business caused him to sit upright on his chair.

"Did something I say – one of the businesses I mentioned – hit a nerve or something?" Richard asked Rod.

"No. Why, should it have?"

"Perhaps not, but I thought you had reacted to something I said. I saw you almost spring to attention."

"Ha ha… Oh, I see. No, sorry to disappoint you, Richard. I was simply going to ask Marion how long until dinner and should I refill our glasses now or wait until we're seated at the table."

Rod received a sceptical look from both Richard and me. We all let the incident go by without further comment, but I felt compelled to say something that might steady the ship again, so I answered Rod's question.

"Dinner is just about ready, Rod. I'll just go and apply the finishing touches. Before I do, Richard, do any of those businesses you mentioned at that industrial site interest you in any way?"

"Not so far, Marion."

"So, I take it you haven't yet established which one of them might have been where McCormac spent that day?"

"If I'm honest, I have to admit I'm still as much in the dark as I was before. My hope is that the camera footage might shed some light on things and at least help explain what he was doing there."

Mere moments later, dinner was dished up and on the table. No 'shop' talk intruded on our meal but quickly resumed later when we were settled on the back deck with our port and coffee.

"How did your meeting with your chairman of the board go, Rod?" Richard asked, and Rod pretended to have forgotten all about it because there was nothing to report.

"All I managed to do was to confirm there was virtually nothing in McCormac's file. Tanya admitted to being concerned about it and can't understand how it had come about. The chairman tried his best to claim ignorance of it, but became tight-lipped when quizzed about it. So, I have zero to contribute to the investigation as a result of my meeting with the chairman."

It was with some relief on my part that Richard chose not to stay long after dinner. As soon as we had seen him off, I demanded to know about Rod's reaction – or lack of what I saw as more appropriate reaction – to Richard's comments about Rothwell.

"Well, I would remind you that we are almost certain Theo Rothwell is Cilla's Joe and, as such, probably has nothing to do with McCormac."

"Okay, but Richard said…."

"Yes, he said they believe there is a contract out on Rothwell, who we know to be Joe. Think about that for a moment. It goes a long way to explaining Joe's sudden disappearance from here."

"Are you suggesting Joe's continued absence and apparent silence, is because the hit was successful?"

"No, I don't think so. What I'm suggesting is that maybe Joe was tipped off about the contract out on him and promptly went into hiding somewhere. It also might explain Cilla's current tense state."

"Uhmm… Yes, I suppose that's logical but it doesn't answer my question. Do you think they, whoever 'they' are, might have found Joe and carried out the contract?"

"I have no way of knowing any more than you do, but the fact that Cilla still hasn't come home might suggest that's not the case."

After considering Rod's comments for a moment or two, I remained unconvinced about the state of Joe's health – or anything else we think we have discovered.

"Right, I hear what you are saying, but that just begs another logical question: How does McCormac fit into all this? Was he somehow involved in carrying out this contract on Rothwell, or was he here to protect Joe?"

"Good question, Marion, but I don't know its answer. While I'm not sure, and it's based on no real evidence, I am starting to have dark thoughts about McCormac's reason for being at Merivale Village."

"Surely no one could possibly know Joe was living here. Everything about him, and about Cilla, is so hush-hush. No one here even knows what Joe's real name is. Isn't it possible Joe has returned to his former employment and has been engaged to look into this contract to kill Rothwell? …And that's why McCormac was at Merivale … So Joe could keep an eye on him and protect him?"

"Marion, might I remind you that we already have established that McCormac was not Rothwell and, therefore, there was no contract out on McCormac?"

"Christ, I am so confused by all of this, but Rod, McCormac was murdered. Does that mean there was another contract as well? If that's the case, are the two situations related or not? Was McCormac's death just the result of a random attack?" Rod sighed and took a deep breath before answering.

"No. Stop and think about it a bit more. Maybe try reversing your earlier scenario."

Chapter 18

I didn't need to belong to Mensa to work out Rod didn't think me bright enough to understand any explanation he might provide, so I flounced off in a huff to clean up in the kitchen. *Reverse my scenario …* what did that really mean? Was Rod telling me something, or was his comment no more than a ploy to cover up the fact that he didn't know any more than I did? Rod appeared unaware of my mood and followed me out to the kitchen and proceeded to help me. As soon as the place was tidy and the dishwasher was happily doing its thing, Rod made noises about going home.

"With any amount of luck, the phone call I'm hoping for might happen some time tonight, so I'll head home now to be ready for it."

There was no protest from me. I remained more than a little put out about Rod's attitude and was happy to spend no further time in his company tonight. As soon as Rod was striding along the footpath, I poured myself another glass of port and took it out onto my back deck. I couldn't help but marvel at how much of Rod's life seems to happen at strange hours of the night, but I suppose it's the way of the world they chose to work in. My hope was that the red mist that had descended as a result of Rod's comments would recede after a few minutes of solitude.

My intention was to clear my mind and just sit and sip while cocooned in the soft, starry darkness of the night and serenaded by the quiet chorus of the resident crickets and other neighbourhood night life. No dogs barked. No cats howled. No traffic disrupted the peaceful interlude. But, clearing my mind and regaining my equilibrium was a challenge too great.

Reverse your earlier scenario… Rod's instruction had lodged in some inaccessible pocket of my mind and kept playing on a loop. No matter what I thought about, or if I tried to wipe all thoughts, that phrase kept repeating – sometimes quietly in the background and at other times at full-blast up front and centre. As I drained the last of the port from my glass, I capitulated and surrendered to its call.

A few moments later, I shot bolt upright on my chair as the thought suddenly hit me. What if it was the other way around? *What if the contract had been on Joe and McCormac was sent to Merivale Village to protect him?*

Then another alternative crashed in from left field almost stunning me. *What if McCormac was at Merivale Retirement Village in order to carry out the contract?*

It was all too difficult, too complicated, to think through alone. I knew I needed to talk it through with someone before any of it would start to make sense. I raced inside, grabbed my phone and keyed Rod's number. His phone was engaged. I waited no more than a few seconds before trying his number again… and again… and again. Who could he be talking to? Surely he could see how urgent it was for me to talk to him. Why hasn't he put his call on hold to at least check if I was all right?

His phone was engaged for far too long … Or maybe it just felt that way when I kept redialling his number every few seconds. After so many unsuccessful attempts to reach him, I even wondered whether Rod had deliberately set his phone so I wouldn't be able to contact him. Nevertheless, I tried a further couple of times before accepting the situation for what it was. Abandoning my phone, I decided a shower to freshen up before turning in for the night was the way to go.

The shower didn't help much and a troubled night ensued. Everything we knew, or thought we knew about McCormac, Joe, and the current investigation kept running through my mind. As a result, I overslept by about an hour this morning and woke feeling groggy and confused. My phone still lay on the kitchen bench where I had abandoned it on my way through for a shower last night. Almost as an automatic gesture, as I sat sipping my coffee, I picked up the phone to connect it to its charger.

That's when I learned I had a missed call. Rod had attempted to return my calls while I was taking a shower before bed last night. I flicked through my contacts and was about to key his number when I realised that, at this time of the morning, he would be out on his morning run and might not even have his phone with him. What to do? Even though it was late, should I go for my morning walk anyway? Or, should I wait until Rod was likely to be home from his run and then go and knock on his door? Such decisions are too hard for first thing in the morning. So, I lingered even longer over breakfast before eventually deciding to go for my usual morning walk – but a shortened version perhaps. Decision made, I laced on my boots and headed off along the street.

As I passed Rod's house, I recalled I still hadn't spoken to Rod about reinstating our mahjong mornings. I wondered if that topic will bring me the same negative response as everything else appears to at the moment. Nevertheless, I made a mental note to broach the subject the next time we were together. Then, I had reached McCormac's house.

Slowing my pace, I studied the house as I dawdled past. I didn't expect to see anything different or any evidence of anything having happened there since the last time I went past. In fact, noticing something different probably would have been a surprise. Then, having reached the corner, I looked up to check the intersection before proceeding further, and that's when I did receive a surprise.

Rod came around the end of the admin building and came towards me as he made his way home after his run. We met in the middle of the intersection and exchanged pleasantries.

"It's a bit late for you to be starting out on your morning walk," Rod said as he eyed me up and down. "Are you okay? Is everything all right?"

"Of course… I just slept in this morning, so my daily schedule is running a bit behind time."

"Well, let's see if we can mess it up further. Go for your walk as planned and then come back to my place for coffee. That will give me time to shower and be decent by the time you arrive."

So far, so good today, I thought as I moved off to continue what would be an even shorter walk than intended. You have to allow him time to shower before you ring his doorbell, I reminded myself. The last thing I wanted was to appear overly eager to be with him. As I strode along, thoughts of McCormac's demise, potential contracts out on Merivale Village residents, and Joe's current situation, kept me company. All those thoughts relating to what appears to be a stalled investigation managed to make me nervous.

Why was I suddenly feeling so nervous? "Stop looking over your shoulder," I muttered to myself as I tried to slow my strides once more to a normal walking pace. "What's brought this on?" I demanded of the universe as I rushed through the little park adjacent to the Village. I told myself I was being ridiculous as I tried to relax my shoulders and slow my pace further to no more than a stroll. Nobody is interested in me. Nobody would have reason to have a contract out on me. Or would they…? What if they – whoever 'they' are – thought Rod and I were getting too close to the truth? What if they thought we needed to be silenced?

Those last couple of questions brought me to a standstill. Stop this nonsense, I mentally chided myself. Getting too close to the truth…? Really…? About what? We don't even know what this investigation is about – except McCormac was murdered while out of the Village on one of our excursions. And, nothing appears to have happened to Rod this morning while he was on his morning run.

Application of logic to my situation achieved nothing other than to speed up my pace again. I stepped up my pace to just slightly below a jog… and arrived back at Rod's sweating and out of breath.

"What's happened? Are you all right?" Rod demanded the moment he opened his door. "Have you been running? Why? Tell me what's happened."

Sometimes there is dignity in lying, I decided, and this morning was one of those times.

"Apologies for my condition. I was jogging this morning and must look a sight now. I'll just slip home for a quick shower and then come back."

"No. No, come in. Just after I arrived home, I had to deal with something and, as a result, I haven't had a shower yet either."

Good one, Marion, I chided myself. Rod would never believe I had been jogging, but he was gentleman enough to act as though he believed me. I was embarrassed by my lie. To make amends, and hide my embarrassment, I volunteered to make our coffee while Rod downed his customary first-thing-in-the-morning long glass of some revolting, bilious green smoothie he makes himself.

Between sips, he asked, "Have you had breakfast? Would you like cereal or something else?"

"No, thanks. I had breakfast before I left home, but you should go ahead and have yours now."

My coffee was tempting, but I felt compelled to wait until he had eaten and was ready for coffee before making a start on my coffee. Decorum and good manners might demand such time-wasting actions but, on this occasion, the delay they caused was killing me. After what felt like forever, his breakfast now dispatched, Rod took a couple of sips of his coffee. Forcing myself to be patient a little longer, I did likewise until we both had lowered the level in our mugs a little before I initiated the conversation I'd been waiting to have.

Just as I was about to broach the subject I had tried to call him about last night, Rod's phone played its tune. After checking the caller ID, he went out onto his back deck to take the call. I looked up as he came back into the lounge room. The look on his face sent my stomach into a spasm and my pulse rate stepped up.

"What happened, Rod? Was the call bad news?" It probably was bad form to be badgering him if he had received bad news, but I was concerned.

"Bad news? No… *Interesting* might be a better way to describe it. Tell me what you make of all this," Rod suggested as he indicated we should return to our lounge chairs.

Once we were settled again, he reiterated Richard's list of businesses located at that industrial site where McCormac spent most of that day. After reeling off the list of business names, he paused briefly before asking his next question.

"Did I miss any of the ones Richard mentioned?"

"No. As I recall it, that was the complete list Richard gave us."

"So, correct me if I'm mistaken, but Richard made no mention of a heavy vehicle maintenance place on that estate?"

"As I told you, Rod, you repeated Richard's complete list and, no, he did not mention any heavy vehicle maintenance operation. Where are you going with this? You are starting to worry me."

"Sorry… That call I just received was from an acquaintance who I had asked about businesses on that industrial estate. Richard's investigation felt like it was moving too slowly for me, so I asked my friend to ferret out the information for me. His call just now was to provide the details of operations on that site. He gave me the same list as Richard gave us earlier… but he also included one other.

It appears Richard forgot to mention – or didn't know about – another business tucked in behind all the others. It is set well back and almost at the rear perimeter of the property. The business purports to be a heavy vehicle maintenance centre, and it has contracts to service buses and transport companies' prime movers. While the business has its own private access road at the rear of the property, there also is access to it via a narrow alleyway from the main area of the estate. At first glance, it almost looks as though the business is not a part of the industrial estate, but is situated adjacent to it. My friend was intrigued and checked the records. He established that, yes, it is located on the site and close to the industrial estate's property boundary."

"How come Richard didn't mention it?" If Rod's friend could find out about it, surely our top cop would be able to do likewise. "Was his not mentioning it nothing more than an oversight on his part? … Or… Or was it deliberate? I know that sounds ridiculous, but why wouldn't Richard mention that extra business if he knew about it? And, if he doesn't know about it, why not – unless it was deliberate?"

"Don't go jumping to conclusions," Rod warned. "A cautious approach is required until we find out more, but I am inclined to much the same thoughts as you."

"Argh… I suppose you're right about viewing this with some caution. After all, we don't even know if this business is likely to be of any interest to our investigation. Did your friend say anything that suggested it might be of interest to us?"

"He wasn't in any position to make any comment in that context as he wasn't aware of why I wanted the information. Is it likely to be of interest to us? I'm not sure yet. I need to think about it for a bit before it makes any sense. So far, I still can't see why that business would interest McCormac any more than any of the others were likely to interest him. I suppose our big hope is that Richard's officers are able to establish exactly where on the site McCormac spent those hours."

"Rod, buses and prime movers travel both inter and intra state. They make long-distance trips. Does that make them interesting at all?"

Instead of answering immediately, Rod just stared at me for a few moments. I braced myself as I waited for him to tell me how ridiculous I was being. When he did speak, it wasn't what I expected to hear.

"I need to call Richard. I'll be back shortly."

With that, he disappeared out onto the back deck but returned soon after.

"Richard's phone was turned off or out of range," he said in response to my curious look, but that was all that was said.

After regaining his seat in the lounge room, he appeared to sit in deep thought for a few moments before rushing back out onto the back deck again. This time, he was gone for a few minutes. I couldn't read his face when he returned but I felt my stomach tightening as I waited for him to settle in his lounge chair again. I allowed him a moment or two before succumbing to my curiosity.

"Is everything all right? You look as though you received some disturbing news. Is it something you might want to share with me?"

There was a distinct gleam in his eyes when he looked up at me and replied. "Not sure yet, but I might just have received valuable information that could provide us with the reason behind everything."

"Did this information come from Richard?"

"No," Rod said, shaking his head. "It came from a reliable source – more of an acquaintance really."

"If the information you received is so good, why hasn't Richard also shared that information with us? If your reliable source has access to the information, surely Richard does too."

"That is the big question – and I don't have an answer. But, what it means is that we have to proceed carefully until we figure out why Richard didn't mention it … Assuming, of course, that Richard did know about it."

"Well, that won't be difficult for me. As I still have no idea what you're talking about."

It is surprising how fast things can happen when excitement drives them. My excitement was running high. It felt like only moments later, we were seated with our coffees on Rod's back deck.

"Rod, I keep coming back to that same question: is Richard's withholding information deliberate or not? I can't quell this uneasy feeling I have about it."

"As I said before, I don't know, but I am prepared to give him the benefit of the doubt – for now."

"Okay, but, before we go any further, Rod, is this informant of yours a reliable source? Is he maybe passing on genuine information or nothing more than scuttlebutt ... or maybe just guessing and making it up to suit?"

"Marion, my informant is reliable or I wouldn't be talking to him."

"Right... Well, maybe I had better hear the information he shared with you."

"My informant says he is surprised by how tight-lipped everyone is being. It's quite unlike his sources' normal behaviour. Despite that, he has managed to gather bits of information that suggest much of our investigation is linked to drug running, and that there also is some sort of association with the trafficking of stolen goods from crimes carried out a long way from here."

"Hmm... I can just about buy the drug-running aspect – maybe – but what's all this stuff about trafficking goods relating to other crimes? And, how is any of this supposed to link to our investigation into McCormac's death?"

"In answer to your first question, trafficking stolen goods is much the same as drug trafficking, except the supply source is different. It involves stolen electrical goods, artworks, and anything else of value from crimes committed in other places, and often from interstate."

"Yeah, I can see how that 'extra mysterious business' on the industrial site could be a perfect set-up for such an operation. If I extrapolate that information, McCormac's time spent at the industrial site might suggest his involvement in such activities in some way and provide a connection to our investigation – albeit a tenuous one. So, Rod, what do we do next? And do we involve Richard in whatever that is, or not?"

"Maybe not at this stage. I need to verify a few things first, and maybe we should test Richard somehow to be sure of his real position in this investigation before we share too much with him."

"I agree we need to be sure of Richard before we proceed much further. How do we do that? How do we test him? When I think of the information he has passed on so far, there hasn't been much. The two things he did give us were the list of the businesses at that industrial estate (except the one we are interested in), and that his officers had obtained the footage from the industrial estate's security cameras." Rod nodded his confirmation and I continued. "Why hasn't he told us which businesses McCormac visited while he was there? Surely, the footage would at least show where McCormac's car went once it entered the industrial estate. He was there for a lot of hours. So, did he spend all that time at just one business, or did he visit a number of places while he was there?"

"Dunno – yet… but I sure as Hell want to know. You might just have provided us with what we need to test our friend, Richard."

At that point, we both lapsed into silence. I didn't know what was occupying Rod's mind, but mine was still trying to digest everything we had discussed since coming to sit on the deck. From my swirling whirlpool of thoughts, suddenly something else surfaced.

"Rod, before I forget again, I've been meaning to ask you about maybe reinstating our mahjong sessions, even if for only one morning each week. What are your thoughts?"

"Good question… and one I hadn't thought about. Now I do think about it, I'd have to admit to being a bit unsure about doing so. What's brought it to the forefront of your thoughts? Has there been an approach about it?"

"No. Well, nobody has spoken to me about it, but I was wondering whether we shouldn't think about kicking it off again. I thought mahjong mornings might help reinstate normalcy around here. We almost went into a type of lockdown after the McCormac incident and nobody has made a move to come out of it yet. Is there some appropriate period of time we should wait before trying to return life to normal? I thought mahjong might be a step in the right direction, at least for the group who are regular players. And, maybe think about reinstating our happy hour get-togethers again – if you are happy to continue to host them at your place. If needs be, we could ease back into them. There wouldn't have to be a happy hour every evening, maybe just occasionally until we see what the response is like."

"Perhaps you are right. It might help at least some of the residents return to a normal life. I'm inclined to have only one mahjong morning per week for a couple of weeks to see how much interest there is. As for happy hours… I'm not sure about this, but I could suggest to the regular group that we're thinking of holding them every evening again and asking for their thoughts on the matter. Happy hours might also provide an opportunity to test feelings about scheduling further bus trips."

"You don't sound confident of support for the idea of more excursions. I think residents are just waiting for something to be organised for them. They don't appear nervous about using the bus. The regulars still fill the bus for every shopping trip Charlie runs to the city. Although, I do admit we don't have a good record with excursions to date. A lost handbag on one trip and lost glasses on another were bad enough before Bert Riley stepped off the side of the access ramp at that small café and broke his leg. McCormac's death on our last trip might just about be enough to convince some that the bus is jinxed and is best avoided."

"Yes, I am aware of all that, but I wonder if residents see shopping trips as different from excursions and, therefore, safer. All right, what I will do is meet with Alice and Maria to discuss some ideas for excursions. If we come up with anything, I will put it up on the Village's Facebook page to gauge the residents' response."

"What about the matter of *the dog on the bus*? Has there been any fallout at all about that incident?" Rod shrugged and shook his head in response. "Might that matter need to be sorted out before any further excursions happen?"

"Probably… but I'm more inclined to 'let sleeping dogs lie' – if you'll excuse the pun. But, if it does come up at all, I will seek a ruling from the chairman on the issue."

I burst out laughing. "You do that … And you'll be lucky to get one by Christmas."

Rod was already busy with his phone organising a meeting with Alice and Maria. He soon reported that a meeting had been set for three o'clock this afternoon to discuss possible excursions. Would I be available to attend? Then he had emails to send out to all the regular mahjong players and to each of our group who used to attend happy hours at his place. It was a good time for me to take my leave. Besides, I needed to think about what I might make to have with coffee at this afternoon's meeting.

Chapter 19

A few minutes before three o'clock, I picked up my container of freshly baked cupcakes and headed for Rod's place and our meeting with Alice and Maria to discuss another bus trip. As I strolled along the footpath, I felt my previous enthusiasm for another bus excursion beginning to evaporate. Although I still believed it would help reinstate normalcy for at least some of the Village's residents, at the same time, something kept telling me such a move was folly.

No time was wasted on socialising. As soon as everyone was there, coffee and cake were on the table and the meeting began. Our first move was to revisit a previously drawn-up tentative schedule of excursions for the coming year. The next trip listed after the one to Jackson Cove was to another seaside community to the north to watch the district's annual sailing regatta. Neither Maria nor Alice thought the destination a good idea so soon after the trip to Jackson Cove. I agreed and it didn't take much to convince Rod we should look for an excursion that didn't involve a seaside setting.

Once Rod agreed, we moved to the next item on the list after the sailing regatta. This was to attend a dress rehearsal of a new show by a local amateur theatre group. Several of such local groups stage performances throughout the year. Alice reported a suitable dress rehearsal night by one of the groups she seems to be somehow affiliated with was coming up in about a fortnight's time. After some discussion of the play they would be staging and its suitability, it was agreed that two weeks allowed plenty of time for an excursion to be organised. But were the residents ready for another excursion yet, I wondered.

After further discussion, it was agreed that Alice should arrange bookings for a busload from the Village to attend the dress rehearsal evening. As soon as Alice advised him that she had tentatively reserved sufficient seats for us, Rod would post details of the possible excursion on the Village's Facebook page to test the level of support. Although the meeting felt as though it had progressed quite swiftly, it was nearing five o'clock by the time Maria and Alice left. I stayed to help tidy up after the others left.

The casserole Rod had slipped into the oven when I arrived for the meeting had wafted its aroma through the house for the rest of the afternoon. It now had my stomach growling as I stacked crockery in the dishwasher.

"If you've finished with all that, let's have an early drink," Rod suggested. "We can watch the sun go down from the back deck and, by then, dinner should be ready, if you're interested in staying."

What was there in those arrangements not to like? Of course, I would stay for a drink and dinner. Unsurprisingly, once we were settled with our drinks, conversation focused on this afternoon's meeting.

"Have we done the right thing?" Rod asked quietly. "I mean, do you think the dress rehearsal outing is likely to appeal to residents, or is it too soon to be planning another outing?"

"No, I don't think it's too soon to test if they are ready for another outing, and I think an evening at the theatre is exactly the right one for the occasion. It is a safer option than another trip to the seaside. More importantly, it won't reopen *the dog on the bus* issue, as a daytime trip to the seaside might. Nevertheless, you need to obtain a ruling on that matter and soon."

"Marion, I'm hoping you are available to stay for dinner, please."

"If that casserole I can smell is what is on the menu tonight, yes, please. I'd love to stay for dinner."

"Good… Then, after dinner, we might take a little drive."

"A drive? Where to and why?"

"I thought we might check out that mysterious business on the industrial estate – that Richard appears to know nothing about."

Dinner and possible excitement… How could I say no to such an evening? But, in the few minutes we had to wait for the casserole to be ready, another question that had bothered me surfaced again. I decided to explore it.

"Rod, what's your honest opinion on why McCormac chose to live in Merivale Retirement Village?"

"Well, in the interests of clarification, he wasn't. Think about it, Marion. Yes, he had a house here in the Village and he was seen around the Village on occasion, but he didn't live here. Think about what we found in his house – or, more precisely, what we didn't find. I don't think you can argue that our search of his house suggested he wasn't actually living here."

"Okay. Well, where then? And, how come no one ever saw him coming to or leaving the Village except for the day that car collected him and he apparently spent all those hours at that industrial site? And here's another question for you to ponder.

Do you think there might be a connection between McCormac's presence here and Joe's suspicious absence? I'm not even game to mention Joe's possible demise in case it tempts Fate." Rod's hesitation before he attempted to deal with my questions was a concern, but he eventually shared his thoughts.

"There's no definitive answer, Marion. The best I can tell you at this stage is that I feel sure it all ties in somehow."

"But, do you think McCormac might have been here to carry a contract? …On Joe?"

"Yeah, I agree that's probably part of it."

This conversation was not going anywhere fast. Well, Rod was answering my questions – in a fashion – but somehow his answers weren't giving me what I wanted. Without thinking, I blurted out my next question – and shocked myself.

"Did Joe kill McCormac?"

For a long moment Rod looked uncomfortable as he appeared to consider my question. Then came the answer I asked for but wasn't sure I wanted to hear.

"It's possible."

Short, to the point, and disturbing… but I now knew I wasn't alone in thinking the darkest of thoughts about this whole McCormac affair. While I was still trying to digest his reply, Rod announced dinner was ready, ending any further discussion of that topic.

Once everything was in the dishwasher, we were in Rod's car and on the way out of the Village. I couldn't help but think it wasn't the best night for a bit of amateur sleuthing on the industrial estate. The moon made only occasional appearances through breaks in the gathering storm clouds. No conversation occurred for some time after we left. I was preoccupied with reflecting on our earlier discussions and, in particular, Rod's answers to my questions. Again, I found myself questioning Richard's actions and behaviour. I imagined Rod might also be assessing progress on the investigation into McCormac's death. But, the sudden realisation that something was not quite as I expected made me sit up and take a hard look at where we were.

"Why are we… I mean, what the hell are we doing here, and exactly where are we?" I demanded.

"What do you mean? We're going to check out that heavy vehicle maintenance place."

"Yes, but why are we using this unsealed back lane? I can't see much out there in the darkness but it looks as though we are travelling through some sort of boondocks area."

As I spoke, Rod eased off the track and pulled up in a cleared area under some trees by the side of the road.

"Feel like a stroll in the moonlight on a pleasant evening in the country?" he asked, ignoring my questions.

"In case you hadn't noticed, I'm not exactly dressed for cross-country hiking … And why have we stopped here? There is nothing here, and we appear to be miles from everything. Are you sure this is safe?"

"Marion, it's up to you. Come or stay in the car, but, either way, I'm not going to stand here wasting time." Having said his piece, Rod strode off into the darkness.

No further encouragement required. It probably was safer to go with him than be left alone in such a desolate place. I rushed – stumbled – after him until I was trailing along no more than a pace behind him. The moon obliged us by completely emerging from the clouds for a few moments. The night suddenly seemed so bright. I looked up to take advantage of the moment and was surprised to see lights not too far ahead.

"Is that our target up ahead?" I hissed at him.

"Yep, that's where we are heading."

Rod's car was quite conspicuous where we left it. I was concerned that a bus driver on his way to the maintenance place up ahead would be suspicious of a strange vehicle parked there, but I was reluctant to mention my concern to Rod. Since we left his place, he had seemed driven by the mission we were embarking on, and I felt he considered me to be excess baggage. Well, he had asked me to accompany him, not the other way around. So, here I am hiking across rough ground and probably ruining my sandals. Still, I had to find a way to mention my concern about his car appearing suspicious without incurring some sarcastic put-down in response. This was not the Rod I knew. I adopted a circuitous route to drawing his attention to my concern.

"Is where we parked beside the access road to the workshop used by buses and semitrailers? Might your car being there cause them concern?"

"The road we parked beside provides access to the properties of local area residents only. It isn't a through road. The access road to the maintenance workshop is about 20 metres off to our right from where we are now."

"Are we too close? What if a vehicle comes along that road? We will stand out in the headlights like the proverbial."

"We should be okay. We have plenty of long grass and shrubbery between us and the access road."

"All the lights appear to be switched on in that workshop. Do you suppose that means they are expecting a vehicle of some sort to arrive tonight?"

"That's possible. A lot of their work is likely to consist of not much more than checks and quick minor service sessions. Where possible such work probably is done at night so as not to disrupt the various companies' operating schedules."

"We are pretty close to that workshop now, Rod. How close are you planning to go?"

"As close as possible."

"Right… And then what?"

"Marion, I don't know how close I want to be. How close depends on what is happening in that workshop, but I want to be close enough to see clearly what is going on in there."

I was about to say something when he cut me off and continued with what he intended to say.

"No, Marion. Don't say anymore. We need to keep quiet. Sounds carry on the still night air, so we are now too close to the workshop to speak at all."

This is definitely nothing like the Rod Maguire I know. His tone and comments bordered on rudeness. Stunned by his behaviour, I was quiet for a moment, but there was still one important question I needed answered. I needed to know what we were supposed to do once we saw what was happening in the workshop – so I didn't get it wrong and earn more criticism. I was about to ask the question when Rod almost frightened the life out of me. Suddenly, he grabbed me by the arm and dragged me over to a thick clump of scrubby plants before pushing me down behind them.

"Stay still and don't speak," he hissed in my ear.

Immediately, and right on cue as Rod delivered his orders, bright lights lit up the clump of shrubs we were hiding behind. A bus roared past. So close and so fast, it created a draught that blew the shrubs about violently. I held my breath. Were we exposed? It seemed unlikely. Surely, if we had been exposed, the bus would have stopped, but it didn't stop and no one yelled out. Despite my pounding heart and shallow breathing, I did manage to register that the bus appeared to be in a hurry and was travelling much faster than I expected.

Without reducing speed, the bus drove straight into the workshop building. Two men climbed out of the bus. Four men emerged from somewhere in the bowels of the building. Two of the workshop personnel spoke with one of the men from the bus. All the other men went around and opened the luggage compartment. The screech of an air tool being used shattered the night air and was quickly followed by the rattle of bolts or screws being removed. Within moments, what looked like the floor of the luggage compartment was removed.

Moments later, I realised the piece I saw removed most probably was a false floor that concealed a shallow compartment beneath it. All the men congregated around the luggage compartment. One of the workmen unloaded a couple of packages and handed them to one of the onlookers. That man carried the packages further into the building and loaded them into a dark-coloured vehicle I previously hadn't noticed was parked there.

As I watched that man, I realised he did not look like a mechanic or tradesman. No tradesman goes to work wearing chinos and a business shirt with its sleeves rolled up to the elbows. He wouldn't look any less like a tradesman if he were wearing a jacket and tie. The vehicle was a pickup truck and the packages were hastily stowed in its cargo tray.

While the well-dressed gent dealt with the packages, three of the men still at the bus began refitting the false floor to the luggage compartment. Then, with the main exercise apparently completed, the focus switched to what the business supposedly was about. The bus's tyre pressures were checked and oil and water levels attended to, while one man brought an industrial vacuum cleaner and started cleaning the interior. Another man, the bus driver judging by his uniform, clambered aboard the bus and started wiping down everything inside. While the bus was being dealt with, the others took care of paperwork.

The bloke in chinos, who had arrived in the bus and had loaded the packages into the vehicle, returned to the scene of the activities and went into a huddle with one of the workshop men who might have been a foreman of some sort. After a brief conversation, those two men disappeared into what looked like a small office situated along one side of the workshop area. After a couple of minutes, the workman emerged from the office and boarded the bus. He appeared to be hurrying along the two men working in there. Then, the man in the chinos came out of the office carrying a briefcase. He walked back to the vehicle where he had stashed the packages and threw the briefcase onto the passenger seat.

By then, work appeared to have finished on the bus. Everyone who had been on the bus, except the driver, disembarked. Almost immediately, the bus roared to life. One of the workmen walked out to a refuelling station off to one side of the building. In the few moments the bus sat idling, the man in the chinos climbed aboard and appeared to give the driver instructions before disembarking again. As soon as that man was safely off the bus, the driver took the bus around and refuelled it. In the penultimate act of this drama, the bus driver signed a slip of paper (probably a chit for the fuel), handed it to the workman who had refuelled the bus, and then drove off.

I heaved a sigh of relief and gingerly tried to move. Cramped from squatting for so long behind those shrubs, I needed to stretch my legs to restore circulation. As I carefully tried to move, Rod planted a restraining hand on my arm.

"No. Don't move. The show is not over yet," he hissed at me.

What else could I do except wait for whatever else Rod thought was still to happen? So, wait we did. Although it was probably only a couple of minutes, it felt like forever but, at last, the pickup truck drove out. Again, I made a move towards easing the pain in my legs, and again Rod slapped a restraining hand on me.

"Wait… not yet," he hissed.

My cramped legs felt as though they were going to give up the struggle to hold me up. I had visions of myself pitching headfirst into the shrubbery before landing flat on the ground.

Fortunately, activity in the workshop distracted me from such thoughts. Lights were switched off and the whole area was plunged into darkness. As luck would have it, that's when the moon chose to come out from behind the clouds and stay out for a few minutes. We listened and watched as the workshop was locked and a few moments later, a hitherto unseen car drove out from behind the workshop building.

It passed by us as it sped away along the access road. I was fairly sure I saw four people in the vehicle as it flew past. If that were the case, nobody should be left in the building. With the place locked up and everyone gone, I felt it was now safe to move and I attempted to stand up. My legs collapsed under me. Rod again stuck out his hand to stop me.

"Sit on the ground and stretch your legs out in front of you," he whispered in my ear. "Get the circulation flowing again while we are waiting before you attempt to stand up."

"Everyone has gone. Can't we leave now?" I demanded as I checked the time on my phone.

"No…," Rod hissed.

"What are we waiting for? There is no one left here and nothing is happening, so why can't we leave?"

"I don't know yet. It might be nothing…."

So we waited – and, no, nothing happened. No one came. No one went. No activity was detected anywhere. I checked the time again, more for something to do than any real interest in the time. It was eight minutes later than when I'd checked it before. I looked over at Rod. He just shook his head at me. Our non-verbal conversation was only possible because of the light from my phone screen. My patience was fast running out. I knew it wouldn't be long before I'd start making rude comments about our present situation, and I also knew I didn't want to do that. I didn't want to initiate any further tension between us. I just wanted to go home. A couple of minutes later, while I was concentrating on biting my tongue, Rod broke the silence between us.

"How are your legs? Are you right to go? Do you think you'll be able to stand? Come on, let's find out."

My self-restraint was admirable. I managed not to fire off the responses that came to mind. While I doubted I was able to stand yet, I did want to be gone, so I struggled to my feet. Yep, I really wasn't able to stand yet. I was wobbly and almost fell over a couple of times, but Rod was already striding back to his car. Somehow, I followed by wobbling along slower and a little way behind him. Rod reached the car while I was still a few metres away.

He opened the driver's door and the interior light came on. Something caught my eye. There was a bulge in the pocket of Rod's light jacket. Where did that come from and what is it? I'm sure he didn't have anything in his pocket when we left home. Whatever it is, he must have slipped it into his pocket just before we started our cross-country trek. Should I ask him about it, or not? Not mentioning it seemed like the safest option. But, unless he mentions it beforehand, I will be asking him about it when we are home again. Then I heard the car roar into life. Rod was becoming impatient. I hurried the last few metres and, without a shred of elegance or dignity, scrambled onto the passenger seat. We were underway before I'd even closed my door properly.

Silence shrouded the first part of our return journey. I didn't mind. The silence provided time to mull over the evening's events. My thinking eventually led to my breaking the silence.

"That was contraband we saw being unloaded from the bus, wasn't it?" I asked quietly.

"Would have to be, I should think. Such a precision operation. You have to admire how well they pulled it off. The planning and timing are interesting. Anyone checking the bus's running record would find it to be just about correct for what the bus was supposed to do today. Even the time the bus spent at the workshop for its quick service and top up would be recorded as about right for that operation."

"Not sure what you mean about the recording, Rod, but I noticed a couple of men checking their watches regularly. What do you mean about the time the bus was at the workshop being recorded? How and why would it be recorded?"

My question sent Rod into a long explanation about how buses are fitted with devices.

"Those gadgets record everything that happens on a trip, including speeds and stops and the timing of everything that happened. The recordings even show whether the driver stuck to the required speeds for the sections of the route, and whether he obeyed the likes of stop signs and other traffic regulations that apply along the way."

"Are semi-trailer prime movers fitted with similar devices?"

"I'm not sure how common they are, but I think some might be fitted with similar devices."

Our return journey to the Village saw us use a more regular route that was devoid of back roads and dirt tracks. As we approached the Village, silence again filled the car. I had been lost in my own thoughts for the last part of the trip and was brought back to reality as I felt the vehicle slowing and coming to a stop. Rod had stopped in front of my house. I didn't want to be dropped off at my house. In fact, I didn't want to be dropped off anywhere. I wanted to continue on to Rod's house.

"No, Rod, I don't want to be let out here. There is more I need to know about tonight. I need a coffee and I want to discuss everything we observed tonight. Now, if you don't want me to come to your place, you may stop here and come inside with me. I will make us coffee and we can sit and discuss things. It's a pity the remaining cupcakes are still at your place. Never mind, we will have to settle for coffee with nothing to go with it."

"In that case, you had better stay in the car and we will have coffee and cakes at my place instead."

Although it was dark in the car and he probably wouldn't have noticed anyway, I tried not to grin.

Chapter 20

In no time, we were seated with coffee and cake in Rod's lounge room. And, mere moments after that, I felt compelled to explore the matter of the bulge in the pocket of Rod's jacket. There was no surprise when he tried to fob off my question, but I was in a mood to persist. He caved in, sighed, and went to fetch his jacket from where he had hung it when we came in.

The bulge in the pocket remained obvious, but I now saw that it wasn't a conventional style of pocket. This one was like a long flap that ran across the front of the jacket, allowing the wearer to insert a hand at either end. The 'pocket' functioned as an excellent hand warmer in much the same way as a muff would. Rod returned with the jacket and placed it across his knees. I gestured at the obvious 'lump' in its pocket.

"While I admit I didn't take particular notice of your jacket when we left here earlier, I am fairly sure I would have noticed that bulge had it been present at that time. So, come on, what is it and when did it miraculously materialise?"

Rod heaved another dramatic sigh before attempting to wriggle a small item out of the pocket. As it emerged, I noted it was some form of small plastic gadget. It wasn't until he held it out to me on the palm of his hand that I realised it was some sort of small camera. Thoughts – and questions – flew through my mind at lightning speed as Rod appeared to fiddle with the 'thing'.

Why would Rod carry a camera on a night almost devoid of moonlight? Did he think the workshop would be unattended? Perhaps he did. I certainly did. If that were the case, then what? Did he plan to break in and take photos? …Of what? Maybe he just intended some shots of the building and its surroundings. But how, when there was hardly any moonlight? No point sitting here thinking up questions without looking for answers, I told myself and promptly set about actioning that line of thinking.

"Is that thing some form of pocket camera?" I asked, trying to sound unimpressed.

"It might be small but I wouldn't call it a pocket camera."

"What did you hope to photograph tonight when there was a fair chance there would be no lights anywhere and not even enough moonlight?"

"Well, this is a special type of camera I came by a while ago. It's been on a few assignments with me in the past. A bit like night-vision glasses, it works well in low or no light."

"I see. It's a pity you didn't get to use it tonight."

"Oh, but I did. Everything fell into place for me and it turned out to be better than I dared wish for … But now it is time to see what I managed to capture."

We moved to Rod's desk so he could connect the camera to his computer. After briefly attacking the keyboard, he sat back. I felt excitement course through my veins. Within moments, as we watched, the screen filled with an eerie green scene from inside the workshop. Rod gave the screen a nod of approval before explaining the image to me.

"As well as taking still shots, this is also a video camera. My hope now is that it continued to record everything at least until they all left the property."

He hit FAST FORWARD and ran tonight's footage through to the end. His excited cheer when he discovered he had captured the entire incident that we had witnessed at the maintenance workshop startled me.

"So, what now?" I asked without taking my eyes off the screen. "What are you going to do with that footage? Do you intend to give it to Richard?"

"Uhmm… No, I don't think so … Not yet anyway. I think we need to know for sure where Richard stands in all this first."

"You don't think Richard is involved in any way in this illegal trafficking, do you?" I felt my eyes open to the size of saucers as I continued to stare at the green scene on the screen.

My tiny mind couldn't handle the thought of our nice guy, top cop, being involved. "I mean, you don't think he might be more involved than by just turning a blind eye, do you?"

"Is that what he is doing?" Rod asked innocently. "I don't have any hard evidence of that. Let's just say it might be wise to play it cautiously for the moment … or until we prove he is not involved in any way."

Rod's answer was no comfort and I couldn't leave it at that. "Okay, I get your point, but how do we go about proving that? Do we just sit tight and wait for him to slip up somehow, or do you have some other plan for us to implement?"

"Er, not exactly, but I do have a couple of ideas kicking about in the back of my mind. The thing is, now that we have tonight's footage, I think it is imperative to establish Richard's innocence – or otherwise."

I watched Rod disconnect the camera from his computer as I started gathering up the mugs and plates to add them to the dishwasher. On my way back from the kitchen, I saw Rod had been checking other stuff on his computer and was now flicking through something that seemed to roll up the screen.

"Well, that seems to settle that," he murmured, probably to himself rather than to me but he had aroused my curiosity.

"What…?" I demanded. "That settles what?"

"Yep," he added as he continued scrolling down the screen. "The residents appear well and truly ready for another excursion, with enough bookings made already to almost fill the bus."

"Okay…So, it appears the dress rehearsal night out will be a success, but what about the next excursion after that on our list, what might that be? Is it too soon to do another 'away' trip given that the McCormac incident remains an ongoing mystery?"

"Argh… I'm not sure yet. I think, for now, I would prefer to adopt a wait-and-see approach. It won't hurt if no further events are scheduled until next month, and who knows what the situation might be by then?"

"Have there been any replies to your email to the mahjong group about resuming our mahjong mornings?" There was a brief pause while he searched.

"Yeah, there are three already – the Furlongs, Luigi and Frank. All those are okay with scheduling one morning per week, but they all question why we can't return to our normal two mornings."

"If I'm asked, I'll say I'm happy to see mahjong happening again. In all honesty, I'd be happy with one morning each week for now. I'm not sure I'm ready for two mornings again just yet. I must admit I can hardly wait to see what Bernard and Marjorie's replies will be – if they bother to reply at all that is."

"Why do you say that? Do you expect a problem of some sort?"

"Rod, let me remind you about your stand-off with Bernard about the dog not being allowed on the bus. When he lost the argument, Bernard probably felt he also 'lost face' in front of the other residents."

"Huh, if they are going to be funny about what happened, perhaps it's as well if they don't return to mahjong."

"Under other circumstances, that might be fine, Rod, but with Cilla and Joe away, we already are a bit short of players. Losing Bernard and Marjorie from the group will impact our games on those occasions when someone from the regular group can't come."

My concerns fell on deaf ears. Rod just shrugged and told me not to worry about it as it probably would sort itself out, if we just ignored it. As there was little else to discuss and it was getting late, I started making noises about going home. As I gathered up my bag and stood up to leave, Rod's phone demanded his attention. After checking the caller ID, he mouthed 'Cilla' at me.

I dithered for a moment. I was confused. Did the fact that he told me his caller was Cilla mean he wanted me to leave so he could take it in peace, or he wanted me to hang around until after he took the call? He sorted the situation out for me by holding up his hand to stop me and then motioning me to sit down again as he answered the call. I complied and sat down again, and found myself enduring another fairly lengthy one-sided conversation.

"Cilla, good to hear from you again. Is everything going all right with whatever you are doing?" was Rod's opening gambit. I waited patiently for what I thought would be a brief call to end but Rod's side of it continued. "… Oh, yeah, sorry about that. I'm sure you have more important things to think about than mahjong mornings, but I just sent out the email to the list I usually use and didn't think to exclude you and Joe. You probably also received the one about happy hours for the same reason … No, of course not. We didn't think either of you would be interested unless you were about to return here soon … Well, thanks. I have received a similar response from those who already have replied … Are we likely to see you back here again soon? … No, I don't think there has been much progress but then, I don't suppose I would know anyway … You're probably right, but have you heard anything via your network connections? … No, as you say, it appears to be going nowhere fast. At least that's the picture I'm getting from Richard, anyway.…"

While I had listened intently to the comments Rod made, I had spent the one-sided conversation studying my devastated sandals. They were my favourites, and they were just not up to cross-country hikes on dewy nights. I was still inspecting the damage when Cilla's call ended. He looked up from his phone, heaved a sigh, and shrugged at me.

"That's another of life's mysteries. As you probably realised, that was a call from Cilla. While I can understand what prompted her call, what I don't understand is why she bothered. Do you have any thoughts on the subject?"

Of course, I didn't have any thoughts on any of it. After all, I hadn't heard anything Cilla had said – and that struck me as odd. Rod had seemed keen for me to stay while he took the call, so why didn't he put it on speaker so I could hear both sides of the story? I tried to tell myself it was just an oversight and that Rod just answered the call as he normally would if he were alone. I didn't convince myself. There was a deliberateness about his performance. But, he had asked me a question and I felt him entitled to an answer.

"No, Rod, I don't have anything to offer… but then, I only heard a part of the story. Still, it was unlike Cilla to call when she was away and supposedly working with her team in Sydney. Did she give you any clues as to what might have motivated her call, other than those emails you sent out, I mean?"

Rod gave me what amounted to an executive summary of his call and, at the end of it, neither of us believed the emails about mahjong and happy hours were likely to be the real reason for the call. Nevertheless, one thing had become clear: neither Cilla nor Joe is likely to be returning to the Village any time soon.

The other thing that had become apparent to me was that Rod seemed a bit hyped up after Cilla's call. From what he told me of the call, there was nothing in it that would have excited him. I suspected he was becoming anxious to do some work – and I was preventing him from doing so. I again made noises about going home. When Rod didn't object, I said goodnight and left.

All the way home and during my shower, my mind toyed with possible reasons for Cilla's call. The same thoughts accompanied me to bed, and a whole raft of new possibilities slammed in: What if there had been some development in the McCormac case? What if Cilla was simply testing to see if we knew about it? What if it had something to do with Richard? Had Cilla – or Joe – discovered something about Richard? Might whatever it was answer some of the questions we had about our top cop?

Joe, having made something of a cameo appearance in my thinking, diverted my thinking from Cilla and onto him. Would Cilla know for certain if Joe were still alive? If he wasn't, would Cilla tell us? That last question went to sleep with me and continued to linger in the background over breakfast. I tried to replay that part of last night when Cilla called Rod. Having heard only one side of the conversation, it was pointless and frustrating. Yes, Rod had given me a rundown later on what was said, but had he given me all the facts? Had it been a truthful and accurate report? Why wouldn't he? What was to be gained by such a move?

After giving the matter some thought over a second cup of coffee, I decided Rod probably didn't deliberately hold anything back. But, being given a second-hand summary of the conversation wasn't enough. How did Cilla sound? Did she sound her usual self or was she on edge? Was her speech strained? If only I had heard both sides of the conversation, I might be able to cross off some of the questions my mind kept creating. Wishing I had heard both sides of the conversation only gave rise to another question – and not a new one: Why didn't Rod put the call on speaker so I could hear it too?

As soon as he saw the caller ID, he indicated to me that it was Cilla and motioned for me to stay while he took the call. Why didn't he switch to speaker straight away? Why didn't he even mention my presence to Cilla, either at the start of or during the call? Was there more to the call than I had been told? That question was developing a recurring theme.

Then, it occurred to me. The big question underlying everything else, and the one I was trying to ignore, slammed to the fore: Did Cilla say anything about Joe? Was there even a hint given about his situation? Was he okay or not? What about where he was? Was he working again, or in hiding somewhere? The whole business of Cilla's call had me feeling I was being kept a 'mushroom'… And I resented it. With no plans made last night for today, I decided I might as well head out for my morning walk as usual, albeit a bit later than usual.

I wasn't more than a few metres from my gate when I encountered Rod coming home from his morning run.

"Can't stop to talk… Maybe catch up later," he shouted as he rushed past and dashed into his house.

Well, how much more do I need to confirm I am on the outer with Rod? I think that was enough to confirm it. Most of the rest of my walk was taken up with thoughts of what I might have done wrong to deserve the insults Rod had started throwing at me. Home again from my walk and with nothing resolved regarding the Rod situation, I set about keeping busy to try to keep my mind off Rod. So, until morning coffee time, I worked on the pile of housework that had been begging for attention. My coffee pot was well into its process when my phone played its tune: Rod.

He called to invite me to coffee. My immediate inclination was to say 'no thanks', but common sense stepped in and I thought better of it. About 20 minutes later, I was trotting along the footpath to Rod's place and being seduced by the aroma of baking that, though I thought it improbable, seemed to be emanating from his house. The sight of the batch of muffins cooling on the kitchen bench left me speechless for a few moments.

"They're still a bit warm but should be okay to eat by the time our coffees are ready," he said when he saw me eyeing off the muffins.

"You have hidden talents, or perhaps they are just talents I wasn't aware of," I murmured as I tried to make light of my surprise.

He laughed. "Don't be too impressed by it. They are only a packet mix, and even I can manage a simple task involving no more than three ingredients."

It didn't take us long to be settled and dealing with coffee and muffins and the muffins were good. I still didn't know why he invited me for coffee, and there certainly hadn't been even a hint of an apology for last night's behaviour. I secretly hoped the invitation was for him to make amends for last night, but, when nothing was forthcoming, all the questions that had bothered me all night came rushing back. Somehow, I managed to decide to stay quiet and ask no questions until I found out what was going on. As if to allow my doubts about his coffee invitation to strengthen, he made me wait until we had almost finished our coffee before making a start on easing my curiosity and my misery.

"On my way home from this morning's run, I encountered the chairman on his way into the Village for an early meeting with Tanya. He said he thought their meeting might last about an hour and asked me to meet him at the Admin building afterwards," Rod said in a flat matter-of-fact way.

"Oh, no… Don't tell me the dog-on-the-bus issue has finally hit home. What did the chairman have to say? He wanted to talk about the dog, didn't he?"

"No, he didn't. He wanted an update on the McCormac case. McCormac's house is still off-limits due to the ongoing investigation into his death, and it appears everyone is becoming edgy about its remaining vacant and not being able to put someone in it."

"Well, that should have made for a short meeting. There was nothing new to tell him. Did you invite me for coffee just to tell me that?" I asked the question a touch more sharply than I intended, but it probably was justified if that was his attempt at making amends for his behaviour last night.

"Of course not… That's not the whole reason. It turned out that the chairman had some interesting news to share."

"So, if there was nothing else to do with McCormac, what was this other interesting news?"

"Right … there was nothing more to say on the McCormac case, but I did have the chairman's ear. So, I figured it might be a good time to talk about Bernard and the dog incident. After all, it was associated with the same bus trip as McCormac's murder and it felt like an appropriate time to acquaint the chairman with the matter.

The chairman burst out laughing when I brought it up. He knew all about it. According to him, the dog's owner, Mrs Carr, contacted him and told him the story. She wanted a ruling on the matter as she was fairly put out by Bernard's behaviour and didn't want to have to endure a repeat performance in the future."

"She was game. There was a real chance the chairman's decision would go against her. What was the result of her approach?"

Rod laughed. "It appears the chairman told her he had never heard such rubbish. There was no rule about dogs going on bus trips with their owners."

"Well, I don't know if that would have been good enough for the woman. She wanted reassurance she would not be faced with the same situation again."

"This old girl is a pretty bright bird. She asked the chairman to give her something in writing to that effect in case a similar situation ever occurred."

"Good for the chairman and Mrs Carr for her initiative. Did the chairman give her something in writing?"

With a smug look on his face, Rod rummaged in his pocket. He produced a sheet of paper and handed it to me. As I read it, Rod continued with his story.

"Oh, yes, the woman got what she asked for in writing. After congratulating me on my handling of the situation, he had Tanya print off that copy of his ruling for me to hold on to."

"Although I said it before, good on him, but I doubt that will be the last we hear of it. Do you know if the chairman gave Bernard a copy too?"

"According to the chairman, he didn't want to precipitate a situation between Bernard and the dog's owner by giving Bernard a copy. My instructions were that, in the occurrence of a repeat performance, we would just need to produce our copies. Oh, and the chairman was disappointed the bus was totally booked out for the dress rehearsal outing. He rather fancied coming with us."

"Damn… That reminds me. I didn't get around to booking myself a seat. I wouldn't have minded seeing that show. As the bus driver, you will be okay for a seat. Oh, well, you will have to tell me all about it later."

"That would be okay if I was the driver rostered for that trip. Luigi will be the driver that night. I don't have a bus seat booked either. Still, all is not lost. Alice used her connection with the theatre group to book extra seats, a few more than those required for a full busload of passengers. So, I have claimed two of those extra seats for us. We can go in my car."

"In case they have returned by then, should we reserve an extra couple of seats for Cilla and Joe?"

Shaking his head, Rod said, "No, that's not likely to happen. Let's not lead to someone else unnecessarily missing out on a seat just on the off chance Cilla and Joe might return."

"Speaking of Joe and Cilla, Rod... Have you thought of some way of testing Richard's handling of the investigation into McCormac's death?"

"Argh, no, not exactly... But the chairman's enquiry this morning regarding progress on the investigation has given me a germ of an idea and a genuine reason to again question Richard on progress. I need to give it a bit more thought as I want to be able to work any such conversation around to the mysterious extra business on that industrial site.

Once I've done that, I can then ask Richard if he has discovered where McCormac was living *actually* living."

Chapter 21

Is our top cop bent, or not? Or was it more a question of someone further up the rankings being not quite all they should be? Are they somehow causing Richard to appear incompetent?

What to do about Richard was becoming something of a vexing question. While Rod had some vague ideas, none was developed enough to be put into action. So, once again, we returned to discussing the lingering question of Richard's behaviour in relation to McCormac's murder investigation. We were brainstorming Rod's ideas on how to test Richard when his phone interrupted us.

After a glance at the caller ID, Rod rushed out onto the back deck to deal with the call. I waited for him to return, but he was gone for longer than I expected. I thought it appropriate to go home, but faced the problem of how to take my leave without interrupting Rod on his call. I decided I would go to the back door, catch his attention, and wave goodbye before slipping away.

My plan was ready, but I waited another minute or so before attempting to implement it. With still no sign of his call ending, I stood at the back door and waved at Rod to catch his attention. Standing there waving didn't work. I needed to make a noise so he would look up. With no better idea, I knocked on the wall beside the doorway to grab his attention. He looked up. I waved goodbye. Rod shook his head and motioned for me to stay. I shook my head and waved again, but he had returned his attention to his phone and didn't notice. The only options open to me were to do as he asked or ignore him and go home anyway.

Did I want to risk straining the relationship further? I shrugged and went back inside. As I was about to sit in my recently vacated chair, I decided that hanging around for a while, required another coffee. When he finally reappeared, I was rattling around in his kitchen.

"I'm sorry about invading your kitchen. I thought that might have been a work call. I didn't want to interrupt it, so I intended to slip off home and leave you to it. When you indicated I should stay, I decided I needed another coffee."

"Good thinking. I could use another coffee as well if you wouldn't mind making me one. No, that wasn't a work call, although I am expecting one of those soon. I'm well past the deadline for an article I was supposed to submit and I expect to hear about it." He checked the time and quickly continued. "It's almost lunchtime. How about I make us a sandwich while you deal with the coffee? We can have an early lunch on the back deck."

Over lunch, his most recent call was the only topic of conversation. It started with his claiming once again (almost as if my understanding of that was some critical factor) that it was not a work call. He said his caller was his contact who seemed to me to be the best informed about some mysterious contract that McCormac supposedly was involved with somehow. Rod gave me an overview of his call.

"My contact thinks Joe is still alive and being kept safe somewhere, possibly in or near Canberra. He believes, but can't be too sure, that the contract has now been terminated or withdrawn in some way."

"Does he think Joe was responsible in some way for that?"

"Well, I shared your thoughts on that one. I asked him if he thought it possible Joe might have killed McCormac. He thinks that might be the case but can't find any hard evidence to support it. So far, the scuttlebutt circulating in relevant circles doesn't indicate whether Joe was the killer or the one to be killed."

"That doesn't make any sense to me. Why would anyone want to kill Joe? He is retired, so doesn't pose a risk to anyone." Somehow, my mind wouldn't accept Joe as a killer so it had to be the other way around.

"It's possible it doesn't have anything to do with his life now. If he is mixed up in it, it's likely to be about something he was involved with in his *other life,* the one before Merivale Retirement Village. My contact did concede that, if the contract had been on Joe, it probably springs from someone he put away back then, or some such incident."

"Rod, if your contact can winkle out this sort of information (unconfirmed though it might be), why can't Richard do likewise? Or, does Richard already have the same – and maybe even more – information? Is Richard just playing dumb with us, and if so, why?"

"Good question, Marion, and one that we need answered. I'll give it more thought this afternoon before I try to engineer another meeting with Richard."

"Today, if possible, Rod. We are getting nowhere fast with this and I am developing a bad feeling about what we might discover. I know it probably would be wiser to walk away from it and leave it to the professionals, but I also know I can't do that."

With nothing more to discuss regarding the investigation, I headed home. As I strolled along the footpath, my mind wrestled with what to have for dinner. If Rod spoke to Richard this afternoon, would there be another clandestine meeting of the three of us this evening? If that were to happen, no doubt the meeting would be at my place … And I would be required to feed the three of us again.

A rummage in my freezer as soon as I was home produced a solid pack of chicken fillets: main course decided. We (or I, depending on how the evening pans out) will be having chicken and mushroom risotto. After a partial defrost in the microwave, the pack of chicken went into the fridge to completely thaw out. With dinner sorted for the moment, I made myself comfortable in the lounge with a book I'd been trying to read for a couple of weeks. I almost have to extend the loan or return it to the library unread.

Of course, reading a book when there is so much going on in your head is an impossible challenge. I sat in the lounge chair with the book open in my lap for a couple of hours without reading more than a few paragraphs. My mind kept reviewing what we know, or think we know, about McCormac's death. The longer I thought about it, the less sure I became about anything. That initiated an invasion of new questions – with no answers. It was a pointless exercise and it was time for my afternoon stroll in the park. After checking that the chicken had thawed, I laced on my trainers, grabbed my phone and headed for the door.

My phone played its tune as I walked out the door: Rod. He has spoken to Richard. As soon as he can get away, probably around six o'clock, Richard will be joining us for a chat … And, yes, the meeting will be at my place again. Life can be so predictable sometimes! Nevertheless, Rod's call caused a minor panic. Of course, they will expect to be fed. Do I have enough chicken to produce enough risotto for three? I believed I had enough when I envisaged this situation, but now I wasn't so sure. Another look at the pack of the chicken in the fridge did nothing to reassure me. That's when I spied the remnants of a barbequed chicken bought a couple of days ago.

Dilemma averted. The cooked chook ensured there was more than enough chicken and the untouched large pack of mushrooms contained more than I needed. With my breathing and blood pressure returned to normal, I was out the door and on my way to the small park adjoining the Village. When almost at the park, I thought better of it and trudged home again. Before tonight's guests arrived, the living area and the back deck required dusting and tidying. As I finished with the back deck and stood back to admire my handiwork, another question hit me: What to have for dessert? God, why hadn't I thought about that until now?

A hurried trip to the kitchen and a rummage in both freezer and fridge produced an unopened tub of ice cream and a smallish tub of fruit salad, but definitely not enough fruit salad. A bottle of cherries hiding in my cupboard added to the fruit salad gave me just about enough for the three of us... and I could always skimp on my serving. At last, I felt reasonably confident dinner was under control, and it was almost time to make a start on preparing the risotto. To reassure myself, I was standing, hands on hips, in the middle of the kitchen mentally ticking off everything when Rod called.

"On the off chance Richard and I might stay for dinner tonight, what's for dinner?"

"Chicken risotto…."

"Okay, I will bring a suitable white wine to have with it. See you soon."

Thank God for that. I hadn't given wine a thought and knew I had nothing suitable in the house. Then, I started on the risotto. Regardless of whether Richard stays for dinner or not, I'm sure I will be feeding Rod. If Richard leaves early, Rod will stay on to discuss any outcomes of our meeting with our top cop. It's a wonder I managed to keep track of what I was doing. My mind was so full of other things. But, when Rod arrived not too much later, I was about to slide the risotto into the oven.

"I thought you said we were having chicken risotto tonight."

"Yes, and that's what just went into the oven."

"But, isn't risotto about standing, ladling, and stirring?"

"If you're a purist, perhaps, but the *à la mode* way is to throw all the stock in with everything else and shove it in the oven. I've decided I'm a new-age woman."

A few minutes later, Richard arrived and we traipsed out onto the back deck for drinks and nibbles while discussing the McCormac investigation. Rod attempted to steer the meeting in the desired direction by opening with the comment that he hoped Richard wasn't too put out that Rod wanted a meeting rather than a long phone call. Richard was okay with the arrangement but curious about the reason for it.

"Has something important about McCormac come to light today? I must admit, I haven't heard anything new. So, I don't know how useful this meeting will be for you if you are expecting to hear something new from me," Richard said as he studied the contents of his glass.

Rod shook his head, and eased gently into the conversation he wanted. "No, Richard, what I have amounts to questions more than information."

He then did the basic *where are we at with the investigation* routine to summarise the situation. Once that was done, he moved to introduce the industrial estate into the discussion.

"Richard, that day McCormac spent at that industrial site, do you know where he actually spent those hours? I mean, do you know which enterprise he spent his time at while he was there?"

"No. That's an ongoing mystery. The CCTV footage from the site for that day shows McCormac went into a couple of the businesses on the site, but only spent a few minutes in each of them. After that, he seemed to disappear."

"Could you see if he bought anything while in either of those businesses? Was he carrying any bags or parcels afterwards?"

"Again, no. He doesn't appear to have bought anything before he disappeared from the camera footage. After that, we don't know where he went or what he did. The cameras did not record his leaving the site. Well, they didn't record the vehicle he arrived in leaving the site that day or the next. We knew he came back here at some point, so my officers checked traffic cameras for that grey sedan and eventually picked it up on its way back to Merivale Village."

"Why did he go back to Merivale?"

Although Rod asked the question in a tone devoid of inflection or hints, I grasped what he was trying to do. It was obvious Richard didn't understand the question and looked confused by it. I felt obliged to become involved. I cocked an eyebrow at Rod before jumping in.

"Of course, he would come back here to the Village. Where else would he be going at that hour? He lived here, didn't he?" I received the hint of a sly smile from Rod before he answered.

"Did he?"

"What do you mean?" Richard demanded. "All my information indicates he lived in that house on the corner of this street. So, Rod, what are you suggesting?"

"You and your men went through – thoroughly searched – that house on the corner. Did it look like he was living there? To me, it looked like he was simply creating the impression he was residing there."

"Yeah, okay, there wasn't much in the house. It looked as though he was waiting for the rest of his stuff to arrive, but I didn't doubt he was living there."

"Aw, come on, Richard. Did you find clothes in the wardrobe, food in the pantry and fridge, or toiletries and grooming equipment in the bathroom?"

Obviously stunned by Rod's comments, it took Richard a few moments before he responded.

"As you well know, we found none of that. I assumed it was due to the fact that he was still in the process of moving in."

I couldn't sit silent any longer. "What an amazing man he must have been. It seems he had perfected the art of living without food or clothes – or anything much else – for about three weeks… Or, perhaps he had somewhere else to live until he had his house here set up properly."

Richard dropped his head into his hands for a moment. He gave Rod a hard look before admitting such a scenario hadn't occurred to him. It took only moments for him to recover and take charge again.

"Okay, Rod, come on. Out with it. What do you know?" Richard demanded none too kindly.

It was all I could do not to laugh. Rod, sporting a pretty good attempt at a confused look, shrugged and shook his head. Richard wasn't about to be put off.

"What have you discovered? If it is relevant to the investigation, what's to be gained by holding it back?"

"That's a good question, Richard. Why would anyone hold anything back unless they didn't want anyone to know about it?... So, Richard, what are you holding back?"

"Me…? I've shared everything with you and risked everything by doing so. Is there something in particular you think I've withheld?"

"What about that *other* enterprise operating on that industrial estate, the one you left off your list?"

Again, it was obvious Richard didn't have a clue what Rod was talking about. I suggested to Rod that it might be helpful if we took time to enlighten Richard. In reality, I was a mere bystander while Rod 'enlightened' Richard with everything we had learned so far. The punch line at the end of Rod's report almost made me giggle.

"So, you see, Richard, we don't actually know anything. All we've managed to collect is a load of assumptions and a little gossip."

For the next few minutes, we discussed all Rod's shared information. Then, it was time to come clean about our late-night cross-country hike and ask Richard if he might like to view Rod's video of our adventure. Until Richard eventually broke it, silence reigned after the video ended.

"So, you think McCormac spent his time that day in that workshop?" he muttered to no one in particular but probably intended for Rod.

"It's a possibility."

"But why? What's there to interest him? Are you suggesting McCormac was somehow mixed up in illegal trafficking operations such as you filmed? I suppose, if that were the case, it could have something to do with his murder. People involved in that line of business seem to be bumped off fairly regularly."

"That's also a possibility. What about the other matter, the matter of where McCormac really was living? In your investigation, have you come across anything that might provide a clue?"

"No, but we believed he lived in Merivale Village. We weren't looking for where else he might have lived. Do you think the issue of where he actually lived is significant?"

Really…? Is this our top cop in action, I wondered, or is he just fishing to find out what else Rod knows? I was running out of patience with this process and felt obliged to comment.

"Well, if McCormac was living somewhere other than the Village, is that where he spent all those hours that day when he visited the industrial site? If it was, what did he do there all day? By using that back access road, he could have slipped away without being captured by the security cameras out the front. He could have gone anywhere and done anything without anyone being aware of what he was up to."

Richard groaned and again dropped his head into his hands for a few moments before addressing Rod.

"I am beginning to suspect you have many more questions, Rod, but I would rather hear your thoughts on this case first. What do you think McCormac's death was all about? Please roll out your thoughts, suspicions, gossip, and whatever else you might have. I admit I'm stalled and there is no information coming from down south. I'm beginning to think that might be deliberate, but I can't say why I feel that might be the case."

Rod looked over at me and raised his eyebrows in question. I shrugged and gave him a half-hearted nod. Rod appeared to consider things before clearing his throat in readiness to tell Richard more.

"Nothing I'm about to say is backed up by any hard evidence at this time. It's important that you understand that before I continue."

Richard nodded enthusiastically as he sat up straight and slid forward onto the front edge of his chair.

"Go ahead, Rod. I'm open to anything, even fairytales, at this point in the investigation."

"Okay, here's how I see it. There are two possible scenarios to consider. Neither one appears more logical than the other. Both scenarios are dependent on why McCormac was here at all and why he chose to pose as a resident of the Village."

"If we knew the answers to those fundamental questions, we wouldn't be having this conversation. I would be out there galloping down the home straight towards solving this case. Sorry for interrupting... Carry on. Let's hear whatever else you might have to offer."

In response, Rod began rolling out everything he had gained from his contact, without indicating its origins. As there was unlikely to be anything I hadn't heard before, I excused myself and went to the kitchen to add the finishing touches to the risotto.

With the table set and the cheese and butter stirred through the risotto, I returned to the back deck in time to hear Rod wind up his summary of our information. Richard nodded a few times before speaking.

"As you suggested earlier, Rod, in many ways, it still all comes down to why McCormac came here and whether or not he was living in the Village."

My intention was to hurry them to the table for dinner. Now Rod had finished enlightening Richard, that's what I did.

"Before either of you decides to speculate further, dinner is ready, and it does not improve if left standing. To the table now, please."

A scraping of chairs followed as they heeded my message. As soon as everyone was in eating mode and the oohs and aahs were done with, I decided it was time for me to respond to Richard's earlier comment about whether McCormac was living in the Village.

"While I have no idea what brought him to this area or why or how he came to be allocated a house here, in my opinion, he was not living in the Village."

"You seem quite sure about that," Richard said. "What makes you so sure?"

"Apart from the basic necessities of life that are missing from the house, there had been no attempt to create the illusion someone was in residence. There were no personal items or trinkets scattered about. No books strategically or casually lying around. There was just one book, ancient and hidden in a bottom drawer and obviously not the current reading matter of the occupant of the house."

Richard cocked his head to one side and studied me for a moment before asking his question.

"I see. So, if you were in McCormac's position, what would you have done to make the place look genuinely lived-in?"

"Look around you. What does an average householder have strewn around their abode? No, if I were in McCormac's position,

I wouldn't have spread quite so much junk about and, after all, he was a bloke. But there would have been nonperishables in the pantry, a couple of frozen meals in the freezer, various bits of clothing in the wardrobe, and a book (complete with a bookmark sticking out) by the bed… Oh, and maybe a pair of trainers by the back door."

To help me think, I had concentrated on my plate as I spoke. As I finished speaking, I looked up to find Rod and Richard staring at me – not in anger but in surprise.

"You've done this often, then?" Richard asked.

"What? What…?" I blurted out in my confusion.

"…Made a house looked lived in when it's not?"

Rod chuckled and Richard shook his head. "Out with it, Richard," I demanded. "Something I said obviously doesn't sit well with you. What's the problem?"

"No… there's no problem, Marion. It's only that you just settled the question of whether McCormac was living in that house at the end of this street. From what you said, it's clear he wasn't. But what I find really interesting is that he felt confident enough in whatever he was doing to believe he didn't need to go to the trouble of creating a convincing scene of someone in residence."

A brief but uncomfortable silence followed as I tried to work out whether I was being ridiculed or not, but Richard wasn't finished and continued.

"So, Rod, what are your thoughts on how we should proceed, and what should we concentrate on first?"

"Well, I wonder if we shouldn't ask Marion for her thoughts." Rod's tone didn't sound sarcastic, but I gave him a hard look to be sure (and to give myself time to think) before I responded.

Chapter 22

Rod's suggestion that they should ask for my thoughts on how the investigation into McCormac's death should proceed had me wrong-footed, but not for long.

"Well, I think that a couple of questions that dogged us all along might be answered if we could determine where McCormac spent those hours when we assumed he was at the industrial site. Unfortunately, that might require more hours spent poring over traffic camera footage."

"We've already scoured traffic camera recordings," Richard retorted. "What would doing it again achieve?"

"Hang on a minute, Richard. Marion might have a point there. We need to look for cameras in the vicinity of the industrial estate's rear access road. Did your officers check camera footage from that area?"

"Probably not… The expectation was that the vehicle would leave the site the same way as it arrived. They didn't know what was at the rear of the site, so they wouldn't have checked anything from back there. Where exactly is that access road you mentioned, and where does it join the main arterial road system?"

A garbled description of the road we found last night followed as Rod tried unsuccessfully to explain the layout of the area we investigated. Everyone had finished eating, so, leaving Rod to explain the workshop and its access road, I gathered up our plates and headed for the kitchen. When about halfway to the kitchen, Rod called after me.

"Marion, may I use your computer for a few minutes?"

"Of course. I was going to dish up dessert. Should I wait until you've finished whatever you're doing before I do?"

As I spoke, the printer whirred into life and, in quick succession, spat out three pages. I looked over and saw the two men huddled in front of what appeared to be a map that filled the screen

"Might be as well to hold off on the dessert for a bit," Rod suggested.

So, instead, I packed everything from the main course into the dishwasher. While I did that, there was a short, murmured conversation between the two men. A few moments later, both men were up off their chairs and coming towards the kitchen with some degree of urgency.

"How much longer do you want to wait before dessert?" I asked.

They appeared not to hear my question and continued their earlier conversation. Although I knew it wasn't a deliberate snub, but I was being excluded from whatever it was. My tone of voice told them I was not happy about it.

"Is this thing you are planning, strictly men's business, or am I to be involved as well?"

I was pleased to see Rod was uncomfortable when he replied.

"Yes and no… Yes, we will tell you what we have been discussing, but no, you won't be directly involved.

Rod knew me better than to treat me that way. I slammed the dishwasher closed, pulled myself up to my full height, and glared at him. He received the message and made a weak bid to smooth my ruffled feathers.

"Sorry, Marion. Richard and I need to go for a little drive. We shouldn't be gone for more than about half an hour. Will dessert be okay if it's delayed that long?"

Rescheduling the dessert wasn't a problem. I hadn't started dishing it out yet. But I wasn't fine about being excluded from the 'little drive' the blokes were planning that would delay our desserts for half an hour. And I knew Rod's 'half an hour' probably would run closer to an hour in reality. I tried not to sound as miffed as I felt as I assured them the delay would not be a problem.

They returned nearly an hour later, and breezed in as though they had only been gone for about five minutes. Rod announced their return by asking if desserts would be out on the back deck. A few minutes later, Richard helped me carry the bowls of ice cream and fruit salad outside while Rod trailed along behind us with fresh glasses and a bottle of dessert wine – that was far too sweet for my taste. I was not yet calm enough to be civil, as the blokes were about to find out.

"Right… Now you have been for your 'little drive' and presumably done whatever you intended to do, perhaps someone might tell me what it was all about… of course, only if it is okay for me to know about it."

"There's nothing top secret about it, Marion," Rod announced in an exasperated tone. "I took Richard to show him that rear access road to the industrial site, and then we checked out the nearby main road for the location of traffic cameras."

"A couple of my men will have the honour of locating the relevant footage from those cameras and spending a few hours searching for a grey sedan," Richard added.

"More wine anyone?" Rod asked as he eyed off my glass. "Marion, you haven't even touched yours."

"Too sweet for me… I would prefer a coffee and port. I'll add these bowls to the dishwasher and then put the coffee on."

"Not for me, thanks, Marion. Thank you for dinner, but I do need to go home. I still have a couple of files to read in preparation for an early meeting tomorrow."

By the time Richard left, the coffee was ready. We took our coffee and port through to the lounge room and made ourselves comfortable in companionable silence for a minute or so before Rod began a new question-and-answer session.

"You seem firmly committed to the notion that McCormac was living somewhere else and that his house here was nothing more than a front for his real reason for being here. Apart from the argument you put forward earlier, is there anything else in your thinking to support that idea?"

"As I said, his poor effort at 'stage setting' doesn't sit well with me. What bloke would be living – or pretending to live –

somewhere without decent a razor of some sort and a toothbrush in the bathroom cabinet? Of course, he wasn't living here in the Village, and I don't think he believed he needed to maintain the pretence for long."

"Yeah, I see your point. If he thought he would be here for the long haul, he probably would have paid more attention to detail when setting the stage for his operation. Is there anything else bugging you about his set-up in that house at the end of the street?"

"At the risk of sounding ridiculous, yes, there is. What about that book, the only book we found in the entire house? Why was it hidden away as it was – or it appeared to be? Are you familiar with that book?"

"No, I'm not. I've been meaning to look it up ever since you found it, but I haven't done so. Why do you think it might be important, as opposed to just an odd choice of reading matter?"

"That's the point, Rod. It wasn't being read, well not recently anyway."

"Okay, point taken. Is there anything else we need to consider?"

"We did not find a computer in that house, or anything that suggested there had been one there … and nobody has found his phone. That is, unless Richard has found one or both of those devices but hasn't mentioned it to us."

"He still hasn't found McCormac's phone, and I haven't heard mention of finding a computer. Is there something significant rather than just odd about that?"

"Baxter McCormac had been a resident of Merivale Retirement Village for not much more than a couple of days, but he knew about the Village's private Facebook page. He knew how to book a seat on the bus for the trip to Jackson Cove. and knew about how to pay for it. The only way any of that could happen was if he had a computer."

"True, but he might have used one of the computers in our library. That's what they are there for, residents who don't have one of their own at home."

"After the fuss about the dog on the bus, I doubt our librarian, Marjorie, is likely to be helpful if we ask if McCormac availed himself of one of the library's machines."

"It might be worth asking Steve Parish if there is some way he can check recent usage of those machines. Residents have to use their private login details, so there might be something he can find if he has a look."

"Steve set those machines up, so he would be the right person to ask. I'll leave it to you to have a man-to-man chat with him."

"Right, I'll try for first thing in the morning. Can we return to that book that you think is so important? Richard hasn't said anything about removing it from the house, so how about we take another look at it?"

"When…? Do you mean now?"

"Why not? It's dark, and no one is roaming around at this hour of the night. We could nip in and be out in about a minute flat. Do you have a clean, large plastic bag I might borrow?"

A search of a kitchen cupboard produced a large Ziplock plastic bag. "Will this bag do?" I asked. Rod said it was perfect and stuffed it in his pocket.

"Rod, it is a dark night. If we visit McCormac's house now, how are we going to see what we are doing? If we use torches, even small ones, they are likely to alert the neighbours, at least one nosy nextdoor neighbour. And stumbling around in the dark in a strange house is likely to create enough noise to wake the dead."

"We won't be stumbling around in the dark. The street light on that corner and the lack of curtains in the house mean there will be enough low-level light to see all right. We know where the book is, so we won't waste time searching for it. We'll go in, grab the book, and be out again. Come on, let's go."

"No. I'm not going anywhere until I change my shoes. I ruined my favourite pair of sandals the last time I went dashing around the countryside with you. You will have to wait until I put on my trainers."

There was almost no moon, but Rod was right about the street light providing enough light for our needs. We strode briskly along the footpath to the corner of the street before strolling along the far side of the house that faced the intersection and was exposed to the street light. Then, a quick dash around to the back of the house and in through the back door. I half expected to find that Richard had locked or bolted the door in some way and prevented our entry. I wondered what Rod might have done had we found our entry barred.

After standing just inside the door for a few moments to allow our eyes to adjust to the gloom, everything went much as Rod suggested it would. We went straight to the bedroom. He opened the bottom drawer, grabbed the book, and shoved it in the plastic bag.

"Are you mad?" I hissed at him. "Are you going to remove evidence from this house?"

"Well, I'm not going to sit here on the bed trying to read in such poor light. Of course, I'm going to take it home to read and examine it properly. Anyway, this isn't a crime scene, and the book isn't evidence … Well, not unless I prove otherwise. Come on... Let's get out of here."

The street light seemed much brighter once we were out on the footpath again. I realised I had no idea about the next phase of our current operation, and thought it wise to find out.

"So, now you have the book, what happens next? Are we taking it to your place or mine to start work on it?"

"What? No, I am going to walk you home, and then I'll go home to bed. I'll look at the book in the morning after I've spoken to Steve Parish if that's possible. I'll call you as soon as I have anything to tell you."

By then, we had reached my front door, and I knew there was no pursuing the conversation further. So, I said a tart goodnight and marched inside, leaving Rod stranded on my doorstep. Why was I suddenly so miffed again? I didn't have to think too long on that one. I suspected Rod had no intention of going to bed yet, and would spend much of the rest of the night poring over that book. And, I had no doubt I would not be receiving a call from him too early in the morning.

With no early morning call from Rod to disrupt my routine, my day followed its now preordained path. There was no sign of Rod this morning, but I didn't doubt that he had been for his usual long morning run. With nothing better to do than think, I extended my walk this morning. The longer walk meant I was out later than usual. More people were about by the time I headed home. The longer walk, combined with chatting with several people along the way, meant I arrived home much later than usual. The time devoted to thinking had produced nothing new. As I strode past his house, I noted I still hadn't heard from Rod.

Although I felt like a coffee, it was still too early for another cup. I indulged in some quiet time at my desk. With so many questions and thoughts roaming around in my head. I struggled to keep track of them all or to properly consider any of them. A page of a new pad divided into two columns sat staring at me. One column was headed 'Questions', and the other was headed 'Anomalies'. After a couple of false starts, the process of recording some of that stuff occupying my mind began in earnest.

"Phew… Have I been carrying all this stuff around with me?" I asked my empty house. I had filled almost three pages. While no answers had jumped out at me along the way, the exercise made me more aware of how complicated the McCormac case was and why we had made so little progress with it. One of my notes made me feel a twinge of discomfort. Although I knew I was being silly, I also knew I would be discussing the matter at length with Rod sometime soon.

Had I listed everything? Were there facts or clues I had forgotten to record? I need to think about it – and thinking about it requires coffee to power my brain. I struggled up off my chair, stretched my back, and headed for the kitchen. After no more than a couple of steps, my phone called me back to where it lay on my desk: Rod. At last, I thought, and then mentally chastised myself for such a mean-spirited thought.

"Are you free to join me for coffee?"

His voice was neutral, so I didn't know whether to be excited or to just accept it as an invitation to coffee. About ten minutes later, I continued to speculate about the invitation as I made my way unhurriedly along the footpath to Rod's house.

As seems to be his way, my arrival did not bring forth any clues to settle my speculation. It wasn't until we were seated on his back deck with our coffees and shop-bought blueberry muffins that the nervous twitch I was close to developing was avoided.

"Steve Parish was only too eager to assist when I spoke to him this morning. He called me back only a few minutes before I called you. His check of the logon files for the library computers showed no access by McCormac. Steve then decided to check who had logged on to our Facebook page in the days before our bus trip to Jackson Cove. He found where McCormac had logged on and had booked his seat on the bus."

"Right, so McCormac used a personal computer... Presumably, his own? It's unlikely one of the other residents would have helped him out. What do you think?"

"It appears safe to assume McCormac had a computer and used it to secure a place on the bus trip. And, no, I know that doesn't answer the question regarding that computer's current whereabouts."

"Something else just occurred to me, Rod. Not everyone bothers with the extra expense and whatever of owning a computer. Some people seem to live on their phones. Maybe McCormac only had his phone and used that for his emails and to access the internet. I know that doesn't help because we haven't found his phone, anyway, but a phone would be easier to lose than a computer ... easier to lose, or maybe steal.

Do you intend to pass this information on to Richard, or will you wait to see what he finds on the traffic camera footage before you say anything?"

"For the moment, I'm more inclined to the latter."

"Rod, I thought that, by sharing information with him last night, we had decided he was the genuine article and it was safe to assume he was not bent. Now, it seems like we are back to withholding info again."

The conversation that followed managed to reassure me about Richard, and it allowed my mind to dredge up the other thought that had caused me some degree of discomfort. I knew I was risking ridicule, but I opted to share it with Rod.

"While I know this will sound ridiculous, I have to admit your contact's comments regarding Joe concern me. While we don't know what his former 'employment' was, your contact's speculation in regard to Joe's involvement in McCormac's death now has me worried. Are we safe associating with Joe and having him living in such close proximity?"

"Eh? Why would you be worrying about Joe? Have you committed some serious offence against Crown or country that you might be held to account for?"

"Of course not, but what about our involvement in investigating McCormac's murder? What if we manage to confirm Joe's involvement? I doubt he would be too pleased about that."

"You've been reading too many of the wrong kinds of novels. We've gotten to know Joe and to know that he is a decent bloke. Everything we know – or think we know – about him suggests he worked in a different kind of world from ours. That doesn't make him a murdering maniac on the loose."

At that point, Rod's phone chirped, cutting short any further reprimand that might have been coming my way.

"Speak of the devil…," Rod murmured as he headed inside to deal with the call.

It seemed a long time before he reappeared. In reality, it probably was no more than five minutes. During that time, I heard nothing from inside the house, no laughter, no raised voice, nothing. It meant his sudden reappearance on the back deck made me jump in surprise. His face told me nothing, but I detected a slight tenseness. So, I asked the question that I hoped might lead to his sharing information about the call.

"Is everything all right? You seem a bit tense after your call."

"My caller was my contact you mentioned earlier. He is still digging around on our behalf and passed on an update. He is now reasonably confident Joe is still alive but is being kept in some form of safe accommodation somewhere around Canberra. He has now revised his earlier speculation that Joe might have been responsible for McCormac's death. The latest info he's picked up is that McCormac might have been the 'baddie' in this story, and his presence here might have been linked to a contract that was issued on Theo Rothwell."

"Theo Rothwell… Isn't that a name we think Joe sometimes uses?"

"Yeah, that was our thinking. I don't have anything definite to tell you, but from the bits and pieces I've been given, it's looking more likely that Theo Rothwell is Joe's real name."

"That could be awkward." I saw my comment confused Rod, so rushed on to clarify. "When he returns, I'm going to have to concentrate on calling him Joe and avoiding the slipup of calling him Theo."

"If nothing else, that could make life interesting for a moment or two when both he and Cilla try to convince you that they have no idea who Theo Rothwell is."

"Rod, interesting as that is, why would there be a contract out on Joe? What would he have done to warrant his death? Whatever it was must've happened some time ago while he was still in his former employment because he's been retired for a while now. Has your contact picked up any hints about the reason for the contract?"

"Again, he doesn't have any definite details, but he has picked up some whispers about a job an agent did some time ago. Apparently, whoever that agent was managed to uncover a corrupt cell operating covertly out of MI5 or MI6. In the process of closing down that cell, a couple of people were killed, and several are spending the rest of their lives behind bars."

"Right… So that agent might have been our Joe, and the contract that was out on him might have been some form of retribution? If that is the case, how did McCormac fit into the picture? Was he simply someone hired to carry out the contract or was he one of those who managed to escape being caught back then?"

"You do manage to ask questions that get right to the heart of the matter, and, as is so often the case, I have no definitive answer for you. For us, the waiting game continues. All we can do is hope more details somehow emerge to answer all our questions."

"I suppose you're right. It's all we can do. In the meantime, Rod, what about that book we 'borrowed' from McCormac's house? Is it likely to tell us anything, and is it likely even to be of relevance to this investigation? Are you familiar with the book at all?"

"No, I've never read it and haven't come across it before. I searched the web last night for information about the book and its author but didn't find anything helpful. As much as I've been trying to avoid it, it now looks as though I'll have to read the damned thing."

"Unlikely to be an exciting read, I suspect. Something that occurred to me since we've been talking about the book. Something about that book was annoying me before I went to sleep last night, but I couldn't get my head around what it was. Don't laugh, but this idea has just occurred to me: what if it was some sort of code book? You know, something to do with ciphers or whatever it is that spooks use."

"As in the source for coded communications…? Is that what you're thinking?" I shrugged, and Rod nodded as though he understood. "Can't dismiss it as a possibility, I suppose. I'll be better placed to let you know what I think after I've read it."

Chapter 23

It was the following morning when I next spoke to Rod. After my morning walk, I experienced a minor panic and called him.

"Are we recommencing mahjong mornings this week? I had forgotten all about it and suddenly realised I hadn't baked anything for morning tea."

"No, we don't kick off again until next week, so no baking required today."

"Will we return to our usual two mornings each week, or are we going to ease back into it gently with only one morning for a while?"

"Everyone was keen to return to what we had before, so I agreed that's what we would do starting from next week."

"What about happy hours at your place, Rod? Are they to resume this week, or are they still on hold for a while yet?"

"Next week promises to be a big one. Mahjong mornings and happy hours will recommence and we also have the little theatre group's dress rehearsal night next Thursday. And, before you ask, there has been nothing further from Richard or any of my other contacts. My tasks for today are to finish and submit that article that's now a couple of weeks overdue and to start reading that book we 'borrowed' from McCormac's house."

Well, that's put me in my place, I thought as I wandered into the kitchen to make a coffee. I'm fairly sure Rod just told me he was busy today and didn't want to be disturbed. Why did I feel so put out about it? There must be plenty of other things I can do – need to do. The reason I felt that way became clear as I sat sipping my coffee. It was frustration ... Sheer, blinding frustration with no possibility of relief in sight. As soon as I finished my coffee (I didn't rush), I went to my desk and the list of Questions and Anomalies I had started yesterday.

Was there anything more – or new – to add to either column? The short answer was a resounding no. Of course, I could always do some housework, I reminded myself, but that wasn't going to happen, not today anyway. That left me with my list to focus on in the hope some hitherto unseen clue might jump out. None did. By lunchtime, I was brain-dead, my eyes were heavy, and I had a headache. I swallowed a couple of analgesics, made a sandwich and plonked down in front of TV to watch the midday news… and fell asleep with my sandwich uneaten.. I might have slept for the rest of the afternoon if my phone hadn't woken me. I found my sandwich now dried and curling at the edges

"Hello…," I mumbled with brain and mouth still not in sync.

"Marion, are you okay?" Rod demanded. "Talk to me, Marion. Has something happened to you?" I noted the anxiety in his voice and its elevated volume.

"Yeah, yeah. I'm fine. Must have fallen asleep for a few minutes."

How easily the lie rolled off my tongue. Those 'few minutes' amounted to more than two hours. God, now I'll have trouble getting to sleep tonight.

"Sorry, Rod. Can I help you with something?"

"Well, if you feel up to it and can spare the time…."

"Sarcasm does not become you. What can I do to help?"

"Come to my place. After I prime you with coffee to wake you up, I'll tell you all about it."

Cheeky sod… Of course, I was up for it, whatever *it* was. After splashing water on my face and combing my hair, I strode along the footpath – until something caught my eye.

The roller door of Cilla's garage was halfway up. While she tends to leave it fully open all the time when she is home, it is always closed when she is away – as it had been this time. Did it mean Cilla had come home? It took a mere moment to squash that thought. If Cilla had arrived home, she would have opened the garage to allow her to drive her car in… and then she would have left it fully open (or fully closed) but not with the roller door at half mast.

She closed all her heavy drapes before she left, so I knew her house would be quite dark inside despite the sunny day. So, what are those pinpoints of light I can see moving about inside her house? Someone… No, more than one, were moving about in there and none of them was likely to be Cilla – or Joe.

"How do I deal with this?" I murmured to myself. "Phone… yes, pretend you have a phone call to deal with."

I needed a convincing-looking reason to stop walking. That one sounded ridiculous even to me, but it was the best idea I could come up with on the spur of the moment. Then, *tie your shoelaces* flashed through my mind. That sounded perfect until I realised I was wearing sandals. Sensible thinking began to seep through. 'Go back to the phone idea', it suggested – but *make* a phone call. Sometimes, I do heed sound advice.

"Rod, without drawing attention to yourself, quickly look across the road at Cilla's house. I'm stalled on the footpath at the moment." I heard him give a low whistle and knew he had seen what I wanted him to see. "What should I do? I can't stand here for too long doing nothing but talking on my phone. I'm bound to give the game away."

"Make a show of ending the call and continue to my place. The door is unlocked. Without as much as glancing across the street, come straight in as though you live here and are just returning home."

In line with his instructions, I marched straight in and closed Rod's front door behind me. A couple of metres in from the door, I stopped and stood still. Rod stood off to one side of his lounge room window intently watching Cilla's house across the street. Uncertain whether I should join him or remain out of the way in the kitchen area, I softly asked him what he wanted me to do.

"Nothing… I've called Richard. He and a couple of his officers happen to be out this way and will be here soon."

"The minute whoever that is in Cilla's house hears a vehicle approaching, they will be off out the back and gone."

"No, I think Richard has a plan that takes that possibility into account."

"Whatever he plans to do, he will need to hurry up and do it. I doubt whoever is in that house plans to hang about in there forever. What can we do? Did Richard suggest any way that we might help with the situation?"

"Yeah, he did. He said we should stay where we are and do nothing. He made it clear that it wouldn't take much on our part to completely stuff-up their operation."

Put firmly in my place, I remained silent for a couple of minutes to sulk. Then, I thought I had seen a movement further back along the street – and close to my house. I tiptoed over to stand at the opposite side of the lounge room window. Rod raised a questioning eyebrow at me but said nothing, so I didn't bother explaining … Not until a few moments later, anyway.

"Who is that coming out of Iris's house across the street from my place? She doesn't have a husband or a son, and it's a bit risky for an 'overnight guest' to try sneaking away unseen in broad daylight."

"They don't look like they are sneaking away," Rod hissed. "They look more like a couple of residents out for a walk, maybe on their way to the bowls club."

"Where the hell are Richard and his officers? Those two blokes could be part of the gang that's inside ransacking Cilla's house. Anyway, at this rate, the show will be over, and the 'birds' will have flown before Richard's mob makes an appearance."

"Don't be too sure. Those two blokes look too young to be residents. I think you might find they are Richard's officers."

"So, if these are Richard's men, where's their vehicle? It doesn't appear much of a well-planned operation. There must be something we can do to help ensure whoever is in Cilla's house doesn't get away. Where is Richard, anyway? I haven't seen any sign of him so far, and I don't know what he hoped to achieve by sending just those two officers. Of course, that is, if you are right and those two blokes are Richard's officers."

I thought I heard Rod give a half-hearted low growl, and I knew he was fast losing patience with me. A few moments of silence on my part might be a good idea, I told myself, but I was a bit too late recognising the situation.

"Just stay quiet and watch for a bit. Instead of harping on, maybe you might stay silent for a while and devote some thought to what we might be able to do if Richard's operation tanks."

Okay, that's me put in my place once again. I remained silent as I watched the two possible officers walking, talking and laughing as they made their way along the footpath until they were out front of Cilla's house. There they stopped. From his actions, it looked as though one of the men suddenly had remembered something. After wrestling a piece of paper out of his pocket, he appeared to scan it. He then leaned on Cilla's gate as he dragged his phone out of his pocket and proceeded to make a call. The other man gave the appearance of being uninterested in whatever his mate was up to and stood casually looking around while the other's phone call was in progress. Then, just as quickly as it had begun, things changed. His call ended, the officer slipped his phone back into his pocket and had a quick word to his mate, who now appeared more interested in the situation.

I gasped in surprise. The bloke leaning on the gate suddenly flung open the gate. Both men rushed up the path to Cilla's front door. Their banging on the door was loud, even in Rod's lounge room. It didn't go unnoticed in Cilla's house. We watched as a flurry of shadows and flittering lights filled Cilla's house for a moment as the intruders appeared to rush to the back door.

Sounds of a scuffle rang out from across the street. The two men at the front door had sprinted through the garage to access the house's back deck. A scuffle probably meant the officers had taken down the escaping intruders. Sure enough, about a minute later, two men in handcuffs were being prodded and pushed through the garage and out to the front of the house.

It felt like the operation had happened for only a matter of moments when a police paddy wagon miraculously arrived and screamed to a halt on Cilla's driveway. I felt myself relax. The situation was under control and the bad guys were about to be whisked away. That was until I saw another light picking its way stealthily around inside the house.

"A light is moving about in there. Someone is still in the house," I yelped at Rod.

Of course, Rod Maguire didn't need me to tell him about it. He had seen it and, quick-thinking man that he is, he had whipped out his phone and keyed a number from his contacts list.

"One still in the house... Appears to be heading for the front door," I heard him tell the person he called.

Almost simultaneously, I saw the unmistakable figure of Richard rush through the garage to the front of the house. A large lump of a bloke escaping via the front door was tackled and added to the list of those in handcuffs. Richard marched his prisoner to the wagon and helped him onboard with a hefty shove. At the same time, the two taken down by the two officers in the back door area, without too much attention to preserving their dignity, were bundled into the paddy wagon to join their mate. Mission accomplished, the paddy wagon departed with its cargo.

An unmarked vehicle drove up to Cilla's house a moment after the wagon departed. Richard and his two officers moved towards it. Before sliding into the front passenger seat, Richard directed a wave and a nod towards where Rod and I stood, watching from the safety of Rod's lounge room. It was all over. Our morning's entertainment was over, and a form of vacuum had replaced it. Both Rod and I remained motionless and silent for a few moments after the last vehicle departed, but the silence couldn't last for long. My mind was a swirling mass of questions.

"Jesus, Rod, what do you make of all that? Who do you think they were, and what were they looking for? No doubt, it's related to McCormac's death, but were they looking for something to do with Cilla, or was it for something to do with Joe?"

Rod took a moment before clearing his throat in readiness to share his thoughts. His reply never eventuated. His phone demanded his attention. Rod awarded it priority. For the first few moments, the caller appeared to do all the talking, but I had heard enough to realise the caller was Richard. Then, when it was Rod's turn to speak, I listened intently to the one-sided conversation.

"Yes, okay. What do you want me to do? … Yeah, I can access it … Right, I'll do that and then what? … Oh, I see. Okay, I'll let you know as soon as I've done it."

Patience is not my strong suit, but I waited at least a minute after the call ended before questioning the reason for Richard's call.

"Is everything okay? Nothing has gone awry with the intruders they captured at Cilla's place, has it?"

"Not as far as I know."

That might have answered my question, but it was not what I wanted to know. Again, I found myself wondering if the phone call had been about more of that 'secret men's business' that Richard and Rod seem to revel in at my expense. I tried to formulate a question that wasn't too rude but would elicit the information I sought. While I was still trying to put something together, Rod seemed to realise I was still there and spoke to me.

"Right, let's see what sort of mayhem they caused and see if we can identify what their search target might have been."

"I assume the mayhem you referenced is what might have happened in Cilla's house, and that we are going to enter her house to find out what was done."

"Yes… I thought I made that clear. Do you have a problem with that? If you're uncomfortable with it, stay here. I'll carry out an inspection on my own."

"If the external doors at her house are the same as ours, it's likely the doors automatically locked again after the intruders exited the place… unless they busted the locks to gain entry, of course. How do we get in? Will a spot of break-and-entry be required?"

"Of course not. Richard is fairly confident the doors are locked, and only the garage remains open. We won't be forcing our way in. Some time ago, Cilla gave me a spare key to her place. She knew she would be spending periods of time away from home with her contract work and felt it wise to have someone who could enter the house if the need should arise in her absence. So, are you coming with me or not?"

"For a journalist, you do ask silly questions on occasions. Of course, I'm coming with you, but I don't much look forward to breaking the news of the break-in to Cilla."

"We don't have a problem. I will be reporting our findings to Richard, who I imagine will inform Cilla of today's events. He's bound to have questions to ask, probably mainly about any connection there might be with his McCormac case investigation."

"Rod, what's your honest thinking on all this? Was Cilla the likely target, or was it Joe?"

"Oh, that it might be so simple to know… Still, that is what we might be able to establish after we have a look around over there."

He made it sound so matter-of-fact and almost ordinary for us to enter a neighbour's home while they weren't there and without her permission. Nevertheless, I suffered a nervousness, a feeling of trepidation, as I accompanied Rod across the street. We didn't have to go far to identify the first evidence of the break-in. The lock on the garage roller door was wrecked when they forced it open. As instructed by Rod, I used my phone to photograph the damage while he made notes in a small notebook.

"You know, that does surprise me," I admitted as I took another couple of shots of the busted lock.

"How else did you think they were going to break in when they didn't have a key?"

"Yes, I knew there would be a busted lock somewhere, but I thought it more likely they would enter the place via the back door. It would have been less obvious than forcing their way in out here at the front of the house. At least Cilla's motorbike is still here and doesn't appear to have been damaged in any way."

Such finer details appeared to be of little interest to Rod. Once he had finished making notes about the busted lock, he made his way through to the back door and checked its lock. He bent down and peered closely at it, before grunting as he stood up.

"Take a look at this lock," he said, gesturing to the back door. "Your thinking was partly right. It looks as though their actual entry to the house was via the back door."

"Really? How did you work that out? The lock on this door looks okay. It hasn't been damaged in any way."

"Have a closer look – and take shots of it. There are scratches on the lock. They didn't have a key but used a tool of some sort to pick the lock."

A key miraculously appeared from Rod's pocket, and moments later, we let ourselves in through the back door. Everything inside looked okay at first glance and in a better state than I expected. But it didn't take long to notice evidence of the place having been searched. Odd things were slightly askew or not quite where Cilla always had them, and disturbed dust was evident in some places. Cilla's house wasn't dusty. It's just that when something remains stationary for some time and then is moved, a light film of dust is disturbed.

More photos and more notes were taken before the house was again locked, and we returned to Rod's place. I was concerned the busted lock prevented the garage from being locked. Apart from her motorbike, Cilla has a lot of expensive-looking tools in there. Rod said he would give it special mention in his report to Richard. While I busied myself in the kitchen, Rod reported our findings to Richard and sent him some of the photos we had taken. When he returned to the kitchen, Rod looked concerned, grave even.

"Richard says he wants to talk to us," Rod announced, "but thinks it probably should be a formal interview rather than a casual meeting. He will get back to us later to confirm arrangements."

"A formal interview sounds ominous. I'd be happy to feed him again if it means we could substitute a casual meeting instead of an interview."

"What's wrong with doing a formal interview? It's the same as recounting what happened in any other setting."

"I dunno… A formal interview sounds like you're almost guilty of something and need to state your case and explain how you had nothing to do with it – whatever it was. Anyway, on a different note, I wonder how Cilla reacted to three intruders searching her house."

"Yeah. I'm glad Richard is giving her the bad news and not me. Harking back to what went on over the road this morning, did you draw any conclusions from our inspection of the place? I mean, did you form any opinion as to what those intruders were looking for or who they were targeting?"

"Not sure… I need a while to think about it before I form any opinions. That's another reason why Richard's suggestion of a formal interview wouldn't work. Well, not with me, anyway. I need time to digest everything that happened before I have anything of any substance to offer."

"Well, hopefully, those three blokes were the last of whatever it is that surrounds McCormac's death. It will be great to have life back to normal around here again, and I am looking forward to our night at the theatre."

"The response to that outing indicates that residents are more than ready for more excursions. I suppose we should look at updating our schedule of bus trips to make sure they fit in with everything else that will be happening here … like the High School plays competition that's not too far away now."

After the morning's excitement, I wandered home with a head full of thoughts. I wanted – needed – to sit quietly and think about what happened this morning and, more precisely, what our inspection of Cilla's place revealed. Something about that particular part of the morning was trying to force its way through the jumble of other stuff going on in my head. I'd probably fall asleep if I sat in front of TV, so I took myself out onto my back deck. Watching the grass in the adjoining paddock waving in the breeze and a couple of hawks circling on the thermals overhead was quite cathartic.

It was only a couple of minutes later when I knew exactly what to focus on. Rod had asked if I had any opinion on who or what might have been the intruders' target. Now, I'm almost sure I know. While there was evidence of things having been disturbed throughout the house, I detected a major focus area… But exactly the *who* or *what* was not clear.

To my untrained eye, it appeared as though there were clearly identified areas that came in for special attention: the bedrooms. I pulled out my phone and checked the images I took of those rooms. The main bedroom looked as though it had undergone a thorough search, but it was the other two bedrooms that caught my attention. Cilla and Joe had taken one each of the spare bedrooms to use as their personal office.

While I didn't know anything of Joe's office prior to the intruders, even I could tell it had been subjected to a thorough search. Cilla's office was a different matter. I had been in her office on a couple of occasions. It was obvious to me where things had been disturbed in the course of their search, and it looked as though the files drawer of her desk had received special attention. The drawer had been left gaping a little. In their hurry to get away, they probably abandoned it when it wouldn't close properly. A file partially sticking up out of its hanger had prevented the drawer from closing.

So, does that mean Cilla was the intruders' target? I couldn't be sure. I didn't know enough about Joe's office prior to the break-in. What sort of information did Cilla keep in her office? She struck me as being extremely cautious, so it was unlikely anything too confidential would be in those files in her home office. It would be handy to know Joe better, but I don't. So, given what I know of the man, what sort of information would he keep in his office?

It was about an hour later before I managed to unscramble my thoughts. Yes, Cilla and Joe were the targets. This was not about a house break-in. This was a search for information. Did the intruders find what they wanted? I think not. Both Cilla and Joe are too canny and cautious for that. I doubted the intruders even managed to learn the true identities of the two residents.

Chapter 24

As I sat there, flicking through the images I took in Cilla's house, another disturbing thought slammed in from nowhere. Before the drama involving Cilla's place began, I was on my way to Rod's house in response to his invitation. I still didn't know why he had invited me or what he intended to discuss with me. When he issued the invitation, I detected a hint of excitement in his voice. Now, a mixture of curiosity and trepidation flooded through me. What was it he had wanted to discuss with me?

He didn't answer his phone. Had he gone out after I left his house, or was he ignoring my call? Something else demanded my attention: I was hungry. I headed for the kitchen to stave off starvation. After eating my lunchtime sandwich at mid-afternoon, I tried Rod's number again. This time, he answered.

"Apologies… I left my phone at home when I went to the gym for a short workout. While I was at the gym, I also remembered we hadn't discussed the reason I invited you for coffee this morning. It's a bit late for coffee now. How about coming at about six o'clock for a drink and then staying for dinner? I owe you a few dinners anyway."

Obviously, whatever he wanted to talk to me about this morning had lost some of its importance, or he would have called me before this. I don't know why I'm so keen to know what it's about. I don't need more excitement today. Curiosity mixed with a dash of excited expectation increased until it was time to leave for Rod's. As I strode along the footpath, curiosity, in its perverse way, had me imagining various exciting possibilities Rod might want to discuss with me, and in Rod's perverse way, he had made me wait to find out.

My stomach grumbled. Our drinks and nibbles were no match for the wonderful aroma emanating from the kitchen. In case Rod planned to make me wait until after dinner to discuss whatever he was excited about this morning, I was about to prompt him when he came good.

"I had another call from my contact. He confirmed that Theo Rothwell is stashed away somewhere safe in the Canberra area. He is now all but convinced that Theo is one of the 'good guys'. The flip side of that is that there are strong indications that McCormac was on the *other team*."

"What did he mean by the 'other team'? How many teams are there and who or what are they?"

"He meant that McCormac more than likely was one of the 'bad guys'."

"Okay, but that suspicion has been around since the outset of this investigation. What's happened to make your friend so sure now?"

"While he is not *sure*, he is fairly convinced. As he sees it, the likely scenario is that McCormac was here in some capacity in connection with a contract out on someone – probably Joe."

"So, who bumped off McCormac? If Joe (or Theo, if you think of him that way) has been squirrelled away in Canberra all this time, is it possible Joe did for McCormac before rushing off to Canberra? And, why was there a contract out on Joe, anyway?"

"No. That's not the story my contact has put together. The contract on Joe appears to stem from a major incident a long way back in Joe's past employment. It seems it has something to do with a dodgy MI6 operative and some of his friends, who Joe was instrumental in uncovering. The dodgy agent, or whatever they are called, was tried and sent away for life. All of that went on behind closed doors and was never made public. Joe's role was never revealed at any time through it, but it seems the bad guys always had their suspicions."

"Why would they come after Joe now? I don't know how long ago it happened, but it sounds a bit like ancient history. Was there a leak of some sort, do you think?"

"My contact suggests it probably was a leak of sorts. He believes a latent member of the bad guys, who has continued to work within the Agency, was recently promoted to a position giving him access to highly classified files. After the original rogue agent, who was serving a life sentence, disappeared recently, his 'comrades' – armed with new information from their 'insider' – decided it was time to balance the books."

"Ri-ight… I suppose someone might carry that sort of grudge for a long time, and would grab at any opportunity to square things. But that doesn't answer the question of who murdered McCormac. Have you heard anything from Richard since this morning? Given your contact's latest information, perhaps we need another meeting with our top cop."

"I was waiting for him to contact us, but you are right, maybe I should call him to suggest another get-together."

It was barely a minute later when Rod's phone played its tune. As usual, Rod wandered off for privacy while he took the call. He hadn't gone too far before he turned and came back. I heard Rod's side of the remainder of the conversation.

"…Well, it is only stew, but you are most welcome … It is almost ready, but it can go a bit longer … Oh, and it's at my place tonight …That's good. See you then."

As he slipped his phone back into his pocket, he announced, "We will be three for dinner. That reminds me. The stew probably needs a bit of a stir."

"While you attend to the stew, I'll set the table. Might I ask who the third diner will be?" I didn't really need to ask.

"Richard… He must be psychic or have exceptionally keen hearing. We had just mentioned him before he called. Anyway, he called to set up another of our casual meetings. What else could I do other than ask him to join us for dinner? He said he would be here in about ten minutes."

True to his word, Richard arrived about ten minutes later, but his arrival came as a shock. He arrived on foot. A glance along the street revealed his car parked in front of my house. I know he thought it was safer to park at my place than at Rod's, and how he arrived at that thinking with a mystery to me. The only worrying thing about it was what his vehicle parked out front of my house was doing to my reputation. Because Rod always arrived on foot, it was likely nobody knew he was there as well … Although, God knows what they might think if they did know he was there too.

Having seen both Rod and me glance along the road at his car, Richard felt obliged to explain.

"Yeah, I know it looks a bit peculiar, but I feel it's safer this way than having my car parked outside a journalist's house."

"That's past tense. I am no longer a journo, although I still do write the occasional article. Nevertheless, I am not and never was a crime journalist. Why are we standing here discussing this anyway? Dinner is ready. We should be getting stuck into eating."

As I was still in the dark as to why Richard was here, I decided to find out exactly what the guidelines were for tonight.

"Will you have to rush off again tonight, Richard?"

"No. Is that important, or likely to cause a problem of some sort?"

"Not that I am aware. I was just trying to establish whether we would be talking 'shop' over dinner, or whether you would have time to discuss such matters afterwards."

"Afterwards will be fine, thanks. I would prefer to devote my whole attention to this dish of delicious stew."

The delay was nerve-racking but proved worthwhile when Richard finally shared his news.

"A couple of my officers again spent hours scanning traffic camera footage and got lucky. They managed to pick up images of McCormac's car leaving the industrial site by that rear access road. With some difficulty due to the convoluted route it took, they tracked it to a three-star motel on the outskirts of town. It's supposedly three-star, but you would need to be easily pleased to believe that. There was no further activity to report until that evening when the vehicle left the motel and headed here to the Village. It explains why they weren't able to pick up the car leaving the industrial estate that evening."

"What happens now, Richard? Can you search his room at the motel after all this time – and will there be anything in it if you do? I mean, would his friends, whoever they might be, have cleaned out his room after his demise?"

"Ah, well, you would be justified in wondering about that, but sometimes you get a break. I didn't need a warrant because of the nature of the investigation and went straight to the motel as soon as its connection was established. McCormac's room remained undisturbed since his death, so everything in it was gathered up as evidence and is currently being rigorously examined."

"Having the room freed up after all this time should please the motel," I commented.

"Everything from the room might've been removed, but the room remains part of an ongoing crime investigation and has been sealed off. There was some debate with the motel owner about outstanding payment for the room, but that's another matter. A laptop was located in the room, but there is still no sign of a phone. So, your suspicions appear well-founded. McCormac wasn't living here. That house on the corner from here was just part of a cover he established for himself."

"Did you find anything else useful in his room?" I asked.

"Like what, Marion?"

"Oh, I don't know… like anything that might prove McCormac's real identity. After all, so far, nobody has been able to find any evidence a bloke called McCormac ever existed."

"Nothing but disappointment on that front so far. Allow us time to go through his stuff, and you never know what we might find."

"So, is it safe to assume McCormac's reason for establishing himself here in the Village was connected with some spurious contract that was out on Joe?"

"Seems like there might be some validity in such an assumption, but remember we still have no hard evidence to support that notion – or that Joe was involved in any of this."

The room remained quiet for a moment or two following Richard's comments as both Rod and I digested what we had learned. Then it was Rod's turn to reciprocate.

"Well, perhaps there is confirmation of sorts," Rod began tentatively. Rod's contact's latest information was relayed to Richard, although in précised form.

"While this information is not the 'hard evidence' you keep on about, Richard, it does tend to confirm Joe as the target, and McCormac's reason for setting himself up in the Village was to be in a good position to carry out the contract."

"Right… Maybe at least some of the pieces are starting to fit together. I've taken it upon myself to interrogate McCormac's laptop – just in case there is anything too political or top secret on it for others to see. So, if you won't think me rude, I'll head off for an early night. I plan an early start on that laptop tomorrow."

"I don't know how you can wait so long," I blurted out. "I wouldn't be able to resist attacking it as soon as it was found."

"…And maybe wiping the hard disc in the process? No, first, the tech boffins are making sure it is safe for me to start digging around in its files before I touch it."

A few minutes later, we watched Richard stride along the footpath to his car out front of my place and drive away. Rod and I wandered out to his back deck in silence. I guessed we both were trying to digest everything we had learned tonight. Rod poured us both a nightcap and, as I sat sipping it, a returning thought generated more questions.

"Rod, that book we borrowed from McCormac's house… You were going to read it or find out more about it. Have you had time to do anything about it?"

"Thanks for reminding me. That was the other thing I was going to talk to you about over coffee this morning. I did read the book from cover to cover. It's true to label: a collection of stories and poems for kids. The language might be a bit antiquated for today's kids. When reading the book didn't give me any clues, I spoke to a couple of people I know in the book world. They weren't much help. Then, I mentioned the book to a friend. He was surprised at my sudden strange taste in reading matter. I explained that it wasn't mine and that I couldn't understand why its owner seemed to treasure the thing."

"I don't suppose that got you very far."

"You would be wrong. After some discussion and a bit of thought, my friend suggested it might be important not as reading matter, but as a cipher code book. Apparently, obscure old books often are used in that way. We agreed Katherine Pyle's book fitted the bill perfectly."

"That could prove an important breakthrough, but where do we go from here? How do we prove the assumption that was the reason for the book? We have no evidence of coded messages being sent or received, so we can't test the theory."

"Maybe not, but I'm hoping that there might be something on that laptop Richard has recovered that might point us in the right direction to discover more."

"Ah hah, so we hurry up and wait some more… We wait to hear what Richard discovers from interrogating that laptop we believe to be McCormac's."

I can't say the possibility of Richard's finding anything had me too excited, but it was the best hope we had. Rod seemed to agree.

"Yep, that about sums it up for now. Of course, the question is, will he recognise anything useful when he sees it."

"While I know there is no easy answer to this question, I feel compelled to ask it: What can we do to support our theory about that book while we wait for Richard to interrogate the laptop? The concern is that he will be obliged to send the laptop to his superiors down south, and we will not have access to it at all," I moaned.

"There is a strong possibility the laptop will leave the area before we have a chance to look at it. Did you have some plan to negate such an outcome?" Rod asked.

"No-o, not really, but I wonder if we shouldn't come clean to Richard about what we've done and why we think the book is important."

We discussed my suggestion and any other possible course of action at some length before Rod finally agreed to think about it. Somehow, the prospect of losing the laptop without getting our hands on it after having come this far didn't sit comfortably with me. Despite my best efforts, no realistic way around this situation came to me. I told myself that it was late, and my creative juices had shut down for the night, but I knew the situation was a bit more problematic than that.

A solution to the problem did not magically occur to me as I made my way home. Nor did one arrive in the hours I tossed and turned before finally falling asleep. The galling underlying thought was that tomorrow could see McCormac's laptop disappear from this area. The question remained: What could we do about it? Although Rod had promised to think about a solution to the problem, I believe we both knew it was an impossible challenge I had given him.

The unresolved dilemma surrounding the laptop occupied my mind as soon as I opened my eyes this morning. By the time I had finished breakfast and decided to abandon my morning walk, a germ of an idea regarding accessing that laptop had started to develop. Finally, I decided.

"Right… I will call Richard and demand access to the laptop so we can follow up on some new information," I told my empty house. "What if he demands to know about this new information and its source? Maybe don't call it 'information'. Call it something else."

Try as I might, no better option presented itself. In the end, and on the brink of mental exhaustion, I decided perhaps a short walk might help the thought processes. The decision taken, my sneakers were on, and I was out the door… and almost barrelled into Rod as he strode up my path.

"Good… I was hoping you were up and about, and I wouldn't drag you out of bed to answer the door. If you could hold off on your walk for a while, might you manage to make us a coffee while I talk to you?"

It was a more appealing proposition than going for a walk. Rod made himself comfortable at my kitchen bench while I fussed with the coffee, but he made me wait until we were sipping coffee on my back deck before launching the conversation he wanted to have.

"After you left last night, I took a punt that Richard had started poring over that laptop. I called him and gave him a sketchy story about a clue I thought I had picked up, but I needed to check something on that laptop to confirm it. Richard immediately invited me to his place to look at the laptop – if I wasn't doing anything else important."

"And, of course, you went to his house – and accessed the laptop. So, what did you find? Anything at all interesting? Come on, don't keep me in suspense."

"Oh, I did better than that. I found exactly what I was looking for, but it did take a bit of searching, I have to admit. Finding it was like finding the 'Mother Lode'. Richard would never have recognised what it was. He probably would have assessed it as McCormac's weekly Lotto numbers selections."

Rod pulled a folded sheet of paper out of his pocket and flattened it out on the table. "This is a printout of one of the items I found. I used Richard's printer to print out a few sheets to take home with me."

"I can see why Richard might have thought they were Lotto number picks. That's what it looks like to me, too. So, what do these numbers mean?"

"Pyle's book is the key. Each group of numbers refers the reader to a page, line and word in the book. When the required word wasn't available in the book, the word was spelled out. In such cases, there is an extra number after the one that refers to a word. The extra number has an asterisk beside it to indicate which letter of the word. I believe his phone – if they find it – will contain more of such coded messages."

"It would take ages to compose a message using this method."

"True. When I explained the system to Richard, he remembered a small notebook found amongst McCormac's belongings at the motel. It appears McCormac composed his short message in longhand and then coded it using Pyle's book. It was an effective system, and Pyle's obscure book made it almost foolproof."

"So, what is Richard's next move? Will all the messages be deciphered here before being sent to his superiors down south?"

"Ah, well, somehow, I don't think that's his plan. I believe he suspects something dodgy is going on 'down south'. Armed with this new information, he might go it alone for a while to see what else he can discover.

By the way, you might be interested to know that operations at that workshop on the industrial estate have come to a sudden halt. The local police evidence room now holds a significant haul of contraband from last night."

After Rod left, I didn't know whether to feel elated or disappointed with this latest development. It didn't answer any questions about Joe's possible involvement or reveal who McCormac really was, but at least a large slab of the 'bad guys' operations was finished. All I could do was to wait to see what else might emerge over the next little while.

It's as well Rod and I wrapped up our part in the investigation into McCormac's murder when we did. The next couple of days were largely devoted to ensuring everything was in place for our big night at the local little theatre group's dress rehearsal performance. In reality, there wasn't much to do except to remind attendees about the importance of adhering to bus pick-up times and locations.

Although Rod and I wouldn't be on the bus with the other residents, we both fussed over making sure everything on the night ran to plan. Initially, I had thought it would be just Rod and me travelling to the show in his car. Then, a couple of hours before we were due to leave, I discovered four of us would be travelling in Rod's vehicle: Rod and me, the chairman of the board, and Richard. Rod had allocated two of the extra tickets Alice obtained to the chairman and Richard.

After fussing for far too long over what to wear, I was now dressed and feeling a certain degree of excitement about our night out as I waited to be collected. After what happened on our last bus outing, I desperately wanted this one, the first since then, to go well for Rod and all the rest of those involved in organising it.

Chapter 25

In front of the theatre group's small playhouse in the city, Rod eased into a parking space behind the Village's bus. I unclipped my seat belt and rushed over to help Alice and Maria assist passengers from the bus. Three or four passengers had already alighted.

Christ, my maroon pants suit looked positively casual by comparison with our other residents' outfits. They looked as though they were attending a gala night at the opera. Evening gowns, bow ties, and even a tuxedo came out of mothballs for this occasion. As I reached up to help the next passenger alight, I did a double-take. It was Henry Tremayne resplendent in a tuxedo, black satin cape lined with similar emerald green fabric, and large felt hat perched rakishly off to one side. I looked around for his wheelie walker to have it in place when he stepped off the bus. There was no sign of his walker – or his glasses.

I gave Alice a questioning look. She shook her head and shrugged. His lack of glasses didn't bother me too much. He couldn't see much when he wore them, unless it was right under his nose. The other piece of kit completing his outfit tonight did worry me. He carried a large, heavily carved wooden walking stick that looked more like a shillelagh than a mobility aid. As he was about to step onto the door's short exit ramp, he paused and brandished his walking stick as if acknowledging a waiting crowd, then cleared his throat before addressing that same imaginary crowd.

"No autographs, please. Not tonight, thank you," he announced in the best pitch and tone his ancient vocal cords allowed.

"What the…?" I murmured to no one in particular.

"Used to be a thespian, you know," a woman beside me replied with just a hint of disgust in her voice.

"A thespian?... When?... Where? ... What do you mean?" I asked without even a skerrick of intelligence in my words but I received a concise reply.

"You must be the only person he hasn't told about it. He was in little theatre for a while before moving on to a few bit-part appearances in films and TV shows."

Her words registered with me, although my focus was on Henry, who now, having delivered his announcement, made a shaky attempt to skip down the ramp. He skipped too close to the edge. Although the ramp was only a few centimetres high at that point, he fell off its edge. His shillelagh went up in the air and landed on the grass beside the ramp. It was quickly followed by Henry himself as, flailing, he fell to join it on the grass. A howl of pain rent the night air. I rushed around the ramp to kneel beside him, instructing Maria to call an ambulance as I raced past her.

Henry had landed on his side on the strip of grass beside the kerb. That strip of grass felt well compacted underfoot, and I knew it wouldn't have done his hip any favours when he landed on it. Of equal concern was the fact that Henry's upper body had landed on top of his elaborate walking stick. I doubted there was any way he could have missed out on some form of rib injury. The howls of pain from the man on the ground were continuous, and I felt overwhelming relief when the ambulance screeched to a halt beside me.

While the young female paramedic gave Henry a 'green whistle' to suck to ease his pain, Stan, the senior officer, gathered some relevant information from me. In reality, he asked a lot of questions, most of which I couldn't answer. We shared the same fear that Henry had probably fractured his hip in the fall. Then I drew Stan's attention to Henry's laboured breathing that appeared to be worsening by the minute.

"Is it possible he damaged a rib when he landed on that walking stick?" I asked.

"Possible and maybe even probable, but we won't know...." Stan didn't finish whatever he was going to say when the other officer yelled for assistance.

The two paramedics exchanged a couple of words before Stan dashed into their vehicle and returned with an oxygen cylinder. Henry became the centre of feverish activity. I didn't consider this to be a spectator sport and started herding the Merivale residents towards the theatre. Some seemed reluctant to move, claiming concern for Henry but, in reality, just wanting to stand and gawp. A man I only know as Roy loudly announced that it was almost 'curtain up time' and, if they didn't take their seats soon, they would be locked out. That did the trick. The bus's passengers surged inside to take their seats.

Rod, Richard, and the chairman remained with me until Rod insisted the chairman join the others inside. There was nothing the three of us could do except watch the paramedics apply their skills and training. Their level of activity appeared to become frantic as we stood watching. Then, Stan looked over at me and shook his head. It was all over. It had been Henry's last curtain call. Richard stepped up and asked Stan for a situation report.

"Most of the deceased's right side rib cage was severely damaged in the fall, and his hip was fractured. Either one of those on its own would have been serious for a man of his age. Together, they became critical. Is there any information on his medical history?" Stan looked to each of us for an answer.

"We can't answer that," Richard stated. "None of us knew the man, but is that information important right now? Are you suggesting he didn't die as a result of his injuries?"

"That's correct. I think you'll find that, while his injuries might have been a contributing factor, the coroner's report will show that he died of coronary occlusion – a heart attack – probably brought on by the fall."

"Ah, now… that is interesting," Rod said quietly. "I heard one of the others say they hoped Henry had his pills with him as he might need them after his fall."

"Sounds like angina medication or something similar," Stan suggested. "He doesn't appear to have any pills or anything else on him, though. Anyway, we'll take him back to the hospital to have him declared deceased and the appropriate paperwork set in motion."

"What on earth was he doing?" Richard asked, shaking his head. "What was all that nonsense on the ramp supposed to be about? Did he think he was Fred Astaire or something?"

"No," I murmured, "just an ancient thespian taking one last bow. It's sad, but, in a way, it's probably the ending he would have scripted for himself."

By the time the ambulance drove off, and we made our way into the theatre, it was only a couple of minutes before intermission. After that, we would be able to take our seats for the remainder of the show. The large subdued segment of the crowd milling about in the bar area during intermission was the contingent of Merivale residents. They all hoped for good news about Henry while believing it unlikely.

The second act of the show was good, but tonight, the occasional stuff-ups that are the hilarious part of a dress rehearsal performance fell flat for many in the audience. After the show, I felt a sense of relief flood through me. Accompanied by Richard and the chairman, I made my way to Rod's car. Rod spent a few minutes with those on the bus before joining us in the car. The drive back to the Village was notable for its lack of conversation. Rod pulled up in front of my place, and we all piled out. Richard and the chairman said their goodnights and made their way to their cars that were parked out front. Richard drove off and was soon followed by the chairman, whose parting remark as he scrambled into his car added a further downer to the night.

"Looks like I'll be back here tomorrow to organise Tanya to clear out Tremayne's house."

Still not particularly up for conversation, Rod and I were sipping our nightcaps in my lounge room when Rod's phone intruded. After checking the caller ID, he took the call out on my back deck. I couldn't read his face when he returned, but I could tell the call had triggered a whole lot of something.

"That caller was my contact, the one who seems to know more about what's going on with Joe than anyone else. It appears a series of lightning raids in and around Canberra over the last few hours have resulted in a handful of arrests. He thinks at least five people have been taken into custody by Federal Police as a result of information received from somewhere up this way. The arrests certainly relate to the contract that was out on Joe."

"Could only be Richard, couldn't it? I mean, who else from up this way had any useful information to pass to the Feds? Is that what 'going it alone' looks like in Richard's world?"

"You might be right about the source. Good on him if that is the case. I suppose the only way we'll know how effective all that has been is if we suddenly receive a call from Cilla to tell us she and Joe will be home soon."

While that seemed highly unlikely, it provided a positive note on which to end the night. So, I didn't argue and simply nodded my agreement. About ten minutes later, I watched him drive off along the street. I suspect I was in bed by the time he had locked his garage and gone inside.

The last thing I felt like this morning was mahjong, but it was Thursday morning, and that's what was scheduled. I had little enthusiasm for baking scones and preparing containers of jam and whipped cream to take with me for morning tea… And the morning went much as expected. Rod and I were at the Recreation Room early to set up the tables and chairs. Then, everyone arrived together in their usual fashion, except today, there were no latecomers.

Cilla and Joe's continued absence did raise questions that went unanswered. Bernard's absence raised comment. I raised my eyebrows at Rod. He simply shrugged in reply. I wondered if Bernard might be boycotting mahjong as a result of his run-in with Rod over the incident involving Mrs Carr's dog on the bus. Then Marjorie Bosworth escaped the library and came in to join us. I felt it safe to assume that her presence, unaccompanied by

Bernard, meant another serious tiff had occurred between the pair.

Perhaps not surprisingly, the buzz of conversation around the morning tea table soon focused on Henry Tremayne's fall last night. It was obvious no one knew the outcome. I sidled up to Rod and quietly asked whether we should enlighten the group.

"No… not our responsibility. Besides, he isn't deceased until a doctor declares him to be. That's why a paramedic kept working on him in the ambulance all the way to the hospital."

"That's true, but those at the dress rehearsal last night probably suspect the truth. No doubt, they will have shared their opinion with most of the Village by now."

"Obviously, some of this mob haven't heard it. By the way, I spoke to Mrs Strambini before we left last night. A couple of the others had told me Strambini and Tremayne were close despite their age difference. They said she tended to look after him, drove him around, cooked for him, and all that."

"Who is Mrs Strambini? I don't think I know the woman. Was she on the bus last night?"

"I'm sure you know her… The big woman wearing acres of red fabric in a voluminous gown…."

"Pearl? Oh, you mean Pearl. I never knew her surname. Did she have anything useful to tell you about Tremayne?"

"She admitted she had worried about him lately. He appeared to be losing the plot a bit. Although aware of it, he was determined not to be seen as some decrepit old fossil. And, yes, his heart problems had worsened in recent days."

"While I don't know how old Henry was, Pearl certainly looks a lot younger than him. Their relationship, whatever it was, surprises me."

"According to Pearl, she is nudging 70, while Henry was almost 90. She claimed they had established a sound relationship; all above board and no scandal, of course. I was taken aback and more than a little wrongfooted when she asked me point-blank if Henry was dead."

"No doubt, you gave her the standard 'safe' reply. You told her no more than Henry had been taken to hospital."

"Well, I tried, but somehow, she seemed to know the truth. Despite that, she appeared calm and accepting of the situation. I suppose that might have been due to the fact that it hadn't sunk in yet for her."

There was no further chance for Rod and me to talk privately as players were taking their places at the tables, and we were being called to ours to allow play to begin. I played like a raw beginner all morning, but Rod appeared unaffected by last night, and made a clean sweep of our games. This morning, no one lingered after the games finished. Today, even those who usually hung about for an extra coffee and scone left with the rest of the mob. With no Cilla and Joe, the cleaning and tidying after everyone left fell to just Rod and me. Later, walking home together provided the perfect opportunity to discuss last night's events and the current status of the McCormac investigation.

"You must have known something, Rod, when you delayed resuming regular happy hours until next week. I don't think I could face a happy hour tonight after what happened last night. There'd be no guessing about the main topics of conversation. The only topics would be Tremayne and McCormac. Oh, and Cilla and Joe's continued absence might merit a mention. I understand why people want to discuss those topics and that it can be significant in helping cope with the events, but it can only lead to speculation. And they probably would look to us for information – that we don't have – not officially, anyway.

And, Rod, the BIG thing on my mind is what impact Tremayne's death will have on future bus trips. The bus might be seen as 'cursed'. I'm imagining future passengers being on edge as they wonder whether their next trip will result in their demise."

"Yeah, I don't doubt recent events will cause some nervousness. As for our need for a bit more information, something might be brewing there. A message came through from Richard during mahjong. I was going to wait until I was home, but I'll give him a call now. No point in delaying learning what new disaster has befallen us."

"Come on in and stay for lunch. You can call Richard while I prepare lunch."

Although I wasn't sure what my larder ran to when it came to producing lunch, I was damn sure I wanted to know what Rod's call might produce. I knew there was every chance it would be a short call that told us nothing new, but I'm nothing if not an optimist. Ham and salad sandwiches don't take long to prepare. Rod's chat with Richard took longer. With every passing minute, I felt my excitement rising. For the call to take so long, there must be an exchange of considerable information. Disappointment is a terrible emotion.

When Rod joined me in the kitchen, there was a hint of a smirk around the corners of his mouth. I did not like the look of it. Although I knew I would regret it, I immediately demanded to know what it was about.

"Don't be smart, Rod. Stop playing silly buggers and tell me what Richard had to say."

"Will you believe me if I tell you there was nothing of any consequence?" I shook my head. "No, I thought not, but that is pretty much the gist of it. We briefly discussed last night's events, and he confirmed Tremayne was declared deceased at the hospital. The most significant part of our conversation was just social. You and I have been invited to join Richard for dinner in his favourite small restaurant. I took the liberty of accepting the invitation on behalf of both of us."

"Great… I suppose. When is this social event supposed to occur?"

"This evening… Seven o'clock. I take it you are available?"

"Yes, I am, and thanks for accepting on my behalf," I snapped.

"You don't seem too sure about that. Do you have a problem with having dinner with Richard and me?"

"Not at all. The only problem I have is whether this is Richard's way of signing off on our involvement in the McCormac case. I know it sounds like the investigation must be close to being wrapped up, but I do want to know all the final details. I don't want to be left wondering how it ended."

"Well, I didn't get that impression from Richard, but then, we really didn't discuss the case at all. So, it looks as though you will have to nurture your curiosity until tonight when we might find out more."

Richard's favourite boutique restaurant must be the best of the city's hidden gems. The ambience was great, the service was fantastic, the food was divine, and only two other tables were occupied, although a large group arrived as we were leaving. 'Shop' talk did not intrude until after the main course – when I could no longer control my curiosity. I felt it safe to lead in with a question about Tremayne.

"Yes, he was confirmed deceased. His daughter, as next of kin, was informed. I don't think father and daughter were close. She announced straight off that there would be no funeral or memorial service. He is to be cremated, and his ashes returned to her for interment with his wife. Strange, I know, but that's how it's going to be."

"Those arrangements will upset some of the residents," I murmured. "They will expect at least a memorial service, and none more so than Pearl Strambini." The two men nodded in agreement, and a moment's silence followed before Richard resumed speaking.

"The other thing I think you might be interested in are developments in the McCormac case. That workshop on the industrial site was closed down, and a number of people were arrested. The operation was one of a chain set up and run by a couple of chaps connected to the McCormac story. So, more arrests have been made in a number of locations in this state and across the border. Only four of them are part of the original core of what's behind all this, but a further three of their group have been arrested in the UK."

"I still don't understand how McCormac fits into all this," I admitted. "Was he one of the group now arrested, or was he simply engaged to carry out a contract? … And who was the target of the contract?" I looked at Rod for support. He was studying the tablecloth in front of him. Richard launched into his story without Rod's encouragement.

It seems a certain rogue MI6 operative was locked away for life after another agent blew the whistle on him. The rogue's operation was quite profitable, and several younger operatives, who he recruited to work for him, also did well out of it. When the rogue was arrested, a couple of his young recruits jumped ship and ended up in Australia. They were the ones who set up the trafficking network, including the workshop here. Nothing much happened for a while, and the other young recruits remained in MI6 and kept their heads down until recently.

About a year ago, the rogue agent was transferred to a new prison in a pleasant area of the English countryside. Then, about four months ago, his one-time recruits somehow engineered his escape. Once he was out of prison, the rogue resumed his vendetta against the agent who had blown the whistle on him. He put out a contract on the man's life. Work by the rogue's acolytes established that the contract's target was now living in Australia, and their focus moved to our part of the world. It now appears that once enough information on the Australian situation was received, McCormac arrived to carry out the contract. However, the rogue and his associates hadn't counted on the support and protection their target might have in this country.

When a whisper went out about a possible contract on an operative working with an Australian agency, that agency went into action. They sequestered their agent in a safe place and went after McCormac. And the rest is history," Richard added.

"The Australian agency made sure McCormac was no longer a threat to one of their own. It is now believed that 'Baxter McCormac' was an alias for that rogue operator, and with him dead and his acolytes all locked away, the Australian agent was now safe. So, thanks to your efforts, this investigation is now closed, and I have come out of it with a whole lot of accolades that will do my career no harm at all. Oh, and I should add, my superiors down south, who were supposedly running this investigation, are now under investigation."

There were a few moments of silence at our table. At last, Rod nodded silently to himself as though indicating his satisfaction at Richard's report. For me, it left a major question unanswered. I sought to correct that situation.

"Thank you, Richard. It's a relief to know at last what the hell it was all about, but there is one more thing I need to know. Who was the Australian agent who was the target of that contract?"

"Oh, did I not say? It appears the target, that is, the agent who blew the whistle on the rogue, was the Australian agent, Theo Rothwell." Nothing more needed to be said, but Rod and I exchanged nods of confirmation.

Our time at the restaurant ended about ten minutes later. Not a word was exchanged in the car as Rod and I drove back to the Village. I was polite enough to invite Rod to come in for a nightcap, but I think it lacked enthusiasm, and Rod didn't hesitate to reject it.

So, the McCormac case was closed, and presumably, Joe (if he is indeed Theo Rothwell) was now safe. Nevertheless, I knew it would be some time before I would find sleep tonight.

Chapter 26

Life at Merivale Retirement Village resumed some degree of normalcy again. Mahjong mornings occurred twice a week, and happy hours at Rod's place were a regular evening occurrence, although a bit hit and miss for a while.

The High School plays competition dominated life in the Village, with residents vying with one another for seats during the heats. The plays took precedence over happy hours. With most of our group involved with the plays, as workers or as members of the audience, it was often just Rod and me sharing drinks on his back deck. Then, the High School finalists had about a month after the heats in which to prepare for the finals.

One night, when Rod and I enjoyed our own happy hour, Cilla called Rod. He answered it out in the backyard, so I didn't hear any of it. I couldn't read the look on Rod's face when he returned to the back deck after the short call.

"That was Cilla. They will be home around the end of the week. She didn't mention McCormac or what she and Joe had been doing."

"Rod, should we maybe do a quick tour of Cilla's place before they return? I know we didn't find much evidence of the intruders' visit, but should we give it a once-over again?"

"Nah… entering her place again could be misconstrued. We could be seen as intruders for entering the place without authority."

Cilla returned to mahjong on Tuesday morning – alone. She arrived as the first games began, and gave the rest of the group no opportunity to cross-examine her about her and Joe's absence. While Rod and I believed Joe had returned with Cilla, he remained invisible until the next weekend when we saw him briefly out in the front yard. His appearance caused concern.

Joe looked pale and gaunt. At the first opportunity, I asked Cilla about his appearance. She brushed aside my concern, saying Joe had caught a bug down south and it had laid him low for a few days. I could hardly argue, but sceptic that I am, I remained unconvinced. Over the next days, Joe gradually returned to mahjong and happy hours.

The other significant event this week confirmed Pearl Strambini as a force to be reckoned with. Henry Tremayne's daughter's snub of Henry's friends – and the Village generally – incensed Pearl. She persuaded our director to hold a memorial service in the Village. A chaplain who made himself available to the Village whenever required officiated. Initially to be held in the Recreation Room, Pearl argued that venue wasn't large enough for the service. Besides being larger, she considered the theatre a more fitting place to farewell a former thespian. With many residents inveterate funeral attendees anyway, the attendance proved Pearl was right. Rod, Richard and the chairman felt obliged to attend. As someone not into attending funerals, I felt no such obligation, and spent the morning dealing with domestic chores.

A couple of days after the memorial service for Henry Tremayne, Rod invited me for morning coffee. Not unusual, perhaps, but he did seem a little insistent when I hesitated to accept. I thought his call a little odd when I had spoken to him only an hour or so beforehand on my way home from my walk. I soon discovered the invitation was motivated by a call from Richard.

"Richard wants to meet with us and suggested that, if we were free, tonight would suit him. I told him I would check with you, but I thought tonight would be fine. Are you available tonight?"

"Apart from a happy hour here at your place, I don't have any other plans. So, how is this going to work?"

"When I explained that we wouldn't be free until after seven o'clock, he said that suited him fine, as he was aiming for a little after 7.30PM. It will be another clandestine meeting – whatever that means – because Cilla and Joe have now returned."

"And, I suppose the meeting will be at my house, and people will be expecting to be fed?"

"Uhmm… Yes, I would think that's the case. So, can I confirm we are okay for tonight at your house and dinner will be provided?"

After gulping down my coffee, I rushed home to see what amazing foodstuffs my freezer might produce at such short notice. My search produced a couple of packs of nice-looking steaks. Right… So, tonight's dinner will be barbequed steaks, jacket potatoes and salad. If I suddenly feel energetic, I'll make something for dessert … otherwise, it will be ice cream and fruit salad. With dinner sorted out, I spent most of the day like any good hostess does, cleaning and tidying the living area and the back deck. Rod is unaware of it, but tonight, he will be in charge of barbequing the steaks.

A call to Rod at about 7.35 told us Richard was about to arrive via my back fence. A few moments later, Richard scrambled over my fence.

"What's with all the cloak-and-dagger stuff, and where's your vehicle?" I demanded.

"I parked on that back track. I'd prefer people remained unaware I was here tonight."

"You mean you would prefer Cilla remained unaware…" I corrected him.

"Well, yeah. Not to put too fine a point on it, but that's what I meant. If she saw my car parked out front, she would be over here in a flash, and that wouldn't suit me at all."

"So, what has brought you here tonight?"

Rod, who was heating the barbeque, glared at me, but I felt justified in asking the questions I did. Richard didn't appear offended by them and launched into his story.

His visit was to update us on the McCormac case, although I thought he had done that at dinner the other night. In the interim, both the Federal Police and his own Police Service advised

Richard that the last of those associated with McCormac had now been neutralised. The Australian trafficking operation run by a contingent of his followers also was shut down.

Richard claimed to be feeling guilty about all the accolades that had come his way when it was largely due to our efforts, especially after his elevation in rank.

"Does your new, higher ranking mean you will be moving to a higher position somewhere else?" I thought it logical that's what would follow.

"No-o, not exactly. It means I have greater responsibilities over an increased area, but I will remain here as your top cop."

"What about Cilla's contract as a special advisor to the police service in this state? Will that continue, and will you continue to work with her?"

"For the moment, status quo is maintained, but I foresee little opportunity for us to work together anytime in the near future."

"Richard, one thing continues to intrigue me. What was McCormac's real name?"

"Well, now, as you know, there always are some aspects of a case that cannot be disclosed." His tone told me I had no room to manoeuvre on that one.

The evening didn't last long and we again were watching Richard negotiate my back fence to return to his car.

We happened upon an interesting event this morning. A couple of weeks ago, Bernard's car was scratched along one side while in a public carpark in the city. At the beginning of this week, it went into the panel shop for repairs. After dropping it off, a friend gave Bernard a ride back to the Village. Originally, it was thought the work would take about two days. Heavy rain that night and all the next day created poor drying conditions and delayed the repaint. The vehicle was in the shop for four days.

By the time the work was completed and the vehicle was ready to go home, the friend was no longer available to take Bernard to collect his car. His only option was to go into town on the Village bus on its next shopping run into the city. As Rod and I strolled across to the bowls club this morning, passengers were boarding the bus for that trip. We heard a fuss and rushed to see what had happened.

Mrs Carr and her dog intended to take the bus into the city as they often did. This morning, Bernard again blocked the doorway to prevent Mrs Carr and her pooch from boarding. Mrs Carr dug into her handbag and produced a sheet of paper which, with a malevolent grin adorning her features, she waved in Bernard's face. It was her copy of the chairman's ruling that dogs were allowed on the Village bus. Bernard had no alternative but to step aside, allow them to board, and then slink onboard after them.

Life never fails to amaze…. So much has happened over the last few weeks, and so much remained unresolved. Then, within the space of a few days, every loose end has been tied up. The McCormac case is wrapped up, the winners of the High School plays competition have been awarded the trophy, Bernard has been put in his place regarding dogs on the bus, and mahjong and happy hours are back on at their usual times. Life has returned to its normal rhythm and can continue in that fashion until the usual flurry of activity that marks the onset of the Festive Season.

I know such evidence of Life's amazing ways will be discussed by Rod and me over dinner tonight and possibly over breakfast… if he forgets to go home tonight.

The End

Thanks

Thank you for reading my book. I hope you enjoyed it. If you did, please consider taking a moment to leave a review at your favourite bookstore or retailer's website.
Thanks

Neive Denis

Other Books by the Author

Sonoma Whittington Private Investigator series:
An Ancient Solution
A Public Service
Missing!
Connections
A Different Obsession
Shattered Illusions
After The Ball
Unholy Secrets
Fateful Reunion
A Dark Place
Layers of Deception
Lost Days

Merivale Retirement Village series:
Close to Home
Growing Pains
One Thing After Another

About the Author

Neive Denis is the creator of two current series. The first series features the Private Investigator, Sonoma (Sonny) Whittington. Neive Denis is the pen name of a writer who was lured from her usual genre to focus on the mystery and excitement that are a part of Sonoma Whittington's world. She came into being specifically for this series and, for the moment at least, intends focusing mainly on stories from Sonny's case files.

That series tells of the intrigue and scrapes – some on occasion life threatening – that are part of the life of Sonoma Whittington, an Australian Private Investigator, based in a Central Queensland coastal city. However, Sonny doesn't confine her escapades to Australia, and that provides Neive with an opportunity to weave some of her other areas of interest into Sonny's hair-raising adventures on occasion.

All Aboard is the fourth book in Neive's second series set in the Merivale Retirement Village. This series takes readers on a light-hearted trip through the world of a group of mahjong playing retirees who are not about to spend their final years being bored. It tells of friendship, intrigue and, perhaps, even romance.

See more about Neive Denis and her work at
www.eaglemountbooks.com.au/neivedenis

or contact her at
admin@eaglemountbooks.com.au

www.ingramcontent.com/pod-product-compliance
Lightning Source LLC
Chambersburg PA
CBHW040520170726
48295CB00012B/270

9781763510968